ETERNITY'S
MARK

ETERNITY'S MARK

MAEVE GREYSON

KENSINGTON PUBLISHING CORP.
www.kensingtonbooks.com

BRAVA BOOKS are published by

Kensington Publishing Corp.
119 West 40th Street
New York, NY 10018

All Kensington titles, imprints, and distributed lines are available at special quantity discounts for bulk purchases for sales promotions, premiums, fund-raising, educational, or institutional use.

Special book excerpts or customized printings can also be created to fit specific needs. For details, write or phone the office of the Kensington special sales manager: Kensington Publishing Corp., 119 West 40th Street, New York, NY 10018, attn: Special Sales Department. Phone: 1-800-221-2647.

Brava and the B logo are Reg. U.S. Pat. & TM Off.

ISBN-13:978-0-7582-7339-0
ISBN-10: 0-7582-7339-8

First Kensington Trade Paperback Printing: March 2012

10 9 8 7 6 5 4 3 2 1

Printed in the United States of America

To my family—for keeping the demons of doubt at bay.
You are my strength.

And to Jasper—for creeping underneath my desk and chomping
down on green squeaky toy at just the right moment.
You keep me vigilant.

CHAPTER ONE

Still no word from the infernal woman. She must be oblivious to her worth. Taggart fisted his hands atop the desk, glaring at the calendar. How long had it been? How many letters had she ignored? Precious time was running out. With her continued silence, she'd force his hand. He would *demand* her attention.

"Thaetus, how long since we sent the last missive?"

The *thwack* of the twined mail packet echoed through the room as Thaetus tossed the bundle on the table. "Long enough for the signed receipt to return stating she's received it and *disregarded* it. Again."

Taggart slammed both fists on the edge of the desk and shoved his chair to the wall. "I canna believe there's still no reply. No response whatsoever. What the hell is wrong with this woman? Ye would think she'd be a tiny bit curious. The women of this world, are they no' supposed to be just a wee bit nosy?"

Thaetus shrugged, peering down his beak-like nose over a pair of dilapidated wire-rimmed spectacles. "If not curious, I thought all Americans were at least supposed to be a bit greedy. Ye would think she'd be thrilled to find she'd inherited a fine piece of land such as Taroc Na Mor."

Taggart launched himself out of his chair and huffed his way across the dense Persian carpet. White knuckling his fists against the damp, cold sill of the window, he stared down into the depressing courtyard below. Where once might have been a garden of well-tended roses stood a clumped circle of mangled thorns choking with shocks of weeds. Dying vegetation surrounded moss-covered flagstones heaved out of place by invading roots of nearby oaks. Overgrown shrubbery sat riddled with out-of-control ivy marauding its way through damaged masonry. A mournful howl filtered from the unseen caverns Taggart knew ran deep beneath the castle. The estate appeared forgotten, the buildings abandoned and battered by the ravages of time.

Taggart blew out a ragged breath. His Taroc Na Mor, his precious sanctuary. The stark vista tore at his heart. Very few individuals on this side of the sacred threshold realized the true importance of this acreage in the remote Highlands. Taroc Na Mor symbolized so much more than just a bit of forgotten land. He'd failed his race's beloved holy ground, failed his duty as protector and lord. He curled his hands tighter, envisioning his helpless charges patiently waiting in the depths below. Grinding his teeth until his jaw nearly cracked, Taggart slammed his hand against the wall. No more waiting. He would get the confounded woman's attention. "That settles it, Thaetus. Hannah MacPherson leaves me no choice. Enough of these certified packets and the blasted receipts she just signs and tosses aside!" Taggart turned from the frosted, lead-paned window. "I will go to this place, this *Jasper Mills*, and track her down. I'll talk to the stubborn woman face to face."

"When ye say ye will go to this place . . ." Thaetus paused with a thin hand resting on the brass handle of the door, his wispy brows stretched into an expectant arch.

"I must use this world's backwards conveyance, Thaetus. Please get me an airline ticket, if ye will. I need to blend in with the general populace as much as possible. We must ease Ms. MacPherson into the ways of Taroc Na Mor. If we're to convince her to stay and become a part of our lives, we must take care not to frighten her away."

With a feather-light touch, she adjusted the zoom one more time and double-checked the focus. There. Now, the object in her lens appeared just perfect. The car aligned between the glowing red dots in her camera's lens showed up as crisply and clearly as if she were sitting on the edge of the hood. She'd bide her time and her prey would show up. She'd rub their little noses in it this time. Now when the little miscreant who'd been moving her vehicle decided to appear, she'd snap the picture. She'd have her proof and she'd convince that hardheaded sheriff that his parking tickets were a waste of time.

Hannah settled herself more comfortably on the seat of her ATV. As she took a deep breath and her plan came together, the knot of tension eased in her chest. She could do this; her plan would work. All she had to do was bide her time. She relaxed and allowed her gaze to wander around the peaceful clearing; she realized she sat in one of her favorite spots in the woods. She loved this little hilltop. A serene wind shushed through the leaves fluttering overhead. The fully leafed-out branches of early summer whispered and sang. The pin oaks, maples, and birches swayed with the playful breeze.

She rechecked her beeper. *Yep*. Battery charged, red light flashing. If anyone needed her, all they had to do was go to the café and Millie would track her down. Closing her eyes, she ticked off her list of patients. She'd just made the rounds of all the farms and everybody was in great condition. Farmer Donovan's mare wouldn't foal for another few days. She'd stopped by the infirmary and checked on Mabry's pups. She worried a little about the runt, but with the bottle-feeding and the liquid vitamins she'd added to his diet, he should continue to thrive.

Stretching her arms overhead, Hannah filled her lungs with the fresh, clean air sifting through the trees. Nothing relaxed her more than the exhilarating scent of greening leaves. Maybe after she nabbed her prankster, she'd sneak a nap later on a stretch of moss-covered ground. A nice slow day, just what she needed, the perfect day to trap a little twerp.

This shouldn't take long. This had to be a couple of local kids one of the town busybodies had paid off. She could hear them now plotting amongst themselves. They would've snickered while they planned where to push her car so the sheriff would write one of his cutesy go-out-with-me tickets. A by-the-book transplant from New York City, Sheriff Matt Mulroney would never write a ticket unless forced to do so. But a flagrant parking violation in front of one of the town's few fireplugs, well, he'd consider that grounds for a ticket for sure.

Fighting against a yawn, Hannah rubbed her eyes as she chuckled to herself. The early summer buzz of the warm woods mesmerized her with a case of the drowsies. If it weren't for the fact they were meddling in *her* life, she'd find this quite amusing. Hannah doted on Jasper Mills, a miniscule town whose population thrived on the smallest bit of gossip. But the biweekly ticketing of her personal vehicle had almost become a news bulletin on the local morning radio show. Apparently, she'd missed the memo, but it appeared the entire town had held a private ballot and decided she and Sheriff Matt needed to start dating.

Hannah shifted on the seat and scanned the area through the viewfinder. Nothing yet, but she had all day. There was no way they'd be able to resist the bait of her unlocked vehicle sitting unattended on the square. They'd show up.

She shook her head. She still hadn't figured out which one of them had managed to sucker Matt into the plot. Evidently, the town had notified Sheriff Matt of the results of their find-Hannah-a-man poll and he'd *also* decided they needed to start dating.

"Fat chance." Hannah snapped a twig in two and waved it at an inquisitive gray squirrel peering down from a nearby limb. "I don't need a man. I'm the only veterinarian in a five-hundred-mile radius. I don't need anyone to take care of me." She could take care of herself *just fine.* She'd been doing it for a while now. You'd think they'd get the hint. A gust of wind shoved against her back, pulling her from her thoughts. A familiar ache fluttered in her chest. That old stab of loneliness that had been her constant companion for the past four years. Hannah turned to face the wind, closing her eyes to the breeze.

Jake. Every time she wandered through this part of the woods, the wind stirred against her like a nudging spirit. It just had to be Jake sending her a message from the other side. They'd walked here often when they'd dated. In fact, this neck of the woods had been their playground as kids. Hannah swallowed hard and took a deep breath. At least she could tick off the years now without bursting into tears. Over four years now, since Jake had made her a widow and she'd sworn she'd spend the rest of her life alone on her mountain.

Hannah exhaled with a shudder as she opened her eyes. It seemed like forever ago, the year and half they'd been married. Damn Jake's need to volunteer to patch up the soldiers in the Iraq War. Hannah swallowed hard against the threat of tears as the wind stroked teasing fingers through her hair. He had been such a great doctor. As an orthopedic surgeon, Jake had wanted to do what he could to support the brave soldiers fighting for his freedom. But they'd sent Jake back to her in a box draped with a flag and

Hannah had laid him to rest on their mountain. Now here she sat over four years later trying to catch some little twerp hell-bent on making her life difficult. Hannah sucked in a cleansing breath of the early-morning air. Enough. Time to focus on the task at hand.

Hannah propped her chin in her hand and glanced around the hillside as she half watched the dots of people milling around in the square below. Even though they tended to go through her mail, eavesdrop on all her calls, and even place and *answer* personal ads for her in other county papers, Hannah loved each and every nosy one of the tiny population of seven hundred and nine, if you still counted Mrs. McCreedy's nephew who'd just left for college in Chicago.

Her quiet little town sat trapped in a time warp and she wouldn't have it any other way. Jasper Mills wedged itself inside the valley of the Great Ridge Line Mountains like wild mushrooms at the base of an ancient tree.

"Now, that's what I'm talking about." Hannah straightened as three figures sidled toward her car on the square below. She rechecked the focus in her lens. Her jaw dropped and her eyes widened as she shifted her position on the ATV, steadying herself on the seat. As she followed the slow roll of the car with the lever of the tripod, she reminded herself to breathe. "You have gotta be kidding me! She knows better."

Hannah watched through the camera lens and snapped the pictures as fast as the camera refocused on the culprits below. The more she snapped, the wider she smiled. Her pile of ammunition mounted with every click of the shutter. "This is unbelievable." Incredulity fluttered in the pit of her stomach as the camera whirred with every press of the button.

At last, the plotters' well-laid plan played out. Her car now not only sat in front of the fire hydrant but also blocked the exit to the fire station. The three had outdone themselves this time. And right on cue, Sheriff Matt Mulroney appeared with ticket pad in hand. Hannah took a few additional shots of Matt as the three individuals who had been kind enough to move her car lined up just behind Matt while he wrote the ticket.

"Oh, I can't resist this Kodak moment. I think I'll even zoom in for a close-up. This is unbelievable. Even Millie!" Hannah adjusted the lens and held down the button. There. The perfect shot of the not-so-perfect crime. As the marauders moved away from her car, Hannah peered over the camera, down into the valley. Her plan had worked. She had her evidence. Now all she had to do was pack it up, take it to town, and end their little game.

Hannah bowed her head against the rising breeze as she packed her camera equipment into the padded ammo box strapped to the back of her ATV. The leafy branches of the oaks swayed overhead and sighed as though responding to her stubborn determination. Glancing up into the sunlit canopy, Hannah shook her finger at the sky. "It's time they accepted the fact that I'm just fine with the way things are now. There's no crime in living alone." The woods understood. Now if she could just convince her friends. She yanked the strap hard, securing the ammo box behind the seat.

The wind whipped harder through the tops of the trees as if in response to this statement. The gust rippled through the branches and whirled the leaf mold into spinning bundles of debris. It tugged her ball cap, ripping it off her head, and tore her ponytail loose from its ties. The wind bounced her hair band and cap to the ground, then tossed them among the multicolored carpet of leaves.

Hannah scooped the hair tie and hat from among the dried leaves and wrestled her thick curls out of her face. "All right now. Enough fun and games. I've got to get

down to the diner with these pictures and end this foolishness once and for all."

The wind died down, fading through the smaller
branches. A stillness fell over the clearing. Hannah shivered as she glanced about the wood. It suddenly seemed
strangely deserted. Hannah whistled her favorite bird call
that never failed to charm a few feathered friends out
of the brush. Nothing. Silence was maintained throughout
the wood. Not a branch moved; not a bird chirped. The
entire forest stood as though frozen in time.

"Great. Everybody's a critic." Hannah packed up,
strapped her helmet on over her favorite ball cap, and
headed down the hill toward town.

"There are rumblings."

"There are always rumblings. Do ye have my ticket and
the rest of my papers? I dinna want to be delayed any
longer." Taggart threw a shirt into a dilapidated, black bag
lying open on the bed, then waved his hand until the gar-
ment disappeared into its depths.

"Why do ye pack clothes for the journey? Ye can man-
ifest anything ye need." Thaetus frowned down into the
cracked leather tote, then glanced back up at Taggart over
the bent rims of his glasses.

"I must *blend in,* Thaetus. Do ye realize how much
trouble I'll have with security at the airport if I show up
for a flight to the United States with no baggage?" Taggart
wandered around the room, spotted a book lying on the
table beside the bed, grabbed it, and tossed it in the bag.

"Then just take an empty bag." Thaetus snatched out
the book and glanced at the spine with a frown. "This one
is mine. Ye canna have it."

"They x-ray the bags, Thaetus. They would question an
empty bag just as much as no bag at all. Now, tell me about
the rumblings and keep your precious little book." What a

fuss over something as silly as a book. With a shake of his head, Taggart stifled a groan, yanked open a drawer, and shoveled up a handful of shirts. Thaetus fretted more over his meager possessions than a female Draecna nesting in her first cavern.

Thaetus hugged his book against his narrow chest and sniffed as he stuck his nose up in the air. "Our sources say they've located our precious guardian. And they know ye travel to recover her."

Taggart slammed the drawer shut so hard the dresser rocked against the wall. "How in the hell did they find that out? If they've found her, they could make an attempt on her life before I get there to protect her." This meant he couldn't get to this Jasper Mills fast enough. Hannah MacPherson wasn't safe. Adrenaline surged through Taggart's veins, pounding the message: *Make haste before it's too late.* Frustration addled him as he struggled with the fact that he still needed to use twenty-first-century means. If just one inhabitant caught him sifting out of thin air, widespread panic would ensue. Creating chaos among the population of Jasper Mills wasn't the way to win the woman's trust.

Thaetus eased a step back toward the door. "The minion confessed. From the information we gathered from his mind, they know where she resides but they haven't quite pinpointed *who* she is. So, she's safe for now. But as soon as ye get there, ye can rest assured, they'll figure out exactly which resident she is."

"Has Septamus disposed of him yet?" Taggart clenched his teeth. He already knew the answer before he spoke the question. He'd once interrogated a minion himself. Messy, wicked little bastards once ye'd broken their will.

Thaetus shook his head. "No. The minion destroyed itself as soon as Septamus twisted the last bit of information from its mind."

"Dammit to hell," Taggart stomped across the disheveled room. "They're getting sloppy. Either that or we are. I want to know how they discovered this information. Minions canna pass through the portals unattended. They must be accompanied by someone with more powerful magic." Taggart waved his hand at the bulging suitcase on the disheveled bed and it sealed itself shut. "I need the rest of my papers now, Thaetus. There's no time to waste."

The diner already swelled with the early lunch crowd, but Hannah managed to snag her favorite spot at the tall counter. She smiled as she slid her hand across the worn vinyl seat, still warm from its last occupant. This particular red stool won the choice seat award because it provided the perfect vantage point for viewing the entire room. From this perch against the gleaming tile wall, you could sit and see everyone as they entered the diner, see everyone at the tables, and still gossip to whoever worked behind the counter. It also spun at the perfect speed. Hannah locked her ankles around the steel pole as she leaned her elbows on the counter. This seat had been Hannah's preferred spot since she'd been tall enough to crawl up on the bright, red swiveling pedestal. And this was where she'd end this infernal parking ticket romance maneuver launched by the population of Jasper Mills.

"Hey, Hannah! I see you got another ticket today! I can't believe you blocked the fire station. Shame on you, young lady!"

It had already started. She didn't even bother looking around. She knew that voice; it was old Mr. Henry. He'd loved Jake like a son. But now he'd become as determined as the rest of the town that Hannah should move on with her life. Well, Mr. Henry needed to butt out and concentrate on chasing Agnes around the library.

"Do you wanna cup of coffee to go with that order of determination written all over your face or what?"

"That would be wonderful, Millie. Thank you very much." Hannah purred a sigh of smug satisfaction as she beamed her slyest grin up into her best friend's face.

"Where have you been all morning?"

Tracing her nails around the rim of the thick ceramic cup, Hannah tapped each one of her fingers in turn as she stared down into the dark, swirling brew. Millie would find out soon enough. The rich aroma of the coffee tickled her nose; her stomach growled in anticipation. She always got hungry after she'd solved a problem. Perhaps a slice of cheesecake would be good while she waited. "I've had a very enlightening morning."

"Enlightening, huh?" Millie repeated as she pulled four plates of steaming food from the window between the kitchen and the bar and stacked them in a line down her arm. "Hold that thought. I'll be right back." Bobbing her head so fast her short blond curls snapped in the air, Millie looked like her head bounced on a spring. Flitting like a hummingbird, she plopped the plates in front of their awaiting patrons and returned to her place behind the counter before Hannah swallowed her first sip of the scalding-hot coffee. "Okay. Now what do you mean by enlightening?"

Hannah held up a finger and shook her head as she glanced up at the oversized clock centered on the bright, red wall at the back of the room. "Not yet. I'm waiting for three more people to arrive and then we're all going to have a nice little chat about my car and erroneous parking tickets."

Millie turned and glanced at the great black and white clock, then frowned as one of the hands shifted. She caught her lip between her teeth and faced Hannah with a pained expression on her face. "What do you mean by a nice little chat about your car and parking tickets? What are you gonna do, Hannah?"

"You never could lie and I know you're in on it too, Millie. You might as well 'fess up now and save yourself some embarrassment."

"They made me do it! I didn't have a choice!"

"Of all people! You know better than anyone, Millie. How could you do this to me?"

"Marty! Get out here and cover for me!" Millie jerked her head toward the swinging doors of the back storage room as she grabbed Hannah's sleeve and yanked. "*You* come with me right now!"

All heads in the diner swiveled to follow the two young women as they stomped their way toward the back room.

As soon as they'd shoved their way through the doors, Millie turned Hannah loose and whirled on her with a shaking finger. "Hannah, you know it's time you moved on. It's been over four years since Jake died. You *have got* to get on with your life. You're a young woman for heaven's sake. You can't just shut yourself down. It's just not natural."

"That is not your decision, Millie! That's nobody's decision but mine!" Hannah yanked her wrinkled sleeve and swallowed hard to keep from screaming. Her entire body trembled inside; she risked collapsing at any moment. It may have been four years since Jake's loss had ripped out her heart, but her emotions still knotted in her throat.

How could Millie do this to her? She wasn't about to let any of them see her cry! She clenched her fists and sucked in a deep shaking breath. She had to make Millie understand. "Are you the one lying in bed at night with the sound of him breathing beside you? Are you the one rolling over with his scent on the sheets, still feeling as though the bed's warm from his body?" Hannah took a step toward Millie, backing her against a rack of unpacked canned goods. "Are you the one that still swears sometimes if you turn around just fast enough he might be there waiting to hold you? Can you swear you just heard the sound of his voice because he just whispered your name? Answer me, Millie. Can you?"

Millie edged away, hugging herself back against the rack. She stood there silent and stared at Hannah.

Hannah's heart hurt like a raw open sore with no hope of healing. Millie should know better. She knew Hannah and Jake had been inseparable. They had all grown up together in Jasper Mills. Everyone had known Hannah and Jake would always be together. Now Jake had gone and Hannah's plans had fallen apart. They had no right to tell her to move on.

"I have photographs. I know you, Tom, and Brodie moved my car today and I'd be willing to bet you're the ones who've been moving it all along. This is over, Millie. It's done! Matt's a nice guy, but I'm not on the market. Fix him up with Lily over at the day care center. She's cute, single, and wants an entire herd of kids." Hannah yanked open the storeroom door, leaving Millie with her lower lip trembling. "I've had enough of everyone's meddling," she hissed over her shoulder. "And I hope everyone heard me." Turning around, she swallowed a groan. *"Oh, great."*

There stood Matt at the counter with his ticket pad in hand, a smug grin smeared across his face. Might as well get it over with and take them all out at once. "Sheriff Matt, I'd like to take the opportunity to give you something that I think will cover all of those parking tickets." With a forced smile stretched across her face so tight her cheeks ached, Hannah fished into her pocket, her gaze locked with his.

Matt's smile widened and he stood a bit taller, glancing around the diner. "So, you've finally decided to give me a few hours of your time and have dinner with me?"

Hannah shook her head as she *tsk-tsked* at Sheriff Matt. "Why, no, Sheriff Matt, I believe that would be unethical. Actually, I thought these photographs of possible tampering of personal property might be of some interest to you. There's also one that looks like you might even know what's going on. See? This one right here?"

The diner settled into a silence as quiet as a tomb. The usual clank of the dishes and silverware evaporated as though they'd consisted of steam. The murmur of voices also disappeared as though Hannah and Sheriff Mulroney stood in between the aisles of a deserted church instead of between the booths of the diner.

"They were just trying to get you to come around, Hannah. No one meant you any harm."

Hannah lifted her chin and stood a little taller. She made a slow circuit and looked around the diner at all the eyes focused on her. She looked deep into the faces, read all the looks that waited to see what she planned to say. She'd known each and every one of these people all her life. She'd thought they'd realize by now how determined she was that they step back and give her more time to heal.

"I appreciate what all of you tried to do here with this little ploy. But you can't do this for me. You've got to let me heal and move on in my own time. I can't get over a lifetime of Jake in just four short years. Your little game has got to stop. It's not funny anymore." Then she turned back to Matt and tapped on his leather-bound ticket book with the packet of digital pictures. "No more hide and ticket with my car. We can be friends, but that's it. If you keep writing me tickets, I'll make sure your house and office is infested with every type of varmint I can find."

"You can't do that!"

Old Mr. Henry cleared his throat as he hobbled his way across the diner toward the cash register in the corner. "Don't underestimate her, son. Everybody knows Hannah has an odd way with the critters. You should've seen her with that pack of skunks a few years ago. *Nobody* messed with Hannah that spring. And that was before Jake died."

"It's no worse than what you did with your little ticket charade. So, like I said, no more tickets. Do we have a deal?" Hannah stood at the door of the diner with one brow arched, waiting for Matt's compliance.

Matt tossed his ticket book on the counter, then raised his hands in the air. "Fine! No more tickets!"

The sunlight filtered down through the ceiling of leaves and danced in erratic spots across the ground. Birches, maples, and fifty-year-old oaks dotted this part of the mountain, along with cedar, dogwood, and pine. The hand-shaped leaves of the birch and maples waved and fluttered in the gentle breeze. The early-morning sunshine still held the kiss of spring as it wafted through the air. It was early enough in the summer that the humidity wasn't high enough to stick the clothes to your body, the kind of warm sunny day where cats became boneless, draping their bodies along the rail of the porch for a lazy, sun-drenched snooze.

Hannah rocked to the rhythmic squeak of the battered porch glider, sipping her morning coffee. She loved the steady rickety-rackety thump of the rusty-hinged swing. It reminded her of Grandma and simpler days. They'd frittered away hours on that front porch swing making up stories about magical places.

She propped her bare feet on the waist-high rail of the weathered veranda, cradling the steaming cup against her chest. The broad covered porch ran the circumference of the house providing the perfect morning oasis. The third-generation home screamed for want of a few replaced boards and a fresh coat of paint, but she just couldn't seem to find the time or the inclination. With a sigh, she flicked at a bubbled-up paint chip with her big toe. A ruby-throated hummingbird buzzed in from the cluster of cedars bunched at the corner of the house. The iridescent flash of green hovered a brief moment in front of her face, dipped closed enough for her to feel the brush of the wind from its whirring wings, then dashed to alight on the feeder hanging from the roof's edge.

Watching the bird dip its needle-like beak into the trumpet-shaped feeder, Hannah inhaled a heavy sigh. Today, she would go to the cemetery. It was their anniversary. She and Jake would've been married six years today. If only. Hannah drew another deep breath and curled her feet beneath her. She hated the if-only game. It had eaten away at her heart and churned at her gut ever since Jake had died.

The wind lofted the faintest scent of sweetness across her face. She closed her eyes against the honey-sweet fragrance and forced down the knot of emotions swelling in her throat. That reminded her: she needed to gather an armload of honeysuckles. She couldn't let their anniversary pass without covering Jake's marker with their favorite flower. A bittersweet ache shuddered through her body with a hiccupping breath as she remembered the first time she and Jake had discovered the sweet-smelling vines. Hannah had just turned six years old and faithfully followed every step seven-year-old Jake took through the woods of their mountain.

Young Jake had sworn they followed the trail of the elusive Big Foot. He'd seen it on television the night before and he'd recognized the massive, old oak of the woods in one of the scenes right before the last commercial. Devoted Hannah had no doubt he must be right. After all, Jake knew everything. Didn't he tell her that often enough?

They'd discovered the opening of a deserted cave hidden behind a tangled abundance of flowering honeysuckle vines. Much to the avid trackers' disappointment, Big Foot escaped them, but the enticing, honey-laced aroma of the flowers caught their immediate attention. Inquisitive Jake discovered if he took the trumpet-shaped flower and pulled the stamen backward out through the stem, they could catch the sweet, sticky nectar on their tongues and rob the local hummingbirds of their syrupy treat. The children forgot Big Foot and spent the afternoon pillaging the tasty flowers.

Hannah swallowed hard again. The memories ached in her throat as she forced herself back to the present. Damn that stupid war, and damn Jake and his need to be everyone's hero. He'd always needed the excitement of any kind of adventure more then he'd ever needed her. Hannah closed her mind against the darkest thoughts that often plagued her ever since she'd known Jake. What other adventure would've robbed her of Jake even if he'd survived that infernal war? It didn't matter now. The hair-trigger bomb wired to that hospital jeep had sent him home to her and she'd laid him to rest on their mountain.

As the liquid met her lips, she realized her coffee had grown cold. Glancing down at her pajamas, she rose from the glider, tossed the bitter liquid over the railing, and padded her way across the porch. Time to get dressed and get the ATV loaded up. Hannah looked forward to the thirty-minute ride up the primitive trail to the gravesite. The peace of the forest would ease her mind. Plus, she needed to get back down the mountain in time to talk to Mrs. Newell's third-grade class about the local raccoon population and the fact that no matter what the children happened to see on television, the animals did not make suitable pets, at least not for the average person.

A chittering noise at the edge of the woods grabbed her attention. Without even looking, she knew who it was and called over her shoulder as she headed toward the back door of the house. "I don't have time today. If you want to meet me up at the gravesite, then go on ahead and I'll see you there." Closing the screen door, she glanced across the yard to make sure the animals had heard her. "Go on. Meet me at Jake's marker. Today's our anniversary, remember?" Three squirrels, a doe, and a very obese raccoon turned and headed back into the woods.

What a quaint small town, this place called Jasper Mills. Taggart rolled his shoulders as he ambled down the narrow strip of sidewalk running alongside the tree-lined lane. Gads, the next time he traversed across several continents he'd sift into a secluded wood; he didn't care if he risked discovery. Hours wedged into a seat inside a plane bordered on unbearable torture. He didn't care if the airline insisted the ticket stated first class. The blasted seats didn't fit his arse.

"MacPherson Clinic," Taggart mumbled, spotting a brilliant blue sign with white letters emblazoned on a white clapboard building. His heart sank when he noticed the blinds drawn in the wide, plate-glass window and a bright red closed sign leaned against the corner. 'Twas the middle of the day, the middle of the week, where the hell could the woman be? Shouldn't she be at her place of business?

Taggart spun on his heel and scanned the street. He had no idea what the woman looked like. But if she came within a few feet of him, he'd home in on her like a bee to pollen. He reached out with his senses into the surrounding area and felt absolutely nothing. Hannah Mac-Pherson wasn't in town.

"Damn, damn, damn." And then Taggart noticed the neat script written on the bottom portion of the closed sign. *In case of emergency, go to the café and ask for Millie.*

"The café and ask for Mille, eh?" Taggart turned and looked up and down the street. "I'd definitely call this an emergency."

"Excuse me, young man?" A wisp of an old lady with shining blue hair squinted up at Taggart through her thick, silver-rimmed spectacles perched on the end of her nose. The glittering blue chain attached to the earpieces dangled down around her neck, swaying with every word she spoke. "Did you say something to me?"

Taggart adopted his most charming smile and bowed as he clasped his hands behind his back. "Would ye be so kind as to give me directions to the café? I'm from out of town and I'm afraid I've gotten a bit turned around."

A hint of a pink blush spread to the elderly woman's crinkled cheeks as she patted a lace hanky to her brightly, painted lips. "Why certainly, young man, it's just across the way. Just cross the lane here and go down a block to your left. You're not very far from it at all."

With another gallant bow, Taggart gifted her with another blinding smile. "Ye are most kind, ma'am. I thank ye verra much."

The woman tittered into her hanky as Taggart headed across the street.

He'd best keep his thoughts to himself. That kindly lady might not have been so helpful had she arrived a few moments sooner to find him cursing the air blue. Taggart smiled as he spotted the café. The first inhabitant of Jasper Mills reminded him a great deal of some of the gentle folk of Erastaed.

The jangle of the bell above the diner door sounded as the smells from the kitchen assaulted him. His stomach roared to attention as the scent of grilled hamburgers, fried potatoes, and sautéed onions reminded him that he hadn't eaten in quite a while. Perhaps he'd do more than just ask for Millie. After all, a man must eat. Glancing around the restaurant, he opted to sit at the counter for now, at least until he'd talked to this *Millie.*

"What'll you have?" A perky blonde asked as she poured a glass of ice water and slid it in front of him.

"Would ye happen to be Millie?" Taggart asked, lacing his fingers around the cold, slick glass and rubbing his thumbs across the rim. He didn't miss her sharp intake of breath or the way she narrowed her pale blue eyes.

"Why?"

"I need to reach Hannah MacPherson. It's quite urgent and the sign at her clinic said to ask for Millie." Taggart suppressed a smile. He read this transparent lass as easily as he would a child's picture book. She stiffened even more, her hand curled into a fist on the edge of the counter when Taggart mentioned Hannah MacPherson's name. What did she hide? Better yet, why was she so protective of his precious guardian?

Millie turned away, snatched a coffeepot from the warming plate, and held it aloft as she edged her way out from behind the counter. "I'm Millie, but today's a very full day on Dr. MacPherson's calendar. I'm not going to interrupt her unless you tell me what you want. Like the sign said, it's got to be an absolute emergency. Do you have an injured animal or something?"

Taggart swirled the sweating glass of water in front him, smiling as he stared down at the rings of condensation swimming on the well-scrubbed counter. Millie guarded Hannah MacPherson as though she were the lass's mother. Good. But he wasn't the one Millie had to fear. He'd come prepared for just such a situation. Pulling a manila-bound packet from the inside pocket of his jacket, Taggart tossed it down the counter toward Millie. "Read this and I'm sure ye'll understand why it's of the utmost importance that I contact Ms. MacPherson right away. I've been trying to contact her for quite some time and as ye can see, the news is quite good."

Millie sat down the coffee urn, opened the packet, and withdrew the sheaf of papers from within. "Is this for real?" she asked with a glance over the top of the papers.

"I wouldna be here if it were not."

She had loaded down the rack of the ATV with sticky bundles of the fragrant honeysuckle flowers. The hillside rising behind her house crawled with the glossy, green flowering vines.

Hannah leaned to the side as the ATV lumbered up the winding trail of the mountain. The growling machine wound between the gnarled trunks of towering oaks. The chunky wheels grabbed hold of rocks and roots blocking the path, grumbling over any obstacle Hannah ploughed through. Her heart grew heavier with every curve in the path. She could drive it with her eyes shut. She'd walked it more times then she'd driven it the first year Jake had been gone. The branches overhead blocked the sunlight, creating a green tunnel up the mountainside.

Hannah loved this mountain with a passionate ache. She and Jake had planned on filling it with generations of MacPhersons when he'd returned from the war. Jake had promised her lots of babies. Jake had been the last one in his family and all of Hannah's family was gone as well. Now Hannah lived all alone on their mountain, just her and all the animals.

Hannah swiped her hand across her eyes. She'd promised herself she'd keep the tears to a minimum. She'd just end up with an aching head, a snotty nose, and a case of the hiccups until she puked. Everything happened for a reason in this world. Wasn't that what Grandma had always told her? At least, she'd had several wonderful years with Jake. She could just hear Granny preach at her to quit whining about her worries now. Granny didn't believe in dwelling on the negative. The stubborn old woman had promised there was always somebody in this world whose lot in life had to be worse than your own. With a sigh, Hannah revved the ATV over a fallen log downed across the path. Sometimes it was just easier to wallow in a quagmire of self-pity than it was to count your blessings.

The trail opened out into a sun-dappled clearing, the ground soft and spongy with years of fallen leaves scattered like a quilt waiting to be pieced. A gray block of weathered stone stood centered in the tree-lined circle, looking as though it had fallen out of the side of some ancient castle's barrier wall. The three squirrels, the doe, and the raccoon nestled together in a contented pile beside an outcropping of elderberry bushes.

Hannah killed the engine to the ATV, blinking hard as she focused on the stone. It had been a while since she'd last been up here, Jake's birthday to be exact. Her hands tightened for a moment on the textured grips before she threw her leg over the side and slid off the seat.

Clenching her teeth, she filled her arms full of the flowers and carried them over to the marker. Jake. With a lover's touch, she traced her fingertips over the cold, chiseled surface and exhaled with a shuddering sigh. It had taken her a while. But she'd finally found it and had the rough-hewn stone shipped over from a disemboweled castle in Scotland. She'd decided it would be perfect as Jake's headstone. She knew he'd never want the smooth, contemporary granite or marble found on all the other graves in the average churchyard. Jake's stone mirrored the man he'd been when he lived: rough around the edges and full of character.

"I still haven't forgiven you, Jake." Her voice echoed around the dogwood-lined clearing of the quiet wood. The pale, heart-shaped leaves rustled and dipped lower from the gnarled stand of trees. Hannah settled cross-legged in front of the stone just as she did every year on this day. "You promised me you'd come back and we'd make babies. You said doctors were safe because everybody knew they were just there to help. You said the press always blew things out of proportion. You lied to me, Jake."

The wind rushed through the trees and swirled in a circle around her, stirring the dead leaves into a flurrying mass of browns, oranges, and reds that flew into the air. The sunlight filtered down upon the stone and danced across Jake's chiseled name and date of his death.

Hannah yanked at fresh green shoots of grass sprouting up around the edges of the stone. She drew in a deep, shaking breath and let her gaze wander through the trees around her. "Just once, I wish you'd answer me, Jake." With a glance toward the trees as though they eavesdropped on her conversation, Hannah lowered her voice and leaned closer to the stone. "You know, Jake, Mama was a witch, so was Grandma and all the women before them. They all believed they could talk to loved ones on the other side. But they left me too soon and didn't show me how. Give me a break, will you? Why won't you talk to me, Jake?"

The wind strengthened and pushed at her back. A forceful gust whipped her hair into her face, lifted one of the bundles of honeysuckles off the headstone, and dropped the flowers into her lap.

Hannah brushed her fingertips across the softness of the yellow petals, closing her eyes against the torrent of emotions threatening to overflow. "Thank you, Jake." She choked back the tears with a muffled cough. Would this ache never go away?

A shrill alarm shattered the serenity of the woods, jerking her free of the memories. Hannah crawled across the ground and fished her beeper out of the side bag of the ATV. She blinked hard and wiped at her eyes. Millie hadn't used their agreed-upon code red, so the beep didn't signal an emergency. It couldn't be Farmer Donovan's mare. That wasn't his number flashing across the display, nor was it the infirmary code. Uneasiness gnawing in the pit of her stomach, Hannah twirled the beeper in her hand and switched off the irritating buzzer. She couldn't believe Millie had even beeped her. Millie knew what day this was and Hannah didn't want to be disturbed. It must be something important.

Plunging into her side bag, she found her cell phone. A sniff and a swallow against the lump in her throat made her hiccup as she punched in the number to the café.

"Millie, did you forget what day this is?"

"No, I know what day this is, but, you *really* need to come into town right now. There's someone here to see you and I don't think you want to miss this." Millie's voice sounded strained, as though she needed to say more but couldn't.

"Is there an injured animal?"

"No. Nobody's injured and he doesn't have any animals with him that I can see."

Hannah pulled the phone away from her ear and glared down into the display. Millie wasn't making any sense and Hannah wasn't in the mood for games today. What was that chick up to now? This had better not be another prank, especially not today. "What do you mean *he*?"

"Hannah, please just come to the café," Millie's voice pleaded in Hannah's ear. "I told him you were out of pocket today, but he's from out of town and has traveled quite a ways to see you. He sort of *insisted*. If you could just come into town for just a bit. I know it's a rough day for you, but just come into town for thirty minutes tops. *Please?*"

Hannah gritted her teeth as she blinked up through the branches laced across the sky. Millie never could stand up to anybody. Her heart melted at the flimsiest of stories.

"Fine, Millie. But I'm on the mountaintop so, it'll be about an hour or so before I make it into town. Can you call Mrs. Newell and see if I can reschedule my talk to her class to another day as well? I don't think I'm up to educating a class full of third graders about pesky raccoons after all."

"No problem. I'll get your raccoon talk rescheduled for next week and I'll see you here in a bit. Bye!"

Hannah stuffed the phone back in the leather side bag of the ATV and straddled the seat. Who could be waiting to see her at the café? Whoever he was, he seemed to have Millie flustered. She glared at the pouch holding her cell phone as she tapped her fingers on the handlebars. "What's going on, Millie? What are you setting me up for now?"

Hannah pointed the ATV back down the trail and paused to glance back at the weathered stone standing in the clearing.

"I miss you, Jake."

The wind rushed around her body with a swirling hug as she turned the machine and headed down the trail.

His back against the wall, Taggart sipped the lukewarm coffee while propping an elbow against the spotless linoleum-topped table situated in the corner. Perhaps this vantage point proved better after all. For the sake of Millie's nerves, he couldn't stay perched close to her at the counter any longer. Poor lass, while he'd leaned against the counter and tried to make polite conversation, she'd spilled nearly every order she pulled from the window. He had her so befuddled she'd toppled his coffee cup across the countertop twice. Besides, he'd discovered from this seat in the corner, he could not only watch every person seated in the diner but also have a clear view of the traffic coming in off the street.

The high-strung blonde fidgeted behind the counter, fretting with the spring-loaded napkin holders she'd already checked twice before. Taggart studied her more closely as he noticed her glance at him for at least the tenth time in the past half hour and then look to the clock hanging over his head. He knew the woman wasn't worried about the level of coffee in his cup. She avoided his table as though he had the plague. For some reason, his presence here had Millie stumbling about as though she had two left feet. He'd overheard her conversation with Hannah Mac-Pherson. Why would today be a rough day for the very important individual he'd traveled so far to see?

He suppressed a smile as he sipped at the dwindling dregs of his coffee. He sensed every thought from every person in the room. Jasper Mills projected the aura of a close-knit community. They shielded Ms. MacPherson, treasuring her as one would a beloved daughter. Good. The guardian of Taroc Na Mor should be pure of both character and soul. If her people loved her, that proved well indeed. The research he'd found about her bloodline and genetics held true.

The bell on the wire hanging above the door jangled. Taggart knew it was her before he raised his eyes; he sensed it by the way the skin tingled at the base of his neck. Her energy sent a shiver up his spine. The sacred guardian's aura flooded the room and he was her protector. He would've known she entered his presence even if he had been blind.

Taggart hid his grin behind the white ceramic mug he clasped between his hands. The collective jaws of the Guild of Barac'Nairn would've hit the floor had they been sitting at Taggart's side. Hannah MacPherson, the blessed guardian, was not what they would've expected. Taggart chuckled into the depths of his cup. As far as he was concerned, the fiery lass beamed the definition of pure delight itself.

The tiny, young woman ordained to be guardian of the sacred Draecna sported a ratty St. Louis Cardinals baseball cap pulled low over snapping green eyes. Her auburn ponytail exploded through the tattered hole in the back. The tangled mass of curls tumbled down her back as though a windstorm had tossed her into the cafe. Grass and mud stained the ragged knees of her jeans. Her well-worn T-shirt clung to her curves like tissue wrapped around a tempting gift. Taggart set down his coffee, stretching back in his chair, unable to resist chuckling again. He'd never seen a woman don such boots. Steel-toed work boots laced tight about her tiny ankles. She plodded across the room like a heavy construction worker.

He held his breath to keep from laughing aloud as she stalked her way over to the counter. He could tell by the way the woman stomped, she was prepared to unleash the hounds of hell if anyone dared cross her. Such a fierce small package, she reminded him of the territorial wood nymphs of Glenoc Mur. She'd barely reach the middle of his chest, yet the woman stood coiled so tight she appeared ready to explode.

The longer Taggart studied her, the more his amusement faded. Hannah MacPherson was gearing up for a fight. Taggart shifted in his seat as the realization hit; he stood centered in her crosshairs. Taggart peered closer. She also suffered; her face revealed a great deal of emotional pain. Her wound simmered deep. Hannah MacPherson might be small, but her heart swelled with sorrow.

Taggart sucked in a slow breath, struggling against an uncomfortable stirring deep within his chest. His precious guardian had been deeply hurt; she fluttered as a wounded bird. Taggart watched as Hannah's head turned with eyes narrowed when Millie whispered and pointed in his direction. He unfolded his frame and stood beside the table as Hannah whirled and barreled his way.

"Mr. de Gaelson? I believe you wanted to see me? I'm Hannah MacPherson." Hannah stuck out her hand as though daring him to take it and fixed Taggart with a green-eyed glare.

Taggart closed his hand around Hannah's cold, stiff grasp and held it as he leveled with her gaze. "Please, call me Taggart."

"What can I do for you, Taggart?" Hannah clipped the words with a jerk of her hand, rubbing her fingers as though his touch disturbed her. She shot Millie a brooding glare, her glance sliding back to Taggart as if blaming Millie for his presence.

Taggart bit back a smile. The woman wasn't going to make his life easy. He read the wariness in Hannah's eyes and the way she'd withdrawn from his touch. Good. She should be wary. It would increase her lifespan and make protecting her somewhat easier, albeit getting close to her and winning her trust could prove even more of a challenge. Taggart nodded toward the table while he motioned for Millie. "Would ye like some coffee while we talk?"

"Not really, thanks." Hannah sent Millie scuttling back around the counter with a single shake of her head. "I don't mean to sound rude, Mr. de Gaelson—"

"Taggart, Ms. MacPherson. Please, I asked ye to call me Taggart, remember?" Taggart cleared his throat. God's teeth, the stubborn woman insisted on doing things her own way. Lucky for her, they were on this side of the threshold. If they were in Erastaed, he would have sifted them to someplace quiet and spelled her. He'd seal her lips and open her ears so she'd have no choice but to hear his words. By Isla's golden beard, she had to see she needed protection. 'Twas time she faced her destiny.

Hannah snatched off her hat and worried with her tangled curls, grimacing as she yanked the snarls. "Okay. Fine. Taggart, as I started to say, I don't mean to sound rude, but I have quite a bit going on today. So, what can I do for you? Can we just get on with it?"

Taggart bit back a rumbling growl simmering just behind his clenched teeth. Protector or no, he'd had just about enough. He'd come all the way from Scotland by uncomfortable, archaic twenty-first-century means. He was in no mood to put up with a surly, hardheaded woman who had no idea of her worth. His gaze wandered from her storming eyes to the disheveled curls amassed about her head; and gads, if his fingers didn't itch to touch the silk of that brandy-colored hair. She needed to put that ratty hat back on her head. Taggart shook himself and pinched the bridge of his nose. What the hell was wrong with him? She was off-limits. He must concentrate on the matter at hand. It must be the jet lag making him daft. The ones of this side always muttered about that weakness whenever he eavesdropped on their conversations.

Taggart cleared his throat, taking a deep breath. He could do this. He hadn't come this far to fail. "Ye wouldna happen to remember receiving several certified packets from Scotland with the legal seal of de Gaelson, Branwen and Septamus, would ye?"

Hannah frowned, then paled an anxious shade of pink as she worried the brim of the ball cap between her hands.

"I paid for the stone, and everything came through customs just fine. Do I still owe some sort of duty or extra taxes to Scotland? Is that what this is about?"

Millie came over and refilled Taggart's cup. She edged her way over to Hannah's side. "Are you okay?"

Hannah shrugged as she leaned closer to her friend. "There must be a problem with Jake's headstone. I guess I didn't file all the paperwork correctly to finalize it through customs with Scotland. You remember all those packets I've been kind of ignoring and tossing into the I'll-look-at-it-later box?" Turning to Taggart, she leaned forward. "Is that what all those packets are about?" Catching her lower lip between her teeth, she shot a guilty look at him before dropping her gaze to her cap. "I never opened them. I just tossed them in a box with the rest of the junk I was going to go through later. I've been really busy."

"Who is this Jake person?" As Hannah's aura darkened with grief, Taggart flinched and felt an immediate jab of regret that he had asked. So this was the source of Hannah's pain. The very mention of the man's name plunged her into darkness.

"Jake was my husband. He died in the Iraq War. Are you here about the headstone or not?" Hannah licked her lips and inhaled a slow, shaking breath while she strangled her ball cap on the table in front of her.

"No, lass." Taggart threw himself back in the chair and scrubbed his face with his hands. The oracle should've provided him with all this information. No wonder she'd ignored all the missives. Hannah MacPherson wasn't going to be easily convinced to leave this place. "If ye had read the letters, ye would know ye have inherited a fine estate in the Highlands of Scotland. If ye had *opened* the missives, ye would've been be pleased to find ye not only own one small stone but actually an entire castle and quite an expanse of land. The name of your place is Taroc Na Mor and it waits for ye to lay claim to it."

Hannah stared at Taggart as though he'd just sprouted a set of golden horns. She worked her ball cap through her fingers while gnawing on the corner of her lip.

Taggart watched her, thinking if she didn't take a breath soon she'd surely faint and fall out of the chair.

Then her eyes narrowed and she leaned forward with a decided shake of her head. "That is impossible. You've got the wrong person. Someone has made a terrible mistake."

Taggart dared her with a jerk of his chin toward the door. "Go get the papers out of your wee box if ye dinna believe me. They'll tell ye what ye dinna wish to accept."

"I don't know of any relatives I've ever had in Scotland. Who would leave me an estate?" Hannah slapped her hat in the middle of the table as she sat up straighter in the chair.

"Go get the papers if ye dinna believe me." Taggart folded his arms across his chest and forced himself not to smile. Today, he was too tired to argue with her and he had yet to win her trust. But he had to admit, it was a temptation to provoke her. He relished a good battle and this one would be easy to win. He loved the way her green eyes snapped when she thought she was right. This woman's fire warmed his blood more then he dared to admit.

"Fine!" Hannah hissed, jumping up from the table. "Don't you dare go anywhere. I'll be right back."

Taggart allowed himself the pleasure of a victorious grin as he tilted his head in admiration of how well her jeans fit the curve of her hips as she stormed her way out of the diner. "Don't worry, lass. There's not a power in either one of our worlds that could tear me away from here now."

★   ★   ★

Hannah burst into her office and tossed her keys across the low countertop dividing the waiting area from the first set of examination rooms. "Sophie, I know you're not in your kennel. I heard you scurrying around when I unlocked the door. Come on out. I promise I won't put you back in there. It's pointless since you're such an escape artist."

A long-nosed dog of questionable breed wormed around the corner. A blond, skinny tail curled between trembling hind legs while pointy ears dripped from a bowed head hanging low to the floor.

"Come here. You're not in trouble." Hannah squatted down, opened her arms wide, and welcomed Sophie's wet kisses while dodging her lunging paws and wildly thumping tail. "Help me find the mail I never open, Sophie. I don't remember what I did with all those boxes. Do you remember where I put them?"

Sophie barked and spun her way out of Hannah's arms. Her toenails clicked as she pranced her way down the gleaming tiles of the hall.

"I really need to trim your toenails," Hannah laughed as she followed the *tick, tick, ticking* of Sophie's nails. Sophie barked again and stood wagging her tail in front of a storage closet, pointing her long, narrow nose up at the black steel door.

"I'm glad your memory is so much better than mine, Sophie. You're the best office help I've ever had." Hannah hugged the dog as she opened the door and spotted the box of mail bulging from the highest shelf.

Hannah took it to the exam room and plopped the box on the table. As she unwound the jute string and lifted the lid, she wrinkled her nose as musty air exploded from the contents. *Whew!* She was going to have to break down and hire some help around the office. Millie's once-a-month overhaul just wasn't quite enough. Hannah held

her breath until the urge to sneeze passed, her eyes stinging with the itchiness of the dust. She tried to keep everything as straight as Millie got it. But it kind of slid right
back to a haphazard mess within a few days' time.

She eased out her breath and flipped through the mail
crammed inside the box. She should've thrown half this
stuff away instead of squirreling it away in this crate. Hannah frowned, pawing through the odd-sized envelopes.
She paused as her mind drifted back to the man she'd just
met, the irritating man waiting back at the diner.

Taggart de Gaelson nagged at her thoughts, demanded
her attention in an increasingly irritating way. When Hannah had seen him, she'd teetered on the verge of remembering something she'd forgotten, a subtle fluttering, a
pulling in the center of her chest. She'd known him, but
she didn't. A jolt of energy prickled across her skin, an
eerie sensation demanding her immediate attention. She'd
shivered with a strange sense of recognition as soon as
she'd walked into the diner and locked eyes with the infuriating man.

Those eyes. Maybe that's what mesmerized her every
time she looked him full in the face. Ice-blue, dark-
rimmed around the iris, they bored into the center of her
soul and pried into her secret places. Hannah shivered
again. If she didn't know better, she would've sworn the
man knew every thought that crossed her mind. And
those hands. Hannah paused as she remembered how her
hand had disappeared in Taggart's muscled grasp as he'd
pulled her a bit closer when he'd greeted her. They'd been
so warm and strong and . . . Hannah shook herself. She'd
sworn there'd been almost an electrical vibration. She'd
never felt a connection in a touch like that before. Hannah coughed when she realized she'd forgotten to breathe.

"Whew. What's wrong with me, Sophie? You'd think
I'd never seen a man before."

Sophie barked and wagged her tail, then curled around Hannah's feet.

"You're a big help," Hannah laughed, returning to the musty carton. Diving deeper into the box, she finally spotted the corner of one the certified packets. With a grunt, she wiggled and worked it loose from where it lay wedged in the bottom of the cardboard box.

With shaking hands, she tore open the letter and removed the sheaf of heavy vellum paper. She scanned through the documents. Hand to her throat, she swallowed hard against the speeding hammer of her heart. A name jumped out at her: Sullivan. She remembered the name from her mother's side. In fact, if she remembered the stories Grandma told her, Gracie Sullivan was the first of her line who had discovered she had talent as a witch. Poor Gracie had paid dearly for that discovery. For consorting with the dead, she had received the death sentence. An oak plank loaded with stones had crushed Gracie Sullivan's life as well as her magical heritage out of her body.

Hannah's breath caught as she double-checked the heavy manila envelope. Pictures had also been included, aerial shots of a castle and grounds. Centuries of abuse by the harsh elements of the Highlands had weathered the keep to a charred, somber black. The skirting wall and the corner guardhouse appeared less battered; the huge rough blocks reflected a lighter gray in the lighting of the photo. The castle itself perched atop a remote cliff overlooking an angry sea. From what she could see, a few more centuries of erosion and the forbidding structure would slide into the waves below.

A tangled, evergreen wood covered the surrounding land, running up to a deep ravine and forming a jagged boundary around the castle. One gated bridge crossed the ravine and led to the skirting wall guarding the keep. Even in the twenty-first century, Taroc Na Mor still appeared an impenetrable stronghold.

Hannah shivered as cold fingers of recognition tickled the back of her neck. How could she know this place? She traced the outline of the slate roof of the keep, almost feeling the jagged coldness beneath her fingers. She swore she heard the cry of the gulls overhead, felt the bite of the wind blowing in from sea. Hannah licked her lips and peered closer at the glossy photo. She pressed her hand against her mouth and tasted the tang of the ocean in the air.

"I have lost my mind," Hannah mumbled, picking up the letter and reading it again. It clearly stated Taroc Na Mor was hers. She was the only living heir.

Hannah tossed the papers down on the table in front of him and slid into the chair. "Why are you here, Mr. de . . . I mean Taggart? What exactly is it you want from me?"

"Ye're no' exactly the trusting sort. Are ye, Ms. MacPherson?" Taggart snorted out a cynical laugh. "Aye, that's verra wise. Ye'll live a lot longer that way. But ye need to remember there's a good bit of difference between caution and bitterness. Ye dinna want to end up a complete solitary, now do ye?"

Hannah tensed, balling her fists at her sides. Who was this guy who'd shown up to complicate her life? Where did he get off lecturing her on her behavior? He had no idea who she was or what the complications in her life were. With gritted teeth, Hannah took a deep breath. She spread her hands on the table and jerked her head toward the photos of Taroc Na Mor. "Just tell me why you're here exactly. I realize I ignored your precious certified packets. But you're here now, so what is it you want from me?"

Taggart reached across the table and fingered the corner of one of the pictures. With a heavy sigh, he traced his thumb along the border of the photo as though wishing he could step inside. Homesickness etched across Taggart's face and longing reflected in his eyes. Hannah read Taggart's love for Taroc Na Mor before he ever uttered a word.

"When we received no response from ye, it was my duty to find ye and explain to ye all that had come to be yours."

"So, what you're telling me is that you're the executor of the estate?" Hannah folded her hands on the table. What he was telling her couldn't possibly be true. This had to be some kind of mistake. She had no kin left in Scotland. For heaven's sake, she didn't even have any living relatives in this country. Uneasiness swept across her like a damp, fetid wind. Something about this whole story just didn't sound quite right.

Taggart paused, leaning a bit closer across the table as he turned the photo in his hands. "Actually, I'm a member of a group of individuals who have watched over Taroc Na Mor down through the centuries. I guess ye might say I'm a protector of sorts."

Wariness swelled in the pit of Hannah's stomach as if she'd swallowed a lead weight for lunch. "You sound like you're in some kind of cult or something." Hannah inched back a bit from the table. This guy didn't look like a nut, but sometimes appearances could be deceiving.

Taggart eased back to his side of the table and returned the photo to the crinkled manila packet. Fixing Hannah with a brilliant smile, he chuckled and shook his head. "I assure ye, Ms. MacPherson, 'tis nothing quite so sinister. We merely tend to the special needs of the estate and when we can find them, we take care of its heirs. Now tell me, what do ye think? Is it not grand? Do ye not think Taroc Na Mor is the most beautiful piece of land on which ye have ever laid your eyes? Are ye not anxious to visit your new property and claim it as your own?"

Hannah forced a polite smile on her face as she gathered up the remaining photos and stuffed them back in the envelope. She'd be kind and explain things clearly and then maybe he'd go away. She took a deep breath and ignored the incessant churning in the pit of her stomach. With a glance into his intense, waiting gaze, she ignored the disturbing scent of powerful male teasing from the man across the table. The sooner Taggart de Gaelson left Jasper Mills, the better. With those eyes and that body, the man in front of her had to be nothing but trouble. She was alone and intended to stay that way. He needed to get back across that pond to Scotland. "I'll admit Taroc Na Mor looks beautiful in these pictures, Taggart. But you've never seen my mountain. I'm sorry, but I'm afraid you've not only wasted your time. You've wasted a lot of money flying all this way to see me. I'm just not interested in coming to Scotland. I'm needed here in Jasper Mills. This is my home."

"What?" Taggart splayed both hands across the table as though ready to lunge across the room.

"My mountain," Hannah repeated. She slid the packet across the table between Taggart's outspread hands and lightly tapped on its top. "My home is here, Taggart. This is where my roots are. This is where I buried my husband and this is where I intend to stay."

"Are ye insane, woman? Ye have to at least go and see the land! Ye canna just toss it aside like scraps of food ye rake from the table after ye've finished with your meal." Taggart slapped his hand on the envelope and shoved it back in front of her.

Okay. So looks could be deceiving. Maybe he didn't have to look the part to be crazy. Hannah stood and planted her hands on either side of the packet. With narrowed eyes, she leaned forward until her nose almost touched his. "If it is my land, I can do anything I want with it, even if it means continuing to ignore it. I'm surprised Scotland hasn't taken it away from me since I haven't paid any taxes on it since you people started sending me all those letters. There's no telling how much money I owe on that land. I'm probably going to have to sell it to pay all the back taxes anyway."

"Taroc Na Mor can never be sold! Are ye daft, woman?" With a roar, Taggart stood so fast his chair flew backwards across the floor of the diner. "There are no back taxes due. We pay all the taxes. It is our duty as the Guild of Barac'Nairn!"

"The what?" Hannah repeated as she took a step back to avoid the ranting Scot. She couldn't help but notice how dark his eyes flashed now that he'd grown so aggravated. If not for the fact that the man was obviously obsessed, she'd fix him up with Millie. Millie had a thing for sexy Highlanders and Taggart definitely had that roll-me-in-the-heather kind of look.

"Hannah, is this guy bothering you?" Sheriff Matt appeared at Hannah's side, his hand resting on the sidearm belted at his hip.

Hannah glanced at Matt; then her gaze swept back over to Taggart. Yep. Matt would definitely have to use his gun. Sheriff Matt stood dwarfed by the angry Scot. Hannah hadn't missed how Taggart had ducked his head whenever he'd walked through the door. She'd also noted he'd had to turn somewhat sideways because the span of his shoulders nearly filled them as well.

His biceps bulged as big around as her head; the man loomed the size of a mountain. She hadn't seen men built like him since she'd flipped through the satellite channels the other night and accidently landed on some weight-lifting program.

"It's all right, Matt." Hannah shook her head. "We're just having a little discussion about some land I didn't know I owned. Taggart is filling me in on Scottish laws of ownership and he's just a little passionate about some points I don't understand."

"Are you sure?" Matt tapped his holster with a tense finger as he fixed Taggart with a warning glare.

"I am absolutely positive." Hannah smiled and patted Matt's arm. A twinge of guilt nipped at her conscience for pushing him off on Lily. Lily could be such a whiny little twit when she didn't get her way. Oh well, Matt was a big boy. Hopefully, he could take care of himself.

Hannah turned back to the table, scooped up the envelope, then beckoned to the glowering Scot with a nod of her head. "Come on. Let's go for a walk and you can explain to me about this Guild of Barac'Nairn without danger of being shot."

His plan had failed miserably so far. This coming to Jasper Mills to sweep the hardheaded Hannah MacPherson off her feet and cart her back to Scotland was proving more difficult than he'd imagined. And he couldn't believe the photos hadn't worked. Taggart worried a hand through his hair. The photos had failed to draw her to Taroc Na Mor. She should've been entranced with the very sight of the land. Perhaps the papers had sat too long and the magic inside the images had fallen dormant. He'd performed the incantation himself, double-checked it before he'd sealed the packets. What had gone wrong? The yearning flowed in Hannah MacPherson's blood; he'd seen it flash in her eyes. Records had verified the Sullivan line on both sides of the threshold. Hannah MacPherson was the last true heir both in this world and in Erastaed.

Gracie Sullivan had been the first of Hannah's gifted lineage. The Guild had sorely fallen short in their protection of their very first charge of the Sullivan line. They'd also failed when they'd lost the thread of the family's heritage to Hannah's grandmother and her mother. Taggart had sorted through centuries of false leads before he'd found Hannah. But he'd finally homed in on her like a bee to nectar. With a sidling glance, he appraised her as she walked along beside him. Such fire! Born to be a guardian, she was. Septamus would dearly love her. All the Draecna of Taroc Na Mor would be thrilled with the lass.

"Taggart!" Hannah whistled and clapped her hands.

"Beg pardon." Taggart bowed his head. "Forgive me. I became lost in my thoughts. What did ye say?"

"This Guild of Barac'Nairn you spoke of? Would you care to elaborate on this elite group you belong to now that we're out of earshot of half the population of Jasper Mills?" Hannah led the way toward the acre of neatly mown grass centered in the middle of town. Inviting white benches dotted the circumference of a black, asphalt jogging path, but Hannah headed for a set of abandoned benches shaded by a gnarled old oak off to the side.

"As I told ye." Taggart cleared his throat. "We have kept up all the taxes on the estate. Ye have no worries when it comes to money and the lands of Taroc Na Mor." If the money was all that troubled the woman, perhaps he could ease her mind and they'd be on their way to Scotland by tomorrow.

As Hannah settled on the bench, three squirrels circled down the trunk of the sprawling oak and scampered to an adoring heap beside her.

"Friends of yours?" Taggart asked with a nod toward the chittering threesome. Relief washed over his body, loosening the uneasy tightness in his chest. The attentive squirrels affirmed part of Hannah's heritage. True guardians of Taroc Na Mor shared a special affinity with creatures on every level of the realities.

Hannah smiled and held out her hand to the chubbiest of the group. "I rescued these three out of the storm drain a year ago last spring. They seem to have a penchant for living on the edge. They've caused a few minor fender benders when they cross Main Street during the busiest part of the day. There's an oak tree on the courthouse lawn that's got acorns they can't seem to resist. Everyone does their best to dodge them since the whole town watched me raise them until they were old enough to release back into the wild."

Either the woman deluded herself or feared he'd think her strange if he discovered her special abilities. A nearby movement in the brush caught his eye and Taggart stifled a smile as his heart warmed with satisfaction. Aye. The heritage flowed strong in her veins. All the beasts loved her. "Another of your friends is coming to see ye. Did ye save that one's life as well?" Taggart pointed toward the edge of the park, where a deer nosed its way out of the dense hedging surrounding the well-clipped lawn.

"Oh, not again." Hannah groaned and jumped off the table. Waiving her arms, she jogged across the park toward the deer, shooing it back into the safety of the woods.

Taggart chuckled under his breath. Apparently, he needed to convince her it was only natural the animals be drawn to her. She was a guardian; that's what she did. Hannah must visit Taroc Na Mor. If he could at least get her to the land, get her in the presence of one of the older Draecna, he knew she would change her mind about everything.

"Okay." Hannah returned to the table. The deer had relented and retreated to the edge of the clearing, nosing its way between a few bowed branches of forsythia bushes until it disappeared into the deeper shelter of the woods.

"Where's your friend?" Taggart smiled as he spotted the flick of the deer's white tail between the greens and browns of the sheltering trees.

Hannah stuffed her hands into the back pockets of her

jeans, pacing back and forth across the path. She ignored his question and gave a jerking shrug toward the woods, staring at the ground as she spoke. "Look. I know it might seem a little strange. But animals are sort of, I guess you could say . . ." Hannah paused, then finally blurted, "They're just attracted to me sometimes. It's kind of hard to explain. Now, could we just concentrate on why you're here please?"

Taggart perched on top of the picnic table, elbows propped on his knees. "I probably understand more about ye than ye think, Ms. MacPherson. Ye have to realize, I know a great deal about your family's history. I'm somewhat of an expert about your past."

Hannah's eyes narrowed as she lifted her head. "I see." She stopped pacing. "Why don't you start by telling me about this Guild of Barac'Nairn since I already know my own family's history."

"I would like to start by callin' ye Hannah, if ye dinna mind," Taggart tersely replied. She'd thrown up her hackles when he'd mentioned her family history. There'd be no telling her the truth about Taroc Na Mor or her destiny until he had her on the blessed soil of the sacred ground. Taggart ground his teeth as his frustration mounted. The woman wasn't going to make this easy. He'd just have to get her there and let the magic in her blood open up her soul to her calling. The Draecna race needed Hannah MacPherson, and whether she realized it or not, Hannah MacPherson needed them.

Hanna inhaled a deep breath through her nose and huffed it out her mouth as though she were about to vomit. With a shrug, she folded her arms across her chest and cleared her throat. "I don't care if you call me Hannah."

Taggart hid his smile behind his hand as he scratched the day's stubble on his face. God's teeth, ye'd have thought he'd asked if it was okay if he could beat the woman. The uneasy snarl in her voice sounded like a mistreated animal. So, perhaps Miss Sass was a bit unsure of herself? Good. By far, Hannah McPherson was the most hardheaded woman he'd ever met. And the greatest challenge he'd faced in quite a while. Damn, if he didna love it.

"Then, Hannah—" Taggart eased her name off his tongue like a lover calling to his mate. He wanted her to hear the music of Scotland, the magic of its sound. "Walk with me and I shall tell ye of the Guild of Barac'Nairn and how we have taken care of Taroc Na Mor down through the ages."

They followed the path winding along the tree line and paused on the tiny bridge spanning a gurgling creek. Rays of sunlight trickled down through the canopy of branches to dance on moss-covered stones below.

"I'm the protector named by the Guild of Barac'Nairn," Taggart began, leaning against the weathered, split-wood railing running across the bridge. "Our group has watched over Taroc Na Mor for more centuries than have been recorded by mortal man."

Hannah twitched her fingers along the gray, wooden beam. She picked off bits of wood and tossed them into the water tumbling over the multicolored rocks lining the bed of the creek. "That doesn't make sense," she interrupted with a shake of her head.

Taggart froze; his body tensed with every muscle thrumming as he scanned the tree line around them. He sensed a change in the air, a tightening in the energies. Danger neared, and it loomed too close too fast. The wind carried the warning to him more surely then a blaring alarm sounding from the town square. Straightening from the rail to search the area, he laid a hand on Hannah's arm and edged closer to her side.

"What doesna make sense?" Taggart mumbled, scanning the uppermost branches of the treetops and dropping his gaze to the darkest shadows beneath the bushes. He did his best to keep his voice low. He must keep her calm. Something neared, something meaning them both ill will. Had a minion followed them? Where the hell was it?

Hannah frowned down at Taggart's hand on her arm, then huffed as she slid out from under his grasp. "If the Guild of Barac'Nairn has watched over Taroc Na Mor for untold centuries and you've known all about my family, then why didn't my grandmother or mother hear anything about this wondrous Scottish Disneyland and inherit Taroc Na Mor before either of them died? That's the part about your little story that doesn't make any sense."

With a warning growl exploding from his chest, Taggart lunged, grabbed Hannah by the shoulders, and dove over the railing of the bridge. He folded Hannah up against his chest and rolled with her underneath the structure. He cradled her head just above the water as she spit and sputtered against his chest.

"What the hell are you doing? Are you out of your fuc—are you insane?" Hannah clawed and kicked against him as the water rushed between their bodies.

"Shut up, woman, so I can hear them!" Taggart jerked her hard against his chest, pressing his back tight against the base of the bridge. He reached out with his senses and listened across the dimensions, strained to hear the slightest sound. They had disappeared into the wind. Attack and leave, like they always did. A quick strike and then fade into the wind or the rain to ensure no one detected the destruction laced with their magic. They couldn't risk those on this side of the threshold discovering their existence.

Taggart hauled Hannah out from under the bridge and unrolled her from his embrace. He patted her arms, felt the top of her head, then finally tucked a finger under her chin and tilted her face up for a closer look. "Are ye hurt? Did I scrape ye when I yanked ye over the railing?"

Blinking the water out of her eyes, Hannah hissed from between gritted teeth. "Bend down here."

"What?" Taggart asked, bending closer to peer into her dripping face.

Hannah balled up her fist and punched him right in the mouth, giving a satisfied huff as blood spurted from his lower lip.

With a yelp of surprise, Taggart clapped his thumb to his mouth and backed a few wary steps away. "Now what did I do to deserve that, ye wicked little beast?"

"What did you do to deserve that?" Hannah's chin dropped to her chest as she paused from wringing out her ponytail. "You drag me off the bridge, yank me into the creek, tell me to shut up, and then you ask me what you did to deserve a punch in the mouth? Are you kidding me? You're lucky that's all I did. And then you call me a wicked little beast?"

"Look over there!" Taggart pointed beyond the bridge to the stand of trees just even with the height of her throat. Several good-sized oaks stood twisted off as though they'd been snapped like toothpicks and now their splintered trunks lay scattered across the path like oversized stalks of harvested broccoli.

Hannah stared at the downed trees. Her fingers traveled to the base of her throat as she caught her lower lip between her teeth. She turned and scanned the surrounding area, searching for the source of the destruction. "We just walked down that path."

Taggart nodded. "Aye. We did. That very same path."

Hannah looked back at the trees. "Those trees weren't down then."

Taggart shook his head. "No. They were not."

Hannah wrapped her hand in the hem of her wet T-shirt and stretched on tiptoe to blot at Taggart's bloody lip. "Bend down here. I'm sorry. I guess."

Taggart bent to accept her reluctant apology. He didn't have the heart to tell her he'd stopped bleeding within a few seconds. The lass hadn't hurt him; she'd just surprised him when she'd popped him in the mouth. He came from the other side. He healed at a much faster rate. But he rather enjoyed the sight of her creamy white belly teasing him as she used the hem of her wet shirt to dab the dried blood at his mouth.

"What could cause that kind of damage? Was it some kind of freak windstorm or something? Do you have any idea? How did you know? How did you hear it?" Hannah pressed the cloth to his mouth, her gaze darting from his face back to the line of felled trees.

Taggart covered her hand with his and gently lowered it from his mouth. "Hannah, there are powerful forces loose in this world. And some of them are nay so friendly toward us."

Hannah's mouth tightened into a grim, determined line. "I see. Then thank you for saving my life." Hannah stepped back. Her eyes narrowed as she studied the felled line of trees then turned back to Taggart. "Is this what your Guild does? Protects the owners of Taroc Na Mor from these *powerful forces* seeking to harm them?"

"Ye might say that." Taggart nodded. Uneasiness stabbed deep in his gut like a demon whispering, *Taggart, ye're no' handling this tellin' well.* It didn't bode well; the tremble in her voice gave away the emotions tainting the color of her aura. Taggart braced himself for the worst. He sensed a storm brewing. Hannah darkened like a lightning cloud about to explode across the horizon.

With a curt nod of her head, Hannah spun on her heel and stomped her way down the bridge. As she left the wood, she shouted back over her shoulder with a single wave of her hand. "Then I suggest you catch the next flight back to Scotland, Taggart. Because first thing tomorrow morning, I'll be telling my lawyer to put Taroc Na Mor up for sale."

"Hannah! Come back here!"

Brushing him off by flinging both hands in the air, Hannah walked faster, with a shake of her head.

"Damn the woman and her hardheaded ways!" With a muttered snarl, Taggart cursed as he scanned the felled tree line to his right one last time before taking off to follow her. As he headed up the path, a snorting buck barreled out of the brush, blocking the lane with his massive antlered head lowered.

"Ye canna protect her the way I can. Now, see reason and step aside." Taggart came up short. He admired the animal's loyalty, respected the multi-pronged antlers the pawing deer tossed with a threatening jerk of his bulging neck. But the creature needed to understand the adversary they faced couldn't be defeated with physical forces of this world.

The deer snorted again, glanced at Hannah's retreating form, then returned a stony glare to Taggart.

"I swear to ye upon my birthing shell, I'm here to keep her safe." Taggart nodded toward Hannah. "Now, let me go. They're still near and she doesna need to travel alone."

The deer eased aside and faded into the trees without another sound.

CHAPTER TWO

With a flick of his wrist, Taggart erased Sheriff Matt's memory. That should make the man forget why he thought he needed to follow him around Jasper Mills. The sheriff's persistent shadow had become a nuisance. The man needed to tend to his regular business and get on with running from that whining lass that herded all those bairns over at the nursery.

Taggart settled back in the seat of his rental car and watched Hannah through the window of the diner. God's teeth, but the woman vexed him. She refused to return any of his calls and left the room whenever he entered. Surely, she hadn't meant what she said about selling off Taroc Na Mor.

Scrubbing the day's growth of beard on his cheek, Taggart heaved a troubled sigh. He had to convince her to come back to Scotland. If he could just get those pretty feet of hers on what she didn't realize was her homeland, he knew she'd be there for life.

Taggart shifted in the seat as he remembered how she'd felt clutched against him under the bridge. He chuckled to himself. What fire she had, when she'd drawn back that tiny fist and bloodied his lip. A woman with such fire would also house great passion. He squirmed again and adjusted the seam of his suddenly too snug pants. Gads, he needed to think about something else.

The late-evening sun glinted through the diner window on her auburn hair and reminded him of brandy swirling beneath the light of a torch. He loved the way she tossed her head when she laughed, although he noticed she didn't laugh very often. She seemed relaxed now that it was just her and her friend. Hannah kept her guard up when others were around.

Taggart sucked in a deep breath; he understood completely. Perhaps, he and the guardian had more in common than either of them knew. Well, guard or not, Taroc Na Mor needed Hannah MacPherson and he wasn't returning to Scotland without her.

"You should at least go see it before you sell it." Millie thunked steaming plates of scrambled eggs and still-sizzling bacon on the table as she settled into the booth.

"I said you could feed me. I didn't say you could lecture me." Hannah scooped a heaping spoonful of the fluffy mound of eggs onto her plate. Millie could be such a noodge sometimes, but man, she sure could cook. Hannah added several slices of thick, hickory-smoked bacon, crisscrossing them atop the crispy mound of hash brown potatoes in danger of sliding off the rim of the dish. She always ate whenever she was troubled over a problem. "Where's the gravy, Millie? You promised me sawhouse gravy too, remember?"

Millie wrinkled her nose as she did a double take at Hannah's overflowing plate. "How can you eat like that and still be so tiny? No wonder everyone hated you in school." Sliding her way back out of the booth, she headed back to the kitchen to get the thick white gravy Hannah requested.

"Everybody hated me?" Hannah pouted as Millie came back through the swinging, double doors of the diner's kitchen. "I thought everybody hated Geena because she was the first one to get boobs." Hannah reached for the gravy and spooned it over her potatoes.

Millie nodded. "Well, yeah. We hated her first. And then we hated you next because you ate anything that didn't bite you first and never gained any weight." Millie slid back into the creaking seat of the booth and began filling her own plate. "Now like I said, don't you think you should at least go see the place before you decide to sell it? I mean, my gawd, Hannah! It's freakin' Scotland!"

"Exactly, Millie." Hannah nodded as she slathered a dollop of butter across a steaming buttermilk biscuit. "Jasper Mills is my home. My roots are right here." Hannah waved her dripping knife in the air, and then she pointed it at Millie's face. "I told you what happened on the bridge in the park. Were you not listening to a word I said?"

Millie stared off into space, flourishing her empty fork back and forth with a slow, purposeful rhythm. "Oh, I listened." With a deep sigh, she fell back against the cushioned back of the booth. "I also imagined what it must've felt like to be wrapped up in those arms and crushed against that muscled chest. I mean *damn,* Hannah."

Hannah rolled her eyes as she licked the melted butter dripping down her thumb. "Oh, Millie, give me a break."

"What? Come on, Hannah! Okay, we won't talk about his fantastic body or that luscious, raven-black hair, but you can't tell me you didn't at least notice his eyes. I mean, come on! I know you've sworn off men, but you've still got to have some hormones somewhere in that skinny-ass body of yours. Vibrators can't take care of everything." Millie nudged Hannah with her foot as she tossed another biscuit onto her plate. "I've never seen such an icy set of baby blues in my life. He's like a wolf. And the way he moves, like he's in constant predatory mode. He looks like a pirate, or maybe a vampire, or both. Wouldn't that be sexy? A vampire pirate who could make you immortal with one luscious bite and hold you captive at sea."

Hannah shook her head as she nibbled the strawberry preserves off the top of her biscuit and then reloaded it with blackberry jam. "I think you've been reading too many romance novels."

Millie tapped on Hannah's plate with the tip of her knife as she nodded toward all the food on the table. "Then why are you gorging yourself like there's no tomorrow? The last time you ate this amount of food was when you decided you were going to finally cave in and let Jake pop your cherry."

Hannah stopped chewing. All of a sudden, the food in her mouth tasted like sawdust and swelled so large she wished she could spit it on the floor. She swallowed hard as she edged the biscuit back on the side of her plate and pushed it to the center of the table.

"Hannah, I am so sorry. I didn't mean anything by it. I wasn't . . . I just didn't think. I shouldn't have said that." Millie raised a trembling hand to her mouth; her eyes widened as she fidgeted along the bench.

"No. It's okay," Hannah said with a shake of her head. "I just suddenly realized I wasn't that hungry anymore." She slid her napkin between her fingers and wiped her mouth as she pushed away from the table. The sad thing was Millie was right. She knew she always ate whenever she was upset, but she hadn't gorged herself this much since the very time Millie had mentioned. So what was her psyche trying to tell her?

"But seriously, Hannah, don't you think you really need to see the land before you sell it? What if you get rid of it and then end up wishing you hadn't done it?" Millie crossed the room to a get a dish tub and began clearing the untouched food from the table.

"I just don't know," Hannah replied as she helped Millie stack the dishes into the bin. "There are so many questions Taggart didn't answer. He never really told me anything about this mysterious Guild of Barac'Nairn. And then what he did at the bridge today when that thing ripped through the trees. I didn't hear a thing out there, Millie, not one single sound. And you know how the animals *always* warn me about everything. How did he know what was about to happen? He never answered *that* question either."

"Well." Millie paused as she balanced a few more dishes into the bin. "I hear it's a really long flight to Scotland."

"So what is that supposed to mean?" Hannah demanded as she followed Millie into the kitchen.

"If you have him hostage on a long flight, he'll have to answer your questions. He can't avoid you on that plane." Millie slid the bin onto the counter, then turned with a scowl to Hannah. "Didn't you say he told you he knew about your family's history?"

Hannah caught her lip between her teeth. "I know what you're thinking, Mill. I wonder if he knows how Grandma died. Or what could've killed Mama."

Millie gave a shrug of one shoulder as she turned back to the sink and started scraping the dishes into the disposal. "You have to admit they were some pretty strange deaths that were never explained, especially for a close-knit community like Jasper Mills. Maybe you better stick pretty close to this Taggart de Gaelson. Aren't you about the same age your mother was when she died?"

With a glance at Millie's worried face, Hannah nodded as a chill shivered through her body. She remembered it as though it happened yesterday, even though she'd only

been six years old at the time. They had found her mother
dead out beside the lake propped against a tree. She'd been
writing in her journal and she'd just died. The autopsy had
proven inconclusive. No heart attack. No aneurism. No
stroke. Her mother had been in perfect health for a
woman of her age. She was just dead. One strange bit of
evidence was that every hair on her body had frosted to a
snowy white, even her thick, black eyelashes. It was as
though the auburn-haired woman had suddenly become
an albino. Another startling finding was that the once vibrant green irises of her eyes had stained to a soulless
black. The most disturbing thing was that her maternal
grandmother had later died in the very same manner.
Grandma had just eluded whatever it was that killed her
until a few years ago, when she reached eighty years old.

"I wish Jake were here. He'd know what to do," Hannah muttered as she walked over to the freezer and yanked
open the stainless-steel double doors. "Is there any of that
mint chocolate chip ice cream left? The one you had listed
to go with the special today?"

"You're gonna puke," Millie groaned as she reached in
the drawer for a couple of spoons. "And Jake wouldn't
know what to do. I wish you'd stop making him out to be
such a flawless hero."

Hannah backed her way out of the freezer, her arms
wrapped around two barrels of chocolate mint ice cream.
Turning to bump the freezer door shut with her butt, she
shot Millie a wilting glare. "I can't believe you'd speak ill
of the dead, Millie. You've known Jake all your life too.
You know exactly what kind of person he was."

"Exactly!" Millie snapped as she yanked one of the barrels of ice cream away from Hannah and slammed it down
on the counter. "The entire time we were growing up,
Jake never treated you as good as you deserved. I never
understood it. You lost your mom when you were just six

years old and your grandmama raised you to be the most independent little brat in Jasper Mills. But when it came to Jake, you followed him around like a starving puppy. Jake MacPherson barely looked down from his pedestal long enough to give you the time of day. The whole town was shocked when he came back from med school and actually married you. Everybody figured he'd bring himself home some diva from the big city. We all nearly fainted when you pulled your head out of Jake's fan club long enough to go away to veterinary school. We hoped then you'd finally gotten over him."

"Jake loved me, Millie!" Hannah bounced the other barrel onto the cracked linoleum countertop and stormed across the kitchen. She couldn't believe Millie had the gall to stand there and say those things, even though a tiny voice in the back of her mind agreed with everything Millie had said. "If you're finished lecturing me on how you can't believe my dead husband could've loved me, I think I'll be heading home."

"Dammit, Hannah, that's not what I meant and you know it!" Millie slammed her hand on top of the counter. "I know Jake loved you in his own self-centered, egotistical way, whenever he didn't have anything better to do. I'm just saying he never showed you the attention you deserved. I just never understood how you never put up with anybody else's crap and yet you took his bullshit by the truckloads. How many nights did we spend in this very kitchen, perched on those wobbly stools, eating ice cream because Jake didn't have time to spend with you? I bet I gained twenty-five pounds the first year you two were married."

Hannah stopped with her hand on the swinging doors, uncomfortable memories of the first year of her marriage wriggling free from the padlocked recesses of her mind. As much as she fought against Millie's words, her friend had a valid point. "I don't know what to tell you, Millie. I guess everybody has a weakness and Jake just happened to be mine. Maybe you're right. Maybe he wasn't such a hero. But I loved him, Mill, and now he's gone. So, let's just leave it at that. Okay?" Sliding her hand off the door, Hannah let her arm drop to her side. "Just dish up the ice cream, will you? Double scoops. You're looking a little thin."

"She canna sell it! Fold time and space. Transport her here immediately. Spell her to the keep this very minute. We'll just keep her here until she discovers the error of her ways. Have ye lost your mind? Why do ye wait? Why do ye tarry when ye know we run so close on time?" Thaetus's high-pitched screech echoed from the depths of Taggart's amulet, which spun in the center of the hotel room coffee table.

Taggart scrubbed his face with both his hands. They'd had to wait centuries for the stars to align and gift them with the Sullivan line. The first age of guardians, the Alexander line, had turned dark and destroyed themselves long ago. He worried his hands through his hair as he paced around the confines of the tiny room. "Thaetus, ye know as well as I that an unwilling guardian would never do at Taroc Na Mor. She will come around. She just needs a bit of time. The attack in the woods frightened her. 'Tis only natural she be a bit put off by that which she doesna understand. It is a well-known human trait."

"Then explain it to her! The next clutch of Draecna are due to hatch in three Erastaedian double moons. 'Twould be nice to have a fully trained guardian this time to ease them into the worlds and on their way to power the portals. Septamus grows surly and asks where the true guardian is and what's taking ye so blasted long. He tires of the Guild members tending the nursery. Ye know how they are, Taggart. The last clutch tried to eat the Guild member bringing the young ones into the world, and then all but one of the hatchlings died. I dinna know if ye've met the one survivor, but rumor has it, he isna quite right."

Taggart waved his hand over the spinning purple jewel as he bent over the short-legged table. "Trust me, Thaetus. Hannah will come around. I have seen into her heart. I just need a little more time to warm her up to the idea. And I could use some help from the powers of the Guild. Have them ramp up the protection surrounding the gateway. There must be no more intrusions from the other side."

"Do ye think it was Sloan?" Thaetus's voice grew hushed and the spinning amulet dimmed as though the jewel itself feared it would be overheard.

"Who else?" Taggart growled as he rose from the chair and resumed his pacing about the miniature box of a room. "It might not have been his own energy I sensed. But the forest reeked of his sinister essence." The stench he'd encountered while scanning the dimensions still clung to his mind like a greasy film.

"Ye looked into her heart?" Thaetus interrupted. "What in the name of Isla's golden beard do ye think ye are doing looking into the woman's heart? Take care, Taggart! Ye know 'tis forbidden. Ye must not become entangled with the one ye are sworn to protect."

"Do not presume to tell me how to do my job, Thaetus!" Taggart snarled down at the purple spinning gem. "I looked into her heart to better understand her. The woman still grieves for a husband she lost to war. Do not question my dedication to the Guild. I'm not only the protector, but I'm also the only one who was able to pick up the lost thread of the Sullivan line. Remember?"

"Aye, Taggart. Ye gave up everything for the cause. Ye

even revealed your true self and sacrificed your precious
Mia." Thaetus's voice echoed from the depths of the
amulet; the transmission weakened as the spinning amethyst
slowed.

Taggart almost choked on his bitter laugh as he moved
to stare out the curtained window. "Mia sacrificed me. I
had nothing to do with it." A familiar ache panged in his
chest. Thaetus *would* have to mention Mia's name and stir
up the ghosts of his past.

"Take care, Taggart. We will mind your back as best we
can. But bring the woman home to us soon." Thaetus's
voice faded from the room as the amulet rattled to a stand-
still on the top of the table.

"Why did you slam his tail in the car door?" Hannah
peered deep into the little boy's eyes as he squirmed beside
his mother.

"Is that why he bit you?" The woman nudged the boy
with her elbow as though they shared a private joke.

"Well, wouldn't you bite someone if they'd snapped one
of your bones?" Hannah clipped the X-ray film to the
light table mounted on the wall and tapped on the glowing white line of the break in the bone.

The puppy on the exam table sidled closer to Hannah
and snuggled against her side. He flattened his ears at the
boy and the woman and bared his teeth every time either
of them moved.

"That's just great! I paid six hundred dollars for that
mutt and now you've ruined him! We'll never be able to
sell him when we get to Chicago." The gum-popping
woman with the snake-print nails slapped her hand down
on the stainless-steel table.

Hannah stifled a shiver of rage as it rippled across her
body; no way would she give this defenseless dog back to

this heartless woman. With his coloring and build, he promised to look a great deal like a pedigreed boxer, especially if he'd had his tail docked when he'd been just a day or two old. According to his thoughts, the poor little mutt was in the middle of a scam. This woman came from out of town and figured Hannah would be none the wiser. Hannah bet her finest scalpel the spike-heeled witch only stayed a few steps ahead of the law. She glared at the woman and picked up the dog to cradle him under one arm. "How many other dogs have you got at home? I don't remember seeing you in my office before."

The woman shook her head as she snapped her gum even louder and shoved her son toward the table. "None. We're just passing through on our way to bigger and better things. We heard you were the closest vet around." Nodding toward the pup Hannah held in her arms, she tapped an impatient foot as she glanced at the instrument table. "Can you just clip off his tail or what? I really need to be able to sell him or something to get some of my money back and besides, won't he be in a lot less pain if you bob it?"

"Hold that thought." Hannah held up a finger as she edged through the doorway around to the countertop phone in the waiting area. Holding the puppy under one arm, she jabbed in a number, then spoke quietly so the woman couldn't overhear. Seething with rage, Hannah clenched the phone so tight she was surprised it didn't snap apart in her hand. On their way to bigger and better things. She'd show that animal abuser bigger and better things. Hanging up the phone, she rounded the corner and fixed the woman with her most professional smile. "I've got a solution to your problem, but it will be just a few minutes before it arrives."

The fidgeting woman's face immediately brightened. "Great! I heard you had a real way with the animals. That's why we brought him here. Maybe he'll be a little money-maker after all. I could really use a break."

"Where are you, Hannah?"

"Exam room one, Matt." Hannah smiled as she scratched the puppy behind the ears. Kissing the puppy on top of his warm, fuzzy head, she whispered against his fur, "You're gonna like Matt. He's a really super guy."

"Ms. Manchester?" Sheriff Matt appeared in the doorway, a notepad and pen in his hand.

The twitching woman visibly paled and she clutched her son to the front of her body. She shot Hannah a narrow-eyed glare before she cleared her throat and squared her rhinestone-covered shoulders. "Actually, my name is Veronica Smith."

"Is it really, now? Well, that's very unusual. You see, I ran the plates on your car outside and my info states the registration as Sylvia Manchester. It also appears there are several warrants out for that name. So, I'm afraid I'll need you and your son to come with me so that we can get this little matter cleared up." Matt tapped his notebook with his pen as he stood in the doorway and smiled.

"What about my son? You can't expect my son to sit in a jail with a bunch of hardened criminals. I'll call the media and every lawyer I can find. I'll make sure everyone knows how you've mistreated my son." The woman hugged the boy tighter against the front of her skintight miniskirt as if he were a human shield.

Matt's smile widened and he winked at the boy. "I've already called Social Services. My best friend Cassie's sitting outside in her van and she'd love to meet your son. They'll be more than happy to take care of him while you and I sit down and have a nice long chat."

Whirling on Hannah, the woman snatched her purse from beside the table and glared at the dog as though she wished it were dead. "You bitch! All you had to do was clip the goddamn dog's tail! Was that so friggin' much to ask?" The woman stormed out of the office in front of the sheriff and yanked her son behind her.

"Bye, Matt," Hannah called after them as she kissed the top of the little dog's head. "We'll get you fixed up in no time, my little friend. See? I told you Matt was a really nice guy."

"Now there goes quite an unpleasant woman. How much did ye overcharge her to tend to her pet? I've never heard such foul language spew out of a woman, at least not all in one breath." Taggart rounded the corner of the doorway, walking backwards as he stared down the hallway. "Your fine sheriff is herdin' the cursing wench with his notebook and she's pulling a squawlin' boy with her down your front steps."

"I didn't overcharge her and that's her poor son, who she's training in her evil ways." Hannah hugged the puppy to her chest. "I took this puppy away from her. She didn't deserve this sweet little guy. He told me all the cruel things she and her son were up to at their house." Turning away, she cuddled the warm pup closer, trying to stave off the tickling shiver that crept over her body as soon as Taggart entered the room. Why didn't Taggart de Gaelson go back to Scotland and leave her alone? He'd done nothing but complicate her life ever since he'd shown up in Jasper Mills.

"Did he now? He told ye all the evils they did at their house?" Taggart grinned at her with a raised brow.

"Umm, well, yes . . . I mean . . ." Hannah stammered as she flipped the light back on behind the X-ray sheet. Damn him. He would have to be a man who actually listened to everything she said. She had never had that problem with Jake. "Take a look at these X-rays. Their story was the boy broke the puppy's tail when he accidentally slammed it in a car door. But they're trying to pass him off as a pedigreed dog that should've had his tail docked at just a few days old. Then the mother wanted me to bob it off just so she could sell him in some sort of dog ring in Chicago. They're trying to run some sort of scam."

"Ye can trust me, Hannah," Taggart whispered. "Remember? I told ye I know your family's history. I know all about their *gifts*."

Could she really trust him? No one but Jake had ever known that she could actually understand an animal's thoughts. Even her family had just thought she had a good rapport with all the creatures. They never realized she communicated with any animal she ran across.

"Hand me the pup. Let me show ye something. I will prove to ye that ye can trust me with all your secrets." Taggart held out his hands and waited; a mysterious smile tugged at the corner of his mouth and twinkled in his eyes.

"Mind his tail. It's fractured in several places." Hannah eased the puppy into Taggart's outstretched hands. Her heart warmed when the little dog planted his clumsy, front paws on Taggart's chest and slobbered a wet greeting across Taggart's face.

"There's a good lad. That's enough now. I think ye are a fine lad too. Hold still now while I heal your wee tail so it willna pain ye any longer." Taggart placed his right hand over the puppy's tail while he held the little dog steady with his left. A faint glow appeared for a brief second around Taggart's hand and the puppy's tail and then absorbed into the little dog's body.

The dog yipped, wagged his tail, and then looked to Hannah with his tongue lolling out the side of his mouth.

"What did you just do?" Hannah took the wriggling pup back into her arms and set him down on the floor.

"I healed him. That is why ye can trust me, Hannah. I too am gifted with the magic." Taggart folded his arms across his chest as he watched the puppy race in circles around the floor. "That is also how I sensed the threat the other day. I've trained years to make the most of my skills. Come with me to Taroc Na Mor, Hannah. At least let me show ye what awaits ye if ye just find the courage to embrace it."

"You make it sound like a training ground for witches, some sort of academy of magic." Hannah glanced toward the puppy and grabbed a handful of paper towels. "Hey, you could've told me you needed to pee," she grumbled as she blotted up the yellow puddle spreading across the floor. Indecision battled within her. How could what he said be true? But he'd healed the puppy and he'd protected her in the woods, so how could his words be false?

Taggart shook his head. "I promise ye, Hannah. Taroc Na Mor is not a school. But it is a great deal more than just a castle hidden in the Highlands. 'Tis not something that can be explained. It can only be felt when ye stand upon the land."

As Hannah sprayed disinfectant on the floor and mopped at the mess, she wished she could clean up her life with just as much ease. Why did he have to show up and complicate things? As long as she had ignored those stupid packets, life had seemed so much simpler. Curling her fingers tight into the damp paper towels, Hannah ventured a glance up into Taggart's face. As soon as her gaze met with his, she found herself locked deep in his stare. And then she shivered and realized she shouldn't have done it. There they were—those damned imprisoning eyes. They pierced right through her soul. But something else lurked in those icy-blue depths. An ache mirrored the pain that throbbed with every beat of her heart. Hannah turned away from the shadows of Taggart's suffering. She couldn't afford to get lost in Taggart's sorrow. She had her own wounds to nurse.

"Come with me, Hannah," Taggart whispered. He edged a step closer and barely traced his fingertips down her arm.

His words meant madness, utter chaos. Everything that meant anything to her was right here in Jasper Mills. How could she consider going to Scotland, to this mysterious Taroc Na Mor? Hannah threw down the paper towels and hugged herself away from his touch. "I can't think, Taggart. I don't know what to do. Why did you have to show up here and turn everything upside down? I had my life all straightened out until you showed up."

"I came here to protect ye, Hannah. If I hadna' come here, ye would have met the same fate as your mother. Or perhaps something even worse." Taggart blew out a heavy breath, dropped his hand, and eased a half step away.

Hannah whirled and stared at him. Her mother? "What do you mean *or something even worse*? Do you know how she died?"

His pained expression spoke more than any words, and the way his eyes dropped when she asked that question reminded her of the guilty look on Sophie's face every time she escaped from her kennel. Hannah took another step forward. "Tell me, Taggart. If the Guild of Barac'Nairn has been around for so long taking care of the Sullivans of Taroc Na Mor, then where were they for my grandmother and my mother? Why is this the first time your so-called Guild of Barac'Nairn has appeared in my life? Where were they when my mother needed them? Where were they when I was left with no one to raise me but my grandmother?"

"We failed them." Taggart's voice cracked with remorse as he clasped his hands together and bowed his head. "I can make no excuses. We lost track of the Sullivan lineage and through our carelessness, we allowed them both to die."

"And now you expect me to uproot my life and go traipsing off to Scotland like a good little girl without any argument?" The sting of the Guild's failure soured in her stomach, the bile burned in the back of her throat. "You stand there and tell me your Guild screwed up and yet now you expect me to trust you with my own life?"

"Yes," Taggart replied with a tired sigh. "Because if ye do not, ye will die, as well."

"You don't know that for sure, and how many times do I have to tell you that my life is here?" Hannah shouted. "Why can't you understand that?"

"I understand more about ye than ye realize, ye stubborn, single-minded woman." Taggart took a step forward with hands fisted as though he wished he could shake her. "It doesna appear that ye've bothered to live since the day your husband died. All ye do is tend to your animals and weep o'er his grave. If ye don't come with me to Taroc Na Mor, the town will soon bury ye beside him up on that infernal mountain of yours. Is that what ye want? Is that what ye sit here and wait for, Hannah?" Taggart's eyes flashed as he came closer. "It's time, Hannah. It is time to live. Jake has moved on. Now that I've come, ye can move on too."

"Jake has not moved on. Jake is just dead. I know. I watched them put him in the ground. Don't you ever speak of him again! You have no right." Hannah choked back the tears closing off her throat. The old blade twisted in her chest; her festering wound cracked open and burned.

Taggart grabbed her wrist. "Enough of this foolish bantering, woman. It's time ye spoke to your husband's spirit and settled this once and for all."

"Ye must do exactly as I say and *do not argue with my instructions*." Taggart glared at Hannah with an arched brow, awaiting her response.

"I can follow instructions," Hannah snapped with a defiant toss of her head. He didn't have to speak to her like she was an idiot. Who did this Taggart de Gaelson think he was? "Let's just get this over with so you can scoot back to Scotland and I can get on with my life. How 'bout it?" She'd show him. She had put all the males in Jasper Mills in their place. By golly, she'd put this Scot in his peg hole with no problem.

Taggart chuckled as he extended both hands and rested them atop Jake's tombstone. "I guess then we shall see just how well your first lesson in necromancy goes."

Hannah rolled her eyes and slid her hands into the depths of Taggart's grasp. She swallowed hard when her hands disappeared as he curled his massive fingers over hers. She hated to admit the intense heat of his calloused touch disturbed her. She stole a glance into his face and immediately wished she hadn't. A surge of emotional energy caught her breath. The floodgates opened, sending a flush of excited heat through her body as his mesmerizing thumbs stroked the backs of her hands. She shook her head. It had to be nerves. What else could it be?

"Close your eyes, Hannah, and dinna speak until I tell ye it is safe for ye to do so."

Taggart's voice echoed rich and mellow through the silence of the woods.

Hannah closed her eyes; the purr of his deep Scot's burr rippled across her senses. An involuntary shiver raced up her spine as the vibrant tones of his voice stroked her mind.

"When I speak the words to lift the veil, Jake's spirit will cross the void from the other side."

Hannah bit her lip. She wanted to ask questions, but Taggart had told her not to speak. She stood and waited, eyes squeezed shut; her heartbeat echoed in her ears. What did he wait for? She wished he'd get on with it. Was he trying to build the suspense or what?

"Taruamis aranu visri!"

Hannah's mind flooded with golden light as though someone had taken a pitcher filled with golden dust and scattered it to the winds. The iridescent beam swam with a distinct purpose across the darkness of her mind. The particles danced and swirled. The energy vibrated with laughter and warmth. Jake's essence filled her mind with light.

"Do not speak aloud to him, Hannah. Ye must only communicate with your thoughts. Ye must not speak aloud." Taggart's deep whisper echoed close to her ear. The touch of his lips brushed against her cheek.

The golden light swirled and twisted through her mind. Its warmth flushed through her body. *"Jake? Is it really you? Can you finally communicate to me?"*

"It's me, baby. Thanks to your new friend here, you're finally able to hear me instead of me just listening to you rant and rave at my gravesite. By the way, now that you can actually hear me, thanks for the headstone. I really like it. All the way from a keep in Scotland? Nice job, hon."

"Do you mean you've really heard me all these years when I've been scolding you about leaving me alone?" The heat of her blush flooded its way up her body. Hannah remembered all the times she'd blessed out her husband for volunteering to go to the war. In part, she'd felt guilty about wanting to keep him to herself; but she'd also resented the sacrifice she'd been forced to make when Jake had left her alone at Jasper Mills.

"Trust me, Hannah. I've heard each and every word, repeatedly and quite clearly across the realities. Now it's time you listened to me and gave us both some well-earned peace and quiet. After all, this is an eternity, you know."

Hannah stiffened. Taggart squeezed her hands as she tried to pull them away.

"I don't think I like the sound of that, Jake."

"It's time, Hannah, and you know it. It's time for you to move on to something and someone else. I guess you could say I've moved on to my next assignment, and now it's time for you to finish yours."

"I can't finish my assignment without you. You promised me children. We were supposed to grow old together. What about that assignment, Jake?" The tears burned out from under her closed eyelids, etching a wet trail down her cheeks as her body started to shake.

"We were wrong about that assignment, baby. You know how much I loved you, Hannah, but we had our good times and our paths turned out to go a different way. I've seen the future, Hannah. You have a bigger destiny and it's time for you to move on, baby.

"I hate you, Jake. You never really needed me."

"No, you don't hate me, Hannah. You're just a little hard-headed. Now get on with it and move on to the next chapter in your adventure. You know there's nothing like the rush of a great adventure. Love can't even measure up to that. You know for me, it never could. Be honest with yourself, Hannah."

"Go back to the hell you came from, Jake. That's where you belong!" Hannah sobbed and tried yanking her hands out of Taggart's grasp.

Taggart pulled her across the headstone and cradled her against his chest. "Hush now, Hannah. 'Twill be all right. Jake has returned to whence he came. His spirit can trouble ye no more." He stroked her hair and curled her into his arms. "Hush now, lass. Dry your tears. 'Twill be all right."

Hannah tucked her face into the curve of his neck and rubbed her tear-stained cheeks against the warmth of his throat. "I don't think he ever loved me as much as I loved him. I can't believe I wasted all those years on him." Hannah hiccupped and choked on a sob as she whispered against Taggart's chest. "Now I know for sure he never needed me like I needed him."

She closed her eyes and sank into the comfort of Taggart's touch. Inhaling another shaking breath, his scent pervaded through her misery, the barest blend of some sort of spice. Hannah leaned closer, breathing in again— oil of clove maybe? Then she shook her head as the fragrance changed. No, Taggart's skin held the barest hint of a fresh sea breeze. She forced her eyes open. Whatever the scent, it lodged in her senses and she found it deeply troubling. Men meant nothing but pain. Look what the last one had done.

Taggart tightened his embrace, stroking her hair as a heavy sigh rumbled from his chest. "Some never love as deeply as we love them, either because they canna do so or because they simply refuse. Come with me to Scotland, Hannah. I promise I will protect ye and help ye forget and heal from your wounds of the past. Taroc Na Mor will make all the difference. I promise. It will make your life better."

Hannah sniffed, risking a glance up into his eyes, then wiped her face with the back of her hand. Maybe she could at least *look* at the land and then return to her mountain. At least, then, Taggart couldn't say she hadn't given it a chance. "Fine. I'll come to Scotland, Taggart, for just a little while anyway. I'll at least have a look at Taroc Na Mor." Twisting in his arms, she peered down at the ground, then turned back and patted his chest. "And you can put me down now. I'm going to be just fine."

Chapter Three

The flames danced behind the grid of the gilt-edged hearth, their golden flickers the only light to pierce the darkness of the room. Mesmerized, he stared unblinking at the glowing coals undulating at the base of the blaze. He traced his forefinger back and forth across his bottom lip, imagining the terror of her screams. He inhaled a deep breath, closed his eyes, and brought to mind the delightful scent of acrid burning flesh as he shoved her face deeper into the flames. His edict had been simple: Destroy the Sullivan line. And yet the woman still lived and breathed. Not only did she live, the protector walked by her side and guided her to the Draecna holy birthplace.

Sloan pushed himself up from the depths of the sumptuous cushions layered in the velvet chair and stalked across the lush carpeting of his private chambers. What good did it do to surround himself with exquisite possessions when all could be lost in the blink of an eye? Sloan selected a gold-inlaid vase off a waist-high marble pedestal and smashed it against a mirrored wall. He'd surrounded himself with more incompetent fools than priceless possessions. Frustration pounded with every footstep as he circled his silver-encrusted desk. With muscles tensed, Sloan rested his hand on an octagonal jeweled box positioned in the center of the green velvet blotter. With gritted teeth, he hefted aside the domed lid and stared down into the depths of the gem-encrusted tomb.

Sloan held his breath as his hands slid inside the satin interior, surrounding a glowing orb within. A thrilling shudder stole over his body; the tip of his tongue wet his lips as his fingertips stroked the oversized egg. The warm pebbled surface hummed with life; the inner stirrings of the incubating creature vibrated against his palms. A Draecna egg. The final cornerstone needed to assure his complete control of the realm portals. He'd ordered it stolen from the Taroc Na Mor nursery. He needed but one of the precious beasts, newly hatched and well on its way to maturity. The magically infused flesh and blood of a young Draecna was all he lacked to fertilize his clutch of synthetic eggs housed in the bowels of the keep. He was one creature short of propagating an entire race. A race that would bow to him. But the beast would never hatch at Tiersa Deun of Erastaed unless Hannah MacPherson breathed life into the egg or he poured her blood upon it.

Between the Guild of Barac'Nairn and the guardians of Taroc Na Mor, the Draecna race had survived for untold millennia. Sloan scowled, his mood darkening as he hefted the egg, cradling it against his chest. The slow, steady heartbeat of the incubating beast thudded steadily against his sternum. The hatchling lay patiently within the egg, waiting for Hannah's touch.

The sacred beasts powered the Portals of the Dimensions. Anyone allied with the powerful Draecna could travel across the webs of time, passing between alternate worlds. Who knew what treasures awaited him beyond the portals? In the past, many Draecna allies had returned with the rare and precious finds from the different universes discovered on their travels.

As ancestral home of the sacred Draecna, Taroc Na Mor also stood as one of the gateways between the realms.

Hannah MacPherson survived as the last of the Draecna guardians and the newest mistress of Taroc Na Mor. While she lived, the beasts' eggs waited in stasis. They paused in this early phase of their life, waiting for her touch. While Hannah MacPherson lived and breathed, Sloan couldn't gain control of the beasts.

Sloan cradled the egg in his arms as if it were a babe as he meandered about the room. Oblong in shape, the diameter of a good-sized melon, the egg felt as if it weighed a solid fifteen pounds. It glowed from within, sparking a red-orange hue as though a sunrise battled for freedom within its shell.

"No mere woman will keep me from this power." Sloan muttered to the shelled beast he stroked within his arms. He tapped a blackened fingernail upon the flashing surface as he circled through the shadows of the room. The beast stirred within its orb, its sliding vibration rubbing impatiently against Sloan's arms. "I know, my little treasure. We must bide our time. Trust me. I shall find the means to set ye free."

"Tor!" he bellowed. "Where is that fool when I need him?" Sloan walked to the window, staring out across blackened cliffs jutting about the stronghold of Tiersa Deun.

"Aye, m'lord?" A bent old man trembled at the torchlit archway, eyes downcast as he wrung his hands in front of him.

Sloan caressed the egg, giving him a wicked smile as he turned from the starless window. "Tell Mia to prepare herself. Taggart returns to Taroc Na Mor with the guardian and I am certain I will have need of her services."

Taggart stared at the length of her lashes resting on her pale, smooth skin. He'd not noticed how amazingly long they were when they framed those sparkling green eyes.

His gaze lingered on the delicate curve of Hannah's cheek while she was unaware. The flight to Scotland took several hours and Hannah had lost her battle against exhaustion. She seemed so vulnerable while she slept. But Taggart knew the woman housed the heart of a warrior and the temper of a wildcat.

Taggart shifted in his seat, glancing around the darkened plane. He couldn't help it. The close confines of the aircraft left him little choice. His gaze returned to Hannah, to her full moist lips and softly twitching eyelids. The steady whisper of her breathing matched the gentle rhythm of the rise and fall of her chest. He eased his hand over and traced the pads of his fingers along the delicate inside skin of her arm. Soft, cool temptation whispered against the tips of his fingers as he smoothed them down to her wrist.

Sheer madness. Taggart adjusted his pants at the crotch and balled his hands into fists on his knees. He was her protector. Hannah was off-limits. And besides, he'd sworn a vow of celibacy since the Mia debacle.

The rustle of clothing as she moved forced him to stare straight ahead. *Son of a bitch.* He didn't have to look. The scent of her assaulted his senses. She smelled of wildflowers after a rain and of woman. A very desirable woman. Taggart shifted in his seat again. *Damn.* Did they think men had arses the size of children's? A man couldn't even spread his legs to give his cock room to breathe.

The silk of her hair brushed against his arm and he risked another glance. She'd curled to her side and now faced him, blouse agape, treating him to an unhindered view of the creamy temptation of her throat and the swell of one luscious breast.

"God's teeth," Taggart groaned, covering his face with his hands.

"Are you airsick or something?"

Taggart jerked straight in the seat, scrubbed his face, and

shifted a bit as he turned slightly away from Hannah. "I guess ye could say I am feeling a bit under the weather. But I shall be just fine. I'm truly sorry if I woke ye. Try and go back to sleep."

Hannah yawned and stretched like a cat, plucking at the blanket pooled around her waist. "The roar of the engines always knocks me out. I'm sorry I'm such lousy company."

Taggart stared at the blanket jealously. He'd give anything to be that bit of wool. A swim in the icy loch was what he needed, as soon as they arrived at Taroc Na Mor. "Sleep, Hannah. That way ye will be well rested when we arrive and we can explore the land with your full attention."

Hannah yawned again, tucked the pillow tighter under her neck, and snuggled deeper into the first-class seat. "Well, I appreciate your understanding, Taggart. Especially since you paid for such great seats." She rubbed her nose, and her voice trailed off as she added, "You really are a nice guy."

"Aye, Hannah, I truly am a nice guy." Taggart readjusted his pants with a muffled groan.

"This is as far as we can go by car. The rest of the way, we must travel by horseback." Taggart swerved the tiny rental car into the lot beside the stable and turned to Hannah with an expectant smile.

Hannah blinked at the view from the square little window, then swiveled in the cramped seat. He couldn't be serious. They'd already driven for what seemed like forever in this tiny matchbox car. They weren't there *yet?* "I thought you said we entered onto the estate an hour ago. How big is Taroc Na Mor?"

"Aye, it fair steals your breath from your chest, doesn't it?" Taggart nodded, heaving a contented sigh.

Hannah climbed out of the car into the Highland

wilderness and immediately understood what Taggart meant. The ancient pines whispered overhead, their feathered tops swaying in the late-summer breeze. The tang of the pinesap wafted through the air as the needles cushioned every step she took. The scent carried her straight back to Christmas and every Christmas tree she'd ever decorated as a child.

A weathered stone stable squatted against the base of the mountainside. Hannah blinked and peered closer since the structure appeared hewn from the side of the cliff. What trees hadn't been cleared away to form the well-trodden center of the paddock area were connected with graying split rails to form the enclosing fence. As the trees grew and the rails shifted too high, Hannah saw the scars on the trees where workers had stripped and lowered the rails to prevent the horses from escaping.

The surrounding woodlands teemed with the voices of all the Highland creatures. Hannah's mind and ears echoed with them all. She shielded her eyes, craning her neck to search the brilliant, blue sky for the golden eagle screaming overhead. She spotted a red squirrel studying her from beyond a cluster of bright yellow Scottish primrose at the edge of the clearing. Following her senses, Hannah turned and found the doe behind the scrub of fir saplings to her left. Apparently, her ability to understand animals spanned continents. Their thoughts came to her as clearly as the ones did back home.

Hannah pulled her jacket closer, trying to keep from trembling, whether from excitement or nervousness, she couldn't quite tell. A strange electricity crackled in the air; she raised her head and sniffed the breeze. She wasn't sure if it was a specific scent she picked up or just a different sort of density to the wind. What was it? The air was different here. Excitement rippled gooseflesh across her skin. She risked a glance at Taggart and rubbed the tip of her nose. Was it the land or the close proximity to the man? Battling with the mess of emotions wreaking havoc with her ability to reason, Hannah struggled not to scream. She didn't need all this confusion in her life. What she needed was the humdrum comfort and safety of good old Jasper Mills.

Pulling herself from the mesmerizing magic of the land, Hannah shivered and rubbed her arms. "So, the stables are part of the estate as well? Even though they're so far from the keep itself?" Hannah nodded toward the structure wedged into the side of the mountain and the horses wandering inside the corral.

With a grin, Taggart motioned for her to follow. "Aye, Hannah, we've been on Taroc Na Mor land for the past two hours. Weren't you listening to me while I was driving and pointing out the sights?"

"*Two hours?* I thought you said one hour." Hannah glared at the back of Taggart's head, willing him to turn around. And he ignored her. Again. He'd been doing that a lot. A fresh horse chip in the middle of the path was almost more temptation than she could resist. She glanced at the steaming patty and gauged the distance to Taggart's back as he sauntered off toward the stable. From here, she could peg him right between the shoulders. Biting her lip, she stepped around the dung pile. She guessed she'd behave and let him off the hook. *This* time.

"I didn't realize I owned the entire tip of Scotland." Hannah kicked a stone out of her path, but it didn't improve her mood. Rubbing her neck, she rolled her shoulders while following Taggart toward the stable. At least they were finally out of that tiny car. The way Taggart had folded up his massive frame to drive, she didn't see how he still managed to walk.

" 'Tis about time ye arrived!" A gnome of a man with an unruly shock of white hair atop his head and a stained leather apron strapped around his barrel waist burst through the weathered stable doors. He held a horseshoe in one hand and a hammer in the other, but neither prevented him from shaking a stubby finger in Taggart's face. "I've had the horses packed for nigh' on thirty minutes and they've grown quite restless with the waiting. Ye need to reach Gearlach's Pass before the sun sets or ye willna have a proper place to make camp for the evening. How many times do I have to tell ye of the importance of maintaining a proper schedule, Taggart?"

"Gothgar!" Taggart brought the man up short with a quick jerk of his head in Hannah's direction.

"Oh, beg pardon." Gothgar shot Taggart an irritated glance and turned to Hannah with a respectful squatting bow. "Gothgar McWinders, chief of your stables, ma'am. Welcome to the glorious Taroc Na Mor."

"It's good to meet you, Mr. McWinders—"

"Oh lordy, no, ma'am. Call me, Gothgar. Don't be a callin' out to a Mr. McWinders. I'll be a thinkin' ye're a talkin' about me father and round these parts, ye just might bring back his contrary ghost." Gothgar wheezed and snorted while he slapped his leg at what he obviously considered his very humorous joke.

"It's good to meet you, Gothgar." Hannah smiled. Gothgar reminded her of old Mr. Henry back at Jasper Mills. "Now, what were you saying about us making camp this evening? Are you telling me we're not going to make it to the castle tonight?"

"Oh, lordy no. 'Tis too far a ride to make it this late in the day. You and Taggart will have to camp at the ledge at Gearlach's Pass. But dinna worry. There's a fine fresh spring and a verra nice clearing there. This time of year should be quite a pleasant evening. I've packed enough blankets and provisions, and Taggart will build ye a fine fire. The night air should nay be too cold for ye to bear."

Gothgar turned to hobble his way back into the stable, waving over his hairy shoulder for them to follow.

Hannah didn't move. She closed her eyes and pinched the bridge of her nose. She couldn't believe Taggart expected her to camp out on a rock in the wilderness of the Scottish Highlands. She was exhausted from the flight and the eternal ride in a car the size of a freakin' matchbox. She wanted a shower, a good hot meal, and a nice soft bed.

"Hannah! Come on, lass. We must get moving. Gothgar is right. We must reach Gearlach's Pass before dark." Taggart called to her from the doorway of the stable, grinning like a schoolboy just freed for summer vacation.

Hannah stomped her way into the stable, kicking up the dust of the paddock until she found herself nose to nose with a chestnut mare. Her heart melted at the horse's warm, reassuring touch and its soft whinny as it pressed its velvet nose against her. Hannah wrapped her arms around the horse's neck and relaxed against its side.

"I knew ye'd love dear, sweet Lisbet. She's a bit older but she has the courage of a warhorse and will love ye true. Ye will find no better friend, Lady Guardian. Lisbet will take good care of ye on your journey." Gothgar patted the horse on the rump as he winked a scruffy brow at Hannah.

"Lady Guardian?" Hannah snagged Taggart by the sleeve. "Why did he call me *Lady Guardian*?"

Taggart's mouth tightened as he shot Gothgar a withering look, then turned to double-check the supplies in Hannah's saddlebags. "'Tis a title of respect and is always given to the owner of Taroc Na Mor. Since ye are the new owner of the estate, ye are now considered its guardian."

"Oh." Hannah rested her cheek against Lisbet's satin neck as she watched Taggart double-check all the straps. "Why didn't you tell me we were going to have to camp out in the wilderness tonight?"

With a wicked grin, Taggart gave her a wink before he turned to check his own horse. "Because I didna want to listen to the sting of your tongue for the two-hour drive to the stables."

The only thing good about following Taggart down this narrow, twisting trail was the fact she had a perfect view of his nicely shaped behind and his fine, chiseled shoulders. Men just didn't realize how much a woman appreciated a man's well-shaped derriere. Hannah sighed and tilted her head. Taggart's butt was perfectly symmetrical. It curved tight and filled out every line of his jeans as though they had been spray-painted to his delicious cheeks. She wondered if he worked out. She'd love to work him out. *Wow. Where did that come from?* Shifting uneasily in the saddle, Hannah fanned her shirt to give her flaming torso a little air. What was she doing? No way was she going there. She wasn't about to get involved with the likes of Taggart de Gaelson. Besides, he was too much of a smart-ass.

Narrowing her eyes, Hannah glared holes through the center of his muscular back. *Didn't want to listen to the sting of my tongue.* Hannah squinted even harder as she visualized several pinecones bouncing out of the trees and pinging off the top of Taggart's head.

"That is not verra nice, Hannah," Taggart called out, his chuckle rumbling out across the deep gully beside them.

Hannah shifted in the saddle again and loosened the neckline of her shirt. "What are you talking about?" She worried the reins between her sweating palms. Surely, he couldn't read her mind. God, she hoped not, especially after all she'd just been thinking about his anatomy.

"I guess I should just be thankful ye visualized pinecones and not boulders." Taggart laughed again.

He *had* read her mind! "How did you do that? But

more importantly, *stop* doing it!" Hannah clenched the reins tighter as a flush of embarrassment flooded through her body.

Taggart's deep rumbling laughter drowned out the steady thud of the horse's hooves crunching along the dirt trail. "Sorry, lass. I couldna help it. When ye concentrated upon me and projected your thoughts, 'twas a natural response for me to protect myself."

Hannah closed her eyes with a silent groan. What had she gotten herself into? And what else had he *heard* her think that he wasn't telling her? "No more reading my mind, or Lisbet and I are turning around right now and going back. Do you understand me?"

His shoulders shook as he snorted with laughter, and Taggart nodded with the rhythm of his horse's gait. "Aye, Hannah. I understand. No more reading your thoughts."

"Why do they call this Gearlach's Pass?" Hannah's gaze traveled over the limestone clearing with interest as she shielded her eyes against the glowing rays of the setting sun.

Taggart paused in the unbuckling of their gear and rubbed the thick leather straps between his hands. What should he tell her? That Gearlach was a Draecna who still inhabited these parts, but Taggart had warned the nosy beast he'd best keep his scaly arse hidden or Taggart would thrash him until his horns fell off? " 'Twas named after a legendary beast. Much like the famed monster of Loch Ness."

A low, deep rumble vibrated through the cliffs above their heads, sending a shower of pebbles and small stones scrambling down the hillside all around them.

"Damn ye, Gearlach," Taggart swore under his breath. The mischievous beast eavesdropped somewhere close by.

He knew Gearlach had never liked the Draecna of Loch Ness. Said she was a narcissistic, snobby little slut who liked having humans vying to take her picture.

Scanning the sky, Hannah frowned at the cloudless strip of sparkling azure peeping through the branches waving in the breeze. "I wonder where that thunder came from? There's not a cloud in the sky." Hannah led Lisbet farther away from the side of the cliff and scowled at the loose stones bouncing around their feet and rolling over the side of the ledge. "Are you sure it's safe to camp around here? I don't want to wake up in the middle of a rock slide."

"It's safe!" Taggart shouted, tossing their gear to the ground and turning to cast a warning glare into the surrounding trees. Gearlach had better take the hint or he'd spell him into another dimension.

"Don't shout at me!" Hannah snapped and turned away to unbuckle Lisbet's saddle.

"I wasna shouting at you," Taggart snorted as he peeled off his shirt and wiped the sweat from his face.

Whirling back around to face him, Hannah fired back. "Well, if you weren't shouting at me . . ." Hannah's voice trailed off when she discovered Taggart stripped to the waist. He stood bronzed in the sunlight, the angular cuts and planes of his upper body chiseled to delicious perfection. "I need to . . ." Hannah stalled, her mind went blank; her awareness shifted to the rising level of heat overtaking her body. It had been so very long since she'd been with anyone. Hannah shook herself. She had to get a grip. She didn't need to get involved with Taggart. "Is there a spring or someplace where I could go wash up or something?"

Taggart nodded toward a narrow trail hugging the side of the cliff on the other side of the clearing. "Down that path, ye will find a spring eddied into a shallow pool perfect for bathing. Ye will find Gothgar packed a bit of soap and a towel in the bag I placed at the base of the pine over there."

Hannah snatched the bag and headed down the path without another word. She had to get away from Taggart's bare chest. The sight of him had her eyeballs sizzling in her head. Now she knew what a thermometer felt like, and her mercury was about to explode.

She rounded the curved wall of the cliff and found the oasis Taggart had promised. The spring had etched out a shallow pool into the limestone shelf, producing a peaceful, cave-like spa perfect for bathing. Hannah stood on the edge of the protruding rock and gazed out across the land of Taroc Na Mor. The surrounding vista stole her breath. She had to admit she'd never seen such beauty; not even her precious mountain back home compared. The jagged horizon of mountains hazed purple and blue in the distance, swathed with the deep greens of the impenetrable pines and dotted with strips of limestone grey. Hannah smiled when she realized the landscape of Taroc Na Mor mimicked the colors of an intricate tartan. It rolled across the land like the proudest plaid. The sweet acrid balm of the endless sea of pines filled the air as the branches whispered their secrets to the wind.

The refreshing breeze kissed at her cheeks and Hannah relaxed with a sigh. This was so much better. Her body cooled down and she stripped off her clothes, piling them beside the bag.

"Yeeeoowww!" Hannah screeched as she slipped her foot into the icy water. She had forgotten how cold spring water could be.

A resounding roar shuddered across the hillside. The ground trembled beneath her feet and the surface of the pool rippled into a thousand rings. Hannah ducked her head and sidled against the wall of the cliff. Earthquake?

She dug her toes into the slippery ooze coating the base of the pool. Lurching along the slime-coated limestone, her heart sank as she realized she'd never manage to make it across the trembling foundation to her clothes.

A great scaly head appeared over the rim of the ledge. Huge iridescent eyes glowed in the half-light of the shadows; heavy lids narrowed, the golden orbs swept from side to side with a watchful gaze across the quaking pool. The beast had twisted horns at both the top of its head and where its great jaws hinged at its mouth. Its scales shone green, but whenever it moved, the smooth plates caught in the light shimmered every color of the spectrum. A long flowing beard trailed down from its lower jaw, snaking down the front of its tiled chest. The creature kept its great muzzle shut; two enormous fangs protruded from under its smooth green lips and curled down from its upper jaw. She remained motionless, clutching a jutting-out bit of rock. *My God, I wonder how many more teeth are in that mouth.*

Hannah eased in a quiet deep breath. *Breathe, Hannah.* She had to stay calm. Surely this creature obeyed the basic laws of any large animal. As long as she didn't make any sudden moves, maybe it wouldn't eat her. Hannah slid her hand along the frigid slab of stone around the edge of the pool. Maybe she could reason with this thing. Get into its mind and let it know that if it ate her, she'd just give it a bad case of heartburn.

She focused on a particularly greenish scale right between the beast's golden eyes. Nothing. Velvety darkness filled her mind. Gritting her teeth, Hannah strained and concentrated harder. Still nothing. *Dammit!* Why couldn't she get inside that scaly head?

Holding her breath, Hannah inched her way deeper into the shadows. She squeezed her eyes shut and projected her thoughts with a decidedly mental scream. If ever she needed Taggart to be able to read her mind, that time was now. *"Taggart! Get your ass down here! You're not going to believe what just slithered up the side of this mountain! It's a . . . it's a . . . damn if it isn't a freakin' dragon!"*

"Gearlach!" Taggart roared, pounding down the trail and rounding the corner of the cliff.

"She screamed," Gearlach explained with a defensive flip of one curled claw in Hannah's direction. "I was merely responding to the distressed call of our beloved Lady Guardian." Gearlach cocked his horned head and gave Hannah a slow wink of a glowing eye. "And by the way, dragons are mythical creatures made up by drunken humans who couldn't explain their sightings of Draecna." Gearlach pounded his scaly chest. "I'm real. I am a sacred Draecna."

Hannah stared open-mouthed at the Draecna. The thing talked. It not only talked, but it apparently had no trouble hearing her thoughts even though she couldn't get inside its head. "Gearlach?" Hannah sagged against the cold rock ledge, then knelt deeper until the water touched her chin and crossed her arms over her freezing breasts. Her teeth chattered as the chill of the spring water settled well into her body. She didn't know which made her tremble more, the shock of talking to what appeared to be a mythical beast or severe hypothermia.

Scrubbing his face with both hands, Taggart nodded and fixed her with a sheepish grin. "Hannah McPherson, meet Gearlach. The Draecna for which Gearlach's Pass was named."

Shivering uncontrollably as she moved toward the edge of the pool, Hannah jerked her head toward her clothes. "Both of you turn around. I'm freezing to death. You can explain this to me once I'm out of this icy water."

"Oh. Icy spring water." Gearlach nodded and displayed the rest of his razor-sharp teeth in a toothy grin. "Could that be why ye screamed?"

"Just turn around!" Hannah snapped, trembling in the water until the surface of the pool echoed with ripples. "Both of you. Now!"

"Is she always this surly?" Gearlach asked, lumbering his great girth in a half circle as Hannah had ordered.

"Always," Taggart sighed as he stepped over Gearlach's tail.

"Why is she having us turn around?" Gearlach bent his horned head close and nudged Taggart with one of his leathery wings. "Doesna she know the spring water is clear and ye've already seen her in all her glory?"

Slinging the water off her arms, Hannah swallowed a growl as she realized she wasn't cold anymore. Thanks to these two, embarrassment and fury surged through her veins like a liquid bonfire. Yanking on her clothes, she stumbled and cursed, fighting to pull them on over dripping wet skin. "Taggart!" she snarled through gritted teeth. "You can turn around now and start with the explanations."

Taggart clasped his hands behind his back as though he were a schoolboy facing detention. "Where exactly would ye like me to start?"

"Oh, I don't know," Hannah mused with an exaggerated shrug. What the hell was wrong with him? He acted like she wanted to talk about the weather when there was an eighteen-foot creature that shouldn't exist standing right in front of them. She jerked her chin in Gearlach's direction. "Why don't you start with that *thing*?"

"Hmmpff!" Gearlach snorted out two great puffs of smoke that curled into the air as he straightened his beard down his rounded belly with his foreclaws. "I will have ye know, I am not a *thing*. I am a sacred Draecna of Taroc Na

Mor, the protected race of the portal keepers. Without us, there would be no time travel or jumping between an endless choice of worlds. As a matter of fact, the continuum itself would cease to exist or remain in balance."

"Draecna? Portal keepers? What are you talking about? What exactly is a Draecna?" Hannah edged a bit closer, wrinkling her nose at the distinct smell of sulfur coming from Gearlach's breath.

"Have ye told her nothing?" Gearlach asked, nudging Taggart again with the hooked tip of one of his wings. "Septamus is going to incinerate you. Ye know he's not nearly as civilized and patient as he would have everyone believe."

"I have not had the time to explain everything." Taggart thumped the Draecna's wing away from his shoulder and fixed Gearlach with a silencing glare. "Hannah, Gearlach is a Draecna. They are sacred beasts who have lived at Taroc Na Mor for longer than your world has been recording time. I meant to introduce ye to them a bit later. Once ye had time to rest and fall in love with your newly acquired land."

Hannah studied Gearlach, circling around him as though he were a new patient. She'd never run across anything like this in any of her veterinary textbooks. This thing was absolutely amazing. He loomed the size of a bull elephant, maybe a bit larger. He reminded her a great deal of the pictures of dragons she'd seen in a Celtic mythology class she'd once taken. "Can you breathe fire?" she asked. With the distinct aroma of sulfur he emitted, there had to be some combustible gas stored in that scaled body of his somewhere.

"Aye! Would ye like to see?" Gearlach inhaled a deep, rumbling breath and prepared to exhale, only to be slapped on the chest by Taggart.

"No, Gearlach. The last time ye did that we lost fifty

acres of trees. How many times do I have to tell ye to think before ye act?" Taggart turned to Hannah with an apologetic shake of his head. "Forgive him. Gearlach is only five hundred years old. He's very immature and has yet to learn the restraint and reasoning of an adult Draecna. He's been in my charge since he was just a hatchling. His heart is pure. He's just a bit impulsive. "

"Five hundred years old? And you say he's been in your charge since he hatched out five hundred years ago?" Hannah clutched at the air, clenching her fists as she tried catching her breath between her pounding heartbeats. She couldn't have possibly heard him right. Her heart drummed so loud it roared in her ears and then everything went dark.

"But they are already on Taroc Na Mor land, Sloan. Ye know 'tis sacred ground. The Guild of Barac'Nairn will sentence me to death if I am discovered anywhere within their borders. It is one of the sacred tenets we agreed to in the last treaty." The cloaked woman stood before an obelisk of crystal, her gaze fixed on a vision of Taggart and Gearlach as they bent over Hannah's unconscious body.

Sloan smoothed his hand beneath the frayed hood of her cloak and caressed the silk of her slender neck. Her body tensed beneath his touch and he enjoyed the sensation beyond measure. Sloan's favorite scent above all others was essence of Mia's fear. He laced his fingers into the hair at the nape of her neck and yanked her face close to his. "Mia, my dearest, my most precious love—" Sloan raked a biting kiss along the edge of her jaw and yanked her trembling body hard against his. "If ye do not do as I command ye, after I have killed them, I will kill you and I promise ye—I will do it slowly."

Mia closed her eyes; her hands shook as she passed them

in front of the visionary crystal. "Ye know I would never disobey ye, my love. Your happiness is the only desire of my existence."

Sloan shoved her away and returned to strolling across the marble-floored room. He pulled a lace-trimmed silk cloth from his sleeve and wiped his hands as though they were soiled. He tired of reminding Mia of her tenuous position in his life. Perhaps her usefulness had neared its end. "Has he bedded her yet?" Sloan twisted the silk between his fingers as he scowled into the mesmerizing flames of the hearth.

"Not yet, m'lord. Taggart holds his resolve. He is her protector and knows he must not touch her." Mia kept her eyes lowered and shuffled toward the door as she spoke, returning her tattered hood to cover her bowed head.

"Ye will not leave my presence until ye are dismissed. Ye know better, Mia." Sloan didn't bother turning from the hearth, just waved the dancing orange tongues higher with a single pass of his hand until the grating roared and popped with a white-hot blaze. "There are still a few members of your family living in the outer regions. Do not think I cannot find them and bring them to the killing cells. Corter grows bored with the few prisoners he has left to toy with. He'll soon run out of victims to disembowel."

"Forgive me, my love. But again, I beg you. If there is to be punishment meted out, I ask that ye punish me." Mia dropped to her knees, closing her eyes as she held her hands out in front of her.

Sloan laughed, walked across the room, and jerked her chin into his hand so he could hiss against her cheek. "Why, my dearest Mia. Ye know my greatest pleasure is when I make ye watch." Then he pushed her to the floor and stepped over her cowering body to return to his place by the fire. "Taggart must seduce her. The Sullivan witch must believe herself smitten. It will weaken them for our attack."

"They are drawn to each other, but they both fight against it. Taggart prides himself on his word and his honor." Mia cowered on the floor, her hands shaking as she pushed her hood to her shoulders.

Sloan turned from the fire and rolled his eyes. The trials he must endure on the path to his dream. Mia had become such a sniveling little beast. "Oh get up, Mia!" Pointing at the crystal across the room, Sloan yanked her up from the floor. "Get over there and see what form ye can assume to win the woman's trust." He shook his head; disgust filled his senses as he studied her cowering form. Mia had become a complete idiot incapable of thinking on her own. What had happened to the cunning vixen he'd stolen from Taggart's side? The seductive minx who'd caused his brother so much delightful pain? Sloan still reveled in the agony and humiliation Mia had put Taggart through when she'd spurned him in front of their people. Now the woman vexed him beyond reason. It was definitely time she was replaced.

Her shoulders hunched, her bowed head trembling, Mia shuffled over to the crystal obelisk and nodded once at the iridescent shaft. The visions shifted and flickered upon the mirrored surface, searching for the subjects of Taroc Na Mor.

Taggart sat by the fire, his shirt wadded in one hand, his chin propped in the other. What would he say to her when she awakened? He covered his eyes and shook his head. He couldn't believe he'd just blurted it out. How could he have told her he was over five hundred years old? Taggart snorted. Wait 'til she found out how old he really was and that he wasn't even from this side of the portal. Taggart threw his shirt to the ground and raked both hands through his hair. Hell, wait 'til she found out his age wasn't the worst of his secrets.

He peered through his fingers and drew a deep breath. She still lay unconscious, curled on her side under the blanket by the fire. Holy blazes, but she looked fine in the flickering light of the flames; her skin glowed as though she burned from within.

Hannah stirred a bit and then shivered. Taggart scowled and leaned a bit closer. God's beard, was the lass unwell? Had she become over-chilled when she'd fainted after swimming in the icy spring? Perhaps the journey from Jasper Mills had been harder on her than he'd thought.

Taggart laid his fingers to the curve of her throat just beneath her ear. "Hell's fire," Taggart hissed. Hannah's skin seared to his touch; her body blazed with fever. Exhaustion must've lowered her defenses, left her vulnerable to some sort of ague.

He stripped back the blanket and unbuttoned her shirt, hesitating but a moment before he spread his palms across her chest. Hannah's fevered eyes flew wide open as she squeaked a weak mewling sound of protest.

"Hush now, Hannah. I only mean to heal ye. Remember how I helped the wee pup back at your office? Just close your eyes and open to the warmth of my touch. My energy will draw the ague from your bones."

Hannah stretched to touch his face, her eyes dazed, her pale hand trembling as her breath came in short uneven gasps. "What? Who?" Her tongue darted out and traced her fever-reddened lips as she moved her fingers across Taggart's mouth. She wriggled closer and pressed her bare breasts against his chest. "So cold. I am so cold."

Taggart groaned and took a deep breath. He had to heal

her. *Ignore the temptation of those sweet breasts. Just heal her, man.* "Ye must be still just a wee bit longer please, Hannah. I beg ye. I canna concentrate when ye wiggle."

Hannah ran her hands around his waist and climbed her fingers up his back. She pulled herself tighter against his body and nestled her face into the crook of his neck. She kissed the skin beneath his jaw and curled a leg around his hips. "I'm so cold. Just hold me and get me warm. . . ." Her voice trailed off and her warm breath tickled the skin beneath his ear.

She trapped him; the velvet of her lips nuzzled against his throat and stole the air from his body. She ran her hands along his face and traced her fingers along the stubble of his jawline. He shouldn't allow this. He must put her aside. Forbid it. He was her protector. "Hannah . . ." *Holy blazes, Hannah.*

Hannah wound her fingers into his hair and pulled his head down to hers. She opened her mouth, inviting him in. Her mouth tasted hot as the fire burning behind them. Taggart lost the battle, crushing her to his chest; he buried his hands in the silkiness of her hair. Hannah welcomed him in, molded her body to his; she vibrated against his mouth with a throaty moan.

Taggart tore himself away from her fiery lips and kissed his way down her throat. With a trembling hand, he cupped a breast and teased a circle around her tightening nipple with his tongue. With half-closed eyes, Hannah arched her back and writhed beneath his touch. As she reached down to fumble with Taggart's pants, she gifted him with a wicked smile.

"Jake."

"Jake?"

Taggart froze, then pulled away from Hannah's tempting body, blinking down into her fevered gaze. God's beard! She was still addled with fever. Here he was about to break his pledge and she didn't even know it was him! Dammit to hell, what was he thinking? Hmmpf! He knew what he was thinking and exactly what he was thinking with. Hell's fire and Draecna scat! He shoved his hand against his aching cock and rolled to his back to stare up into the stars. Risking another glance at Hannah's parted lips and half-closed eyes, Taggart sent another silent curse up into the starlit night. By Isla's beard, he'd heal her this time and there wouldn't be any more blasted distractions! Taggart clenched his teeth and plastered his outspread hand across Hannah's face, pressing her back against the blankets.

She batted at his wrists, sputtered, and kicked, as though fighting to breathe.

"Be still, woman!" Taggart grabbed her flailing arms with his other hand and held them over her head. A bright, golden glow surrounded his fingers, which covered her face, and it flowed all around Hannah's head.

Hannah grew still and soon the slow, steady rise and fall of her chest told Taggart she finally slept. Then he spread his hand between her breasts and drew the fever from her body. He lifted his hands, glaring down at her as he clenched and unclenched his fists. He'd almost done it, almost broken the pact. He'd almost tossed it all aside, just so he could feel alive again one more time. He couldn't resist tracing a finger across her now cooling cheek. Her skin slid as pure velvet beneath his fingertips. He drew a shaking breath and damned the burning ache throbbing the length of his body. His gaze traveled over the rest of her frame. Her breasts had been just as soft.

This was madness! Taggart tore himself away, stomped to the edge of the clearing and grabbed more wood for the fire. "Gearlach!" he bellowed into the silent darkness. "Where the hell are ye, ye oversized lizard?"

"I am right here. Must ye bellow? We Draecna do not

have the weak hearing of ye half-deaf hybrids, ye know." Gearlach emerged from behind a pile of boulders, scrubbing his fangs with a branch ripped from a nearby pine.

"Watch over her!" Taggart barked through gritted teeth with a jerk of his head in Hannah's direction.

Gearlach shrugged a half-spread wing, then continued picking at his teeth as he settled down beside the fire. "I can watch over the lass if ye like. But where are ye going to be?"

"Just watch over her." Taggart snapped as he stomped down the narrow trail leading to the secluded springs. He didn't bother stripping off his jeans before diving into the deepest end of the icy pool.

Something poked her in the middle of her side just below her ribs. Hannah shifted atop the thin padding of the pallet covering the cold, hard ground. That felt worse—now it stabbed her even higher. Either a sharp rock or a clump of dirt dug into her back right above the kidney. The chilled night breeze ruffled her hair across her face and invaded the folds of the plaid gathered loosely about her neck. She shivered, pulled the woolen blanket higher, and scooted over again. She opened one eye, searching for a source of heat, and scowled as she spotted the dwindling flames of the dying fire. This was ridiculous. An involuntary shudder rattled her teeth until she almost bit her tongue as another chill stole across her flesh. That fire needed stoking with a lot more wood. Time to build the inferno. Hannah yanked the blanket tighter around her shoulders and rolled to scan the clearing.

"Taggart?" Her voice echoed off the sheer wall of the cliff and faded out into the darkness.

The nocturnal woods stood murky and silent except for the shushing of the wind through the swaying tops of the pines. Hannah swallowed hard against a passing moment of homesickness. She missed the sweet night songs of her mountain back home, the chirp of the crickets, the *ching ching* of the katydids tucked away in the trees. Why had she left her safe little sanctuary and wandered halfway across the globe?

"Taggart!" Hannah hissed again. Still no response. Taggart appeared to be missing in action. Apparently, he'd left her alone. Well, maybe he'd needed to pee. Hannah rubbed her nose with an irritated shiver. That didn't change the fact that the ground radiated the cold and the fire burned as low as a birthday candle. She'd just have to get her own firewood.

Worming her way to her feet, she hitched the blanket higher around her shoulders, then paused as the material scratched against her bare skin. Bare skin? Wait a minute. As she peeped down between the folds of the rough woolen blanket, Hannah gasped at the sight of her ruined blouse baring her chest and hanging from her shoulders in shreds. The buttons were gone, popped from the threads; the holes were tattered as though they'd held the buttons just a bit too long.

Hannah stepped closer to the circle of firelight and spread the blanket wide. Branded between her creamy breasts appeared a bright red imprint of a very large hand.

"Taggart!" Her enraged cry echoed across the mountain as she kicked a nearby log into the fire. Embers crackled and popped up into the darkness, sending a beacon of sparks spiraling into the night. What the hell had he done while she slept—branded her as if she were some sort of cow?

Taggart stormed out of the shadows, his claymore fisted between his hands and swinging in a menacing arc above his head. His icy eyes flashed as he burst into the clearing, his body poised for the attack. Bare-chested, hair loose and dripping rivulets down tensed muscles of his body, he looked like a wild barbarian in the half-light of the fire. "What is it, Hannah? What threatens ye?"

"Nothing threatens me!" Hannah whirled upon him, opening the blanket and exposing his handprint, as well as a clear view of her breasts. "Would you care to explain to me how this got here?"

Taggart coughed; his hands tightened to a white-knuckled grip on his blade as he lowered his arms to his sides. "Ye were sick with a fever." Taggart cleared his throat again, wiping the back of his hand across his eyes and trying to look anywhere but at Hannah's chest. "Ye had to be healed. Ye were delirious, out of your mind. Trust me. Dammit, woman, there was just no other way."

Snapping the blanket back around her body, Hannah fixed Taggart with her best I-don't-think-so looks. Did he really think she was that gullible? "So I was delirious with a fever? You really expect me to believe that?" How stupid did he think she was? She might've been sick, but what could she have done that would've been so bad? Babbled a little bit of nonsense maybe?

"Yes, Hannah. Ye were delirious." Taggart raked his wet hair away from his face, then sheathed his claymore at his side.

Stomping over to her bag to rummage around for another shirt, Hannah stumbled and tripped over the folds of the blanket. She silently cursed the rock that had just jammed her big toe. As she hopped and yanked the blanket out of the way, Hannah snapped, "Well, if I was so delirious with a fever, what did I try to do?"

His jawline rippling with his clenched teeth, Taggart folded his arms across his chest. "Ye don't believe me? Ye don't think ye were delirious? Be careful what ye wish for, my little Guardian, because with just one word and a wave of my hand, I can return every memory to your stubborn little head."

After she fished a shirt out of her bag, Hannah moved back closer to the fire. She should've never come to Scotland, especially not with such an infuriating smart-ass. "I haven't known *you* all that long, but I know *I'm* not a bad person. What could I have possibly done that was so bad in this dreadful state of delirium?" Pulling the fresh shirt underneath the blanket, she returned his narrow-eyed glare. She wished he'd just spit it out. She was freezing to death and still jet-lagged. She wasn't in the mood for twenty questions. "And you're the one who'd better be coming up with some explanations, Taggart. As soon as I finish getting dressed and get this fire built up, we're going to discuss this little chronological announcement you made down at the spring that started my little roller-coaster blackout."

With a muttered curse, Taggart strode across the clearing in a ground-eating stride, clapping his hands in her face. "*Esromer!*"

Hannah tasted Taggart on her tongue as though he'd just lifted his mouth from hers. She rubbed her fingertips across her lips; the fresh rasp of his stubbled jaw throbbed anew across her flesh. Her body flushed hot. Her nipples tightened; her breasts ached for the return of his touch. She remembered. She'd kissed him, reached out to him; she'd wanted more but . . . no. It hadn't been him. Oh good gawd, she had called out to Jake. "Well, it wasn't like I was really kissing you. You know I thought it was Jake."

Taggart whirled away from her, stomping his way back across the clearing, where he shot her an angry glare across the fire. "That explanation makes it so much better. Thank ye very much, Hannah."

Hannah fumbled out of her ripped blouse, yanked on the fresh shirt underneath the cover of the blanket, and then wadded it up into a ball. She kicked it over beside her pack. She had no trouble maintaining her body temperature now. Taggart's attitude kept her plenty warm. There wasn't any reason for him to be a jerk. He still owed her many explanations. "Well, apparently, you weren't all that wild about kissing me anyway. I don't remember anything about you pushing the advantage."

Taggart rolled his eyes and held up a warning hand. "Oh no! I am *not* taking that bait. Many a man down through the centuries has met his downfall by following that line of conversation with a woman." He circled around the edge of the clearing, gathered a few sticks of wood, and tossed them on the fire. "Have ye seen Gearlach? He was supposed to be watching over ye while I took a swim in the spring."

Hannah frowned and shook her head. "No. I was alone when I woke up, and why would I need someone to watch over me? I'm perfectly capable of taking care of myself. Believe it or not I've lived this long without you watching my every move."

Worrying his hands through his still–dripping hair, Taggart eyed Hannah as though she'd lost her mind. "I've just finished healing ye from a delirious fever. And need I remind ye of the attack on your life but a few days ago?"

"Oh—well. I guess you have a point there." Hannah picked up a stick and stirred the coals of the fire, grudgingly mesmerized by the glowing embers. She'd tried to put the memory of the felled trees from the attack at Jasper Mills to the back of her mind. "Which reminds me, you said you'd tended to Gearlach since he was a hatchling and he's now five hundred years old. So exactly how old does that make you?" Hannah raised her stick from the depths of the coals and watched the flame dance about on the tip. Not a sound could be heard except for the *hiss* of the fire and the distant *hoot-hooting* of an owl serenading the stars.

Hannah turned from the fire, the flaming brand in her

hand, her temper simmering hotter than the tip of the stick. "Taggart, I'm waiting. How old are you? I know you've got to be older than five hundred years if you've been babysitting Gearlach all that time."

His face drawn, Taggart approached Hannah as though he trudged to the gallows. "Why does my age shock ye so, Hannah? Ye didna bat an eye at the sight of an eighteen-foot Draecna, but ye fainted when ye learned I was over five centuries old."

He's not human. Hannah tossed the stick and hugged the gooseflesh of her arms as she peered deeper into the iciness of his gaze. She'd seen his smile. No fangs that she'd noticed. Then what exactly was he? Hannah swallowed hard at the knot lodged in her throat. Her voice rasped around her uncertainty. "Answer the question. How old *are* you, Taggart? And more importantly, what are you?"

His lips tightened as he lifted his chin, fierce blue eyes filled with challenge. The chiseled planes of his body tensed as he stalked around the dancing flames of the fire. "I am Taggart de Gaelson, eldest son of the Royal House of Cair Orlandis. I am seven hundred and seventy-seven years old and I come from another reality. I come from Erastaed, from the world on the other side of the portal of Taroc Na Mor, ancestral home to the race of the sacred Draecna. I am chosen protector from the Guild of Barac'-Nairn, watchers over the blessed guardian."

"Blessed guardian?" Hannah swallowed hard before licking her lips. That movement proved futile; her mouth had gone drier than the sands of the Sahara.

Taggart nodded once in her direction. "Aye, that would be you."

Hannah sank to a fallen log and leaned back against a tree. Digging her fingers into the sponge of the rotted bark, she gulped a ragged breath of the dank, loam-scented wood. Hannah ground her palms against the log until it splintered between her fingers. She plunged her nails deep into the damp crumbling bark; maybe if she clenched something tight enough the reality of Taggart's words might somehow make more sense.

"Seven hundred and seventy-seven years old." Hannah repeated the words as though mumbling a spell. "A world called Erastaed." Maybe if she said it aloud it might make it easier to accept. No, this couldn't be real. She must still be delirious from that fever. She pressed the back of her hands to check the heat of her forehead as she choked out a whisper, "I've never heard of that place . . . that Erastaed, and nobody can live to be over seven hundred years old. At least I've never heard of anyone living that long. I just don't see how what you're saying could be true. There's got to be a more logical explanation." She closed her mind against the nagging inner voice. The voice whispering that if Taggart's words weren't true, then how could she explain Gearlach?

With a bitter laugh, Taggart turned away and tossed another log into the middle of the fire. A shower of sparks exploded into the night and the flames licked higher into the air. "Do ye no' think it a bit conceited to believe this world ye're standin' in is the only reality in existence?"

Hannah covered her face with shaking hands as an icy shiver of recognition tickled teasing fingers up her spine. Grandma had repeated wondrous folk tales to her when she was a little girl. The eerie bedtime stories often portrayed Hannah as the heroine and never failed to lull her to sleep. But surely, that's all they had been—stories to entertain a lonely child. Weren't they? She couldn't wrap her mind around this. Jet lag. Strange country. A freakin' creature that looked like he'd stepped out of one of her mythology books, and now an annoying, sexy guide who turned out to be from some other reality.

Not bothering to open her eyes, Hannah pinched the

bridge of her nose. "Well, you know how self-centered we earthlings can be. But why don't you humor me and just tell me the name of your world again. I'm afraid I'm in information overload right now and I didn't quite catch it earlier. Could you please repeat it so I'll know exactly where you're from?"

The log shifted as Taggart joined her, causing Hannah to lurch against his side. Scrabbling her way to the other end of the teetering seat, she glared at the mischief flashing in his eyes. He did that on purpose. He delighted in baiting her. Did he want her to split his lip again? Hannah gritted her teeth. "Are you going to tell me where you are from or not?"

"Erastaed is the name of my world. Cair Orlandis is the Royal House or the bloodline from which I descend." Taggart folded his hands as he rested his elbows on his knees. "Ye reach my world through the portal located at Taroc Na Mor. There is a powerful gateway there permitting passage to many wondrous worlds, or dimensions. Gearlach and his kind are the conductors of the portals. Without the awesome power of the mystical Draecna, the gateways would cease to function."

Royal bloodlines, portals to other worlds that needed mystical beasts to power them? Hannah closed her eyes and massaged her temples. He'd said he was the eldest son. Hannah opened her eyes. "If you're the eldest son of a royal house, then why aren't you back at the castle leading your people or something? Or isn't that how it works in your world?"

A groaning sigh pulled Taggart's face into a troubled scowl. Rising from the log, he stoked the fire until the flames licked even higher toward the winking stars piercing through the darkness. Lifting his face toward the pinpoints of light, he turned a slow circle as though searching for a particular set. "The hour grows late, Hannah. Pull your pallet close to the fire and try to get some rest. There will be time for more answers tomorrow. I promise. The longer we're at Taroc Na Mor, the more you will come to understand."

Hannah's head snapped up in disbelief. Did he actually presume to send her to bed? Was he serious? Taggart's face glowed by the light of the blaze as he stared down into the depths of the coals.

"I am not tired," Hannah retorted. "I want information. I think it's important I know more about you before I go any further."

"Please, Hannah," Taggart begged without pulling his gaze from the snapping flames. "I'm weary and I'm askin' ye. Please leave it until tomorrow."

Something in his voice wrenched at her heart. Hannah heard utter bleakness, a deeply felt sorrow; she sensed a sadness sifting into his tone. Taggart sounded defeated. She didn't like it when he went belly up. It just didn't fit his protective nature.

Rolling her aching shoulders as she rose from her seat on the stump, she headed over to fetch her pallet. Another glance at his drawn, weary face stayed the questions on the tip of her tongue. No. She'd bide her time. Find out more when Taggart was ready. After all, there wasn't any need to cause him pain. Hannah scooped up the blankets and hugged them to her chest. "Well, maybe I'm more tired than I thought. Good night, Taggart. We'll talk about it in the morning."

"Sleep well, Hannah, and thank ye."

CHAPTER FOUR

"Why did you leave her after I specifically asked ye to watch over her?" Taggart risked a glance back over his shoulder at Hannah as Gearlach fidgeted in place before him. Good. She still slept. At least while she snored beneath the mound of blankets, she didn't batter him with questions he wasn't prepared to answer.

Gearlach hung his head and worried a splintered claw around one of his crooked horns. He wrinkled the mottled skin on his great, greenish snout as he stubbed the foreclaw of his right foot deep into the soft earth. "I heard something prowling about in the wood and I thought I should go have a look-see." He fretted and scraped an odd-shaped symbol in the dried silt he'd knocked loose from the limestone shelf extending around the base of the cliff. He balanced himself with stubby forearms held akimbo; his scaled body swaying back and forth as he scratched jagged glyphs deep in the darkened soil with the curved claw on his biggest toe.

"Stop that, Gearlach! Ye know that symbol will call up a storm and I am sick and tired of getting soaked." Taggart rubbed out the markings with the toe of his boot as he shoved against the sulking Draecna's chest.

"Well, if ye would go ahead and mate with the snippy lass, ye wouldna have to keep dousing your cock in every bit of icy water ye can find." Gearlach shoved back, knocking Taggart across the clearing into a thicket of newly sprouted rowans.

Rage surged through him as he disentangled himself from the weave of silvery branches. With teeth clenched, Taggart stumbled out of the brush and knocked broken branches off his sleeves. He'd strangle that insolent, over-sized lizard. With a glance over at the motionless mound of blankets by the fire, he bit back the response he longed to roar. Hannah still hadn't moved. Thank the fires of all Erastaed; the longer the woman slept, the better. He dreaded all the questions she'd launch at him as soon as those accusing eyes popped open.

"It—is—forbidden," Taggart hissed through gritted teeth. "And ye know there are several reasons why."

Gearlach rolled his golden eyes as he stretched out a tip of his hooked wing and scratched behind his scaly pointed ear. "Do ye truly think she will mind the fact ye are a Draecna hybrid and ye've hidden your form in that human shape she seems to favor so much? She seems to be the sensible sort. After all, she didna mind me. She didna even scream."

"*Ecnelis!*" Taggart snapped with a nod of his head. "Ye will be silent until I decide ye have found the wisdom to know what information should be spoken aloud and what should not be shared with any who happen to be in your presence."

"What is all the yelling about?" Hannah's muffled growl emerged from the depths of the blankets piled beside the fire.

"God's beard," Taggart groaned. "Now look what ye've done. Ye've awakened the raging beastie herself." Taggart shot Gearlach a withering glare as the Draecna fixed him with a sharp-toothed grin and returned to cleaning the dirt from underneath his claws with the pointed tip of his tail.

"I heard that," Hannah snapped, throwing back the covers as she rolled to her knees. She wrestled her way out of the wad of blankets and stumbled toward the dwindling fire while rubbing her lower back. "Why did you let me sleep so long? We should've been up and going hours ago."

"Ye needed your rest," Taggart grumbled. He wasn't about to tell her the real reason. He cringed and waited for the arsenal of questions he knew perched on the tip of her tongue.

Shaking out the blankets, Hannah winced with a roll of her shoulders and folded the blankets against her chest. "I guess I was pretty tired. Jet lag must've nabbed me after all. But we really need to get moving. Instead of bothering with a campfire breakfast, can we just eat some of that dried trail mix while we ride? Where's the bottled water? If you don't mind, I'm not all that up on drinking water out of that spring."

Taggart cut a glance over toward Gearlach, who merely tapped a claw across his pale green lips and returned a wink before ambling off into the woods. "Ye don't even want some of that noxious coffee ye favor so much? I have a coffeepot in the pack. I can have some of the black wicked brew ready for ye in no time at all."

Hannah rolled the blankets into a tighter bundle and belted them behind her saddle. "As tempting as that generous offer sounds, I'm anxious to see Taroc Na Mor. I'll just wait until we get there for my first cup of the day. I'd rather we got going if you don't mind."

The minx plotted something. He'd bet Gearlach's oversized arse in gold. Did she think him some sort of fool? Taggart scratched the stubble peppering his face while he admired the temptation of her fine, round backside as she bent to shove gear into another bag. She hadn't mentioned a word about last night. Not one prying question or comment about anything they'd discussed. He'd been certain she'd launch a verbal assault as soon as those fiery green eyes popped open. She had to be setting some sort of trap. "Aye, perhaps that would be best. The sooner we get ye settled at Taroc Na Mor, the sooner ye shall see what a fine place ye have come to call your own." Taggart kicked dirt on what was left of the night's fire and smothered out the orange, glowing coals.

As they rode down the trail, Taggart rolled his shoulders as though feeling an itch he couldn't reach. Hannah's stare burned through the center of his back. Her mind hummed at him with questions she longed to ask. Dammit to hell, the woman electrified the very air with everything she wished to know. She fair ticked aloud like an activated bomb set to detonate at any minute. Taggart slowed his horse and turned in the saddle to face her. "Hannah, for heaven's sake, by all that is holy. Just ask me what ye want to know."

Hannah arched a brow and stared back at him, her hands folded atop the horn of the saddle. "Wow. Aren't we a little tense this morning?" She popped another handful of raisins and nuts in her mouth as she rocked to the rhythm of the horse's gait.

With an irritated growl, Taggart swung back around in his saddle and urged his horse to a faster trot. The woman bordered along the edge of impossible. He knew she wanted to ask him questions. Why didn't she just do it?

"I learned a long time ago no man is going to tell me anything until he's quite good and ready. I figure when you're ready to talk, you'll tell me everything I want to know."

The little minx. Taggart pulled on his reins and brought his horse to an abrupt stop. He turned in the saddle just in time to catch Hannah's grin. "Last night ye asked me why

I wasn't the leader of my people since I am the eldest son of a royal line? Do ye remember that, ye wicked woman? Never ye mind, dinna answer that." Taggart arched a brow well into his hairline while his hands tensed into a strangle hold on the reins. He wasn't about to give her the opportunity to answer, knowing Hannah would just piss him off. "I guess ye could say my father found me to be bit different. So, he chose my younger brother in my stead."

Hannah shifted, leaning forward in the saddle and scrutinized him up and down. "What do you mean different? Is it your magic? Grandma always told me to keep quiet about the magic. You know people fear what they don't understand."

Her observation almost choked him as he swallowed a bitter laugh and shuttered painful memories back in their tightly kept closets. If only magic was all it was. Taggart nearly snapped the reins in two. Better she believe it was just the magic. She need never know the entire truth. If all went well, Hannah would never see his true form.

Taggart jerked his head forward with an acerbic snort. "Not everyone on Erastaed is capable of magic. Especially, the *abilities* I possess. Many fear it, which seems to be a universal trait. As ye said, people fear what they dinna understand."

Hannah studied him as she laced strands of Lisbet's black mane between her fingers as though she wove a tapestry. "So you lost your birthright just because you were born gifted? I'm so sorry, Taggart. I don't understand how a father could do that to his son."

A stab of uneasiness clawed at his bowels. Taggart hated a half-truth as much as a lie. But he couldn't help it. He wasn't prepared to reveal all of Taroc Na Mor's secrets, not just yet. He hadn't won Hannah's complete loyalty and trust; she still teetered on the edge. He couldn't risk losing her now, not when they'd come this far. "Don't worry yourself o'er much about it, Hannah. I've adjusted and am quite satisfied with my life. After all, I'm the protector of the guardian of Taroc Na Mor. I'm most pleased watching over ye and helping ye settle in to your new life."

Hannah waggled a warning finger over Lisbet's head as she eased the horse into a comfortable swaying gait up the narrow trail hugging the side of the mountain. "I told you I'm here on a trial basis only, remember? Now swivel around in your saddle there, cowboy, and let's get on our way to this heaven on earth you've promised me."

A chill wind howled around the skirting wall, whistling its way in from the churning sea. An early-evening mist swirled atop the chopping waves battering against the base of the gray, jagged cliffs. Hannah shivered as she scanned the black, weather-worn stones of the castle. She hugged herself, tightening her jacket closer as she rubbed the tingling skin at the back of her neck. Wow. All this place needed was some eerie organ music, a howling wolf, and the rattle of chains echoing in the background.

And that smell. *Whew.* The air reeked with an unbearable fog. Hannah choked back a gag. Heaven above, what caused that stench? Something pungent and acrid, like a cross between rotten eggs and singed hair, battered against her senses. Hannah wrinkled her nose and covered her face with one hand as her eyes watered until tears streamed down her cheeks. The memory of lab experiments with smoking sulfur came to mind, but something indescribable layered along with the noxious vapor . . . decayed fish, maybe?

"Taggart, what is that god-awful smell?" Hannah mumbled behind her fingers.

Taggart lifted his head and sniffed. "I dinna smell anything unusual in the wind. What does it smell like to ye?"

Hannah squinted more water from her eyes and prayed

the tears would relieve the ferocious burning caused by the toxic ammonia-like fumes cutting through the air. She tightened her grip on her nose and gasped a quick intake of air through her mouth. "I caddot belieb you caddot smell dat. It sbells like sodedody's filled a hair bag with chidden shid and sed id on fire!"

"What did ye say?"

Taking another quick breath through her mouth, Hannah released her nose and repeated, "I said I cannot believe you cannot smell that. It smells like somebody's filled a hair bag full of chicken shit and set it on fire!"

"Oh that." Taggart nodded. "That's Draecna scat. Dinna worry. When the tide comes in it will cleanse the feces from the rocks below and the odor willna be nearly as offensive."

Hannah stared at him and clamped her hand back over her face. Did he just tell her she smelled Draecna shit? This enchanted wonderland that was supposed to sweep her off her feet reeked so ripe it nearly burned her eyes out of their sockets. "Can't you teach them to shit out to sea? Or will it destroy the ecosystem in this part of the ocean?"

"Ergonomics," Taggart replied with a shrug. "They canna fly and shit at the same time."

Hannah swallowed hard and fixed him a narrow-eyed look. Surely he didn't expect her to believe that load of bunk. Even a common sparrow could drop a load while soaring overhead. "Let's just go inside."

With a wicked grin, Taggart shouldered open the double oak doors gracing the front of the keep. The blackened hinges creaked and groaned, protesting at being disturbed. Their footsteps echoed throughout the hub of the main entryway and into the honeycomb of tiled hallways shooting off in every direction. Enormous supporting beams stained black with age staggered across the vaulted ceiling like the ribs of some prehistoric beast. Hannah slowed until her steps came to a sliding halt and she found herself open-mouthed in the center of what appeared to be some sort of welcoming room.

Hannah spun in a slow circle, entranced by the elaborate furniture, the exquisite artwork, and the sculptures gracing the halls. *Mouth shut,* she reminded herself as she craned her neck and stared at the massive architecture of the interior of the castle. Taggart would think her some kind of fool walking around the keep like a slack-jawed tourist. The heart of the castle appeared to be the perfect opposite of the dilapidated exterior. Glancing toward the doorway, then back at the room, she almost wanted to go back to make sure she hadn't lost her mind. While outside, the castle had seemed a beaten-down Scottish keep, neglected and ravaged by the winds of time. Once inside the door, she felt like she'd taken some sort of potion and found herself the size of a tiny doll within a giant's house.

This room consisted of flooring inlaid with gold-streaked marble and vaulted ceilings supported by satin-finished granite pillars. Burnished mahogany formed the panels of the walls and gleamed along the curved banisters of the winding stairways. The finest inlays of ivory, silver, and gold, as well as metals Hannah couldn't identify, decorated every surface. Tracing her fingers along the sumptuous velvet of a chair, Hannah fingered the ornate tassels of an overstuffed pillow and let the satin threads tickle across her palm. The furnishings amazed her. Pristine antiques strategically adorned the heavy-legged tables scattered through the halls. Love seats and settees clustered about in cozy seating areas. Hannah's jaw dropped at their gargantuan proportions. The comfort of giants appeared to be the clear intent the designer of the home had in mind.

Craning her neck as she walked under the chandelier, Hannah squinted at the teardrop-shaped facets as the crystals twisted in a shaft of sunlight glimmering through the window. "Why is everything in this place so huge?"

"Because this is our ancestral home, honored Guardian, and it was built for our comfort, not yours."

Hannah whirled from her perusal of the chandelier to face the owner of the deep, rumbling voice. A battered Draecna with gray, faded scales wavered in the shadows of the doorway with eyes half closed into glowing, watchful slits.

Taggart stepped forward and placed himself between Hannah and the Draecna, his arms crossed over his chest. "Septamus, that is no way to great the guardian. Do not be such an ass."

"My quarrel is not with the guardian, Taggart. My irritation is with you. Why did ye tarry so long?" With a hitching slide, as though movement pained him, Septamus grimaced and showed a bit of yellowed fang as he worked his way into the room.

"Are you all right?" Hannah pushed around Taggart as she noticed Septamus's odd, tormented gait. Her heart went out to the aging Draecna who still carried himself with pride.

Septamus drew back, holding up his forearms as though he feared Hannah's touch would singe him. "It is nothing. I just grow weary. I am too old to power the gateways for as long as I have. That is why I am anxious for the hatching of the next clutch of young ones."

"He lies," Taggart interrupted. "Septamus hasn't been required to power the portals in years. The old coward has snarled and gimped around these halls for centuries, but he refuses to allow anyone to help him."

Pride could endanger the best of health, and apparently Draecna were as susceptible as humans. She could see the stubbornness flash in his great luminous eyes; sensed it in the way he growled. Hannah grabbed hold of Taggart's hand and pulled him to Septamus's side.

"I can understand him, but I can't heal him. I don't have your ability to heal. Help him, Taggart. Lay your hands on him, like you did me. Help him. Make him better."

Septamus's eyes widened and he retreated a step as Taggart gave him a quick shake of his head. Turning to Hannah, he pulled back a step and put her hands aside. "Hannah, I cannot heal a Draecna. I'm verra sorry. My powers canna help them. I've tried in the past and it doesna work. I canna explain it to ye. I just know that the magic fails to return a Draecna's health."

Hannah shook her head. "No, there's something different in the air. I can feel it. Can't you feel it, Taggart?" She couldn't explain it. The air about them tingled. If she had a lightbulb, she bet she could illuminate the room by merely holding it in her hand. An electrical current surged through her body; the hair on her arms pricked and stood on end. A strange knowing settled in her mind. An eerie familiarity with just this type of situation nudged her. It seemed so simple. She knew exactly what to do. "Give me your hand."

Hannah grabbed Taggart's hand and tucked it under one arm while she placed her other hand flat on Septamus's scarred, yellowed chest. As soon as she connected her palm with the cold, scaly flesh of the gasping Draecna, Hannah detected a subtle warmth surge into her body. With a smile at Taggart, Hannah closed her eyes. His healing essence rushed into her veins like a burning sip of brandy on a cold winter's night. A warm, golden glow washed through her being and soothed across her with a gentle wave. The sensation flowed through her; the energy concentrated in her belly and traveled up into her palm. The glow dissipated into Septamus's chest, leaving Hannah missing its warmth.

Septamus roared and pumped his arms. His once-faded

gray scales pulsed with brilliant color as though he'd returned to the age of a young hatchling just emerging from
his shell. "I am young again. She has taken away the dreaded
pleurisy. This guardian is blessed beyond all the others."

Hannah struggled to catch her breath as she stood with
Taggart's hand still clutched to her chest. Keeping her eyes
closed, she ignored the tiny voice in her head nudging her
to release his hand. Her heart pattered out an excited
rhythm against her rib cage, drowning out all other sound.
My gawd. The sensation she'd felt while healing Septamus.
Taggart rushed through her like a drug; she needed—no,
she *wanted* more. She wondered what it would be like,
what he'd be like. Have mercy, her deserted libido. . . . It
had been so very long.

"Hannah?" Taggart brushed the back of his fingers
against her cheek. "Hannah, are ye all right?"

She forced herself to pry her fingers from around his
hand and slowly opened her eyes. Hannah missed his
warmth already, digging her fingers into her palms as she
tucked her arms close to her sides. "I'm fine." No way was
she anywhere near fine. She ached for Taggart's warmth
already. What the hell had she gotten herself into when
she'd decided to follow him to Scotland?

Septamus rumbled with a throaty chuckle as he filtered
his silvery beard through his claws. "I believe she's a great
deal better than mere fine. I'd rate this guardian as classic."

"Aye," Taggart agreed with a wink toward Hannah.
"She's not half bad at all."

"So, ye do not think it necessary she be told your natural form is that of a Draecna hybrid?" Septamus perched
on the edge of the skirting wall, his silhouette highlighted
by the white-yellow glow of the waxing moon.

"I am the only human-Draecna mix left in existence,
Septamus. I am the last of the Goddess Isla's magical

clutch. While watching over Hannah, I just need to make sure that I do not turn. Over the past six hundred years, I've gained control over my emotions and can maintain my human form indefinitely." Taggart stood beside Septamus, frowning down at the hypnotic moonlight glistening on the waves as they rippled and danced against the wall of the keep. He yearned to unleash his Draecna self, unfurl his wings, and soar above the ocean. He loved flying out into the night. He missed the exhilaration of the frigid wind lashing across his scales. "I've silenced Gearlach with a temporary spell. I think everyone else can be trusted." Taggart looked to Septamus with an expectant cock of one brow and received a haughty nod in response. As he turned his attention back to the sparkling waves, he added with a heavy sigh, "Besides, Septamus, I am her protector. Hannah is forbidden to me. I can never touch her."

Septamus chuckled as he stretched his grey, leathery wings and curled his tail around the carved outer stones at the top of the curtain wall. "I never said anything about bedding the lass, Taggart. I just asked if ye were going to tell her ye were really a Draecna. But now that ye mention it, since when did some silly rule ever slow ye down when it came to a lovely maiden?"

"I have taken an oath of celibacy." Taggart fisted his hands atop the rough stone of the wall. Sly old Septamus. The beast always could see right through him.

"God's beard, Taggart. Not that Mia business again." Septamus snorted and rolled his great, glowing eyes. "Ye know Sloan put her up to it. He wanted her to breed with ye to produce a legion of hybrids he could bend to his will. Ye were told she couldna be trusted."

"She loved me!" Taggart slammed his fist into the crumbling stone block, causing the rock to shatter into the ocean below.

"Take care, hybrid. Mind your temper lest ye turn

whether ye wish it or not." Septamus took his tail and nudged Taggart in the chest, pushing him back from the edge of the wall.

Taggart clenched his eyes shut against the raw, blinding pain surging through his body. Conniving Mia, with her lies and humiliation. She'd sworn she loved him, pledged she'd always be his. She'd even offered her soft throat for his mating mark. He raked his hand across his mouth, remembering the sweet copper scent of her blood racing through the tempting blue veins running beneath her ivory skin. He'd almost made the mistake of marking her as his own, but instead he'd done the honorable thing. He'd shown her his true form first. He'd been honest with her. And then she'd spurned him, cast him aside. She'd chosen his brother, Sloan, instead.

Shoving Septamus's tail aside, Taggart faced the biting wind; he reveled in the sting of the heavy sea mist pelting through the night. He inhaled great gulps of the brackish night air to cool the rage from his mind. His pain dulled with the rising crash of the pounding waves against the jagged rocks below. Taroc Na Mor had healed him once from Mia's cruelty. Taroc Na Mor would shelter him again.

"Leave it, Septamus. I have it under control." Taggart rolled his shoulders and flexed his neck as he stalked across the wall. "And speak no more to me of my past. I am the guardian's protector. That is all."

Septamus slid from his perch on the highest ledge and stretched his expansive wings to the gusting wind. With a nod, he called back over one scaly shoulder as he caught an updraft and soared into the night. "As ye wish, Taggart. But dishonesty to one's self does greater harm than any dishonesty to others."

Now this was what she had in mind. Hannah purred a sigh of pure contentment as she stretched between the cool, crisp sheets. As the perfumed linens caressed her skin, she appreciated the definite advantage to the Draecna-sized furniture. The overstuffed mattress swallowed her up in its satin-covered softness. Pure heaven. She could stay in this bed forever. And the scent! Hannah inhaled a slow, appreciative breath. She couldn't quite place that delicious, sweet fragrance. Lilacs maybe? No, something more delicate; the floral aroma enticed and tempted her senses but fell short of being too icky sweet. She took another deep, cleansing lungful. Whatever it was, she loved it. Every tensed muscle in her body relaxed as she lost herself to the aromatic caress.

And what was that sound? A delicate chime pinged in the distance; sweet metallic bells *ting-tinged* like water droplets tapping against the windowpane. Very soothing. Hannah stretched her arms across the pillows, eyes closed as she floated along with the melody as it trickled along in the breeze.

"*Yeow? Reow!*"

A pitiful wail shattered the serenity of the room. Hannah jerked upright in the center of the bed, searching for the source of the pleading caterwaul.

A kitten. And it sounded terrified. She searched the room for the poor little mite. "Kitty, kitty, kitty?" She cocked her head and waited, straining to home in on the exact location of the little varmint when it decided to sound again. Where was it? "Come on, kitty. Sound off, so I can find you."

"*Reow . . . reooww!*"

The balcony. Fighting her way out of the depths of the pillowed bed, Hannah stumbled her way free of the tangle of covers. She padded barefoot across the lush Turkish carpets layered across the floor to the partially opened balcony doors. "There you are! How did you get up there? Did Septamus or Gearlach scare you?"

The balcony faced a private garden where a sprawling oak with gnarled and twisted branches created an intricate canopy covering most of the enclosed courtyard. Hanging on to one of the knotted branches, a scruffy, mottle-colored kitten with a white-tipped tail mewled a pitiful wail.

Hannah stretched across the railing of the stone balcony and held out her hands toward the tiny, wild-eyed cat. "Come here. It's okay. Come on. You'll learn you can trust me, little cat, just open up your mind and listen."

The cat flicked a tattered ear in response and perked up straighter on the wavering branch. It whipped its little tail around its haunches as it tensed its body into a tighter ball. Then it wiggled its butt as though testing its rear springing mechanism and launched itself into Hannah's arms.

Hannah caught the kitten as it jumped from the branch and landed in the center of her chest. The kitten bumped its head against her cheek, purring as it pushed and kneaded its front paws into her hair.

"You're welcome. I know you must've been frightened to climb that high up in the tree." Hannah scratched the kitten behind the ears as she carried it into the room. As soon as the kitten spotted the bed, it leapt out of Hannah's arms and dove into the pile of bedclothes. It scampered across the mountains of pillows and blankets as though in search of prey.

"Now, come here, you little scamp." Hannah circled the bed as the kitten wormed its way deeper under the blankets piled against the headboard. "What are you looking for? Are you just cold or something? If you'll come here, I'll take you to the kitchen and get you something to eat."

The kitten peeped out from under the bedclothes, flipped its tail, and edged just out of Hannah's reach. It bounced its pink nose against the pillows, alternately sniffing and glancing up at Hannah as it switched its tail.

"I know. I love the scent too. But come here and we'll

go find you something to eat." Hannah clambered up on the side of the bed and stretched for the little cat.

A gentle knock on the door echoed through the chamber causing the kitten to explode into a hissing fur ball. It shot off the bed, darted across the room, and disappeared back out the balcony doors.

"It's okay. Don't be afraid!" Ignoring the louder rapping on her chamber doors, Hannah hurried out to the balcony. "You're just going to be stranded out on that tree again! Come back here, little cat."

The balcony was empty. The arm-like limbs of the old oak stood bare. The morning breeze whispered through a cat-free private garden. Leaning over the railing, Hannah searched the cobblestone yard. How could the little scamp just disappear?

A loud crash followed by a roared curse brought her attention back to her bedchamber. Taggart stood in the doorway, sword drawn, chest heaving, and eyes aglow with a murderous light. A tall, wispy man with thin, silver hair trailing down to his belted waist stood quietly by his side.

Padding into the room, Hannah crossed her arms over the front of her skimpy nightgown and scooted for her robe draped across the end of the bed. She glanced at the strange man with the breakfast cart, then turned to Taggart with a frosty hiss. "Would you mind telling me what you think you're doing? All you had to do was give me a few minutes and I would've eventually answered the door."

Taggart sheathed his sword with an irritated thump as he glared about the room. "Why in the *hell* did ye no' answer the door when Thaetus knocked and asked ye to allow him entry?"

As she yanked the belt of her robe tight about her waist, Hannah envisioned wrapping it around Taggart's neck. How dare he talk to her as if she were a child! Who did he think he was? "He only knocked twice and I was busy.

All he had to do was wait a minute. Since when do you break somebody's door down when they don't open it after a couple of knocks?"

"Actually, I knocked thrice." Thaetus cleared his throat and folded his pale, narrow hands atop the brass handles of the cart. "And I called out to ye twice and asked if ye were unwell. When ye didna answer, I could only assume something had gone awry and ye needed immediate assistance."

"Thaetus, I swear I didn't hear you call out to me. If I had, I would've answered." Hannah stalked across the room, struggling to keep her voice leveled to a reasonable tone. Obviously, Thaetus was only trying to do his job, but the man needed to learn not to panic. "In the future, please give me more time to respond. After all, I'm safe here in Taroc Na Mor. What could possibly make its way into this room?" She gave an impatient flick of her wrist in Taggart's direction. "Especially with all of you lurking around every corner just itching to hack something with your swords."

Thaetus raised his chin and his bespectacled eyes narrowed as he replied with a delicate sniff. "One can never be too careful, Lady Guardian. We must never let down our guard."

Hannah glared at the stone-faced servant. The man's stubbornness obviously mirrored Taggart's hardheaded ways. She might as well save her breath. "Thaetus, I'm not going to argue with you. But I want you to know that I think you're really overreacting." This was ridiculous. They guarded her like she was some national treasure. There hadn't been any attacks since they'd left Jasper Mills. How could she not be safe here at Taroc Na Mor?

"What were ye doing, Hannah? Why did ye no' call out and answer Thaetus?" Taggart slapped at the twisted hinges dangling from the chamber doors, scowling at the damage he'd done to the wood and the surrounding doorframe.

"I just told you that I didn't hear him. And besides, I

don't believe that is any of your business." With a huff, Hannah poured a cup of coffee and curled up on the settee to return fire at Taggart's fuming stare. She had to admit she rather enjoyed the results when he was irritated. And this was the second time she'd gotten a little more than breathless by seeing him rush to defend her. When he brandished his sword, those wondrous muscles pulsed and she had no doubt he'd slay anything foolish enough to get in his path. Hannah cradled her cup between her palms and remembered the warmth of Taggart's essence when she'd helped him heal Septamus. She shifted on the settee, drawing in a rapid breath. These chambers suddenly seemed very warm.

Thaetus's eyes widened with a horrified look and he tapped nervous fingertips atop Taggart's arm. "Ye need to leave this room and allow the Lady Guardian to compose herself. Ye have upset her and you know that is *forbidden*."

With an arched brow, Taggart studied Hannah more closely, then sidled his glance back to Thaetus's bug-eyed expression. A roguish grin crept across his face as he crossed his arms over his chest. "Truly? Are ye absolutely certain, Thaetus?"

"Aye, Taggart. Ye know the rules. The Lady Guardian must be *left alone*." Thaetus plucked at Taggart's tunic with long, narrow fingers and jerked his head toward the door.

"Thaetus, I know we might've gotten off on the wrong foot, and please don't take this the wrong way. But you are acting a bit strange. What exactly is your problem?" Hannah stretched forward and slid her china cup onto the marble-slab table squatting in front of the damask settee.

Taggart's warm, rumbling chuckle bubbled up from the depths of his chest and echoed off the walls of the high-ceilinged room. "I have to tell her, Thaetus. 'Twould no' be fair to keep the lass in the dark. Ye've already given yourself away."

Thaetus shook his head and backed against the wall, pulling the breakfast cart in front of his body as though it were a shield. "She will not be pleased. Consider yourself warned, Taggart. And ye might want to step behind here with me."

Taggart rubbed his nose with the back of his hand as he gave a wink and a nod toward Thaetus. "Thaetus is an empath, Hannah. Ye might say he's very sensitive to your . . . um . . . *needs*."

Hannah looked from Taggart to Thaetus and then back to Taggart's knowing grin. *That son of a bitch.* Thaetus had picked up on her very private case of the hornies and alerted Taggart in code. Embarrassed heat of this revelation stormed its way through her body. Her cheeks burned hotter than they had in high school when the zipper had split on her jeans during her speech in the middle of assembly.

"Get out." Hannah pointed at the door hanging off the hinges and stared at the middle of the coffee table.

"It's all right, Hannah. I understand how ye might be excited."

"I said, get the hell out!"

Thaetus took the lead and hurried toward the door, dodging the coffee cup Hannah lobbed at their heads. He only paused long enough to hiss to Taggart, "I advised ye she would not be pleased."

"They still havena lain together. Neither the bed nor her body held a trace of his scent nor has he placed his mark anywhere upon her. Moon lilies fragranced the entire room—no other oil or aroma inhabited any other surface. I saw no mark upon her skin indicating she was his mate." Mia knelt before Sloan's chair, head bowed, hands limp and lifeless on her bended knees.

"Ye do realize she communicates with animals. She will have access to the recesses of your mind since ye have chosen the form of a beast." Sloan scowled at Mia as he worried his fingertips across the intricate carvings running down the arms of his chair. If she botched this task, he would twist her delicate neck until her bones snapped. She'd failed him once by not mating with Taggart. She'd best not fail him again.

Mia's hands fluttered to her throat as she bowed her head even lower. "Yes, my love. I took great care to shield my true inner nature. The guardian had no idea I was anything more than a stray cat wandered in from the courtyard."

With one long, blackened fingernail, he tapped the grooved arm of the chair and studied the woman before him. A wave of disgust shuddered through him at the phenomenal disappointment cowering before him. Mia's weakness with his brother had ruined his well-thought-out plans. She'd best redeem herself with this latest task or he'd take the greatest pleasure in separating her soul from her body. Through Mia and Taggart, he could've built and controlled armies of some of the strongest beings across all the realities. But she had failed him. He'd counted too much on her deceptive heart and not realized how truly inept the woman actually was. In the end, her cowardice had failed his plan. She had been terrified of Taggart in his natural form. Sloan blew out a heavy sigh. He'd lost count of the times he'd wished his conniving father had sired him as a Draecna hybrid as well.

"Taggart is slipping in his old age. What is he now? A little over seven hundred years?" Sloan steepled his fingers under his chin and stroked his goatee as he mused aloud. "Perhaps his carnal lusts have slowed down over the centuries. Although, I have seen the lass. I wouldna have a problem bedding her."

Mia clenched her hands into a shaking knot on her lap, glancing up as she inched closer to Sloan's gilded chair.

"Seven hundred years is quite young for a Draecna, m'lord. Taggart is merely holding true to his pledge."

Sloan traced his sharpest curved nail along Mia's pale cheek as she rested her head on his knee. "Perhaps, he fears she'll react the same way you did when she sees the true monster residing within him. 'Tis one thing to be a guardian of the Draecna race. 'Tis another to find one between your legs."

He pressed down harder, slicing into Mia's ivory skin. He adored how the ruby-red droplets beaded up, then trickled down the gentle curve of her face like a stream flowing down a hillside. He hated Taggart, hated his power, his immortality, his magic and everything about him. Taggart had ruined his plans of an army of hybrids. He'd not ruin his plan of controlling the next clutch of Draecna waiting to be hatched.

Sloan stroked Mia's hair as she crouched beside his chair. With a disgusted hiss, he jerked his hand away from her head, spit, and shoved her away with his boot. "Your hair has become as coarse as straw since ye've aged. Is there nothing ye can do to make it more pleasing to my touch?"

"I will try, my love. Please forgive me for being so repulsive." Mia backed away to her pillow by the fire, where she curled up as though she were a dog.

"No." Sloan snapped his head and pointed toward the door. "Ye have not finished with the guardian. Return to Taroc Na Mor. When the time is right, I want her brought to me. I will not accept a failure from ye this time. This is your last chance, Mia."

Mia bowed her head and closed her eyes. "As you wish, my love."

CHAPTER FIVE

A solid block of wood, monstrous in size, formed the worktable running down the middle of the kitchen. Trunks of trees, twelve inches in diameter, provided the spindled legs hammered into its base. Centuries ago, Erastaedian artisans had coaxed the work of art from a single Rowanian tree. It had been a treasured gift to one of the original guardians of Taroc Na Mor from the world of Erastaed.

Taggart sat and traced a finger along the honey-colored grain of the wood, sulking with his chin propped in his other hand. "Thaetus, for once in your miserable life, why did ye no' keep your observations to yourself?"

With a disgruntled huff, Thaetus stuck his nose into the air as he splashed the remaining coffee into the gleaming porcelain sink. "Ye needed to be warned! The woman is in high lust for ye, and she doesna know it, but her body is hell-bent on breedin'! If I didna warn ye, she might have jumped on your bones and raped ye before ye knew what happened."

"Ye canna rape a willing soul," Septamus observed from his seat at the other end of the table.

Gearlach pounded his fisted claws on the table, then pointed at his sealed snout when Taggart finally looked his way.

Taggart shook his head, leaned back in his chair, and crossed his arms over his chest. "No, Gearlach. Ye havena learned your lesson yet and I'm in no mood to hear what ye have to say on this matter." He closed his eyes and pinched the bridge of his nose. This morning hadn't gone well at all. Thoughts of Hannah had tortured him through the night, and then Thaetus had falsely sounded the alarm. *God's beard*. Every one of his seven hundred and seventy-seven years ached in his bones. He hadn't been this weary in centuries.

"The Barac'Nairn tenet stating the protector will fail the guardian if he grows too close to her is idiotic. More than likely, 'twas written by a jealous wimp who couldna achieve a healthy rising whenever he found a buxom maiden waitin' for him in his bed." Septamus drained his mug with a resounding slurp and tapped it on the table with a pointed glare at Thaetus.

Snorting, Thaetus rolled his eyes, snatched up the tankard, and headed for the tap. "Might I remind ye, I'm here to serve the guardian, Septamus, not the Draecna of this keep. Ye would do well to keep that in mind when ye're bouncing your bloody dishes on the table."

Septamus fixed Thaetus with a knowing smirk and allowed a single puff of smoke to thread up from one glistening nostril. "I read your contract, you pompous little squirt. Ye're here to serve us all."

"Enough!" Taggart slammed his hands on the table. This banter wasn't solving his problem. This morning had increased the tension with Hannah. At some point, something had to give or she'd never connect with her heritage and the magic of Taroc Na Mor.

"For Isla's sake, Taggart. What is the penalty if ye sleep with the woman? Do they castrate ye at the opening ceremony for the Solstice Moon of Cair Orlandis or just string ye up by your cock at high noon?" Septamus drummed his claws on the table while glaring at Thaetus, who was dawdling at the ale tap with his still-empty mug.

Raking both hands through his hair, Taggart rose from the table. "There is no penalty, Septamus. It's just . . . just ill-advised." And what happened if he opened himself to Hannah? What happened when she found out the truth about him? When he'd revealed his true form to Mia, horror of the revelation had been reflected in her eyes. He didn't want to relive that pain with Hannah. With Hannah, the humiliation would be much worse. A piercing ache clenched deep in his chest as he imagined the same recrimination flashing across Hannah's face. He couldn't. No. More than that. He wouldn't bear it.

"She doesna fear us, Taggart. From what I perceived from Gearlach's thoughts, she reacted well the first time she saw him." Septamus rose from the table, looped a claw in the back of Thaetus's shirt, and hung him from a hook on the wall. "Now ye can lollygag all ye like, ye skinny little bastard." He lifted the keg off the stand on the counter and returned with it to the table.

"It's different, Septamus. Ye know that," Taggart whispered while staring out the window. Hannah was different too. He closed his mind against the image of horror reflecting in her eyes if she ever witnessed his true form. Although he'd loved Mia, she'd always remained aloof, even before he revealed his Draecna form. A distant coldness had echoed in her touch. In all honesty, they'd never bonded and Mia had reveled in humiliating him in front of his people. She'd publicly scorned him; the blow to his pride had hurt worse than losing her. He knew in his heart Hannah was different. He found himself attracted to Hannah's warmth like a lost soul drawn to a welcoming hearth on a bitter, cold winter's eve.

A fluttering movement past the window tore him from his musings. A lone figure stumbled along the rim of the cliff's edge, arms extended as though walking along a tight rope.

"What the hell is that hardheaded woman doing now?"

Septamus and Gearlach crowded next to him at the tall, narrow window while Thaetus fumed and kicked on the hook next to the door. "Never mind me. I'll just hang over here until ye decide ye need me or need something from the kitchen. But if ye want your dinner served to ye on time, ye'd best be mindin' the clock and lettin' me down from this bloody hook!"

Ignoring Thaetus's sarcasm, Septamus pushed Gearlach out of the way and stretched to get a better view. "It looks like she's taking the hard way down to the caves. Did you tell her they were there?"

"Dammit!" Taggart slapped Septamus between his folded wings and stormed his way out of the kitchen. "I've got to stop her before she falls and breaks her stubborn little neck. The woman is a challenge sent by the fates themselves as punishment for all my sins."

If Taroc Na Mor was supposed to be hers, what better way to get to know it then by enjoying a little rock climbing? She'd always loved wandering around the great outdoors, and maybe the fresh air would cleanse the disturbing morning from her mind. Hannah paused in picking a foothold through the jagged black rocks jutting along the cliff's edge and licked the salt spray from her lips. Wrestling against the wind whipping in from the sea, she combed tangled strands of hair out of her eyes. From this precarious vantage point, the churning, white-capped ocean reached the horizon. The waves crashed below her, exploding on impact with the shore with sparkling fountains of frothy spume.

The gulls circled overhead, fluttering white ribbons against the stormy blue of the sky. They keened out a warning; someone was approaching across the top of the embankment. Hannah shielded her eyes against the glaring sun and the punishment of her whipping hair. She twisted to look back up the cliff from which she'd just edged her way across. Taggart loomed over the horizon. Great. He was the reason she was out here in the first place. Perhaps she'd gotten lucky and he hadn't seen her yet.

Her arms stretched for balance like a circus performer, Hannah picked her way faster through the protruding clusters of rock. Centuries of wind and waves pounding against the volcanic land mass had beaten the shores of the cliff to razor sharpness. In her haste, she slid, scraping her shin but catching herself before she tumbled headlong into a deep fissure yawning into inky blackness.

"Hannah!"

Well, so much for him not seeing her. Hannah picked up a loose stone and aimed for the direction of Taggart's voice. Maybe she could scare him off as if he were a stray dog. As she drew back, she fell off balance and stumbled on the brittle stones.

He closed his hand over hers and curled an arm around her waist. "Now, that's no' verra nice. Ye could put out my eye by throwing such a sharp stone. Then how would I protect ye from all the evils of the worlds?"

Hannah blinked and almost lost her footing again. How the heck did he appear at her side when just a moment ago, he'd stood at the top of the cliff? Clutching at his arm, she pushed off his chest and peered down into the abyss below. Suddenly losing the ability to breathe, Hannah fought against the tightness crushing her chest. She would've fallen if he hadn't caught her. Irritation flared through her body. Of course, she wouldn't have stumbled in the first place if he hadn't appeared out of thin air. "How?" She glanced back up the cliff where he'd stood but a few seconds ago. She fixed him with a suspicious glare, tightening her fist around the rock she still held in her hand. "I thought you said your only magic was healing, not zapping across distances at super speeds."

Taggart chuckled, pulling her closer while edging them to a smoother patch of ground. "I never said healing was my only magic. I just told ye I could heal."

"You . . ." Hannah licked her lips, her mouth suddenly very dry. The caress of his heartbeat tickled against her breasts. Her traitorous nipples tightened, straining toward him. Rebellious desire battled with her common sense. She wished he'd press her closer. *No. I'm not going down that road again.* She pushed against his chest. "You can let me go now. I won't throw the rock and I'm sure I've got my balance."

"Are ye certain, Hannah?" Taggart smoothed his hand up the middle of her back, pulling her closer as though he'd read her mind.

Damn his eyes. Hannah cursed their intense blue depths that fluctuated whenever he spoke. Hypnotic eyes ordered her to let him in, mesmerizing her into melting wherever he touched her.

The rock slipped out of her hand and she raised her fingertips to stroke the stubble of his jaw. "No."

"No?" Taggart trailed his hand along her arm and laced his fingers into her hair.

"Don't let me go," she whispered against his mouth while leaning her body into his. A gust of wind shoved against her back as though urging her to complete the kiss. Icy spray peppered across her body, but only heat surged through her veins. She opened to him. It had been too long. He tasted of ale, fresh air, and the sea. Hannah molded her body tight against the hardened length of him. Dear God, she risked bursting into flames.

"Hannah." Taggart pulled away, his breath ragged as he mouthed the corner of her lips. He curled his fingers deep into her hair. With a groan, he delved into her mouth with his tongue. He pulled her closer, the softness of her body tantalizing him. He smelled the fragrance of his home world's orchids lingering in her hair. The aroma triggered visions of Hannah sprawled across the perfumed pillows of her Draecna bed. *This was madness.* He deepened the kiss. He scented Hannah's need pulsating through her body; her senses called out to him. The caves. The mineral springs heating the nursery. He could take her to the seclusion of the caves. Damn the tenets. He would have her. To hell with the Guild of Barac'Nairn, his monstrous ancestry, and his past. She belonged to him.

With a groan, Taggart tore his mouth away from hers, shuddering as he lifted his head. Cradling Hannah's face between his hands, he traced his thumb across the softness of her lips. "Do ye trust me, Hannah?"

With a silent nod, Hannah snuggled tighter against him as she slid her hands up his back underneath his leather coat.

"Close your eyes then," he whispered. He couldn't believe he dared risk it. But she had to know *before.* He wanted her so badly his entire being ached, but he wouldn't deceive her, not his Hannah. He'd danced around the truth long enough.

He tucked her head under his chin and cradled her to his chest. God's beard, he hoped he'd become enough for her. He prayed she wouldn't run screaming back across the Atlantic. With a great shaking breath, Taggart reached deep inside and removed the barriers blocking his Draecna form from the physical world. As the barricade came down, every fiber of his body burned as though acid pumped through his veins.

As his body tensed, Taggart concentrated on not crushing Hannah in his arms. The metamorphosis to his natural form pained through his tissues like lightning splitting the air. He grimaced as wings erupted from his back and unfurled to the rising wind. He shifted as the ledge started crumbling beneath them. It was now too small to hold them.

Hannah opened her eyes and screamed.

Taggart's already muscular body increased tenfold and sheathed itself in dark, iridescent scale-like armor. He shimmered a mesmerizing purple-black, depending on how the rays of sunlight hit him. His hands armed themselves with retractable, razor-sharp claws. His black leathered wings spanned out behind him as though he were a minion straight from Hell. Horns of blackest obsidian sprouted out of his forehead, glistening as though buffed to a high sheen and silver-tipped at the end of their long curved points. He retained the body shape of a well-muscled man, just amplified with Draecna attributes. Disbelief tore Hannah's breath from her body as she squeezed her eyes shut, then reopened them. All Taggart missed was a Draecna tail on his deliciously defined derrière.

"Hannah, it's still me. I will never hurt ye." Taggart held out a clawed hand, a pleading look reflecting in his icy blue eyes.

Hannah winced, curled her hands to her chest, and tried to back away. This thing sounded like Taggart, even though the voice resonated much deeper and echoed as though coming from the center of the earth. What in the world had he become? Magic was one thing, but she'd never expected this demon thing standing before her.

"Please, Hannah. Look into my eyes. My eyes are the one thing about me that will never change, no matter what my form." Taggart let his hand drop and waited, his wings folded against his back as he spoke.

She peered closer. "But, how is this possible? Why . . . *what* exactly are you?" Hannah whispered, struggling to find her voice. She wrapped her arms around her body, hugging tight to keep from collapsing. A raging shiver, a sudden chill not caused by the blustering wind, shook her body. What she wouldn't give to be back in Jasper Mills. Why had she ever followed him to Scotland?

With a sidelong glance at the darkening sky, Taggart exhaled a great, rumbling groan as he unfurled his wings and held out his hand. "A storm is coming. Let me take ye to the caves. I will try to explain everything there."

Hannah clutched her hands about her throat and glanced first at Taggart's wingspan and then the size of his outstretched hand. She could fit her entire ass in that hand and still have room to spare. Her heartbeat out-pounded the crashing waves battering the rocks below. *Breathe, Hannah, before you pass out.*

"Please, Hannah. Please try and trust me." Taggart's voice lowered to a throaty whisper; the pain in his eyes begged her to give him a chance.

She moved her lips, but no sound came out. Then she coughed and tried again. "I . . . I will try." She edged closer to him, touched the tips of her fingers to his palm, and flinched. She couldn't help it. His new form made him look as though he was about to rip her to shreds.

Taggart remained motionless. He held open his hand. His corded tendons rippled as his muscles tensed while Hannah stared at his outstretched arm. She edged her hand deeper into his waiting hand and exhaled when she realized she'd held her breath. The feel of his hand wasn't that much different in this strange new form he'd taken. His palm scraped a bit to her touch; still warm, leathery, and maybe just a bit tougher, sort of like a tortoise shell, but still similar to a human's touch. A bit strange, not what she'd expected. "I thought you'd be cold."

That observation elicited a bitter laugh from his armored chest. "I'm not a reptile, Hannah. I am still just as warm-blooded as you."

"I didn't mean . . . what I meant was . . ." Hannah

stammered when she saw the hurt flash in Taggart's eyes. Her heart wrenched as she realized the depths of his pain. So this was Taggart's secret, one of humiliation and pain. He'd been an outcast because of his Draecna heritage. "Taggart, I am so sorry."

"Do not pity me, Hannah."

With a curt nod, he scooped her into his arms, cradled her against his armored chest, and launched them both into the sky.

A myriad of caves honeycombed the land of Taroc Na Mor, hiding the location of the sacred nurseries. Several entrances dotted about the estate, all well hidden and guarded by mystical wards and trusted members of the Guild of Barac'Nairn.

Taggart touched down on a narrow strip of beach littered with weather-stained bones and debris. The tide was in and there was barely enough room to stand in front of what appeared to be a sheer wall of impenetrable rock bleached white by years of exposure to nature's abuse.

Hannah pulled her collar higher about her face and glanced up into the black, thunderous sky. She'd kept her eyes squeezed shut while Taggart flew them the short distance around the tip of the cliff. Flying in an airplane was one thing. Hang gliding in the arms of a winged creature was a little more then she'd ever imagined.

A gust of wind yanked at her body, nearly jerking her off her feet. She grabbed at Taggart's wing to keep from toppling into the chopping waves below. Taggart curled the leathery shield of his wing around her and waved a hand over a shimmering obelisk imbedded in the face of the sheer wall.

"Greetings, honored prince. Greetings, honored Guardian. Is it time for the clutch to be released?" The faint outline of an extraordinarily tall, wispy man appeared on the rock wall, his features elongated and wavering with the wind.

Taggart nodded. "Greetings, Luthor. No. Not at this time. We only wish to view the nursery, please."

Hannah shivered, peeping out from the protection of Taggart's leathery wing. What the heck was Luthor? A glance around her feet took in all the scattered bones. She swallowed hard against the bile burning at the back of her throat. Some of those looked like human bones. She pressed closer against Taggart's side and tightened her arm around his waist.

A rumbling sound interrupted the hysteria hammering inside her head and the rock wall in front of them shuddered and began to shift. As Hannah watched, what she thought was a fissure in the impenetrable rock wall widened into a dark, yawning entrance.

"Thank you, Luthor. Please close it behind us. When we've finished viewing the clutch, we'll leave through the internal passage and go up to the castle." Taggart nodded his thanks to the transparent man as he pressed Hannah toward the opening in the wall.

"As ye wish, my prince. I am here to serve." Then Luthor disappeared into the mottled surface of the limestone cliff.

As Hannah slid through the opening of the cave, she paused and glanced back over her shoulder. "Why did he keep calling you prince?" she whispered with a shiver against the damp air of the cave. She wrinkled her nose against the wet, earthy smell. She'd never liked close places.

"Luthor is one of my oldest followers. He found it difficult . . . *still* finds it difficult to accept the fact that my father left the House of Cair Orlandis and the rule of Erastaed to my younger brother, Sloan." Taggart waved his hand at the unlit torches along the walls, causing them to erupt with flames.

Hannah turned in a slow circle, blinded by all the blazing torches. "I see." What other secrets had Taggart been hiding? She turned back to Taggart, now standing before her in his handsome, *human* form. "So, is your brother like you?"

Sending a bitter laugh echoing through the dripping rocks of the cavern, Taggart shook his head. "No, Hannah. Why do ye think my father selected him? I am the last of my kind."

Hannah flinched at the acidic spike in Taggart's voice. His bitterness oozed like a raw, open sore, tainting the air between them. "Taggart, I'm so sorry. But I'm a bit confused. How can you be what you are and then your brother *not*. Dammit! I'm trying to figure this out without hurting your feelings!" She wished she could reel back her words. It seemed like the more she babbled, the darker the pain flashed from the depths of his eyes.

"My dear sweet Hannah." Taggart chuckled as he nodded toward a pile of large, rounded stones for her to have a seat. "Ye're the only soul I've met in over seven hundred years who has truly given a damn about my feelings. Have a seat and I'll try to explain exactly how my dysfunctional family tree is laid out."

Hannah perched on the edge of the flat rock shelf. Wrapping her arms around her knees, she waited for Taggart to begin his tale. Poor Taggart. She noticed he always paced whenever he fretted, as though it enabled him to speak. If he didn't stop soon and begin talking, he'd have a trench pounded waist-deep in the damp loam of the cave.

"Not only was my father the ruler of Cair Orlandis—" Taggart paused, inhaling a deep, groaning breath as he rounded another lap of the cave. "He was a time-traveling, sorcering, scheming bastard who always looked for ways to use the universe for his own selfish means."

Hannah bit her lip and held her tongue. Wow. Surely the story could only go up from here.

As Taggart paced, he locked his hands behind his back, stared at the ground, and kicked a few stones from his path. Hannah's heart hitched a sympathetic double-clutch as Taggart walked out his demons. Her body tensed as Taggart's face strained with the effort of laying out his painful memories to the light of day.

"Some would say my father was a handsome man. And there have been several historical references of female Draecna enamored with humans. However, these feeling are usually not returned and these Draecna learned to put their unrequited loves aside." Taggart paused; a thunderous scowl darkened his face as he raked a hand through his black, windblown hair. "But my father was also a powerful sorcerer; he decided to con a young Draecna female into giving him children. He couldn't charm any of the Draecna of this century into giving him young. They wisely feared the insanity of the magical beings that would result from a mixture of Draecna DNA and my father's tainted blood. So, my father traveled back in time and found a young unsuspecting female. He found my mother, Isla."

Taggart's words caught her off guard. Shifting on her cold, hard perch, Hannah couldn't help but interrupt. "Taggart, you said *children,* but you said your brother isn't like you. I'm sorry, but I still don't understand." Hannah rubbed her temples. She was having trouble keeping up. He'd sprung so many surprises on her lately; she wanted to get this one straight. She wished she could write it down.

With a heavy sigh, Taggart shook his head and turned another lap in his circle. "Sloan has a human mother. He is my *half* brother and is only thirty years old. Sloan is from this century and has very little magic flowing through his blood. But dinna make the mistake of underestimating him; he is quite capable of basic elemental magic."

"Then where are your other siblings?" Hannah stood and rubbed the feeling back into her rear. Enough of that chilled, damp seat. She knew she remembered him saying his father conned Isla into giving him *children*. Taggart had spoken as though he had siblings.

Taggart fixed Hannah with a look that chilled her to the bone more than the stones of the cave. "They are dead, Hannah. I am the only one left. My mother killed them all."

Hannah's hands flew to her pounding chest. "What? What do you mean she killed them? Why?" She struggled against the nauseating bile rushing to gag her.

Taggart's jaw rippled as he clenched his teeth; the pain in his eyes begged her to understand. "They were insane, Hannah. They were a danger to themselves and any world they happened to enter. The strength of their powers required a great deal of responsibility and they had no conscience at all. Mother tried guiding them, but when they refused to change, she made the only choice she could. That is why Mother is now a goddess among the Draecna. Her unselfish sacrifice to the race and the worlds has been deemed truly great."

Hannah swallowed against the lump of emotions knotted in her throat as tears welled up in her eyes. Draecna or not, the poor female had to kill her own babies to save the worlds from their cruel insanity. "How many?" Hannah choked on her whisper. "How many did she have to kill?" She almost couldn't speak the words. She couldn't fathom what Taggart's mother had endured.

Taggart stopped pacing. A barely discernable shrug rippled across his shoulders as he stared at his feet. "There were seven of us in the clutch. I am the only one left."

"Where is your mother now?" Hannah edged closer across the sand-covered floor. The echo of the wind howled through the cavern, magnifying the loneliness of Taggart's life.

With a hollow laugh, Taggart stretched and rubbed the

back of his neck. "Ye never quite know where or when Mother is going to show up. She has a habit of popping up when ye least expect her."

"Oh, so surprise tends to run in the family?" Hannah gently teased as she veered from the mouth of the cave and turned toward the rear of the cavern, heading for one of the darker tunnels. She sensed Taggart didn't want closeness right now. He'd shut down on her. If anyone understood needing a bit of distance, she certainly did. With a shuddering sigh, she hugged herself. Perhaps a bit of distance would be better for them both. Besides, what would an emotional wreck like her know about helping an isolated soul like him?

"Not that way, Hannah." Taggart took her arm and steered her toward the tunnel to the left. "If ye wish to see the nursery, we need to follow this one."

Hannah tensed. "Could you light some more torches? I just felt something rather damp slither beside my foot and I'm really hoping it was just a clump of seaweed." She hadn't felt any vibes from whatever it was on the ground so she hoped it wasn't any type of creature.

The walls sweated, radiating the steady cool of the moist earth, but the farther they traveled down the torch-lit tunnel, the warmer the air grew. Taggart brought the torches lining the passage to life. Hannah's feet sank into the soft, white sand sparkling in the light of the flickering flames. The farther they walked, the finer the grain became and her feet sank deeper into the path.

"What is that sound?" Hannah stopped. She cocked her head, straining to listen to the music floating down the passage. "Is that Mozart I hear playing in the distance?"

Taggart closed his eyes, turned his face in the direction of the nursery, then smiled and shook his head. "No. Vivaldi. Ye missed it because the song neared the end and they have it programmed to fade out when it's time for the next selection."

"Classical music for the nursery?" Hannah turned to Taggart as another aria began.

With a shrug and a knowing smile, Taggart nodded toward the door up ahead. "It seems to lessen the frequency of frenetic lightning activity in the eggs. When there is less lightning activity in the eggs, there is less distress among the hatchlings."

"I see." Hannah nodded. She really didn't see at all, but she didn't want Taggart to think her an idiot. Maybe once inside this wondrous nursery, she'd figure out what Taggart meant. She'd read studies about classical music played for human babies in the womb. Why not baby Draecna?

At the end of the passage, a metallic arched door blackened with centuries of age awaited them. Taggart waved his hand over the archaic script and whorls carved on the disk in the center of the door and waited. In a few moments, the elaborate metalwork responded to his movement; the whorls burnished to a rich golden glow and then spun in a counter-clockwise circle. Shouldering it open, he stood aside and waited for Hannah to step inside.

The first thing Hannah noticed was the familiar aroma wafting through the cavern. The breeze of it brushed across her face as soon as she walked through the archway. The stale, dank air of the caves disappeared. This same scent lingered on the pillows and sheets in her room. It greeted her every morning when she opened her eyes and every evening when she retired. Lifting her chin, she sniffed the air to seek out the source of the fragrance. "What is that smell?"

"Dahliacieos." At her answering stupefied stare, Taggart pointed to several niches carved out in the walls where clumps of deep purple orchid-type flowers tumbled from moss-covered clumps of earth stuffed into wired baskets.

Edging her way around the narrow stone walkway surrounding the room, Hannah stood on tiptoe and studied the strange-looking flowers. "How do they grow down here without any type of light? I've never seen anything like them before."

"They are the moon orchid. They abhor any form of sunlight at all," Taggart explained. "They come from Erastaed."

A gentle thump drew her attention to the center of the room. There were twenty-one indentations smoothed into a raised stone pedestal approximately twenty feet in diameter. Each indentation was padded, velvet-lined, and twenty of them held softly glowing Draecna eggs, the size of large melons.

"One is missing." Hannah pointed to an empty spot adjacent to a freshly cemented-off tunnel on the other side of the room.

Taggart's face hardened into a stony mask as he nodded toward the tunnel with a thunderous glare. "Sloan," he hissed. He spit his brother's name as though it poisoned his mouth. "The bastard stole the egg. He is as greedy as our father. He seeks the power of the Draecna race."

Hannah circled the room, mesmerized by the blush-colored eggs and the kinetic flashes of light erupting from within their thick, stony shells. Dancing, flashing to twenty frantic heartbeats, the air around her swirled with intensity of the energy from the little beasts. Moving closer, she covered her ears with her hands. Her mind hummed with tiny voices. How could she hear them? She thought she couldn't connect her mind to Draecna after the failed attempt with Gearlach. Yet dozens of whispers floated together into a muddled chaos. A cacophony of singsongs chattered like magpies inside her head. "Stop!

Not all at once. You've got to take turns so I can understand you."

"Ecnelis!" Taggart clapped his hands together. The lightning activity of the eggs slowed to just one or two. He turned to Hannah. "Any better?"

Biting her lip, Hannah eased open her eyes and tried to relax. Mercy, all their tiny voices had been like a stereo blasting too loud. She cringed at what she feared she might hear as she opened her mind again. Much better. Two very delicate voices nudged the back of her mind. Her eyes widened. What they whispered didn't sound very good. With a glance at Taggart, she fixed him with a confused frown. "We need to get the other egg back before it hatches. They said their hatching moon isn't very far away. What are they talking about?"

Taggart turned from the eggs with a heavy sigh as he walked around the upraised platform. "Dinna worry. Sloan's hatchling is as good as dead. His egg will never hatch."

"What?" Her heart wrenched at the thought of an innocent creature abandoned and left for dead. Hannah swiped the back of her hand across her forehead. The warmth of the nursery had the sweat trickling down into her eyes. "Why would you say that? Do you think he damaged it when he stole it from the nursery?"

Holding out his hand, Taggart beckoned for Hannah to follow him around the pedestal to yet another tunnel leading out of the secluded room. "Sloan is missing one very important element when it comes to bringing a young Draecna into the world."

"What?" Hannah took one look back at the sparkling eggs as she followed Taggart out into the tunnel.

Pulling her close as he reached around her to bolt the door, Taggart fixed her with a meaningful wink. "He doesn't have you."

* * *

The lights flashed with less erratic frenzy as long as he played the music. The little beast responded best to the sweetness of the violins; the string music floating through the air seemed to lessen the creature's building hysteria.

Sloan leaned forward, resting his fingertips on the warm, pebbled surface of the egg and wished for the hundredth time that he'd been born with the powers of a guardian. Untold power and access to endless riches coiled right beneath his fingertips, and yet he couldn't obtain it. Blast the rules of Draecna magic and their ridiculous, tenuous existence. Sloan ground his teeth as the hatchling shifted positions within the egg and slithered against the shell. "If ye weren't so damned particular, I could call ye forth rather than wait for some weak human from the other side."

A shuffling grunt at the doorway interrupted his brooding conversation with the egg and resulted in an immediate flash of fury pumping through his veins. Who dared interrupt him in his private chambers? Mia wasn't due back from Taroc Na Mor, and all the other servants knew better than to bother him unless he summoned them.

"This better be good!" Sloan sneered at the polished slate door as it shushed its way open across the thick plush of the carpeted floor. Curling his hands on either side of the egg, he scowled at the doorway, waiting to see who was stupid enough to put their own neck in a noose.

As the figure hitched its way out of the shadows of the hallway, Sloan relaxed back into the depths of his wingback chair. "Ah, it is you, my friend. I hadna expected to see you this evening. I thought ye had returned to the caverns." Sloan drummed his nails on the desk. In fact, Sloan hadn't expected to see the dark one unless he summoned him for another delicate assignment.

The lone soul remained silent, pointed at the egg resting in the center of Sloan's oval desk, then pointed back at Sloan.

"Yes, I appreciate your getting me the egg and I paid ye for your troubles, remember?" Pushing back from the desk, Sloan tensed his satin-clad legs against the front of his chair and tapped his fingers in time with his words. He studied his guest and controlled his voice. By the infernal fires, he wasn't in the mood to be patient this evening.

His visitor reached over, tapped once on the egg, then raised his head and looked up at Sloan with an expectant frown.

Rubbing the back of his fingers against the silver stubble gathering beneath his chin, Sloan's irritation flared. His well-paid thief had served his purpose. It was time for him to disappear into the mountains of Erastaed until summoned again. If not for the fact he might need him in the future, Sloan would have disposed of him in a more permanent manner. He was a secret weapon that could still prove useful especially the way things were going on the other side. Lowering his hands to the wide arms of his chair, Sloan dug his nails deep into the sumptuous leather as he attempted to reign in his ire. "The egg willna hatch without the touch of the guardian. Our little Mia is in the process of extending our *invitation* to the guardian now. Then our little hatchling can be born and a new dawn of the Draecna race can begin. Ye must be patient, my friend."

A growling laugh rumbled up from the belly of the guest and echoed off the mirrored walls until the crystals in the chandelier tinkled overhead. Then he turned around, shuffled out of the room, and closed the door behind him.

"That one's more insane than I am," Sloan muttered to the egg.

CHAPTER SIX

"Ye had her that close and ye didna do anything about it? I am so disappointed in ye. Ye were my hero. Now who in the world am I going to look up to when it comes to beddin' the lasses?" Gearlach moaned into his tankard and shook his head as his voice echoed off the blackened beams of the high-ceilinged kitchen.

Septamus reached over, picked up the keg, and slid it down the table out of Gearlach's reach. "No more for you. Five hundred years old and ye weep in your cups after only six kegs of ale. What the hell is wrong wi' ye? Ye shame us, Gearlach. A Draecna who canna hold his grog before the sun rises above the horizon! Ye're a disgrace to the entire race."

Taggart slumped at the wide table with his chin propped in one hand and his tankard clenched in the other. They were right. He'd had her so close. And then he'd gone and gotten gallant and obviously very stupid. And now here he sat in a steamy kitchen with two half-sotted Draecna and his cock throbbing between his legs. "I had to show her the truth. I couldna take her before she knew me for what I truly was." He drained his tankard and threw it across the table. God's beard, he tired of dousing himself in the depths of the frigid sea. He might as well be cursed to be one of the selkies, he spent so much time swimming the waters of the loch.

Septamus nodded as he drummed his claws in time with his words. "Aye, that's true. There would've been hell to pay if ye had taken the lass and *then* shown her what ye were. But tell me something. . . ." His eye slits flexed in the gas light of the lamps as he frowned at Taggart over the top of his cup. "Once she didna run screamin' from your form, why the hell did ye not take her after ye got to the caves?"

A tortured moan escaped from his chest, as Taggart buried his face in his arms. "The moment had passed. She asked me so many blasted questions about how I came to be. The magic of the kiss had left us." He'd always had such lousy timing with women. They were such complicated creatures. Draecna had it easy. A Draecna mate never became an issue. Since they were genetically matched at the time of birth, nothing was ever left to chance unless they were unwise enough to wander from tradition as Taggart's mother had.

"This is so verra sad," Gearlach blubbered as he plopped his snout to the edge of the table.

With a jerk of his head in Gearlach's direction, Septamus rolled his eyes. "Did ye have to lift his silencing spell?"

"I couldn't verra well leave him silent forever," Taggart mumbled from the depths of his arms as he gave a defeated shrug. He might as well let Gearlach speak. Lord knows Hannah was probably finished talking to him.

"I don't know why not," Septamus muttered as he nudged the snoring Gearlach with his tail.

"Well, ye better sober up because she's on her way down here from her rooms and she wants to see you, Taggart." Thaetus smacked his hand on a copper pot hanging on the wall as he bounded into the room.

"Down here?" Taggart jumped up from the table. Sheer panic exploded through the numbing effect of the grog. What in holy hell could she be coming down here for? Why did she want to see him?

"Gearlach! Dammit, wake up ye drunken oaf!" Septamus whacked the snoring Draecna with his tail and sent him sprawling on the floor. Pottery rattled in the cupboards as Gearlach crashed to the marbled tiles.

"All of ye, out. Out of here, now!" Taggart pounded on the table and pointed toward the rear kitchen door leading to the outer pantries.

"We're trying, dammit! He's drunk on his arse. He'll no' wake up until late tomorrow afternoon." With a jerk of his head, Septamus hooked a claw around one of Gearlach's horns and started dragging him toward the door. "Grab the bastard's tail, Thaetus. Ye may be scrawny but ye can help me wedge his wide, scaly arse through the door."

"Here, move out of the way, Thaetus. Ye'll throw your back out again." Edging past Thaetus as the man turned a strained shade of purple, Taggart grabbed Gearlach's meaty hind legs at the bend of his leathery knees. Gads, the beast weighed a bloody ton. Gearlach must've already packed on his weight in preparation for winter. "Now, Septamus, lift him now. Thaetus, get the damn door."

Thaetus scurried around the table in front of Septamus and swung the door wide while they shoved the snoring Draecna across the kitchen. Shoving the inert mass of Gearlach across the threshold, Taggart slammed the door, then smoothed his hair away from his face. As he rubbed the sweat from his face against his shoulder, he cringed and wrinkled his nose. By the fires of hell. He reeked of ale and much worse. *God's beard*. He'd repulse the lass before she entered the room.

In a panic, Taggart glanced around the ancient kitchen. The indoor spa built into the side of the room was his silent salvation. He couldn't greet her smelling like a Highland sheep. With a clap of his hands, he lit the fires beneath the stone spa entrenched along the wall. He ran to the door, pressed his ear to the wood, and listened for the sound of footsteps echoing down the hallway. Good. Silence greeted his ears. Perhaps he'd finish bathing before she came down from her rooms. Now that the ale had begun to wear off, he couldn't even stand his own stench.

He glanced at the door, then turned back toward the waterline as it inched its way up the stone enclosure. He willed the water to flow faster into the tub. He thanked the gods for the ancient spring flowing directly beneath Taroc Na Mor and the spa from one of the earliest guardians. Reportedly, the woman complained of a constant chill even on the balmiest of Highland days. Chiseled stone blocks stood mudded together in the shape of an inviting tub in what she deemed the warmest room in the castle. She had ordered it built in one corner of the overly large kitchen. Fire pits surrounded the perimeter of the tub. The roaring fires kept the magical spring water within the stone tank heated for as long as the fires burned. The complex system of ancient piping no longer functioned, but the original sluicing mechanism had been quite impressive indeed. Stripping off his clothes, Taggart hesitated before stepping into the water. He'd always heard the spring had strange powers, unexplained magics from this side of the portal. It didn't matter. There wasn't time; he had to get clean.

Taking a deep breath, Taggart groaned as he eased into the steaming hot water. He knew he didn't have to light the fires to keep the water warm. But he had to admit, he liked the flames.

"Taggart, are you in here?" Hannah shouldered open the door, her dinner tray in her hands.

Holy blazes, she'd gotten down here quicker than he'd

thought. He grabbed the sliver of soap wedged into the hollowed-out side of the tub, submerged, scrubbed his armpits while he held his breath, then slid back above the surface of the water. "Aye, Hannah. I'm over here in my bath. Would ye mind handing me a fresh cake of soap and a rag?"

Hannah stared at him, her knuckles whitening on the dinner tray she held in her hands. "There's a bathtub in the kitchen?"

As he smoothed his dripping hair back out of his face, he leaned back into the recessed seat of the tub. With a nod, he gave her a teasing wink and propped his feet on the edge of the tub. "It's a bit of a long story." The lass had no idea the length of the *story* and wouldn't he love to tell her. Taggart scrubbed a bit lower beneath the surface of the water, stretching farther back in the tub.

"Hmmphf!" Sliding the tray on the marble countertop, Hannah muttered as she searched the shelf above the sink for a bar of soap. "Is there anything about you that *isn't* a bit of a long story?" She bent to rummage through the cabinet.

Taggart took a deep breath as he rubbed his wet hand over his face. Damnation, the woman had a fine, round bottom. His hands itched to cup its firmness. "Hannah."

"What?" She came across the room and stood as far away from the tub as possible, holding out the soap and the small towel she'd found.

"Come closer." Stretching over the side of the tub, Taggart reached for her, ignoring the bar of soap she offered in her outstretched hand. He wasn't going to miss his chance this time. The woman wanted him. The burning filled her eyes. Passion danced in the darkness of their depths and he smelled the scent of her need.

"I . . ." Hannah paused, licking her lips as her gaze raked across the delectable expanse of his sculpted, glistening body. "I don't want to get wet."

With a wicked chuckle, Taggart crooked a finger to summon her closer. "I can tell by the look in your eyes, lass, it's a little too late for that."

Color flamed high on Hannah's cheeks as her eyes widened with realization. "You know what I mean!"

Taggart chuckled again, leaned forward, and hooked his finger into the front of her jeans, tugging her body toward him. His voice rasped deeper as he caressed the curve of her cheek. "Aye, Hannah. I know exactly what ye mean." Yearning blazed hotter than the fire pits heating the water. He'd grown tired of waiting and the tenets could be damned. "Come to me, Hannah. Let us be done with these games. I'm weary. I'm lonely, and I need ye."

Hannah wet her lips again as his gaze entrapped her. She'd heard all she needed to hear. His words, paired with the eyeful of battle-hardened flesh, filled her with liquid fire. She retreated a step, peeled off her shirt, and shucked her jeans. *Breathe, Hannah.* Hannah hugged herself to stop the shaking. The drumming of her heart drowned out all other sound. The pounding in her chest choked her. She'd only been with one man before and there hadn't been anyone since. But lord, she wanted Taggart. She ached to wrap her legs around him and ride. The depth of the water did nothing to hide the fulfillment his body promised. He was right. She'd already soaked her clothes.

And then he stood, scooped her into his arms and cradled her against his slippery chest. Her chilled breasts hardened against his steaming-hot skin as she pressed against him. He settled with her into the hollowed-out corner of the tub. She straddled his body, rubbing against his deliciously, hardened shaft.

Taggart cupped her breasts and thumbed her nipples into aching, demanding points. He swallowed Hannah's moans with a claiming kiss while she writhed upon his lap. Hannah shuddered, clenching him tighter. A glorious ache possessed her body, threatening imminent, mind-reeling explosion. How could he make her come so quick? He wasn't even inside her yet. She panted against him, ground her hips and locked her legs around him. *Dammit.* She needed more and she needed it *now.* "Taggart, take me now."

"Slow down, *maemos.* We have all night." Taggart nibbled his way along the trail of her throat while cupping her breast with an excruciatingly slow caress.

The heat of the water. His prodding erection against her aching nub. *Dammit.* He didn't understand. She wanted him inside her *now.* She grabbed him and attempted to slide down the length of him. "Oh . . . my . . . G—" she hissed with an ecstatic groan. It had been so long. She held her breath while her body struggled to accommodate his size. "Oh yes," she purred as she buried him to the hilt.

Taggart grabbed her waist and held her still. *"Maemos ma dao! Uthe dina cuma!"*

Hannah hadn't had sex in forever, but apparently, this was so damn good she'd lost her ability to understand words. "What did you just say?" Hannah gasped as she flexed her thighs and gyrated her hips again.

With a guttural groan, Taggart cupped her face between his hands and fixed her with a threatening glare. "I spoke Erastaedian! I said, *Slow—down—love—before I come!"*

Hannah turned her head, suckled one of his fingers deep into her mouth, and pulled his other hand to her breast. Tickling her tongue into the palm of his hand, she smiled as she half-closed her eyes. "You talk too much. I'm not about to gear down this ride." Raking her fingers down his side, Hannah moaned and rode him hard.

The water overflowed the confines of the tub. The waves increased with the fervor of her thrusts. The wet friction of his skin sliding against hers increased her pleasure with every delightful lunge.

Taggart reveled in Hannah's cries; he growled in unison with her throaty purrs. She clenched him with every swivel of her hips. He pulled her hardened nipple deeper into his mouth. Hannah caught her breath as he suckled harder. Her moans reached a fevered pitch; the sound drove him over the edge. Taggart tensed as Hannah gyrated harder and faster. He couldn't hold out any longer. He filled his hands with her buttocks and roared his own claiming as she pushed him to his release.

A frantic scratching sounded somewhere in the distance. The faintest hint of a muffled tap as if sharp little claws scrabbled against a roughened surface. Hannah raised her head, dragged one eye open, and scanned the dimly lit kitchen. Where was that noise coming from? A herd of mice must be on the move. The digging noise finally stopped. Good. Her gaze shifted back to Taggart's delicious warm body stretched out on the blanket beside her. They were alone on their pallet beside the spa.

Who cared where the sound came from? She had everything she needed right here. She dropped back down with a purring sigh, nestled deeper into the haven of his arms, and inhaled deeply as though she sought the scent of her mate. He smelled heavenly, pure lusty male and the sex they'd enjoyed all night. Tickling the tips of her fingers down the ridges of his abdominals, Hannah released the delicious air of him she'd just breathed in. She couldn't remember the last time she'd been this contented and it wasn't just the sex. Taggart truly seemed to need her a lot more than anyone else ever had.

With a mental shake of her head, she scolded herself. She shouldn't do that. She shouldn't compare Taggart with anyone. She shouldn't taint the pleasure she'd just enjoyed with painful memories of the past. Hannah traced the pads of her fingertips across the taut planes of his chest. She loved the smoothness of his skin. She wondered if the Draecna blood kept him from sprouting any hair? Her husband had been like a sasquatch. Damn, she'd done it again. Hannah squinted her eyes shut and pressed her forehead against Taggart's warm skin. No more comparisons! Well, maybe just one more. Her heart pulled as she snuggled closer. Last night with Taggart had made her feel like he cared for her more than anyone else ever had.

A sharp crack echoed from the depths of the caverns beneath the kitchen, followed by louder scratching. No way that sound came from mice. But if not mice or even very large rats, then what kind of varmint roamed in the depths of Taroc Na Mor? Fully awake now, Hannah sat up and scowled at the door leading to the tunnels. The sound had definitely come from the nursery.

Smoothing her hand across Taggart's bare shoulder, Hannah gave it a squeeze and a gentle shake. "Taggart. Taggart! Something's going on in the nursery. I think you might want to go see."

No response. Taggart just reached for her, mumbled something incoherent in his sleep, and pulled her body closer. Hannah swallowed a wicked giggle. Poor baby. He was exhausted. And well he should be. Hannah tried to ignore the flash of heat that flooded her belly at the mere thought of all they'd done the evening before.

The thump and scratch from the caverns repeated. It did kind of sound like some sort of very small varmint. Surely, she could just handle this by herself and let him get some rest. Hannah grinned and planted a kiss in the center of his chest. She'd have a look and then pop back upstairs where they could test out the lovely pillowed nest of her Draecna-sized bed.

Hannah eased over Taggart and gathered up her clothes. After she slipped them on, she tucked the blanket about him and kissed him on the forehead before slipping out the door leading downward to the tunnels.

"There will be no eating on this table until it has been thoroughly disinfected." Thaetus stood with his shirt sleeves rolled above his elbows, a bucket in one hand and a scrub brush held in the other.

"Let me run a flame across it once or twice. That'll kill anything that might be a crawlin' about!" Gearlach rubbed his front claws together and filled his lungs with a great gust of air.

Jumping up from the pallet on the floor, Taggart whipped the blanket around his waist as he blinked the sleep from his eyes. "Don't ye dare! Ye'll burn the entire keep to the ground. Ye know ye have no control over your blaze." Scrubbing the bleariness from his eyes, he fixed Thaetus and Gearlach with a narrow-eyed stare. "What the hell are ye both doing? What is going on in here?" Ye'd think they'd have the decency to let a man sleep.

Releasing his precious wind with a huff of disgust, Gearlach jerked his head toward Thaetus. "He won't feed us breakfast in the fancy dining room 'cause he says we're too messy, and he says we can't eat off this table until he cleans it because ye probably had Hannah spread all over it."

Taggart glanced at the table, then cocked a brow at Thaetus and gave him a slow, satisfied smile. Thaetus had a point. But that was none of their damn business. "By the way, there is no whipped cream for this morning's straw-berries."

"What happened to the whipped cream?" Thaetus plopped the bucket on the table with a splash and soused the brush inside as he turned a darkened scowl upon Taggart.

Taggart broadened his smile as he scooped his clothes up from the floor. He hadn't been this contented in centuries. "Never ye mind." With a nod toward the door, he turned back to Thaetus and tossed the blanket over the bench. "Did ye see when Hannah went up to her room? Do ye know if she's still in her bed?" He just might sneak up there and surprise her. The memories of the creativity of the erotic whipped cream had given him quite the rising.

The swishing sound of the swirling motion of the scrub brush stopped. "I havena seen Hannah since last night. I thought perhaps she'd gone for a morning walk in the gardens and left ye to sleep off the effects of your evening." Thaetus's face paled with his words as he looked up from his spread-eagled stance at the table.

"Gearlach?" Taggart yanked on his shirt as a sense of dread unfurled in his gut and clenched the very air from his lungs.

With a shrug of one wing and a shake of his head, Gearlach confirmed Taggart's worst fears. "She's nay in the gardens. I've already been there and called out to her. I never received an answer. When I came in here and saw ye curled up like a wee hatchling, I figured she was still somewhere in the kitchens with you."

"By all that is holy." Taggart gaped at the empty pallet in the corner of the room, willing it to spill Hannah's whereabouts. "I break my vow and the verra next morning I have already lost her!" Taggart tore across the kitchen, yanked his sword out of the corner, and belted it to his waist. He didn't even know where to begin looking. They had passed out in each other's arms on the stubbornly silent pallet. He vaguely remembered her shaking him at some point this morning, but he thought she just wanted him to hold her.

"Taggart! Man, dinna be a fool. The woman knows ye

to be a hybrid. Why do ye go for your sword?" Thaetus lobbed the scrub brush across the table and yanked his apron away from his chest. "Change, man! Use your Draecna senses to find her. Have ye gone daft with exhaustion?"

His chest pounding, Taggart heaved the sword across the room and stared at the blade where it shuddered in the whitewashed stones of the wall. "This is why I should've kept the vow and never touched her. I broke my word and now my judgment has disappeared with my priorities. I am a complete disgrace."

Septamus clouted him across the shoulders and knocked him toward the door. "Enough, Taggart. Ye can berate yourself later. Change now and find her! Use your powers, hybrid. We will worry about your useless vows later."

With a ripping sound echoing through the kitchen, Taggart shredded his clothing as he assumed his Draecna form. He cocked his head and strained with all his senses for a hint of where Hannah might be. Finally, he heard a sound that lessened the weight on his heart: a tinkling melody of happiness like water trickling down the streambed of a mountainside after a gentle rain. Hannah's distant laughter floated through the air.

His clawed hands curled into trembling fists as he turned in a slow circle and scanned the area. Where was the laughter coming from? Where did the little minx hide?

"Do ye hear it?" he asked Septamus, nodding toward the tunnels.

"She canna get into the nursery. The gateway would never open for her." Septamus shook his horned head at the door, a puff of smoke escaping from both flared nostrils.

They both turned and glared at Gearlach where he sat at the table dipping his claws in the bucket of soapy water. "Did ye leave the gateway to the nursery open again?"

Taggart flexed and refolded his wings, trying to keep his anger in check. Thieves had already stolen one Draecna egg from the nursery. They couldn't afford to be careless, especially not with Hannah in their midst.

Gearlach shook his head and rose from the table with a sullen look on his face. "The gateway is sealed! I swear to ye. Thaetus doesn't let me anywhere near it. Ye should know that by now. Do ye think I would be foolish enough to cross any of his magical wards?"

Thaetus held up his hand toward Taggart and patted Gearlach on the wing with a sympathetic shake of his head. "Have ye forgotten your texts, Taggart? The guardian has entry to the nursery anytime she wishes. She merely has to stand in front of the door and wish to go inside."

With a smirk plastered all over his scaly face, Gearlach bobbed his head and pointed his claw at all their chests. "Ye see? Ye canna always blame me when something goes wrong around this place. I'm no' as stupid as ye like to give me credit."

Yanking his sword out of the wall, Taggart ignored Gearlach's defense. He battered open the door leading down to the tunnels. The sound of Hannah's giggles bubbled up clearer from the depths now that the heavy metal door no longer blocked the music of her laughter. The louder Hannah's laughter grew, the harder his stomach churned. She'd slipped away and he'd panicked like a fool. He'd completely lost his sense of reason.

When he reached the end of the tunnel, he was relieved to find the gateway to the nursery tightly sealed. He rolled the haft of his sword in his palm, toying with the glyphs cut into it as he stared at the locked patterned door in front of him. What was Hannah giggling about? What was the woman up to this time? And why had she gone to the nursery alone? Blast, the woman! She knew she shouldn't go anywhere unprotected. What did it take to get through that stubborn head of hers?

"Gavrana!" Taggart snarled; his guttural Draecna growl echoed through the tunnels like thunder. When he got her in front of him, he had half a mind to turn her across his knee.

The thick metallic disk covered by whirls and crescents groaned as it slowly rolled to the side. A different scent, one stronger than the usual fragrance of the moon lilies, buffeted his face as soon as the door shifted to the side. *New life. God's beard.* Hannah had released a hatchling. The smell of moist, loamy earth mixed with the tang often scented in the wind from the sea. An ancient primeval scent known only to a chosen few allowed at the ceremonial births.

Hannah sat cross-legged beside the warming pedestal with an iridescent green bundle cradled in the crook of her arms. Tiny, damp wings stuck to the scaly back and fluttered a transparent pink as the baby Draecna wriggled in Hannah's arms. Lifting the little beast beneath its forearms, Hannah laughed as the creature belched a tiny ring of smoke, then nuzzled her face with an affectionate chirrup. Its dripping green tail curled up between its chubby hind legs as it squirmed and wriggled between her hands.

"I think William is a lovely name."

"William?" Taggart snorted as he stormed into the room. "What kind of name is *William* for a Draecna?"

Cuddling the hatchling closer into her embrace, Hannah kissed *William* on the end of his glistening green snout. "William is an honorable name." Giving Taggart an up-and-down glance, she added, "And why are you in lizard mode?"

"Lizard mode?" Taggart ground his teeth so hard he

swore he heard them crack. He'd show her lizard mode. Shifting back to his human form, he stretched before her in all his naked glory. "None of us could find ye this fine, wonderful morning. How many times have I warned ye about your safety? What does it take to convince ye that ye must not go anywhere unprotected?"

Rising up from the floor, Hannah balanced William on one hip and nodded toward the remaining eggs. "I figured we're here in Taroc Na Mor. How could I be in any danger, especially down here in the nursery? William was ready to hatch. I heard him scratching at his shell. If I hadn't helped him, I'm afraid he might've died. He was having a lot of trouble breaking through and he called out to me, Taggart." Moving closer, she traced a finger down Taggart's chest and stretched to steal a kiss.

Grabbing her by the wrist, Taggart spun her away and turned her toward the warming pedestal. She wasn't going to distract him again. He had to make her understand. "Look, Hannah! Do ye no' remember the stolen egg? What if the scratching ye heard had been a trap? What if a minion had lain in wait for ye? I couldna have gotten down here in time."

Hannah stared at the empty indentation, then yanked her wrist out of Taggart's grasp. "Then I would've handled it. I'm not stupid, Taggart. There's plenty of places down here I could've hidden until you came to the rescue. I haven't been down here very long."

William glared at Taggart over Hannah's shoulder, curled back his tiny green lips, and hissed.

Taggart snorted and shook his head as he yanked a plaid off one of the drying racks in the corner and slapped it around his waist. "Well, it appears ye have another protector now. 'Tis just as well, since it's obvious I'm no' the man for the job." Why the hell did she refuse to see reason? Had she forgotten the destruction in Jasper Mills so quickly?

"What are you talking about? You've been protecting me." Hannah settled William down on the floor, grinning as he wobbled across the smooth paved stones.

How could he tell her how he'd panicked this morning? Taggart stared at her, standing there with her arms crossed, her stubborn little chin stuck up in the air. As soon as he'd discovered she was gone, he should've shifted to his Draecna form, scanned the area, and been at her side within seconds. Instead, her disappearance from the kitchen had thrown him into a misguided frenzy; he'd lost direction, lost his way, forgotten all the strength and magics coursing through his veins. It had taken Septamus and Thaetus to snap him out of it, to tell him what he needed to do. What sort of protector waited for orders like a common foot soldier at the front line of the battle?

"Last night," Taggart began and then he stopped. Turning away, he sucked in a deep breath and paced around the stifling room. By the fires of Eras, the nursery seemed smaller than ever before. The scented air blew hot against his skin, stirred by the gently undulating branches of Rowanian saplings fanning over the eggs. His heart wrenched with the pain of the words he was about to say, but he had no choice. Hannah's safety was all that mattered. "Last night should've never happened, Hannah. I broke a sacred vow."

Her eyes glittered cold as the color left her face. She'd shut down on him; he sensed it. She didn't understand it was for her own good, her own safety, but he didn't know how to explain it. *Dammit to hell.* Why didn't she say something? "I have to keep ye safe, Hannah. Above all else, your safety is more important than anything. Worlds depend on it, Hannah. Please tell me ye understand."

Hannah's eyes narrowed as her mouth hardened into a cold, flat line. "Fine," she retorted, then turned on her heel, scooped up William, and headed toward the door.

"Fine?" Taggart scrubbed his face with a defeated groan. God's beard, he knew that dreaded word. When a woman said *fine* in that tone of voice, it surely doomed a man straight to hell. He hadn't lived over seven hundred years without hearing horror stories about men's wives using the word *fine*.

Standing in front of the door, tapping one foot, Hannah shrugged and repeated, "Fine."

Taggart reached for her, then let his hand drop. The look on her face said it all. "Holy blazes, Hannah, please. Ye have to try to understand. I have to keep ye safe. As I said, worlds depend upon it; countless races depend upon it. Can ye no' see what I'm trying to tell ye, woman?"

"I understand perfectly," Hannah snapped in a voice that said a great deal more than her words.

William propped his scaly chin on Hannah's shoulder and licked his forked tongue out at Taggart with another threatening hiss.

"Don't sass me, boy!" Taggart warned and shook his finger at the young Draecna's nose. That's all he needed, a smart-ass Draecna hatchling to deal with while he tried to protect Hannah.

"Just open the door, and William and I will go up to the gardens where Septamus and Gearlach can babysit us until it's time for the next shift to tag-team out and watch over every move I make."

"*Gavrana,*" Taggart sighed, with an exhausted wave of his hand. So it was to be like that. All their carefully built closeness shattered. "There, Hannah. But how did ye get in here to begin with?"

Pausing just after she'd entered the tunnel, Hannah shot Taggart a warning glare. "Apparently, when I'm not so pissed off I can't see straight, the door will open up if I just stand in front of it."

"I see," Taggart replied.

CHAPTER SEVEN

Unbelievable. Taggart clenched his teeth until his jaws ached as William fidgeted before him. Three months and still no improvement. Why was training William proving to be so much more difficult than guiding Gearlach through his formative years? For the life of him, Taggart never remembered Gearlach being this much trouble.

Scrubbing his jaw with a tensed fist, he studied the downcast youth. The willful hatchling should know better by now. How many times had they told the boy to keep the wind at his back to avoid pissing on his oversized feet?

From the corner of Taggart's eye, Gearlach's sheepish expression haunted him. And then there was the *other* matter. Where in the hell had Gearlach come up with the idea to ignite William's farts into exploding fireballs?

Returning his attention to his squirming charge, Taggart heaved an aggravated sigh, "Aye, William. Gearlach told ye the truth. None of the other Draecna have ever accomplished your trick." Taggart folded his arms and sidled his unblinking stare back to Gearlach. He couldn't imagine why the fool had taught the young one that idiotic stunt. Of course, Gearlach had always held an obsessed fascination with flame and any type of explosion.

Turning back to William, Taggart blew out another irritated breath. "I hold Gearlach responsible, William. But ye're getting old enough now to realize what ye should and shouldna do. Show some sense, boy. Use yer damned head for something other than a place for the midges to land." With a nod toward the castle, Taggart raised his voice. "And I want ye to start spending a great deal more time with Septamus rather than Gearlach. He's a *much* better influence upon ye. Do ye understand me?"

"Aye." William nodded and cut his flickering golden gaze over at Gearlach as if silently accusing him of sending him straight to the gallows.

Kicking his toe in the soft dirt of the clearing, William's face suddenly brightened. "Mother wants to know if we can keep the kitty inside the keep when the dead of winter comes."

Kitty? What the hell was the boy talking about? Drawing closer to William, Taggart swallowed hard and barely choked out the words. "There are *no* cats allowed at Taroc Na Mor, William. Ever. The beasts are considered ill-omened."

Gearlach scowled at the young Draecna standing by his side. "What filthy cat are ye talking about, William? Ye never told me there was a feline slinking about the keep."

Shrugging his wings, William backed away from Gearlach and Taggart, his nervous gaze shifting back and forth between their faces. "It's Mother's cat. It comes to her private courtyard beneath her window. 'Specially in the evenings. She feeds it all the time. It's soft and grey and when I'm verra still, Mother helps me hold it."

Taggart's gut wrenched as his gaze locked with Gearlach's knowing look. There wasn't a cat on this side of the portal that would get anywhere near a Draecna. Natural enemies since the beginning of time, the two species detested one another. Something wasn't right. "Is your mother with Septamus now?"

William shook his head. "No, I left her in the garden with Thaetus and the kitty."

"With the kitty? Thaetus wouldna be caught dead near a stinkin' cat. He detests them as much as we do." Gearlach worried a claw around one of his horns as he ambled closer to William.

"Oh, Thaetus didna know the cat was about," William volunteered. "She was sneaking up on him from behind. Kitty likes to hide in the bushes until no one but Mother or me is about."

The more she thought about it, the angrier she got. She couldn't believe she'd been so stupid. Holding her cup clenched between her hands, Hannah envisioned snapping Taggart's wondrous neck. She couldn't believe he'd actually said it. A mistake. He'd said their fantastic sexual marathon had been a terrible mistake. Was he saying he hadn't enjoyed it? Like hell, he hadn't enjoyed it. He was the one who hadn't even woken up the next morning when William couldn't break through his shell.

She couldn't believe she'd finally relented, finally caved and opened to another man, and then he'd said it'd been a mistake. She'd even admitted to herself that she might care for him just a bit. And where had it gotten her? Sitting alone on a cold concrete bench. In her garden. Fuming over her coffee.

She took another sip of the delectable brew Thaetus brought her every morning. It had been three months now since their *mistake* and Taggart treated her like a delicate porcelain doll. He'd practically placed her on a shelf under a crystal dome to ensure not even a speck of dust settled anywhere on her body. Explosive sex after such a long dry spell was worse than no sex at all. Now she ached for him every night. He'd reawakened every nerve ending in her body and she craved a repeat performance. She clutched her coffee in a stranglehold. *Damn you, Taggart.*

"Thaetus, why don't you go do whatever it is you need to do and stop hovering around like a buzzard waiting for something to die? I'm just sitting here in the garden enjoying my morning coffee. I promise. I'll stay right here. What could happen here in the middle of the garden?" Swiveling on the bench, Hannah glared at the man fidgeting close to the outer door of the keep.

"Ye're not to be left unguarded under any circumstances. Ye know that. 'Tis been discussed with ye many times before." Thaetus made a show of plucking withered leaves off a nearby bush and tossing them over onto the lawn.

"Then why don't you get yourself a cup of coffee and join me?" Hannah nodded toward the bench on the other side of the glass-topped iron table and smiled.

"Join you?" Thaetus looked horrified at the thought of following Hannah's suggestion.

"Okay. I see by the look on your face that you've got a big problem either with coffee or with my company. Which is it?" Hannah asked.

Thaetus didn't reply. His knees buckled, his eyes rolled back in his head, and he collapsed and rolled to the ground.

"Thaetus!" Rushing to his side, Hannah crouched beside him, checking his condition by pressing her hand to his throat. A faint pulse feathered an erratic beat beneath her fingertips while the muscles of his neck clenched and twitched as if his body tightened down.

A sultry voice rose up behind her. "He is not dead. I've merely paralyzed him. But it would be best for him if ye moved away from his body." Still squatting beside Thaetus, Hannah whirled and stared into the linen folds of a young woman's threadbare robes. As her heart pounded into her throat, Hannah's eyes traveled up the length of the rough weave to meet the amber-eyed gaze of a hooded girl. "Who are you? What have you done to Thaetus?"

With a lazy dip of her blond lashes, the girl shoved her tattered hood to her shoulders. "I am Mia and as I told ye, I have only paralyzed him. Ye should be thanking me. I should have destroyed the insolent servant." Pressing her lips together into a tight-lipped frown, she darted a glance over Thaetus's convulsing body, then returned her bored gaze to Hannah. "He will recover in time." She motioned for Hannah to rise. "Come now. We have little time. My master grows quite impatient and waits to meet ye."

Mia's detached, pale-eyed gaze stole Hannah's breath from her lungs. Her heart hammered so loudly in her head it drowned out any other sound. As much as she hated to admit it, Taggart had been right. She wasn't even safe in Taroc Na Mor. But she'd be damned if she'd go without a fight. While she stared at Mia's outstretched hand, a plan crystallized when her gaze shifted to Mia's right. A gaping hole in the leafy shrubbery jumped into her line of vision.

Hannah leaned forward and slid her hands deep into the loose dirt as though steadying herself in the soft earth close to Thaetus's body. She pressed her mouth close to the twitching man's head and whispered, "Tell him I didn't go without a fight."

Mia shifted to the side and nudged Hannah's leg with her toe. "What do you say to him? Ye must come now. I told ye I have chosen not to kill him, but if ye tarry any longer I will change my mind. We must leave now. My master grows impatient."

"I'm coming," Hannah said. Taking a deep breath, she curled her hands shut. *Now or never.* With one smooth motion, she slung two handfuls of the sandy topsoil into Mia's pale, amber eyes. Then she vaulted through the thinned out bushes beside the retaining wall and rolled down William's favorite mudslide to the creek. Thank goodness the little Draecna had shown her his latest invention. Just yesterday, he'd shared how he'd perfected sliding to the waterway using the back of his tail.

Landing in the rocky creek bed with a splash, Hannah flailed across the shallow stream. The icy water numbed her flesh, only adding to the panic pounding through her body. Her teeth chattered until her jaws ached. Her body trembled more from spiked adrenaline than from the frigid water. Hannah clawed her way up the muddy embankment of the other side and collapsed as she pulled herself up into a moss-covered ledge. Her stomach churned as she risked a look back; terror threatened to close off her throat. She hadn't heard a sound of Mia giving chase, not a single snap of a branch. Had she given up so easily?

Hannah gave up looking for Mia and reached for the root system of a washed-out tree. She pulled herself behind the blackened mass of roots and into a hollowed-out cave deep within the embankment. Curling her body as far back against the soft earth as she could, she decided she'd hide here until Taggart found her. He'd use his senses to locate her. Pressing her back against the cool, damp earth, she closed her eyes and tried to slow her breathing. It was going to be all right. She was safe. She just had to wait for Taggart.

"He will not find ye because ye will not be here." Mia's bony white hand snaked through the protection of the tangled roots and lightly tapped Hannah in the center of her forehead.

"Thaetus, ye must tell me. What do ye remember?" Taggart strode in tight circles beside the four-poster bed. The miasma of emotions pounding through his body prevented him from remaining in one spot for very long. His Hannah, spirited away, perhaps already dead. God's beard, how had he allowed this to happen? Once again, the Guild and the protector had failed the sacred Sullivan bloodline. But far worse than any ancient trust, he had failed Hannah, his beloved Hannah.

His lips gray, his red-rimmed eyes receding deep in their darkened sockets, Thaetus appeared ready for the grave. Mia's vicious poison still raged within his body; his limbs twisted and twitched uncontrollably beneath the sheets. "I never saw her," Thaetus rasped. His voice was so weak Taggart ceased his pacing and leaned forward to hear him better.

Cold hatred clenched tighter in his chest as Taggart looked down at his beloved friend. How could he have ever considered such a woman as a mate? *If she hurt Hannah . . .* His hands fisted as he envisioned Mia's neck between his fingers.

"She posed as a wicked cat!" Gearlach hissed. "It was the prophecy! We shouldha warned the boy against trusting any type of feline. How could we have been so lax?"

Holding up his hand to silence Gearlach, Taggart shook his head. "Even if we had warned the boy, he still would've been no match for Mia. William is an innocent, still young and untrained. Mia can be verra convincing when she wants to be. God's beard, I should know." Mia had once been such a wondrous creature of light, filled with hope and promise. Then she'd turned, become poisoned and unforgiving. She'd become as maniacal as Sloan.

Returning to the side of the bed, Taggart repeated his question. "What do ye remember, old friend?"

Running his blackened tongue over his cracked lips, Thaetus drew a shaking breath before he replied, "She told Hannah she could've killed me but she had chosen not to. Then she told her she had to come with her because her master grew verra impatient."

"She showed you mercy?" Taggart stroked his chin as he turned and circled the dimly lit confines of the room.

Mia could've easily killed Thaetus. In fact, Sloan had probably ordered her to do so. Ruthlessness and cruelty marked Sloan for the hated ruler of Erastaed; many died without reason by his hand every day. He had an edict against housing prisoners any length of time. Sloan's standard theory remained very simple: If you kept prisoners, they had to be fed.

"Why would they want Hannah alive? Why would she spare Thaetus?" Septamus entered the room with a tray of herbal medicines clinking in tightly stoppered bottles. "By the way, the young one wants to see Thaetus. He is greatly troubled that he left Thaetus and his mother unguarded with the cat. He blames himself for leaving them unprotected and not seeing through Mia's evil glamour."

"It is not his fault," Taggart retorted with an irritated snap. If anyone was at fault, it was he. He was the one who had failed everyone concerned. After all, he was the supposed protector.

Septamus paused in his grinding of the pungent herbs and arched an accusing brow. "I will leave that for you to explain. Now as to my other question, why would they suffer Hannah and Thaetus to live?"

The caustic aroma of the herbs wafting through the room yanked unbidden memories from the recesses of Taggart's mind. Mia knew every herb from every reality and the effects it wreaked upon any creature's body. Mia claimed herbal magic as her greatest power and apparently, under Sloan's tutelage, she had become demonic in its use. To this day, specific scents still raked vicious claws across Taggart's emotions. They reminded him of Mia and the future they'd planned, then the pain she'd inflicted when she'd publicly shunned him for being a monster.

"Taggart!" Septamus banged the stone pestle on the edge of the mortar; its sharp *clink* ricocheted across the room. "Enough! You will cease giving Mia this power over you or I will do something I should have done long ago."

Shaking himself free of the bitter aromatic trance, Taggart pulled his gaze from the rain-spattered window. "And what would that be?" he snapped.

"I will summon your mother."

"You wouldn't dare."

Septamus scraped the herbal mash out of the mortar and rolled it into a noxious, oily egg-shaped ball between two of his claws. "Try me."

Not looking at Taggart, Septamus forced the greasy brown mass between Thaetus's dry, cracked lips. Then he slid his scaled forearm beneath Thaetus's trembling shoulders and supported him while holding a glass of water to the gagging man's mouth. "Now answer my question. Why would Sloan suffer Hannah to live? Do ye think it has anything to do with the stolen egg?"

With a sympathetic swallow in Thaetus's direction, Taggart rubbed his throat and tried not to gag. He knew the god-awful taste of that potent concoction. The smell alone made him want to retch. "I think it has everything to do with the egg. Why else would he keep her alive? He'll prefer she release the Draecna from the egg, but if she provokes him and he knows of the tenet, he'll sacrifice her and hatch it with her blood. My greatest fear is she'll make the mistake of releasing his hatchling and then he'll kill her before we can save her."

"We'll need many to lay siege upon Tiersa Deun." Septamus eased Thaetus back against the pillows and pulled the blankets close about the trembling man's chin.

"Few would be better," Thaetus whispered, his eyes closing as he turned his head into the pillow. Few would stand a better chance of slipping past the warning barriers.

Stroking his chin, Taggart resumed his pacing and made a slow circle around the mahogany table centered in the room. "How long would it take to summon the other Draecna from all the gateways? Gather them from every portal, bring them forth to cross over to Erastaed?"

Septamus shook his head. "We canna leave the portals neglected. Not even for something as great as rescuing the guardian. The balance of time and space must be maintained or the very grid itself will implode and chaos will result. There are no Draecna to be spared."

"The nursery is full," Gearlach interrupted. "Ye have at least nineteen eggs down there ready with nineteen healthy Draecna young. Bring forth the hatchlings and meld with them to advance their training to your level."

Taggart stopped his pacing and turned to stare at Gearlach. He knew Gearlach was trying to help, but had the fool lost his mind? "Only a guardian can release the hatchlings, Gearlach. Guild members have tried but havena had much success. Do ye no' remember the last time? Almost all the hatchlings and the Guild members died except for the one youngest Draecna and ye know how he turned out. How long has it been since ye've read your texts? Have ye forgotten all your history?"

Swaggering his way across the room, Gearlach thumped Taggart with a knobby claw to the center of his chest and knocked him back a couple of paces. "Ye need to reread your own in-depth texts, ye uppity little hybrid! When ye joined with the guardian, ye marked her for your mate and whether *she* knows it or not she accepted ye and mixed her blood with yours. I know ye both did it! She fair reeked of your scent. Hell, the kitchen still crawls with the very essence of your union. Ye need to pay closer attention, ye stubborn hybrid. Ye now have the power to call forth the hatchlings just as well as she."

God's beard. It couldn't be true. Could it? Had he unknowingly placed his mark upon her? Taggart glared at Gearlach, unease rumbling in his gut as he tried to remember every ancient text he'd ever read. Mated? He thought back to that night and his body thrummed to attention. Holy blazes, he hardened at the very memory. It hadn't just been the magic of her body. Taggart had experienced an unexplainable bonding with Hannah; he shivered now as he realized she'd electrified him to the depths of his very soul.

"Son of a bitch," Taggart muttered as he raked his hands through his hair.

Gearlach snickered, wagging his great horned head to and fro as he swaggered about the room. "For once I am right and you are wrong. Now, what do ye think about that?"

"Shut up, Gearlach," Septamus huffed as he rolled his great, iridescent eyes. "Taggart, as much as I hate to agree with him—" Septamus paused and flashed Gearlach a warning look before he continued. "Ye are now mated to Hannah and ye do possess the power to bring forth the remainder of the brood."

Scrubbing his face with both hands, Taggart groaned and collapsed into an overstuffed chair beside the hearth. "And what good does this newfound power do me? If they are all as immature as young William, what can I hope to accomplish with an army of inexperienced Draecna?"

"William is innocent because Hannah brought him forth and he has been allowed to advance at the natural rate of acceleration. He has not experienced the advantage of connecting with your mind." Septamus rebottled the herbs on his tray, carefully tightening the stoppers on each of the glass vials. "However, if you bring forth the hatchlings and meld with their minds as soon as they emerge from their shells, ye can advance their level of maturity and battle experience to that of your own. They'll no' have your magic, but they will be able to control their blaze and should grow to nearly Gearlach's size."

Nineteen Draecna ready for battle and that didn't include Septamus and Gearlach. Taggart scraped his fingertips through the stubble of his beard and winced as he weighed the odds. The ancient texts had only hinted at what Septamus proposed, as a possibility. Taggart searched his memories as growing uncertainty settled like a weight in his gut. As far as he remembered, no one had ever tried such a melding. Sorting through his teachings of the sacred tenets, Taggart recalled why. The final chapter describing the untried ritual warned of irreversible insanity for both participants if the melding failed.

But nineteen Draecna flying against his brother and saving Hannah from a cruel death. How could he not try? Cunning and evil, Sloan excelled at every level of war, be it outright battle or cloak-and-dagger stealth. The young Draecna would only know what Taggart's DNA transmitted into their minds. They would only possess his knowledge. Taggart's thirst for vengeance would remain entirely his own. Sloan had his Hannah. Taggart had no choice, and the nineteen eggs awaited him.

CHAPTER EIGHT

A distant whip cracked through the air and echoed down the hallway, followed by a rattle of chains and a muffled thud.

Hannah eased open one eyelid and listened for the source of the sound. A moaning sob followed another air-piercing crack and heart-wrenching lash of the leather. Hannah slid back farther into the darkest corner of her cell and curled her hands over her ears. If she kept her back pressed against the cold, hard wall, maybe she could disappear into the darkness. At least this room smelled better than the first one they'd thrown her into, and the only thing crawling on the floor was her. The slab flooring radiated the chill like ice and appeared as black as an oil slick. The walls loomed above her dark and bleak as though drawn from the bowels of the earth. The only light filtering into the room glimmered from the one tiny window notched high overhead.

Uncurling from a tensed little ball, Hannah stretched and tried peering out the window. No such luck. Even if she stood on the tips of her toes, she couldn't reach the tiny rectangle. Feeling her way along the thick icy walls to the door, Hannah pressed her ear to the crack beside the hinges and listened. She cringed when pathetic moans and high-pitched wails vibrated the walls of the passage.

With a jolt, she recognized the distinct clomp and drag of booted heels on the heavy tile steps, perhaps the boots of a good-sized person. The stomp grew louder as the steps drew near, then scraped to a halt as they reached her cell. Moving away from the door, Hannah backed into the corner and held her breath as keys rattled in the lock.

"Good. Ye're awake. Sloan tires of waiting and I damn sure ain't gonna carry ye to him. Move yer ass." A scowling man jerked his double chins in the direction of the hall as he stood scratching his belly with the end of the keys dangling on the large ring held in his hand.

Hannah glared at the squat, balding guard. With those fat, stubby legs and that oversized gut, she bet she could outrun the man easily. The problem was, where would she go once she got out of the cell?

"Don't even think about it, bitch. I may be short and fat, but I can zap yer scrawny ass back in this cell so fast it will make yer uppity little head spin off yer spindly neck. I may not have as much magic as your glorious protector, but I gots me enough to keep the likes o' you in line. So, keeps that in mind before ye go gettin' stupid." Digging at his crotch, he swung the door wider and jerked his head again. "Now come on. Sloan's in a pissy mood and I ain't takin' no clubbin' o'er the likes of a bitch like you."

Hannah cringed and wrinkled her nose. This guy's stench matched his looks. Sidling by him, she moved into the hallway, trying to take note of all her surroundings. She couldn't remember how she'd ended up in this place, but she had to figure out a way to get out.

"That way." The guard shoved her down the hallway to the right, snickering as Hannah slipped on the highly polished floor. "Kinda slickery, ain't it? Yeah, Sloan likes the place kept spotless. It's easier to drag the bodies out that way."

"Bodies?" Hannah swallowed hard against a wave of

churning nausea. A distinct whiff of rotted flesh floated up from the hallway to her left. Her gag reflex kicked in at the stench and she slapped her hand over her mouth. She'd be damned if she'd give the guard the satisfaction of making her retch.

"Yeah, bodies." With a glint in his eye, the guard leaned his sweaty face close and tapped the keys as he nodded toward the doors lining the halls. "Every day when we hose out the cells, the slick floors make it easier to drag the bodies out to storage."

"You have prisoners die every day?" Hannah asked, remembering the sounds she'd heard while listening at the door.

"Sure." The guard nodded as he splattered her face with a wet belch that smelled like putrefied fish. "They die because I gets to gut 'em."

She'd held out against the nauseating odors and sounds of torture as long as she could. Hannah gagged and projectile vomited all over the hall. Her head spinning, she stumbled to a squatting position before she risked blacking out and lost her footing completely. Closing her eyes, she held her head in her hands. She couldn't believe this was happening. This had to be a nightmare and she just needed to wake up. None of this horrifying suffering could be real. She just needed to open her eyes and it would all be over.

"Now look what ye did!" the guard hissed. "They'll make me clean that shit up."

The bolted door in front of them clattered open to reveal Mia's hooded face. "I thought I heard Corter's lovely voice." Glancing at the splattered mess all over the hallway, Mia shook her head. "This will not do. Corter, please clean this up. Ye know Sloan will not be pleased. I will escort Hannah the rest of the way into the sitting room."

"I'm gonna enjoy it when it's time to rip out your guts!

They promised I get to be the one to kill ye." Corter snarled against her face as he yanked Hannah up from the floor and shoved her into Mia's arms.

Mia caught Hannah and graced her with a sadistic smile as she dug her nails into Hannah's upper arm. Brushing Hannah's hair back from her face, she patted her cheek a little too hard. "There, there now. Pay no attention to Corter. He enjoys killing all of our guests here at the hall."

With a shaking breath, Hannah yanked her arm out of Mia's grasp. "Somehow, I don't find that very comforting." The cold glint in Mia's eyes reminded her of a snake about to strike.

Shrugging a narrow shoulder, Mia pushed back her hood and motioned for Hannah to follow the rest of the way down the gleaming hallway. "Each of us has a time to die, Guardian. Corter merely enjoys sending people on their way. I just did not want ye to feel he singled ye out because ye are supposedly sacred. When ye have served your purpose, Corter will not enjoy your death any more then he enjoys the death of any other."

"When I have served my purpose?" Hannah repeated as she retreated a few steps away from Mia down the hallway. "What purpose?"

Mia turned; her forehead furrowed with obvious frustration as she glanced first toward the larger doorway up ahead, then back to where Hannah stood. "Ye will learn your purpose soon enough. Your fate is sealed, Guardian. Ye might as well accept it. It will make things much easier for all creatures concerned. Now, please follow me."

"Uh-uh." Hannah crossed her arms over her chest and took another step back. This chick hadn't met hardheaded yet. She might be their prisoner, but that didn't mean she was going to make it easy on them. "If you think I'm going to let you lead me like a lamb to slaughter, then you don't know who you're dealing with. I'm not moving until you tell me what's going on. I deserve a fighting chance."

"I will not tell ye because Sloan will kill me, and I will not die for one such as you." Mia floated forward, her eyes darkening into narrow slits as she edged closer to Hannah.

Hannah stiffened, her muscles tensed, and her heart pounded so hard she swore the sound echoed off the blinding white walls of the hallway. Knotting her hands into trembling fists, she waited for Mia to make the first move.

Mia raised her hand, opened her palm, and blew into Hannah's face. A choking green dust cloud enveloped Hannah's head and seized all of her senses. Her eye watered, her nostrils burned, her lungs clenched as though a vise clamped them shut. Gasping, Hannah dropped to the floor, clawing at her flaming throat. Kicking and writhing, Hannah fought to free herself of the noxious herb. Blinded by the tears burning her eyes, Hannah flailed and clutched at her chest. *Air.* She needed precious air. The lining of her lungs raged and burned as though dipped in acid. *Damn Mia.* She didn't fight fair.

Mia raised her voice as she bent over Hannah; her words rang clear and sadistic in her tone. "Do not challenge me, Hannah. If ye feel ye have learned your lesson, I will cleanse ye of the poison. Are ye ready to follow me down the hallway?"

Hannah managed a weak jerk of her head between spasms and bleated out a cry of relief when Mia dusted her body with a pale yellow herbal cloud. Hannah wheezed a shuddering gasp and trembled in a curled ball at Mia's feet. Before she escaped this accursed place, she'd snap Mia's infernal neck. She'd never been much for revenge before, but something about being tortured really pissed her off.

"Now follow me to Sloan," Mia instructed and waited at the door.

Hannah raked the back of her hands across her face and pulled herself up from the floor. She couldn't remember when she'd been so enraged. Fury thundered with every beat of her heart, replacing the icy terror of the unknown. Where in the hell were Taggart and the cavalry? There was a war to wage.

As she staggered down the hallway, Hannah blinked away the residual poisons and followed Mia through the doorway into an opulent sitting room. Garish and swathed in purple, red, and gold velvets, Hannah cringed at the gaudy décor of the chamber. Sloan's private decorator must've gotten a hell of a deal on velvet. Glancing around the room, a chill of nausea shuddered through her again, this time from the assault of tacky colors. The room looked like a cross between a western whorehouse parlor and a velvet circus tent.

"I take it ye do not appreciate fine décor?" Sloan observed from the shimmering settee beside the blazing hearth.

Hannah spun to face the source of the voice and caught her breath. Sloan of Cair Orlandis wasn't what she expected. Where Taggart stood dark, his brother Sloan glowed light: his hair shimmered the color of molten silver. The long, flowing tresses framed the sides of his chiseled face, accentuating the perfect angles of his seemingly angelic features. He remained seated, but the breadth of his shoulders hinted at the massive size of the man. His long, blackened nails matched his glittering black eyes as he tapped them along the gilt trim of the crushed red velvet settee.

"Are ye deaf, rude, or just inept? I thought guardians were supposed to be intelligent beings, since their touch brought forth the sacred Draecna. Ye've done nothing of interest since ye've arrived except vomit in the hallway."

Sloan ran the tip of his tongue across his perfect, full lips. Flexing like a cat, he leaned back in the chair, crossing his long legs at his well-muscled calves.

That did it. She'd had all she could take. "You know, I've had just about enough of your bullshit." Hannah took a step toward him, brushing off the remaining dust of Mia's poisonous powder and the antidote as she moved. "You kidnap me, lock me in a cell, drag my ass through a hallway that smells like rotted corpses, threaten to kill me once you're done with me and then you ask me if I'm deaf, stupid, or just rude? Well, it's curtain number three. I'm a rude bitch. What are you gonna do about it?" Hannah ignored Mia's sharp intake of breath behind her. She'd passed the point of giving two shits. If they were going to take her down, then by golly, she was going to go down in a blaze of hellatious glory. She'd had enough. They'd better bring it on right now.

Sloan's eyes widened, one corner of his mouth twitched, and he leaned forward to the edge of his chair. "You. You have had enough. Of my *bullshit?*"

Clenching her fists at her side, Hannah lifted her chin. "Yes." She wondered what method he'd try to finish her off. She widened her stance; whatever it was, maybe she'd at least get one good kick at his crotch.

Sloan slid forward, stretched to his full height, threw back his head, and roared. His laughter echoed throughout the chamber until tears streamed down his face. "*Bullshit.* Ye have had enough of my . . . bullshit. I find that so verra amusing." Strolling over to Hannah, he traced a cold fingernail along her jaw as he continued to chuckle and snort. "Such a beauty and such wondrous fire. Perhaps we shall come to an *understanding.*"

"I very much doubt that," Hannah hissed, recoiling from Sloan's touch. Bitter bile burned on the back of her

tongue. She wished she had something left in her clenching stomach to vomit all over Sloan's tacky, iridescent
dressing gown.

"Pity," Sloan hummed as he spun on one fine leather
heel and returned to perch on his velvet seat. "I grow
bored with Mia and need a replacement in my chambers.
Although from the stench of ye, it smells like ye've already
mated to my brother."

"Mated?" Hannah's stomach flip-flopped and nether regions fluttered at Sloan's choice of words. "What exactly
do you mean by *mated*?" They'd had unbelievable sex, but
nobody had said anything about a permanent arrange-
ment.

Idly rubbing his thumb across his lower lip, Sloan fixed
Hannah with a seductive smile. "Did ye or did ye not have
sex with Taggart?"

Hannah caught her lower lip between her teeth. She
flushed hot as a sea of memories flooded through her body
of the night she and Taggart had shared. "I don't believe
that's any of your business."

Shaking his head, Sloan gifted her with an evil chuckle.
"Well, dearest Guardian, my business or not, Taggart
made it quite evident when he marked ye as his own."
Sloan motioned toward her chest with a flutter of his
hand. "It is our *way*, woman. When we find one we are
no longer willing to share with any other males. Any male
from Erastaed, or several other realms I might add, who
gets anywhere near ye can clearly smell Taggart's scent
upon ye. *You* are his mate. There is no mistaking it."

"He didn't tell me," Hannah whispered. Why hadn't he
told her? Hannah ached at the thought of Taggart.
Dammit! Why hadn't he told her?

Sloan's smile widened and his eyes narrowed as he
stroked at the silver stubble sprouted on the very tip of his
chin. "Truly?" Leaning to the side, he looked around Han-

nah and cast a malicious sneer in Mia's direction. "Did ye hear that, Mia? Taggart marked Hannah as his mate, but forgot to tell her about it. What do ye suppose that means, Mia? How long were ye with Taggart? How long were the two of ye betrothed and Taggart never chose to mark ye as his mate? As a matter of fact, I don't even think the two of ye even had sex, did ye? Whatever could have happened there? Could it be ye were a coward, perhaps? What say ye to that, Mia?"

"Taggart loved me," Mia hissed as she shot Hannah a hate-filled glare.

"Ah, but he never marked ye, not once in all the times ye professed ye were his betrothed. Not once in all the times ye stood together before the council. Are ye sure he loved ye, Mia? If he loved ye, perhaps he marked ye and ye didna know it. Did ye check to be certain? Did he mark ye? Even once? I don't detect his scent upon ye." Wagging his finger, Sloan winked at Hannah as he rose and sidled closer to Mia.

Mia dropped her eyes and avoided Sloan's gaze. "No, my love. He never marked me. Not once."

Sloan frowned at Mia and jerked his head toward the corner. "Go over there until I summon ye. As usual, ye are a complete disgrace to me."

Taking a deep breath, Sloan shrugged the tension from his shoulders and returned his features to that of a benevolent host as he turned back and extended his arm to Hannah. "Walk with me, Hannah. Ye have nothing to fear. I assure ye. I will not harm ye."

Hannah believed that about as much as she believed she'd picked the winning lottery numbers on this week's ticket. Pure evil radiated from the depths of Sloan's cold, black eyes. Death reflected in his gaze.

"Mia and Taggart should've mated and brought forth an army of Draecna hybrids." Sloan stroked his silver-tipped nails across the back of Hannah's hand as they walked across the sumptuous carpet to a raised pedestal at the far corner of the room. "But instead, when Mia realized Taggart was, shall we say, a bit different, she could not bring herself to consummate the deal. I told the boy he should've taken her before he turned, but Taggart always did have a twisted sense of honor."

As they walked, Hannah yearned to yank her hand out of Sloan's moist, cloying grasp. The repeated stroke of his blackened, silver-tipped nails made her skin crawl. Gritting her teeth, she kept her eyes straight ahead and concentrated on her breathing. "I get it, Sloan. They never had sex, but they were betrothed and Mia backed out when she found Taggart was a hybrid. Is that pretty much it in a nutshell?" Hannah spat it all out in one explosive breath. Lord, she wished he'd send her back to her cell. She'd rather sit on that cold, damp floor than have him touching her skin.

"My, aren't we a bit tense?" Sloan tapped the tips of his nails on the back of her hand until her flesh stung with every rap of his fingers.

Gritting her teeth, Hannah steeled herself against her throbbing hand and concentrated on the softly glowing Draecna egg she'd just spotted on the raised pedestal before them. Nodding toward it, she turned to Sloan. "So, is that why you stole that Draecna egg? Because you want to start your own army of Draecna?"

"Something like that." Sloan chuckled as he released her to slide his hands beneath the Draecna egg. With a loving smile, he cradled it into his arms and hugged it against his chest. "What has Taggart taught ye of these delightful beasts? Has he told ye of all their wondrous possibilities?"

Uneasiness roiled in the pit of Hannah's stomach and churned like an angry sea. Taggart had told her very little about the Draecna, but she couldn't let Sloan know that.

With a nod toward the rose-colored egg in Sloan's grasp, Hannah fixed Sloan with her most convincing smile. "I know that little one needs me to be able to see the light of day." She hoped that was true. William had needed her help to emerge from his shell, and Taggart had hinted at that when they visited the nursery at the caves.

As Sloan brought the egg closer to Hannah, the corner of his right eye twitched with an uncontrollable tick. The inner light of the egg strengthened in its intensity the nearer he brought the egg to Hannah. "Then bring forth life, Hannah. This one has waited a very long time to, how did you put it? See the light of day?"

No way. Did he think her a fool? Hannah shivered with the cold certainty that if she released that Draecna, Sloan would order her immediate execution. No matter what, that little hatchling had to stay inside that egg. Clasping her hands behind her back, Hannah shook her head. "I don't think it's ripe yet."

Sloan's face darkened as he frowned first at the egg, then back up at Hannah. "I can see its heart beating strong with every flash of the light. I can see every movement of the little beast. How much longer before it will be ready to hatch? How much longer until ye can release it?"

Making a great show of looking over the egg but taking great care not to touch it, Hannah kept her hands behind her back and racked her brain for every bit of information Taggart had ever told her. "Not much longer. I'll be able to sense it when the time is right. I just helped hatch William, so I'm sure it won't be too long." That wasn't a lie, so if Sloan's magic enabled him to read her mind, he wouldn't catch her in an untruth.

"Mia!" Sloan barked as he returned the egg to its velvet-cased pedestal and waved his hand to increase the heat of the warming stones.

Mia scurried to his side, her head bowed but raised

enough to shoot a murderous glare in Hannah's direction. "Yes, my love."

"Return the guardian to her cell."

"Corter will inquire about today's killing hour, my love," Mia said as her gaze darted in Hannah's direction. Her pale eyes glittered with anticipation as the tip of her tongue snaked across her lower lip.

With a benevolent smile at Hannah and a sneer at Mia, Sloan gave a gracious shake of his head as though his audience should be grateful he deigned to give them an answer. "Don't be an idiot, Mia. We shall suffer her to live for now, at least until I grow bored with her. Simply shift her to a different cell at the stroke of each killing hour. That will amuse Corter enough. He can pretend he's emptying her cell. He can even hose her down if he likes."

Mia's shoulders slumped and she glared at Hannah from beneath her tattered hood.

"Oh and Mia," Sloan sniffed as he pulled a lace-edged handkerchief from his gold-trimmed sleeve and pressed it to his lips. "She's not to be tormented overly much, for if she is, I will ensure whatever happens to her is visited thrice upon you."

"Yes, my love."

"I dinna know what to do," Taggart grumbled betwixt gritted teeth. He stood centered in the nursery and glared at the remaining eggs scattered in their spots upon the pedestal. His hands clenched at his sides, he focused on the eggs until he finally exploded. "Kill that damned music! By all that's holy, I need blessed silence to figure out this impossible task." The delicate strains of the violins faded away into the shadowed crevices of the jagged ceiling.

"Now it feels like we're in a tomb," Gearlach grumbled. His voice bounced against the polished gray walls and echoed across the circular cavern.

"At least it's nice and warm down here and we can still smell the pretty flowers." William raised his snout in the air, snorted a loud breath, and sneezed.

Inhaling a deep breath, Taggart closed his eyes. The young Draecna was right. The scent of the moon lilies calmed his nerves as the fragrance stroked his senses. Sweet and clean, like Hannah. His Hannah, who had accepted him for the monster he was and still opened both her body and soul. Shaking himself free of the intoxicating memory, he forced himself back to the present. "Septamus, what is the rite to bring them forth? What do I need to do?"

Septamus shook his head as he circled the platform, one gnarled claw waving over the softly glowing eggs. "We need your mother. She helped with the last hatching, even though it proved less than successful. She would know for certain what ye need to do to call them forth out of their shells."

"It's close enough to the hatching moon. Why don't they all just come out?" William reached over and tapped his claw on one of the eggs, jumping when Gearlach thumped him on the back of his horned head.

"Stop that, boy! Are ye daft?"

William sulked as he tucked both forepaws behind his back. "I was just trying to help."

"Well, stop it," Gearlach snapped. "Ye're acting just like me and ye're supposed to be smarter than that."

"I *will not* summon Mother," Taggart insisted, rubbing his chin as he studied the eggs. He hadn't seen Mother since Mia had spurned him just before their matrimonial rites. He wasn't in the mood to see the superior glow of *I told you so* gleaming in her eyes. The Goddess Isla had warned him repeatedly against an alignment with Mia's house. Mother had despised Mia's bloodline for centuries, and she detested Mia personally as well. She had lectured Taggart more than once against pursuing the match, even going so far as to threaten to spell him if he didn't heed her words.

"Just because your mother was right about Mia doesna mean she's going to make you miserable. She knows the conniving woman caused ye a great deal of humiliation and pain. The goddess willna reprimand ye for not heeding her warning." Septamus raised his head to meet Taggart's narrow-eyed glare. "Well, she willna remind ye o'er much. She'll just remind ye of the need to listen to her the next time she chooses to give ye advice." Septamus warned William away from a cluster of moon lilies with a stern jerk of his head.

Much his hybrid arse. Taggart knew better. His mother never missed an opportunity to lecture him on the error of his ways. How gullible did the ancient Draecna think he was? If they summoned his mother, the first words out of her mouth would be that she warned Taggart about that—what was it she used to call Mia?—*useless herb-wielding trollop.* Taggart shuddered. His mother's insistence that Mia was nothing better than a piece of universal trash not fit to wipe the slime from her grandchildren's behinds still echoed clearly in his mind.

"We will do this *without* Mother." Taggart took a deep breath, lifted the nearest egg into his arms, and cradled it as though he held a child. Stroking the smooth surface, he concentrated on the pulsating light and listened to the thrumming heartbeat within. He wished the tenets had been more explicit. They could've at least recorded the steps. There had to be a way he could do this task. He would do this for Hannah. Together, the Draecna would storm Erastaed before it was too late.

The egg warmed in his arms, the play of the light sped to an excited frenzy as the little beast's movements inside the egg became maniacal. Taggart held his breath, stroked the egg, and concentrated on the hatchling within. A cracking sound echoed through the chamber; then frantic scratching against the inside of the shell ensued as the little beast struggled to be free.

"Help him, Taggart. The magic binds the shell tight around us. That's why Mother had to help me." William tapped Taggart on the arm, pointing excitedly to a piece of the shell rising and falling back against the hatchling as though firmly glued in place.

"What did Mother do to help ye, William? Do ye remember what she did?" Taggart kept his concentration centered on the egg as he lowered the egg closer to William.

Shrugging his wings, William nodded toward the undulating shell and extended a hesitant claw. "She peeled the shell away and called out to me. She called me by name and told me not to be afraid. She said she wanted to meet me."

"It canna be that simple." Septamus frowned, edging closer to peer down at the egg in Taggart's arms.

"I guess we'll find out," Taggart muttered. With a hesitant grasp, he grabbed one edge of the rising shell and gave it the slightest tug. An electrical shock jolted up his arm, burst into his shoulder, and exploded with a rupture of searing energy into the muscles of his chest.

"Son of a bitch!" Taggart stumbled backward and nearly dropped the egg as he jerked his hand away from the splintered shell.

"Wow," William observed. "I guess that must be the protective magic."

Rubbing his tingling fingers, Taggart shook his throbbing arm and glared at the little Draecna standing at his side. "The protective magic? Aye, it works verra well. Any more suggestions, William?"

"You forgot to call his name out, remember? Before Mother pulled away the shell, she called me by my name."

Closing his eyes and inhaling a deep calming breath, Taggart reminded himself William was not only extremely young, he was also Hannah's pride and joy. He must be patient. Hannah loved William. "I thought she named ye after she drew ye out of the shell. When I walked in the nursery and she held ye up before me, I distinctly remember her saying, she would call ye William."

William shook his head with a decided frown. "Nope. Ye heard wrong. She said she thought William was a fine name. She had already called me by my name before she pulled the shell away. I heard her say it before I was born. I remember it now. 'Tis the only way the magic knew 'twas safe to release me into her arms."

"How are ye supposed to know their names?" Gearlach asked as he looked out across all the remaining eggs.

"Listen to their whispers." William nodded toward the egg in Taggart's arms. "Can't ye hear him? He's crying out to ye even now."

Taggart frowned at William, then eyed the rumbling egg in his arms. He didn't hear anything other than scratching and the occasional thump accented with the odd-placed hissing growl. Hitching the egg closer up against his chest, he held his breath and leaned his head closer.

"Nostradamae." The whispered growl murmured from the depths of the shell.

"Nostradamae," Taggart repeated, flinching as he grabbed the cracked edge of the shell and pulled. He braced himself for another painful jolt, but instead found himself nose to nose with a moist, green snout.

The struggling hatchling pushed his head through the membrane of the egg with a pop as the rest of the shell gave way. Nostradamae purred and rubbed his slimy muzzle against Taggart's chin as he clambered the rest of the way out of his shell.

"See? All ye had to do was call his name. Now ye've only got eighteen more to go." William triumphantly bobbed his head, bouncing excitedly around Taggart.

"William, hush!" Septamus growled, drawing closer to examine the newly hatched young Draecna Taggart held in his arms. "He must also meld with each and every one of them. They must all taste of Taggart's DNA to accelerate to the level of maturity needed."

"Taste of Taggart's DNA?" William asked. He glanced at the hatchling squirming on Taggart's chest, then tugged on Septamus's wing. "How?"

"I can hear ye both and I don't need the additional step-by-step commentary. I need silence to accomplish this task!" Taggart shot them both a withering glare. Septamus knew better. He was an upper-level Draecna. He had even served in Taggart's mother's court.

Septamus bowed his head in Taggart's direction and silenced William with a thump on the tip of his snout. "Forgive us, Taggart. Please continue your task and we will monitor your progress in the *peace and quiet* you require."

Rolling the tension out of his shoulders, Taggart assumed his Draecna form. Nostradamae trilled and flapped his damp, little wings, his glowing eyes widening at Taggart's sudden metamorphosis.

"I willna hurt ye little one. Ye will soon be nearly as big as I." Unsheathing one of his silver-tipped claws, Taggart opened a gash in the center of his left palm. As he held his hand over the hatchling's forehead, he allowed three drops of his blood to fall between Nostradamae's horns in the center of his tiny, wrinkled forehead. Sending up a silent prayer for the melding to work, Taggart placed his right hand firmly atop the little Draecna's head and concentrated his memories of the last seven hundred years. As Taggart's right hand glowed, the blood soaked into the hatchling's hide and disappeared as though it had never been there. Nostradamae's physical size increased over a matter of minutes until he stood nearly as large and muscular as Taggart.

When Taggart broke the connection, the young Draecna opened his eyes. His deep voice rumbled from the depths of his broad, sparkling chest. "I am ready to battle at your side, Father. When do we leave for Erastaed?"

Taggart exhaled. Thank the heavens. The melding worked and no sign of poisoned sanity shone in the Draecna's eyes. The tension in his chest eased a bit as he smiled at the powerful young Draecna in front of him. Then he cast a narrow-eyed glance at the rest of the eggs waiting on the warming platform. "As soon as I awaken the rest of your siblings, Nostradamae, we leave for Erastaed."

At least the floor of this cell caught the warmth of the afternoon sun as it beamed in from the one narrow window overhead. Hannah hugged herself away from what appeared to be a fresh bloodstain splattered across the farthest wall.

Several winged insects buzzed about her head, circling close to her eyes. Flinching, Hannah batted them away from her face. The scent of the blood must be drawing some sort of gnats or flies in through the uncovered window.

"Cease your attack, Lady Guardian. We bring word from Taggart. Ye must not release the hatchling. Your very life depends on it."

Great. She must be losing her mind. Now she'd started hearing voices. Sitting up straighter, Hannah flattened her back against the wall and stared out into the emptiness of the cell. "Who said that?" Hannah croaked; her throat flinched as she forced the words out of her parched lips.

One of the flies buzzed in her tangled hair. "Taggart sent us to warn you. Do not release the hatchling. You will be safe quite soon."

Hannah sat very still and prayed what the fly said was true. Her heart pounded so hard it nearly closed off her throat as she swallowed hard to control her excitement. "I already figured out not to release the hatchling. I know once I do, Sloan won't need me anymore. But tell Taggart to hurry up. I can hear the little Draecna constantly scratching. I don't know how much longer she's going to be able to wait. She really wants out of her shell."

"She?" The fly vibrated near Hannah's ear. "Are ye certain the hatchling is a female?"

Hannah nodded, almost shaking the fly from its spot on her shoulder. "Yes. This one is a female. Her name is Esme. Why do you sound so surprised?" She struggled to tamp down her rising hysteria; she had never realized until now that the buzz of a fly could ever sound surprised.

"Another female isn't due to be born for at least several hundred years. Most hatchlings are male. It's the way of the Draecna, Lady Guardian. 'Tis verra complicated."

Hannah closed her eyes and leaned her head against the wall. Great. This news must not be good. She wished Taggart had given her a handbook on Draecna lore. It seemed like every time she turned around, she found another tidbit she should've known. "Okay, I'll bite. Why are Draecna females so rare? And is this a good thing or a bad thing?" She dreaded the fly's answer. She had a niggling suspicion that a Draecna female hatching right now wouldn't be a good thing.

The fly fluttered its wings and rubbed its forelegs together as it repositioned itself on a strand of Hannah's hair. "Draecna females have the power of bringing forth new life and bestowing the gift of immortality to humans.

Their mystical powers are much greater than those of the Draecna males. Female Draecna are truly precious indeed."

"That's just great. So, I've not only got to keep Esme in her egg to save my life, but we've got to keep her out of Sloan's hands to keep him from becoming immortal. Is that what you're telling me?" Dropping her head forward into her hands, Hannah dislodged the fly. Lack of sleep and spoiled and meager food had her head throbbing like a fiend. She couldn't think straight, couldn't function. When would this nightmare end?

Buzzing around her head, the fly whizzed close to her ear. "Keep the female in her egg. Taggart storms Tiersa Deun soon. I will tell him her time nears and the news that the hatchling is a female. Ye must stay strong, Lady Guardian. Ye must not give up hope."

"This cannot be real," Hannah muttered into the darkness of her arms as she cradled her pounding head. She'd thought Grandma's stories were just weird fairy tales. Apparently, she should've been taking notes about those magical creatures resembling the mythical dragons. It might've prepared her for a lover who turned into a hybrid-mix of one of those mystical beings. If she'd listened more closely, she might've known what to do when she found herself imprisoned in a strange new world.

Squeezing her eyes hard against the threat of stinging tears, Hannah choked back the aching knot in her throat. "Why didn't you tell me the truth, Grandma? Why didn't you make it more clear what you were trying to teach me?"

The cell door swung aside with a clattering bang and Corter slapped his iron hoop of keys against the wall. "Wake up! The egg is cracking, but Sloan says somethin' is wrong. Get yer ass in gear!"

Now what was she going to do? A wave of nausea burned the bile up into her throat; a cold sweat trickled down her spine. Pulling herself up from the floor, she searched her memories for all the tales her Grandmother had ever told her. She frantically tried to remember everything Taggart had said. There had to be something to delay Esme's hatching. Stumbling as she pushed herself up on her trembling limbs, Hannah came up blank. There had to be something. What had she missed?

"Come on! What the hell's the matter with ye? Ye'd think ye'd be ready for this to be over. Ye may as well quit yer stallin'. Look at it this way, once we kills ye, ye ain't gonna be in these here cells no more." Corter grabbed her by the arm and shoved her into the hall.

"Do not touch her like that again, Corter!" Mia snapped from farther down the corridor. "Until the hatchling is released, the guardian is not to be harmed. Remember Sloan's words. I do not wish to be tortured just because ye canna control your actions with the woman."

"I didna hurt her," Corter snapped. "Did I hurt ye?" He pushed Hannah toward Mia, who awaited them at the great arched doorway.

"Let's just get on with it," Hannah sighed. What was that old saying? If she knew then what she knew now? If only she'd known Mia was that cute little kitten, she would've snatched her up by the scruff of her neck and fed her to Gearlach.

"Get her in here now or I shall be forced to destroy the lot of ye!" Sloan's bellow echoed out into the hall from beyond the opened doorway.

As soon as Hannah entered the room, she sensed it wasn't good. The egg illuminated the entire room; its rosy internal life-beat heightened to a frenzied glow. Trailing up the midline of the egg crawled a series of ever widening hairline cracks. As Hannah concentrated on the pulsating aura emanating from the center of the watermelon-size egg, her heart fell as the crackling started to spread.

"The beast struggles. The cracks grow, but then they re-
cede, and every time I touch it the wicked little bastard
electrocutes me." Sloan extended the blackened fingertips
of his swollen right hand and nodded toward the egg.
"Release the beast, lest it dies. If the hatchling dies . . ."
Sloan whirled on Hannah with a piercing glare. "So do
you."

Taking a deep breath, Hannah avoided Sloan's gaze and
concentrated on the egg. She couldn't allow Esme to
hatch. Studying the egg, she wondered how well her gift
of communicating would work when she was under so
much stress. She had spoken to William before he'd
hatched. He'd heard her words without any problem. She
had to communicate to Esme and convince her to stay inside her shell.

Esme. Please be still and listen. With a glance at Sloan, she
placed her hands on the egg. He needed to think she was
trying to help Esme hatch.

Closing her eyes, Hannah cleared her mind and concentrated on the young hatchling she could already hear
fussing in her head.

*"Help me toss the shell aside, dearest Guardian. It is so very
stubborn!"*

*"Esme, I need you to stay in your shell a few days longer.
These people are evil and it's not safe for you to come into the
world just yet. You need to wait until Taggart and the other
Draecna arrive to rescue us."*

*"I'm afraid that's not possible. I have waited to hatch for over
three hundred years. I am truly ready. Please, Guardian. Please
help me emerge into the wondrous world."*

*"Esme, it's not safe. Please try to understand. These people
stole your egg. You are not in the safety of Taroc Na Mor. They
want to control you and make you their slave. Please stay inside
your shell just a little longer. Taggart is coming to save us both,
and then I promise you can come out."*

"I can wait but three days more, Guardian. I can wait no longer."

"It may take longer, Esme. I'll let you know when it's safe to come out. Please promise me you'll wait until I tell you it's safe to emerge."

"Three days is all we have left, Guardian. After that time, I shall die."

Hannah swallowed hard, smoothing her hands across the warm egg, relieved to see the cracking shell smooth over and seal itself shut. Esme would wait the allotted three days. Taggart better hurry.

"What the hell did you do?" Knocking Hannah out of the way, Sloan bent to examine the now flawless shell.

Hannah held her breath as she cringed on the floor. Sloan's face flushed to a decided shade of enraged purple. As he turned from his perusal of his precious egg, his hands clenched into shaking fists as he loomed closer to Hannah's face.

Hannah skittered backwards away from Sloan until she bumped into the corner. "It wasn't time. If the hatchling had come out now, he would've died," she lied. She kept her eyes wide, hoping Sloan would believe her. She'd never been good at telling tales.

"You lie!" Sloan accused through tightly clenched teeth. "I see it in your eyes!"

"No!" Hannah shouted, ducking her head. "That's why the egg shocked you so badly whenever you touched it. The shell was damaged and needed to be healed." God, she hoped he'd buy that lie. Since he hadn't seemed to have known why the shell had zapped him, maybe he would buy her story.

Sloan paused, his eyes narrowed as he studied Hannah's face. Turning to Mia, he jerked his chin toward Hannah. "Is the bitch telling the truth or not? Ye know Draecna lore better then I."

Mia shifted her gaze first to Hannah, then to the egg, then back to Sloan's enraged face. Tightening her thin lips in her pale, drawn face, she gave a regal nod of her head. "The guardian knows all things when it comes to the hatchlings. I watched her with a young one at Taroc Na Mor. While I detest her, ye had best heed her words on the health and well-being of the young one."

"When?" Sloan spit, yanking Hannah up from the floor. "When?" he repeated, sinking his sharp nails deep into the flesh of her upper arm and twisting until Hannah dropped to her knees.

"Three days," Hannah gasped as spots flashed in front of her eyes from the pain ripping through her shoulder. That wasn't a lie. One way or another, three days was all the time Esme had given her and Taggart to make something happen.

Throwing her into Corter's greasy chest, Sloan barked, "Bring her back to me in three days' time."

"A female?" Taggart worried his hand through his hair. A female Draecna complicated matters tenfold. "Are ye certain she said the hatchling was a female?"

"She was quite clear, my prince. She said the female's name was Esme."

"Septamus!"

"I heard him. Stop bellowing. Do ye wish to announce our presence to everyone in Erastaed?" Septamus wrestled his snout through the narrow opening of the tent and shoved his way through the canvas flap. "By the way, how the hell do ye expect to fit inside this infernal thing when ye assume your Draecna form? I have to hunch over just to keep my horns from snagging the rigging and yanking down the poles."

"Septamus, ye've done nothing but complain ever since we crossed the threshold and led the Draecna through the pass at Ruarke Ridge. Can ye no' survive beyond the walls of the nursery? Can ye no longer stomach the mountains of Erastaed?"

Septamus huffed two clouds of blackened smoke as he yanked his horns free of the lines holding the canvas tent tight between the shining black poles. "Mind your tongue, ye rash hybrid. Ye know as well as I, 'twould be much more efficient to campaign across Erastaed with equipment well-fitted to the size of a full-blooded Draecna rather than a puny human."

Waving away his words, Taggart continued studying the map draped across the table and ran his fingers along a jagged blue line. "Once I assume my Draecna form, we won't be returning to this infernal camp overlooking Sloan's keep."

"The flies say they keep her in the death cells and relocate her to a new one at the stroke of the killing hour. They are not able to tell us the location of the egg. But I am certain Sloan keeps it with him in his chambers." Septamus peeled back the map to show a detailed schematic of Tiersa Deun and tapped his claw on a highlighted wing. "And ye realize when ye steal them both out from under his nose, your brother will not be satisfied until he sees ye both dead."

"The death cells," Taggart hissed. Hannah was interred in the bowels of Tiersa Deun, the same place where Sloan tortured his prisoners for his own amusement until death brought them merciful release. "I think 'tis time Erastaed had a cleansing. This time, I willna go quietly to another world."

Septamus responded with a single nod of his gray horned head. "I will spread the word. I am sure there will be many ready to join us. Ye have had centuries of followers waiting for ye to decide to reclaim your throne."

Taggart ripped aside the tent flap and stormed to the

edge of the cliff overlooking the densely wooded gorge hiding the fortress of Tiersa Deun. He glared out across the mist-covered landscape, the purple-hazed mountains, and the jagged, unforgiving terrain. A mournful howl trebled across the barren vista. Home. What a mockery of the word. He snorted; his breath fogged in the chill of the evening air.

Humiliated at the altar, stripped of his birthright, and forced to watch everything he loved destroyed. How could he think of Erastaed as home? A cold, bitter wind whipped at his back as though trying to shove him even closer to the painful memories. The sea lay just a few miles to the west of the gorge. The stench of rotted fish hung heavy in the air. Taggart rubbed his hand across his face. Sloan had hunted to extinction the graceful blue terns that kept the beaches picked clean of any carrion. He said their early-morning keening annoyed him whenever he tried to sleep.

"Taggart! Where are you?"

Gooseflesh shivered the hair straight up on the back of his neck. Taggart whirled and scanned the grove of gently swaying trees behind him. He had clearly heard Hannah's voice.

"Hannah! Hannah, where are ye?"

The first of twin Erastaedian moons swelled full in the early evening sky. Whisps of clouds raced across its mottled surface, streaming through its eerie light. The blue white sentinel illuminated the encampment almost as brightly as a burning torch.

"Taggart, please . . . please tell me you can hear me."

Looking up into the brilliant light of the swollen moon, Taggart realized he heard Hannah's thoughts. *"Hannah! I hear ye. Are ye looking at the moonlight? If ye are, ye must not look away or we will surely lose the connection."*

"Yes! It's shining into my cell. Please, you've got to hurry and

save us. Esme only has three days and then she's going to die if she doesn't hatch. I'll have to release her in three days. I can't allow her to die."

Only three days? Taggart's wind expelled from his chest as though Hannah had sucker-punched him.

"Taggart. Did you hear me? Are you still there?"

"Hannah. I will come for ye, I swear. Ye must not give up hope, my love. Promise me ye'll not release the hatchling. I give ye my oath, I will be there in time." Taggart paced along the edge of the cliff, kicking at the clumps of dried grass. Hannah mustn't free the young Draecna from its egg. As soon as she did, Sloan would kill her. *"Hannah, promise me?"*

Nothing but silence echoed across the ridge as the wind smothered the glowing beacon of the night with a blanket of impenetrable clouds.

CHAPTER NINE

"And on the third day, she brought the hatchling forth and then was relieved of her head." Sloan chuckled as he clicked his blackened nails together beneath his silvered goatee.

Her hands behind her back, Hannah held her breath as she peered at the egg. Esme lay coiled tight as a spring, more than ready to emerge. Hannah sensed the impatient young female knew what day had arrived and longed for Hannah's touch.

"I will protect ye, Guardian. I have been listening to the evil ones. I know exactly what to do."

Hannah swallowed hard and reminded herself to breathe as she rubbed her hands together. She appreciated Esme's bravado, but she remembered her precious little William and couldn't imagine an immature young Draecna protecting much of anything. *"Protect yourself, Esme. You don't have a flame since you're a young one. As soon as you hatch, I want you to run and find someplace to hide. Promise me you'll run as fast as you can. Don't worry about me. I'll try to distract them so you can get away."*

A warm, comforting giggle erupted through Hannah's mind, perfectly matching the pulsating glow emitting from the egg. *"Females are born fully matured with complete knowl-*

edge and control of all Draecna powers, dear Guardian. It is the silly males who require all the patience and training because they are so immature."

"Well, score one for the females," Hannah muttered under her breath. Maybe that would level the playing field just a little.

"What did you say?" Sloan rose from his chair and clamped a hand on her shoulder.

"Do you want me to hatch the egg or not?" Hannah flinched as Sloan's nails dug into her flesh. She hoped Esme fried him to a crispy crunch but used a nice slow flame when she did it. "I have to call the hatchling out of the egg. Now, if you'll step back, I'll get on with it."

With a narrow-eyed glare, Sloan lifted his hand and retreated half a step. Folding his arms across his chest, he jerked his chin in the direction of the egg.

"It's showtime, Esme," Hannah whispered. "Are you ready?"

The shell splintered into a thousand fiery cracks, blinding light rays shot out from the interior of the egg. A roaring wind filled the room as pieces of shell exploded away. A darkened form inside the whirling light unfurled, stretched, and uncurled, filling the room. The egg pedestal groaned beneath the weight of the expanding Draecna. The structure collapsed beneath Esme's feet and crumbled to dust beneath her full-grown form.

"By all that is holy, the hatchling is a female." Mia edged her way behind a marble likeness of Sloan reclining on his favorite chaise lounge.

Sloan eased a few steps back and placed the bug-eyed Corter between himself and the glowering, newly hatched Draecna. "Ye will never escape Tiersa Deun. The magical wards will kill ye both as soon as ye pass between them."

"Order them disabled, Sloan of Cair Orlandis, or feel the heat of my very first blaze." Esme widened her great, golden eyes and bent her iridescent, blue head closer to his face.

The room shook as a blast echoed beyond the door. Masonry dust and chunks of gaudy painted plaster spattered loose from the vaulted ceiling and rained down all around them. Alarms sounded. High-pitched sirens pealed through the air as more explosions followed.

Hannah stumbled against Esme's side, dodging flying debris as bits of stone and marble whizzed past her head. Choking on the dust, Hannah held tight to the edge of Esme's wing. Taggart. It had to be Taggart and his army; Hannah's heart soared.

"If ye let them take either one of them, I will impale ye in the center courtyard and let the dogs rip out your entrails while ye're still alive to watch them." Sloan shoved Corter through the rubble toward a doorway beside his settee. "Release the Waerins. Taggart willna' expect an army of those beasts."

"Come on, Esme. It's time to go." Hannah tugged on the Draecna wing and motioned toward a gaping hole in the wall. More blasts shook through the building and rattled the foundation under Hannah's feet.

"If ye take one more step . . ." Sloan started toward her only to come up short as a wall of flames spread across his path.

"Very impressive." Hannah smiled up at Esme. "You're going to be able to teach Gearlach quite a bit about control. Did you fry him or just delay him?"

With a slow turn of her graceful, horned head, Esme urged Hannah toward the opening in the wall with the tip of her tail. "A Draecna does not take a life unless absolutely necessary. There is a history to be settled between

Sloan and his brother. If I killed him, it would leave loose ends for Taggart. It is not my battle to fight."

Pausing to peer one last time into the cloud filled room, Hannah fell back against the pile of rubble when she spotted Mia's crushed body trapped beneath a collapsed column. Closing her eyes against the gruesome carnage, Hannah shuddered and swallowed hard. Apparently, Mia's karma came back to bite her with a vengeance.

"We must find Taggart, Guardian. The Waerin are a cruel and vicious entity that are difficult to overcome." Esme nudged Hannah once again as another blast rattled around them.

Hannah scrambled over the loose stones and paused, glancing up and down the passage. This hallway differed from any of the others she'd seen. The slate flooring that wasn't destroyed or covered with debris appeared to have plush, red carpeting running down the center.

"This looks like an entry hall. Which way do you think we should go?"

Cocking her head, Esme spread her leathery wings and stretched her graceful neck closer to the ceiling. "That way," she murmured, nodding in the direction of several grotesque golden statues lined in front of mirrored panels along the wall.

As a blast shattered the walls, the end of the hallway disappeared into a cloud of billowing debris. Waving the dust out of her eyes, Hannah coughed and forged ahead. She barely made out the dark outline of several forms edging toward them through the cloud. "Esme, can you see who or what that is up ahead? I can't make out a thing." Her eyes burned, her chest tightened as the air thickened with exploding debris.

"Hannah!"

She'd know that voice anywhere. Taggart! Relief thrilled

through her body, electrifying all her senses. Hannah rushed to claw her way across the rubble.

"No, Guardian!" Esme blocked Hannah with her wing and seared the hallway with a blast of scorching flames.

"What are you doing?" Hannah pounded on Esme's heaving side. "Esme, stop! It's Taggart and the other Draecna."

Esme ignored Hannah and increased the intensity of the blaze to a white-hot inferno until the high-pitched shrieks faded into silence.

Hannah fell to her knees as Esme's fire dwindled away, not wanting to look at the charred remains smoking in their midst. She couldn't comprehend that Esme had destroyed them all. "Esme, it was Taggart. I heard his voice. What have you done?" With a choked sob, she hugged herself, kneeling in the smoking debris scattered all over the floor. She couldn't deal with the pain coursing through her body. She couldn't deal with this misery again.

"It was not your Taggart, Guardian," Esme assured. "I did not have time to warn ye. It was the Waerin. They shape-shift into whatever a human's heart desires most to get close enough for the kill. It is their way. Draecna are able to see through them. Humans cannot."

"Hannah!"

Stepping around the scattered bodies of the still-smoking Waerins, Taggart, in Draecna form, shoved his way through the wreckage.

With a nod in his direction, Esme bared her fangs in a gleaming smile. "There is your true Taggart."

Like an avenging angel, the streaming sunlight behind him created a halo around his outspread wings as Taggart shoved his way through the crater created in the blown away outer wall. Fresh blood glistened on the armor of his Draecna hide; his eyes glowed with the lust of sending his enemies to an early grave.

"Taggart!" Hannah launched herself into his arms and landed onto his chest with a thud. Wrapping her legs around his waist, she clamped her arms around his neck. "My God, I thought she'd roasted you. Esme says he's turned loose Waerins. Sloan says there's an army of them out there. They're attacking your people."

Wrapping his arms around her, Taggart closed his eyes, nuzzling his face deep into her hair as he held her close. "Aye, well, what Sloan doesna realize is that we've got an army of Draecna and that trumps an army of Waerins every time."

Running her palms along the smoothness of his scales, Hannah pressed tighter against him and shivered. A warm glow stirred deep in her belly as she wriggled against his broad, armored chest. Draecna form or not, she relished the safety of his arms. "I missed you," she whispered against the leathery side of his face.

His voice fell to a husky groan as Taggart set her on her feet. "Words canna begin to tell ye the agony I went through when ye were stolen from me." After a tender stroke against her cheek, Taggart reluctantly drew back his scaled hand and sucked in a shuddering breath. "But now is not the time to say all that is in my heart. We must first get ye to safety."

Pulling his hand to her chest, Hannah held it tight. "We just need to get back to Taroc Na Mor and find a way to seal that gateway." The quicker they kissed the land of Erastaed good-bye, the better.

An explosion rattled overhead, shaking debris down all around them. Esme sheltered Hannah with her extended wings and directed Taggart's attention to the collapsing hole in the wall. "Shall we join magics to transport the guardian somewhere a bit safer than the halls of Tiersa Deun?"

Baring his fangs in a grin of agreement, Taggart nodded. "Excellent idea, Esme. We shall wish her to Mother's stronghold in the Crystal Mountains."

He turned to Hannah and steadied her by the shoulders, centering her directly between himself and the calmly waiting Esme. "Stand here. Close your eyes and don't say a word until I tell ye 'tis safe to do so."

Too tired to spar with Taggart about his curt instructions, Hannah closed her eyes and hugged her arms around her chest. He was so bossy. The cramping tension in her shoulders eased a bit. She had to admit, after the torment of the past few days, it was kind of nice to let him take charge. A relaxing sense of security spread through her. She had noticed the warmth and concern echoing in his voice. They'd talk later about his poor choice of words. Taggart and Esme joined the tips of their wings in an arc over Hannah's head. Energy crackled through the air as they laced their claws together. Hannah squinted against the flashing sparks and covered her ears against the deafening roar. The ground around her undulated and surged. She stumbled and fought to maintain her balance as though trapped on a ship tossed about in a storm. Dropping to her knees, Hannah closed her eyes. They had better land soon or she was going to puke. The roaring in her ears finally stopped. She lowered her hands and eased open her eyes.

"Oh my g—it's just like Grandma's fairy tales." Hannah straightened and spun in a slow circle, craning her neck to stare at the ceiling. *Breathe, Hannah.* She twirled more slowly to take in the unbelievable surroundings. The endless cavern glittered with crystal-covered ceilings as high as a Roman cathedral. Chiseled-out walls sparkled with gemstones: emeralds, rubies, sapphires, and garnets. Stalactites and stalagmites shimmered and glowed, reflecting flickering torchlight with the semiprecious stones trapped within their depths. A great stone hearth housed a roaring fire at one side of the monstrous cavern. The inviting flames twinkled and danced off every gemmed surface of the cave. Huge pillowed couches and chaise longues beckoned from a seating area holding a table with several tall pitchers and ornately carved tankards.

Torchlit hallways flickered off from the main room, sparkling like diamonds in the distance. Tunnels and cul-de-sacs honeycombed in every direction. The obsidian walls held niches lit with flaming sconces and sumptuous furniture scattered throughout the rooms. Other than the jewels bedecking the walls, red dominated the décor.

"This is really nice. So . . . regal." Hannah kept her hands clenched behind her back. She did her best not to touch anything. During her imprisonment, she'd shifted from one dank cell to another with barely enough food and water to survive. She'd lived like a caged animal, crouching in the corners praying for her release. She couldn't even stand her own smell. "Is your mother here right now? I don't really want to meet her when I'm like . . ." Hannah held her arms aloft as though she'd just risen from a vat of dung. *"This."*

"Yes, Guardian. I am here. Ye wouldna think I would miss the opportunity to greet my honored guest?"

Hannah shielded her eyes as blinding white light exploded into the center of the room.

"Mother likes to make an entrance," Taggart grumbled under his breath.

"And there is nothing wrong with my hearing, Taggart," Isla intoned as the light dimmed and her shape solidified.

Hannah took a step back and edged in close beneath the protection of Taggart's wing, shivering at the sight of the Goddess Isla. The scales of the ancient Draecna who had sacrificed so much gleamed a pure and startling white. Her long trailing beard and the tips of her horns shone as golden as her huge, luminous eyes.

"Welcome to my home, Guardian Hannah MacPherson. I have monitored your journey and ye have done quite well." With a pointed glare in the direction of her son, Isla stretched and resettled her gold-veined wings along her iridescent back. "I have also watched my son's behavior and will speak to him about some of his choices later."

Should she be offended at the goddess's tone? Hannah glanced from Isla's face to Taggart's guarded expression. Was his mother referring to the fact they'd slept together, or something else Taggart had apparently done? Unable to quite pin down their expressions, Hannah's curiosity overcame her reservations about her physical appearance. "Would you mind explaining what you mean by that? I don't mean to sound short, but I've had a *really* long day and I'd just as soon have everything out in the open between us right now. If we're not going to get along, I'd rather we both were up-front about it. I'm not good at games of innuendo."

Stroking a gold-tipped claw through her trailing beard, Isla's snakelike irises flexed. The shimmering skin of her long, smooth face crinkled at the corners of her eyes. "The fire of honesty. Verra good. It will serve ye well in the difficult days that lie ahead." Chuckling, she turned, waddled over to the table, filled the tankards, and nodded for them to sit. "Rest easy, child. I was not referring to the fact that he marked ye as his mate. I look forward to the day when ye place grandchildren at my feet. I am not pleased with the way he accomplished it. He didna honor ye as he should have. It is my son I have issues with, not you."

"Mother," Taggart groaned through tightly clenched teeth. He shot a pleading look in Hannah's direction.

Hannah relaxed and stepped forward. Taggart's mother seemed quite reasonable. "Taggart and I just want to get back to Taroc Na Mor. We've rescued Esme, so now we can return to the nursery and see to the other eggs." She accepted a tankard from Isla and sniffed at the contents. *Wow.* Now that's some potent stuff. Her eyes watered at the fumes wafting up from the depths of the cup. With a slight cough, Hannah moved the cup away from her face and concentrated on Isla's understanding face. "I appreciate all that the Draecna have done, but it's over now. They can return to guarding their portals or wherever it is they came from before Taggart asked for their help."

Isla turned to Taggart, one golden brow rising in a questioning arch. "Ye didna tell her where ye obtained your forces? Ye told her nothing about all that transpired while she was imprisoned in Sloan's keep?" Taggart's tense expression darkened with a meaningful scowl. "I havena had the chance to tell her much of anything *yet.*"

"Taggart?" Hannah risked a sip of wine, choking back another muffled cough as the fiery fluid seared her throat. "What's your mother talking about? What did you do?"

Taggart waved away the wine his mother held out and kneeled at Hannah's side. "All that matters is that you're here . . . safe." Taggart slid her hand into his. "But I can no longer turn my back on my people, Hannah. Please try to understand. We have to stay here. We have to fight and save Erastaed from Sloan."

Sliding her glass onto the low marble table, Hannah drew her hand out of his grasp. *Absolutely not. Not another war.* She'd lost one love to war. She'd be damned if she'd risk another to a senseless battle. "No, Taggart. We can go back home, to Taroc Na Mor. We can go through the portal and seal it off. He'll never find us and we'll be safe. Let the Draecna take care of Sloan. All we have to do is leave here and never come back."

Taggart shook his head, stared down at the floor, then took Hannah's hand back into his. "No, Hannah. I canna desert my people again. I left them once when my father took away my birthright. They've suffered immeasurably under Sloan's rule. Ye've seen him, Hannah. Ye know his cruelty firsthand. If not for the people of Erastaed, the coup would not have been such a success today. They helped us, Hannah. Now, we must help them. I canna turn my back on my people again."

Hannah searched his face, her heart falling at his words. But she had to admit, he had a point. Sloan's ruthlessness . . . Hannah shuddered, reaching out to touch his cheek. Taggart's eyes had changed. Their depths glistened with newfound pride and determination. All the humiliation and loneliness was gone.

"I can't lose you," she whispered through the knot of emotions closing off her throat. Why couldn't he understand? Her soul ached for him to be safe in her arms and never leave her again. She'd risked opening the rusty hinges of her heart. How could he ask her to do this?

Brushing her hair away from her face, Taggart smiled his reassurance. "I've lived over seven hundred years, my love. I'm as close to immortal as I can get. Ye're not going to lose me, Hannah. I promise."

Hannah glanced at Isla, then at Esme, then returned her gaze to Taggart. All of them watched her as though they held their breath. What choice did she have? She'd witnessed Sloan's barbarity in the short time of her imprisonment. Who knew what the populace of Erastaed had suffered over the years? "Fine. We stay until we rid Erastaed of Sloan, and then we go back and seal the gateway."

Pressing his forehead against hers, Taggart wrinkled his nose as he stroked her cheek with his thumb. "Ye're a wonderful woman, my dearest love. Now, all we must do is get ye in a bath. Lest your aroma give away our position."

"You are such an ass." Hannah shoved him away, causing him to topple back on his heels as she rose from the chair and pushed past him.

"The ass will stay here while ye relax and get refreshed. I need to have a few words with him. Gilda will take ye to your bath." Isla nodded to a much smaller, gray Draecna waiting at the farther end of the cavern.

With a haughty nod, Hannah cut her gaze back to Taggart, now sitting in the floor. "Thank you, Isla. I appreciate your hospitality. Obviously, you attempted to teach your son some manners. He just forgets to use them."

Taggart enjoyed the sway of Hannah's hips as she made her way down the cavern toward Gilda. The tightness in his chest had finally eased now that she was safe.

"Ye lied to her, boy. When are ye going to learn to be honest? It makes your life more complicated every time ye turn around. Taggart, how many times do I have to tell ye—"

"Dammit, Mother!" Taggart snarled. "Do ye even take a breath between any of those words?" He hadn't seen her in several hundred years and she'd already started in on him.

"Do not curse at me, young man!" Isla's roar echoed through the cavern, making the gemstone chandelier tinkle as it trembled from the blast.

"Forgive me, Mother." Taggart took a deep breath. Scrubbing the weariness from his face, he reminded himself his mother didn't care he was seven hundred years old. Some things never changed. He'd just let her rant and get it over with.

"When are ye going to tell her ye already destroyed the gateway to Taroc Na Mor?" Isla circled her son as though ready to pounce if he dared answer her in the wrong way.

"I can still send her back." Taggart defended, turning to keep his front to his mother. He'd learned long ago: never ever turn his back on Mother. It didn't prove wise.

"Aye, and if ye send her back, ye know as well as I, ye must send her back alone. When are ye going to tell her that? Are ye also going to tell her that 'tis permanent since the portal has been destroyed?" Isla cuffed him on the back of his head, catching him before he turned to face her in time.

Flinching from the sharpness of the blow, Taggart rubbed his throbbing skull. Holy blazes, Mother truly was pissed this time. "I'm hoping she'll want to stay here with me. I'm hoping it willna matter."

"Ye're hoping." Isla shook her head. "I canna believe I raised such a blithering idiot."

"Mother!"

"The woman is intelligent. Tell her all the facts. She accepted ye as a hybrid, didn't she?"

There was that. "I will tell her soon. As soon as she is rested. Ye have to admit, she has had a very big day."

Pointing a razor-sharp claw within inches of the tip of his nose, Isla growled until the chandelier shuddered again. "Ye will tell her as soon as she finishes her bath. I want no more secrets between the two of ye before the battle is waged. The mating ritual is not complete even though she has been marked. Now make me proud, Taggart! Ye grow too old for this type of nonsense." Clapping her claws together, she disappeared into a mist of shimmering droplets.

Taggart turned and looked at Esme standing quietly in the corner.

"Ye appear to be in a great deal of trouble, Taggart," Esme observed with a subtle nod.

She stood in the center of the crystal alcove in front of the shimmering fountains. By all that's holy, she was a beautiful woman. What had he done to deserve her? Taggart's breath stilled in his chest as need blazed through his body. Her still-damp hair curled down over her shoulders and across the silk wrap clinging to her lovely curves. An ebony wrap shot with silver embroidery encased her like a second skin. Taggart shuddered and swallowed hard. Gilda had chosen well. Taggart clenched his hands; he already felt the black sheen of the material polishing the roundness of her hips and breasts.

His mother's voice nagged at the back of his mind, while lust inflamed his body. He had to talk to her. He had to tell Hannah the gateway back to Taroc Na Mor was gone. Surely then they could move on with their lives. She would accept the reality of things. He knew she would, just as she had accepted him.

"I've been waiting for you." Hannah prowled over to him with a promising smile curling her inviting lips.

Pulling her close, Taggart breathed in the perfume of her hair and the honey-sweet warmth of her still damp skin. "Mother kept me o'er long. Did ye enjoy your bath, my love?"

As she buried her face into his chest, Hannah slid her hands up inside Taggart's shirt. "Not as much as I'm going to enjoy being back in your arms."

Swallowing a groan, Taggart pulled away and tucked her hands into his own. "First, we must talk. I'm afraid there's something I must tell ye, Hannah, about the portal to Taroc Na Mor."

A confused look darkened her eyes as Hannah searched his face. "What are you talking about? You said as soon as we saved your people from Sloan, we could go back to Taroc Na Mor. Enough talk, I missed you and I need you to hold me." Hannah stretched forward and nipped at his chest.

With a groan, Taggart shuddered and took a step back. She wasn't making this any easier. Patting her hands, Taggart hedged and pulled her closer to the bubbling fountains. "Not exactly. I believe I told ye I couldna desert my

people. I never actually went into any details about returning to Taroc Na Mor."

Hannah's eyes narrowed as she jerked her hands out of
his grasp. She circled him slowly, smoothing her robe and
yanking the belt tighter about her waist. "Out with it,
Taggart. What are you *not* saying? You've got a bad habit
of omitting extremely necessary details. You're a great deal
like the little boy who only steals *some* of the cookies from
the cookie jar."

"The portal to Taroc Na Mor has been destroyed."

Hannah stopped in her tracks, clenched the neckline of
her gown, and scowled as if she couldn't believe what she'd
just heard. "Destroyed? As in, gone, like I-can-never-go-
back-ever-again destroyed?"

Taggart tilted his head with a weak shrug of one shoulder. "In a way." She wasn't making this easy on him. The
curve of her cheeks flamed a decided shade of red. A clear
indication the fires of her fury blazed higher. Uneasiness
wrapped icy fingers of worry around his spine and raked
their nails across his gut.

"It's a simple question, Taggart. Either I can go back to
Taroc Na Mor or I can't. Which is it?" Hannah's voice increased several decibels, nearing an irritated shriek.

This wasn't going well. She shouldn't be this upset. After all, at least they were together and she no longer sat inside Sloan's prison. "Hannah, I can use my magic once to
send ye back. But I can only send ye back alone." Taggart
paused, allowing his words to sink in and his frustration
fermented when she didn't say a word. "I canna go with
ye when I send ye back and I can never bring ye back to
Erastaed once ye've gone. We would be separated *forever.*"
God's beard. Why doesn't the woman understand? All that
mattered was the fact that they were together.

Hannah stood with her fists clenched. Her lower lip
trembled as her eyes glistened with unshed tears. "How

did the gateway get destroyed?" she asked with a trembling voice.

Ducking his head, Taggart turned away. He couldn't bear the hurt and recrimination in her eyes. "We overloaded it," he admitted. "Too many of us came through at one time when we brought all the Draecna through."

"So, what you're telling me is," Hannah choked out in a quivering voice, "if you had been more careful, more patient, and had only sent through a few at a time, then I wouldn't have to make the choice between everything I've ever known and loved and the man I've only known for a few months. The man who's brought nothing but chaos into my life."

Somehow, it sounded really bad when she put it like that. Perhaps that was why mother had been so very pissed. With a nod, Taggart replied, "Aye."

"Get out and leave me alone. I can't stand to look at you right now." Hannah pointed at the door as tears spilled down her face.

"Hannah."

"I said, *out.*"

"How many of the outer provinces are still ablaze?" Sloan paced the length of the table, which was in the center of the room and had all the regions of Erastaed mapped out on its surface. Outside the window, the smoke of the burning villages still darkened the horizon. The putrid scent of charred bodies and decaying flesh hung heavy in the air. Sloan inhaled the delectable perfume of the carnage. He just wished his brother's scent reeked among them.

Corter stood in the doorway with his bandaged arm lashed to his side. "At least half a dozen still burn bright. A few more are no more than smoldering piles of ashes."

Studying the table, Sloan traced a nail along a silver-edged line running along one of the mountains to the north and turned his head to read the inscription. "And yet no one has given up Taggart's whereabouts? No one has seen the newest female Draecna or the guardian?"

With a snort, Corter shook his head. "Not even when we stretch them across the fire pits and turn the dogs loose on 'em."

"Such loyalty," Sloan muttered. The people had always loved his brother. Sloan had never understood it. The man was half beast. Were they complete fools? He could turn on them in an instant. "Has anyone sighted the goddess lately? I'm sure with the guardian traipsing about, Isla and her royal guard won't be too far away."

Corter shrugged his unbandaged, hairy shoulder, swiping a grubby hand across his face as he limped closer to the table. "I'm tellin' ye, Sloan. Ain't nobody talkin'. And now that slinkin' Mia's dead. We ain't got no good spies left."

Tapping the table with his longest black fingernail, Sloan scowled up into Corter's face. The man best be glad he'd changed his mind and decided to let the fool live. "Order the Waerins to gather information. Have them use their shape-shifting abilities to source out Taggart and the guardian, but they are not to leave a trail of bodies in their wake. There will be no more killing unless I personally approve it. Is that understood?"

"Why not?" Corter asked. "It'll just save us time later."

With a roll of his eyes, Sloan tugged his handkerchief out of his sleeve and pressed it to his lips. Corter's stench reeked worse than usual, accentuating the fact that he was such a bloodthirsty little minion. "If we allow things to calm down a bit, perhaps Taggart and Hannah will relax and show themselves."

Corter's eyes widened with understanding. "Ahh. I gotcha now. I'll talk to Metador and have him take it from there."

Sloan inhaled the perfume scenting his lace-trimmed handkerchief. Mia. Pity the little chit had decided to splatter herself all over his chamber floor. Scowling at the table, Sloan slipped the cool cloth between his fingers and thought how her lifeless eyes weren't that much different from how they'd been when she'd lived.

No matter. He'd easily find a replacement once this sordid business with Taggart and his bothersome guardian was resolved. Crumpling the handkerchief into a ball, Sloan focused his gaze on the collapsed pedestal that had once held his precious egg. A female Draecna. If only he'd known. He could've better prepared. Clenching his teeth, he remembered his father. By the fire of all Hades, he could've sired his own generation of Draecna hybrids.

The chaos of rebuilding echoed all around him. Constant hammering and shouting battered his sensibilities throughout each day and late into the night. A curse upon his brother and his army of Draecna! Leaning on the table, Sloan glared at the map and willed it to give up the hiding place of his brother.

"I will find you, Taggart," Sloan hissed down at the colored topographical vista. "And when I do, I will dine on your heart while ye watch."

Chapter Ten

"Is she speaking to ye yet?" Thaetus settled himself into the chair beside Taggart, wincing as his body hit the seat.

Eyeing his friend's pained movements with a sympathetic cringe Taggart shook his head. "Not yet. I'm sure she'll come around. Hannah is a sensible lass."

"And your mother?" Thaetus wheezed into his cup as he sipped his morning grog.

"My mother never *stops* speaking," Taggart retorted while massaging his temples. Gads, her voice still pounded in his head. He wondered if she'd spelled him with a nagging hex to keep her words constantly drumming in his brain.

"I heard that, Taggart." Isla's voice echoed down from the rafters as golden particles sifted into the room.

" 'Tis very rude to eavesdrop, Mother," Taggart noted as he fixed the sparkling ceiling of the kitchen with a murderous glare.

The golden particles swirled and solidified into the shining form of the Goddess Isla. "I was not eavesdropping. I was in this room before the two of ye decided to come in for your morning grog."

"Aye, the fact that ye just weren't visible isn't a factor?" Taggart drummed his fingers on the table, wishing he had something stronger in his cup. It appeared he was going to need it.

Isla glided around the table and poured herself a drink. "I was merely keeping out of the way until I was called upon to finalize the mating vows."

Draining his cup, Taggart pounded it down on the table and fixed his mother with a baleful glare. "Well, since one of the participants in the ceremony refuses to speak to the other, there's a slight problem with the *I do's.*"

"Then I suggest ye get busy and fix it."

Don't say it. Taggart bit back the first words springing to mind. He had to be respectful to Mother. He rose from the table to pace about the room. Something about walking helped him think. "Tell me, dear Mother. What exactly should I do? Ye never seem short on advice."

"Mind your tone," Isla warned as she settled herself in her seat at the head of the table. "Thaetus, ye're looking stronger every day. Don't forget the herbs I prescribed."

Sliding farther down in his seat, Thaetus bobbed his head. "No, ma'am. I shan't forget. Thank ye ever so much."

Isla sipped her steaming drink. Her long, graceful snout fit perfectly into the oversized tankard and she curled a dainty claw from the handle. Setting her mug aside, she turned back to her son, her eyes narrowed as she leaned forward in her chair. "I know ye must have *some* of your father's seductive genes running in your veins. Woo her, Taggart! Ye must convince her she canna live without ye. Are ye daft or just a bit slow?"

Thaetus choked on the mouthful of grog he'd just sipped and showered the table with the amber-colored liquid.

Pummeling Thaetus on the back, Taggart shot his mother a heated glare. "Have pity on the poor man, will ye, Mother? He still suffers from the aftereffects of Mia's poison."

Isla rose from the table and pulled a braided cord hanging beside the hearth. "Rub his back, Taggart. Do not beat the poor man, and *I* am not the one who caused him to choke."

A half-grown Draecna scurried into the room in answer to the silent summons. His head was bowed, his narrow chest heaving, as his gaze darted furtively between Taggart and the goddess across the room.

"Dasim, please help Thaetus back to his room and let Gilda know 'tis time to prepare the meals."

With a bob of his head, Dasim scooped Thaetus up into his arms and cradled him like a babe.

"I can walk!" Thaetus sputtered as the Draecna carried him from the room. "I have never been so humiliated in my entire life."

Isla closed her eyes with a resigned sigh and turned her attention back to her son. "Dasim is the one survivor from the hatching the Guild attempted. I'm afraid he doesn't always quite understand."

Frowning in Dasim's direction, Taggart searched his memories with a shudder. The botched attempt at bringing forth the young Draecna without a proper guardian had proven fatal for most concerned. "I heard one had suffered ill effects while all the others had perished."

"Only young Dasim survived, and still suffers greatly with the results of the struggle."

Circling the room to stand beside her son, Isla combed a claw through Taggart's hair, then rested it on his shoulder. "Now promise me ye'll get on with this wooing business. I wish to see ye properly joined and moving on to the task of gifting me with grandchildren. Ye're over seven hundred years old, ye know. How long do ye expect a mother to wait?"

Taggart leaned his elbows on the table and propped his chin in his hands. "Ye know, Mother, I havena been around for ye to meddle with in several hundred years. Ye really need to pace yourself lest ye burn yourself out."

With an affectionate cuff to the back of his head, Isla chuckled as she left the room. "Don't give it a passing thought, my boy. I've been saving up."

She'd never see them again. Her stomach churned with a mixture of frustration and homesickness as she stared down the mist-covered mountain. Her beloved mountain of Jasper Mills would be lost to her forever. She'd not even get to revisit her newly favored landscapes of magical Scotland. No. She blinked back the tears that came to her eyes from the sight of strange mountains in a foreign world where people wished her dead. Hannah hugged her legs tighter against her aching chest and rocked back against the cold, hard ledge.

She'd never see the folks of Jasper Mills again. Never see any of her friends. The woods would take over Jake's grave and wipe it from existence. Vines of ivy and bushes of wild sumac would engulf the stone, causing it to be lost forever until some hunter stumbled over the marker. Burying her face in her arms, she released a shuddering sigh, hoping at least some of the honeysuckles had taken root around Jake's headstone to bloom on their anniversary.

There was no question that she would stay here. When she'd thought Esme had burnt Taggart to a crisp, she'd felt the same ripping open of her heart that she'd felt when Jake had died. She didn't know when she'd made the mistake of allowing herself to love him, but somehow she'd given her heart completely to Taggart. But why did he have to take her choices away? Why hadn't he been more careful?

"Guardian, it is not safe to be outside of the cavern. It would be best if ye returned inside with me, please." Esme edged her way out on the ledge beside Hannah, scooting her feet sideways along the rim of the path as she curled her tail around her body.

Hannah wiped the back of her hands across her face, sniffing with a shrug of one shoulder. "I needed somewhere where I could think. No one's going to bother me out here."

"Why do you cry? We are safe with the goddess. Her caverns are well guarded by the most trusted Draecna. I would think you would be pleased."

"It's complicated, Esme." Hannah pinched the bridge of her nose. Ugh, she hated crying. It stuffed up her nose and made her head throb. She knew better. Tears never solved anything.

"Males?"

"You're extremely wise for one so young," Hannah observed without opening her eyes. "What do you know of males, Esme?"

"Entirely too much, since the crystal caverns seem to be crawling with them." Esme folded her paws across her stomach and rocked back on her heels. "They appear to think quite highly of themselves and don't seem to think females know very much at all."

Massaging her temples, Hannah paused. "Ah, you've been talking to Septamus. He just takes some getting used to. He should be able to help you with your lessons. He's helping William."

Two rings of smoke puffed out of Esme's glistening nostrils as she expelled a snorting huff. "Lessons!" She sat bolt upright on the ledge and fixed Hannah with a narrow-eyed glare. "I am a *female*, Guardian. Females *never* require lessons. I thought you understood that."

"Well apparently, *I* need lessons," Hannah muttered as she scrubbed her face with her hands. "Esme, I really came out here to be alone. I discovered I can never return home again and I'm having a hard time letting go."

"But ye will be with your mate, correct?" Esme tilted her head and waited for Hannah's answer as though she were a teacher waiting for a student's response.

Hannah nodded. "Yes. I'll be here with Taggart. But I'm still going to miss all the people I loved back home. And I'm going to miss my homeland and everything I left behind." How could she explain the aching homesickness battering her heart to the logical, fact-based Esme?

Esme studied the sky for a moment, wrinkled her brow between her horns, then turned and shook her head at Hannah. "Is not being with the one who makes your heart sing all that truly matters?"

Hannah closed her eyes and leaned back against the ledge. Yes. That was all that truly mattered. Esme had hit the nail on the head. No wonder female Draecna didn't need lessons. Leave it to Esme to boil it down to the facts.

Her auburn curls shone by the light of the fire like fine brandy swirling in a snifter. Taggart's groan caught in his chest; his fingers itched to lock in those silken tresses and lower Hannah beneath him on the bed. The silk wrap she wore as she sat reading clung to the swell of her breasts and traced the path his hands and his mouth longed to enjoy. His mouth watered for the taste of her velvet skin and the luscious sweet buttons of her nipples.

She'd bathed in scented water and perfumed herself with oils. He drew a deep breath and shuddered. The lilies, the same scent she'd worn the first night they'd made love. She'd forgiven him; she wanted him as much as he wanted her. *Holy blazes.* If he kept this up, he'd soon be so hard he'd be unable to walk over to her.

First things first, he'd give her the gift he'd fashioned

from his own birth shell his mother had entombed in the depths of the caverns. Then they'd make love the rest of the night and plan the date of their official joining.

"Hannah."

She raised her head, her eyes dark with need, her wrap barely closed at the waist. Setting aside her book on the couch beside her, Hannah leaned back against the pillows and smiled an invitation for him to sit. "I've been waiting for you."

As he settled onto the couch beside her, Taggart slipped her book to the floor. Stroking the curve of her cheek with the backs of his fingers, he whispered, "God, I feared I'd lost ye again."

With a sigh, Hannah closed her eyes and turned her face into his palm. "I was a little worried there myself for a bit. But we're together now and that's all that really matters. I'm sorry it took me a while to realize it."

"I'm sorry, Hannah." Taggart took her face in both his hands. "I'm so verra sorry I destroyed the gateway."

"It doesn't matter," Hannah whispered. "All that matters is that I'm here with you."

"Do ye truly mean that, Hannah? With all your heart? I would never wish for ye to be unhappy." Taggart searched her eyes and held his breath, waiting to hear her answer.

"I promise with all my heart."

Leaning forward, he touched his lips to hers as though they were delicate petals of a cherished rose. With a choking whisper, he placed a golden chain around her neck and kissed the closed lids of both her eyes. "I made this for ye, Hannah, as a small token of my love."

Hannah opened her eyes, looked down, and gasped. At the end of the golden chain was a carved locket reflecting every color of the rainbow. The oval-shaped structure of the locket itself consisted of gold with panels of polished shell refracting iridescent like abalone shell.

"Open it." Taggart nodded at Hannah's questioning look.

Hannah undid the intricate gold clasp, gasping again as soon as she opened the locket. With the power of his magic, Taggart had burnished Hannah's image into one side of the oval and his own into the other.

"It's beautiful," she whispered and caught her breath as the images shimmered to life and joined in an impassioned kiss. "How?" She raised her eyes to Taggart as the images separated and became inanimate once more.

With a grin, Taggart cupped her hands between his own and closed the locket between them. "Ye canna expect me to reveal all my secrets just yet, my love. Ye have your whole lifetime to ferret them out. Is it to your liking?"

"It's wondrous," Hannah sighed. Snuggling closer, she smoothed her hands up his throat and opened her mouth to his.

"Aye, now that's more like it," Taggart rumbled as he settled into the kiss. God's beard, she tasted better than before. Had her mouth been this wondrous last time? His mind flashed back to the other talented uses of her lips and tongue. With a groan, he smoothed her wrap down from her shoulders.

"OUCH!"

An electrostatic shock zapped the palms of his hands. Blue sparks crackled and popped in the air between them.

"What the hell was that?" Hannah rubbed her shoulders and glared at Taggart as though he'd just slapped her.

Working his hands as though he'd just singed his fingertips on a red-hot brand, Taggart shrugged as he fluttered his hands. "Son of a bitch! It's no' that cold in here and that's a silk wrap. I would no' have thought I'd have built up that much static electricity by walking across this floor." Damn, if she hadn't stung his fingers as though he'd touched an electrical grid.

"That was a heck of a lot more than any static electric jolt I've ever gotten," Hannah muttered as she twisted to eye the red marks on her shoulders.

Pulling her close, Taggart grinned. "Here, I'll kiss them and make them better."

As soon as his lips touched her skin, fiery sparks repeated, and Taggart jolted backward rubbing his mouth. "Dammit to hell!" His lips burned as though he'd kissed a fiery poker.

"Okay, that's it. You stay at that end of the couch." Hannah shook a warning finger in his direction as she tightened her wrap around her throat.

"Mother!" Taggart roared. "Show yourself. I know this has to be your doing."

Glittering gold dust filtered down from the crystal ceiling and formed a curtain with the image of the Goddess Isla's face. "Did ye call me, my son?"

"Ye know damn good and well I called ye, Mother. What spell have ye cast on me so that I canna even touch my mate?"

"There will be no more pleasuring of one another until *after* the joining ceremony. It is not considered proper." Isla fixed both Taggart and Hannah with a look as though they'd both been caught sneaking in after curfew.

"Mother, I am over seven hundred years old. I have already marked Hannah as my mate and it's no' like this is the first time we've known the pleasure of one another's charms." Taggart risked a glance at Hannah's face and couldn't decide if her face burned that decided hue of red because she was embarrassed or because she was about to burst out laughing. His mother wasn't being reasonable. And Septamus wondered why Taggart hadn't returned home in over three hundred years? Septamus didn't have a mother like Isla!

"This is not negotiable, Taggart. Ye will not know the rapture of Hannah's flesh again until *after* the union is blessed." The golden curtain shimmered and Isla gave a haughty sniff as though daring her son to challenge her. "Now, bid Hannah good night so she may return to her reading. Gilda waits in the hall to show ye to the new chambers ye will use until after the ceremony."

With a growl, Taggart swiped his arm through the golden curtain and scattered Isla's image into the air. "I canna believe she's cast a spell of celibacy upon us! Of all the controlling, manipulative, scheming—"

"Taggart," Hannah interrupted with a giggle. "It's not going to be that bad."

"Not that bad?" Taggart roared as he grabbed her to his chest. "Woman, I needed to make love to ye until the sun crests over the horizon!"

"Take care, my hot-blooded Taser. You're gonna get us zapped again." Hannah wriggled out of his arms, cringing as she skipped away before the next electrical shock hit.

"The spell will only zap us if it senses we are attempting to go too far. It allows us minimal physical contact."

His mother had pressed her limits too far this time. As soon as they'd freed Erastaed from Sloan, he'd make sure it was another three hundred years before she laid eyes on his hybrid arse again. Which reminded him, he needed to speak to Esme about blessing Hannah with immortality.

"By the way, how do ye feel about growing old?" Rubbing his chin, Taggart circled Hannah, pretending to eye her body up and down. He needed her to crave immortality. He couldn't bear the thought of watching Hannah die and leave him behind. If Hannah didn't accept the concept willingly, Esme's blessing wouldn't take hold.

Hannah's eyes narrowed into a pair of suspicious green slits. "Well, you certainly veered off onto a different subject." Pulling the belt on her silken wrap, she turned and faced Taggart while he circled her. "Growing old doesn't bother me. A lot of people never get the chance."

That's not what he wanted to hear. Why couldn't she be one of those vain women who were terrified of growing old? "But as a human, Hannah, your life is so short. Do ye not often feel cheated by the lack of years ye've been given?" Maybe that was the route to take, not growing old but the fact that she didn't have as much time as he did.

Hannah's eyes darkened as she stared off into space and an intense sadness filled her face. "Not so much cheated. I feel like I've wasted time I've been given because by the time I've finally figured things out, it seems like I've frittered away my very best years."

"If ye had an endless supply of years, or at least what seemed like an endless supply added to your lifespan, then I doubt I'd see the sorrow and remorse for wasted time shining in your eyes." Taggart ignored the stab of guilt gnawing at his gut. He'd stirred her painful memories with his query. He avoided the directness of her gaze.

"What are you getting at, Taggart?" Hannah sighed as she bent to scoop her book off the pile of pillows beside the couch.

As Hannah bent, she treated him to an unhindered view down her décolleté to her luscious, forbidden breasts. Taggart groaned as his groin tightened with a lust-filled throb. *Dammit, Mother, I will see to it that you never lay eyes upon your grandchildren.* Scrubbing his face, he shifted his stance to adjust his leather breeches. "Esme has the power to grant ye immortality so the years of your life mirror mine."

Hannah hugged the leather-bound book to her chest, clutching it as though it were a life preserver helping her stay afloat. She curled her brightly painted toes into the plush carpeting as she stood slightly weaving to and fro.

"You're saying Esme could hocus-pocus some sort of spell over me and then I would live forever?"

Taggart took a deep breath and edged a step closer, taking care to keep his voice to a low rumbling purr. *Careful, lad, choose your words well or she'll bolt. She's barely nibbling at the bait.* "All Draecna females are born with the Fire of Immortality. If Esme so chooses and you choose to accept, ye can increase your lifespan by thousands of years."

Hannah curled her toes tighter into the loops of the rug and bit her lower lip. Tucking the book under her chin, she repeated, "Thousands of years?"

Taggart held his breath. He wanted to shout, *"Say yes!"* but he held his tongue. What was there to decide? She'd be with him. Isn't that all that mattered?

Tapping her thumbs on the cover of the book she hugged against her chest, Hannah eased closer to the hearth to stare down into the fire. "What exactly does this Fire of Immortality entail? Besides a longer life, I mean."

The tightness in his chest gradually uncoiled as Taggart heard acceptance in Hannah's voice. With her curiosity piqued, she'd only move forward. He could tell by the lift at the end of her words and the shift in the hue of her aura. She warmed to the idea even now. He blew out his breath and realized he'd been holding it, waiting for her reply.

"'Tis just a small rite. Quite painless. We can add it to our joining ceremony." Brushing her hair back from her neck, he risked nuzzling the silk of her throat. "Then nothing can ever part us, Hannah. We'll be together for all time."

CHAPTER ELEVEN

"Isla's stronghold, the Crystal Caverns." Sloan traced his fingertips around the top of his wineglass as he stared into the swirling ruby liquid. "So obvious. So bloody, bloody obvious. We should've known they'd go there from the beginning." He wrapped his fingers around the bowl of the goblet and crushed the glass in his hand.

Corter cringed, shifted back a step, and widened his stance on the elaborate Turkish carpet. "He waits outside for your orders. He said the ceremony is to be held in three days' time."

"Three days," Sloan repeated as he plucked out the shards of glass embedded in his hand. Three days gave him plenty of time to plot the perfect revenge. As he licked at the blood streaming down his wrist, he savored the copper, salted tang. His brother's blood would taste the same after Sloan ripped him open with his own dagger. "Tell him to listen and relay any more news. Tell him he has done well. Give him his usual payment. In fact, Corter, pay him double."

"Double?" Corter's mottled face darkened into a frustrated scowl. "Do ye know how scarce virgins are these days? And 'tis no' like he uses them for pleasure. He just eats them, ye *do* realize that?"

"I don't give a damn what he does with them. It's his

payment. Their bodies are none of my concern." Sloan
rose from his settee, wrapped his hand in a silk handkerchief, and tucked the ends into his sleeve.

"In three days' time, balance will be returned." Sloan
strolled about the room, wandering around the collapsed
columns and blown-away walls still left from Taggart's attack. Revenge against his brother would truly be sweet
when he held Hannah's dripping heart in front of Taggart's
face and took a slow, succulent bite.

William snickered as Taggart entered the room.

Septamus arched a brow and glanced first at Taggart,
then back to William, who stood with several of the
young Draecna hatchlings.

Stalking to the front of the training room, Taggart
homed in on William. His lips tightened as he contem-
plated the irreverent hatchling. "William!" he thundered.
His voice echoed off the crystals imbedded in the walls
and rattled the torches on their hooks. "Step forward and
explain the Eleven Tenets of the Draecna Elders of Barac'-
Nairn."

William's horns sagged and his wings drooped as he
shuffled to the front of the cavernous room. The rest of
the young hatchlings stood tall and silent, their iridescent
eyes narrowed into sidling glances toward one another.
They lined up, eased back a step, and locked their front
claws behind their backs.

William turned, faced his peers, and assumed their
stance even though he was half their size. With a sheepish
glance at Taggart, then one at Septamus, he squinted one
eye closed and mumbled. "The first tenet says—"

"William! Ye will explain the texts with proper eti-
quette and format. Begin again." Taggart loomed over the
young Draecna, circling around him until the youngster's
eyes glistened with unshed tears.

William dropped his head. "I cannot," he whispered. "Forgive me. I am so ashamed."

"Then I suggest ye concentrate on learning your lessons rather than mocking your elders." Taggart jerked his head toward the rear of the cavern. "Find your place in the back of the training room."

William shuffled to the farthest corner of the classroom, his Draecna scales shimmering to a brilliant hue of embarrassed pink.

"Well done," Septamus murmured. "Ye've grown nearly as fearsome as me."

"Hmm." Taggart grunted as he watched William skulk to the back corner of the room. He didn't like shaming the lad in front of the others, but with the war, disrespect could not be tolerated. Everyone knew Hannah favored William because Hannah had discovered him first and the boy was the only hatchling allowed to mature at a natural rate. He'd not melded with Taggart. William remained an innocent youngster. The lad was more or less Hannah's baby and she'd spoiled him rotten. Taggart had to bring him under control before they engaged in full battle. William's life could depend upon it.

With a glance at Septamus, Taggart inhaled a ragged breath. "Any word on whether Sloan has advanced?"

Without waiting for an answer, he returned his attention to the group still standing tall with their feet spread. They looked good. Strong. Well-trained. But the only direct confrontation they'd had so far had been the breakout at Tiersa Deun. The young Draecna had done well. Not a single hatchling had been lost. But freeing Erastaed from Sloan's rule would be a different battle altogether. Sloan would expect them and be prepared; his claws would be fully unsheathed.

Septamus cleared his throat and leaned closer to Taggart. "More provinces have been destroyed. Nearly a third of Erastaed lies in ruins. The villagers . . ." Septamus exhaled a pained sigh. "He's truly slipped off into madness, Taggart, worse than ever before. We must take a stand soon or there won't be any Erastaedians to save. The cruelty of the bastard." Septamus shook his head. "Are ye quite sure you and Sloan share a bloodline?"

Taggart shrugged. "Perhaps I'm a throwback or maybe I'm the one who's insane. My heart tends to rule more than my head. Mother had to destroy all the siblings of my clutch. Perhaps she missed and destroyed the wrong one."

Septamus shuddered. "I remember your siblings. I had to help your mother hunt them down. Trust me, Taggart—you're not the one who's insane. The truth of your heart is a boon."

Looking over the room at all the young Draecna still standing proud, Taggart swallowed hard. He didn't want to lead them to their deaths, but Erastaed cried out for a cleansing. Curling his hands into fists, Taggart gave the group a curt nod as his voice echoed across the room. "I am proud of each and every one of ye. Your dedication is beyond compare. Ye not only saved the guardian from her death but ye saved my beloved mate. Tomorrow, Hannah will accept the Fire of Immortality and our blessing rite will complete our joining." Taggart took in the dedication shining in their eyes, his heart swelling at the electrifying bond of trust pulsing through the room. "If not for your strength and protection, tomorrow wouldna be possible. Ye have my eternal gratitude. And once we free the world of Erastaed, the people will be grateful to ye as well. Never forget the sacred honor of the Draecna race. Always take pride in your heritage."

As a group, the young hatchlings raised their snouts and filled the ceiling of the cavern with brilliant flames.

Taggart raised his hands, clapping them together with a sharp report. "Warriors!" Taggart clapped once more.

"After the ceremony, we will declare full war." As the Draecna warriors raised their muzzles to blast their flames again, Taggart lifted his hands for silence. "More Draecna have joined us from the farthest reaches of Erastaed. The mercenaries of Ruarke and the assassins of Glenoc Mur are also counted as our allies. Our numbers are great enough to flank Sloan on every side. After tomorrow, we will seize control. Erastaed will know freedom from Sloan's bloody reign before the next double moon."

"Oh, it's absolutely beautiful," Hannah breathed. She twisted and turned in front of the full-length mirror, admiring the gown Isla had sent to her chambers. The white satin framed her bare shoulders. The heart-shaped neckline accentuated her throat and the corseted bodice uplifted her bosoms. Seed pearls and crystals sparkled across the length of material wrapped around her waist. Layers of silk and chiffon swirled like veils around her hips and whispered down to the floor. Shimmering white ribbons strung with more diamonds and pearls trailed from the back, creating an eye-catching train.

Hannah fingered the locket hanging at her throat and smiled at her reflection in the mirror. Who would've thought? Gilda stood behind her fussing with her hair, using both claws and the tip of her tail to adjust all the curls. Hannah stifled a giggle. Molly the hairdresser back at Jasper Mills always wished she had an extra set of hands.

"Is something wrong?" Gilda asked, pausing with the tip of her tail wrapped in a strand of Hannah's hair.

Hannah bit her lower lip and swallowed hard. "Absolutely nothing is wrong, Gilda. Thank you. You're doing a wonderful job."

At the sound of her chamber door softly closing, Hannah adjusted the angle of the floor-length mirror to see who had just entered. "Esme! Good. I wanted to ask you a few questions before the ceremony."

With her tail swishing against the thick golden carpeting covering the floor of Hannah's chambers, Esme padded across the room. "Ye look very presentable, Guardian. Taggart will be well pleased."

Hannah smiled. Presentable. That was quite the compliment coming from Esme. "Thank you, Esme."

"You had questions for me?" Esme folded her hands across her shimmering tiled belly and patiently tapped a claw.

Gilda swept her hair up off her neck and piled the mass of curls high upon her head. "Oh no. Can I please just wear it pulled back a little bit and flowing down my back? My ears are big and stick out like car doors. See?" Hannah turned toward Gilda, stuck her fingers behind her ears, and waggled them at the confused-looking Draecna maid.

With a nod of her head, Gilda released Hannah's curls. "Whatever ye wish, honored Guardian."

Turning back to Esme, Hannah pulled the strapless bodice of the dress a bit higher up around her breasts and continued, "Please explain to me just exactly what this Fire of Immortality entails."

Folding her claws back across her belly, Esme peered closer at Hannah's ears as she replied. "I enclose your body with the Fire of Immortality and increase the years of your life. What are car doors? Is this some sort of human imagery reference?"

Hannah whirled from her image in the mirror. "What do you mean you breathe fire around my body? I saw you crispy-critter all those Waerins in Tiersa Deun. What if you accidentally pick the wrong heat setting?"

Esme's eyes widened as though Hannah had slapped her.

"I would *never* make such a simple mistake! Just because I'm newly hatched, do not take me for an inexperienced fool."

Gilda dropped the brush she held between her claws and stood trembling with her head bowed. "Forgive me," she whispered. "But take the greatest care. I made just such a simple mistake many eons ago. That is why I no longer possess the magic. I had the powers stripped from me. But the goddess saw it was truly a mistake and not malice as some accused. That is why she suffered to allow me to live under her protection here in her crystal caverns."

"And you wondered why I was nervous?" Hannah shot Esme an accusing glare as she retrieved the brush from the floor.

"I *will not* make the mistake Gilda was unfortunate enough to make." Esme huffed two tendrils of smoke in short impatient bursts.

Hannah rubbed the gooseflesh on her arms as she compared the two female Draecna. One self-assured and one self-effacing. She wondered how many times, in the history of Draecna, Gilda's type of mistake had actually happened. Or did she really want to know? Her stomach gurgled as though filled with a thousand flopping fish. She inhaled through her nose and exhaled out her mouth. *Deep breaths.* She could do this.

"Don't fry me, Esme. Think cool thoughts, okay?"

Esme's eyes narrowed into insulted slits. "Ye still havena described a car door."

She hadn't been in this sector of the caverns. The crystals imbedded in the walls and the ceilings reflected the purest white. Even the floor of this part of the cave consisted of great slabs of crystal striated with silver and gold. Rows upon rows of black shining pews disappeared down each side of the colossal room. This section was so massive that even though it was well lit, she couldn't tell where the cavern actually ended.

Hannah rubbed her hands together and forced herself not to wipe her damp palms against the folds of her lovely gown. Nervous perspiration rolled down her back, trickled down her butt, and threatened to roll even farther. She swallowed an anxious giggle. There was no way she'd ignite even if Esme did mess up. She'd drenched the lining of her gown with nervous sweat.

A raised platform stood several yards into the room surrounded by several pews. The pews held every Draecna she'd ever met, all waiting for her to join Esme, Taggart, and Isla on the center dais.

Taggart. Hannah raised her hand to her pounding chest as a surge of need stole the ability for her to breathe. Decked in black leather that strained across every muscle her hands ached to stroke, Taggart watched her with those eyes that said he wanted her as much as she wanted him.

"Come forth, Hannah, and receive Esme's gift so ye might know many years of happiness as Taggart's mate." Isla motioned her forward with a wave of one claw, smiling as she nodded her great white head.

Breathe. She had to remember to breathe. Fingering the locket at her throat, Hannah made her way down the aisle. Stepping up to the platform, she glanced at Taggart before she turned to Esme.

I love ye, he mouthed with a slight nod of his head.

Hannah shivered. It was the first time Taggart had actually said the words. *I love you too,* she mouthed back. A warm glow released throughout her body.

"Are ye ready, Guardian?" Esme cleared her throat.

"I hope so, Esme." Hannah took a deep breath as she turned her full attention on the young female. Esme seemed so determined and sure of herself. Hannah hoped she knew what she was doing.

"It will be fine, Guardian. Ye must trust me."

"I do, Esme. Or I wouldn't be here," Hannah replied. "Please do whatever it is you're going to do."

Esme took a deep breath; her tiled chest expanded and shimmered beneath the torchlight flickering in the hall. Then she exhaled and enshrouded Hannah's body in a cloud of silver-white flames, keeping them burning brightly as Isla's voice echoed off the crystals scattered throughout the room.

"By the power of blaze, by the power of flame, death shall no longer have any claim."

Inside the circle of flames, Hannah squinted against the brilliance of the light, reaching out to touch the flickering tongues of the fire around her. The flames licked through her fingers, but she felt no heat from the yellow-white tongues of fire. How odd to watch something that should be so painful and not register the normal feeling at all. But she felt *different*. She couldn't quite place it; a strange coursing of energy pulsated through her body. Turning, Hannah raised her arms in the enveloping light, lost in the miasma of brightness surrounding her. Warmth seeped through her, like a sip of brandy as it burned down her throat and coursed through her entire system. Her hand to her chest, Hannah frowned and concentrated. Had she died? She pressed a finger to her wrist. She couldn't detect the beating of her heart. She pressed down hard against the general area of her jugular vein. Wait, there it was. Finally, she felt it. Her heart had slowed to a rare beat every now and then. She exhaled and looked down at her hands. With a smile, she noticed the skin had smoothed to a lustrous eerie glow.

The flames gradually withered away and everyone's smiling faces came into view.

"Ye see, Guardian? I told ye I would not *crispy-critter* ye, as ye so succinctly put it," Esme stated with a disgruntled sniff.

Reaching out to clasp Esme's front claws between her hands, Hannah bowed her head. "Thank you, Esme, for this precious gift, and I'm very sorry if I offended you."

"Your gratitude and your apology are accepted."

With a cough, Septamus stepped up to the platform with a curved dagger clutched in one claw. "Allow me to present this gift to ye, Guardian, from all your beloved Draecna. Ye now have the lifespan and the sight to see through the Waerin's glamour. Unfortunately, there is no way to arm ye with the holiness of the Draecna fire. The claw of an ancient Draecna crafted this sacred dagger. It possesses the magic he controlled while he lived. Always keep it connected to your body. It will protect ye when others cannot be there for ye."

Hannah hefted the knife in her hands, amazed how it immediately molded itself to her palms. It bonded to her as though it lived. She raised her head to meet Septamus's thoughtful gaze.

"It will protect ye, Guardian."

"Thank you, Septamus."

"And now for the joining," Isla's voice rang out once again. "Taggart and Hannah, please face each other."

Esme took the knife out of Hannah's hand and tucked it into the back of Hannah's dress. "It must always be touching your skin to keep ye safe. Ye must always keep it with ye."

"Thank you," Hannah murmured as she fixed her bodice and turned to face Taggart.

"Taggart, reveal the mark for everyone to see." Isla nodded to her son as she stood in front of Hannah and Taggart.

Reveal the mark? What mark? Hannah arched a brow at

Taggart. She didn't know if she liked the sound of that or not. Glancing around at the expectant faces, Hannah backed up a step from Taggart. "Reveal what mark?"

"Shh, easy now, love. Watch." Taggart smiled down into her eyes as he caressed her cheek with the pad of his thumb. Bending closer, he blew a warm breath down the base of her throat and bare décolleté, tracing his fingertips along behind it.

In the path of his touch appeared dark whirls and icons of an intricate ornate script. A tattoo of sorts, a black-patterned writing, started at the base of Hannah's left ear, flowed down her throat and collarbone, and ended right between her breasts.

Hannah bent her head, staring down at as much of her chest as she could see. Catching her breath, she blinked twice at the detailed tattoo trailing down her body. "What is that?"

"It is my mark," Taggart replied, opening his shirt to reveal an identical symbol on his chest.

"I don't remember seeing that on you before." Hannah ran her fingertips across her skin, frowning at the raised edges she felt running along her throat.

"It is only visible if we wish it to be, like today," Taggart explained.

"Hannah, the mark is Draecna tradition. It is how Taggart implanted his DNA in your system so all know you to be his mate. It is irreversible. There is no question of fidelity with Taggart." Isla expanded her chest with pride and nodded toward her son.

"It was just a bit of a surprise," Hannah said, shooting Taggart a look that said he should've told her about it before he'd done it. At least with her extended lifetime, now she had an eternity to discover all his secrets.

Taggart just smiled.

Isla looked over the couple's heads to the gathered Draecna. "Do ye accept the proof of Taggart's mark?"

In unison, each Draecna in the room raised his snout and blasted a short burst of flames into the air.

"Taggart of the bloodline of Cair Orlandis, your proof has been accepted." Isla nodded in Taggart's direction and raised a golden brow when he failed to move. "Taggart?"

"William!" Taggart hissed to the young Draecna sitting on the pew closest to the platform.

"Now?" William jumped as though Gearlach had just elbowed him in the ribs.

"Yes, William, now," Taggart groaned.

William stumbled up the steps and planted a good-sized rock into Taggart's hands. "Sorry," he mumbled, turned back around, and tripped back to his seat.

"Poor William," Hannah whispered as she watched his scales flash a bright shade of red. Her poor little Draecna, younger and more innocent than all the rest, he was having such a hard time growing up.

Crumbling the rock between his hands, Taggart revealed two polished bands of a dark, lustrous metal. Sliding one of the bands over Hannah's ring finger, he exhaled as it slid perfectly into place. "Draecna steel. Indestructible and pure. Just like my love for you."

The metal warmed around her finger and sent a surge of energy pulsating through her veins. Her fingers trembling, Hannah blinked against the tears stinging her eyes as she reached for the other ring to slide onto Taggart's finger. As she felt the ring settle in place, she raised her gaze to his. "I never thought I'd be happy again. I don't know how you found me. But I'm so very glad you did."

Taggart bent to accept the gift of Hannah's kiss just as the ceiling exploded.

★   ★   ★

Taggart pushed Hannah to the floor and covered her body with his. "Septamus!" he roared as chunks of the cavern rained down all around them. He couldn't see for the clouds of exploding crystals dusting all around them. Another blast shook the platform beneath them as Taggart transformed to his Draecna form. Spreading his wings, he shielded them both from the shards of gemstones pelting through the air.

"How did they get through to the caverns? I thought we were safe in here?" Hannah shouted, cringing and covering her eyes as debris bounced off Taggart's wings and rattled to the floor beside them.

Taggart flinched as a larger clump pegged him squarely between his wings. Anger roared through his veins like liquid fury. So, Sloan had chosen today as the day of reckoning.

"I canna tell ye how he found the stronghold or why he chose this day," he ground out between gritted teeth. Raising his head, he released his blaze and welded the loose gemstones against what was left of the ceiling. "That should hold long enough for William to lead ye out of this room and get ye both to the shelter."

"I'm not leaving you." Hannah shook her head as she wriggled her Draecna dagger out from the back of her dress. "That son of a bitch ruined my dress and my day. Do you think I'm leaving here without a fight?"

"William!" Taggart bellowed, not taking his eyes from the enraged gaze of his hardheaded mate. By all the gods, she would go to that shelter with young William even if he had to paralyze her with a catatonic spell and toss her over William's back.

"I am here," William panted, ducking as a boom echoed from a lesser cavern deeper to the north. "I will not fail ye, Taggart. Tell me what ye will have me do."

Pulling Hannah's wrist into William's front claw, Taggart closed it around Hannah's hand. "Take your mother to the shelter, William. Do not come out until I come for ye." Taggart paused and stared down at Hannah's tiny hand swallowed up by William's clawed hold. His heart clenched at the sight of her delicate arm, so pale and fragile in William's grasp. She had to be safe. He couldn't comprehend living a moment without her. "Keep her there, William. One of us will come for the two of ye. Make certain ye do not open the door for anyone unless ye know ye can trust them."

"The others have gone to fight the intruders." William nodded toward one of the tall narrow doors dangling halfway off its hinges.

"I know, William." Taggart nodded. "I'm glad ye stayed here as ye were taught. Ye did well and this is why. 'Tis your duty to lead the Guardian to the shelter. I must go and join the others to fight off the intruders."

"William, I want you to go to the shelter, but I'm going to stay and fight at Taggart's side. Now let me go. Uncurl your claw. I promise I'll be just fine." Hannah squirmed and tried to pry her hand from William's clenched claw as she spoke, frowning when William shook his head.

"No. Taggart has given me a direct order, Mother, and it sounds as though it's for your own good." William tugged on her arm and encircled her with his wing as he edged them toward a curtained off alcove toward the side of the room. "Come on, Mother. The shelter is safe. We must make the passage before another volley hits and seals off the corridor."

"Dammit, Taggart! I said I am *not* going!" Hannah planted her feet and grabbed the tip of his wing with her free hand. "I can stay and help you fight. I'm an immortal too now, remember? I'm not leaving here without you."

Touching her forehead with the tip of his claw, Taggart

rendered her limp as a child's rag doll. "I love ye, Hannah," Taggart whispered as he caught her up in his arms and settled her across William's back. Smoothing her green eyes closed, he pressed his lips to her temple. "I will come for ye when it is safe. Until then, ye must stay with William." He hated to leave her, but he couldn't bear the thought of her facing Sloan.

With a nod to William, Taggart rose up and spread his wings. "The spell will render her motionless, and *silent,* for three days, lad. Hopefully, I shall be back to save your poor hide before she recovers and regains her tongue."

CHAPTER TWELVE

"How many still live?" Sloan pressed his finger along the top of the crystal, relishing how much the squeal of the glass mimicked the cry of a victim in pain.

"Gearlach is the only confirmed Draecna kill, my lord. The Waerins have placed his head on a spike outside the tents. I havena bothered to count the villagers. I didna think ye gave a damn about them." Corter ran his thick tongue across his bulging lower lip as he ogled Sloan's glass of wine.

Swirling the blood-red liquid in the long stemmed glass, Sloan frowned as he pondered Corter's report. "Ye mean to tell me, we've only killed one of those infernal beasts? What the hell seems to be the problem?" They'd been blasting the caverns for nearly three days. They should've mangled a few more of those monstrosities than that. "Are the vermin that difficult to kill?"

Corter didn't answer. He stood hypnotized by the ruby-red temptation swirling in Sloan's glass.

"Corter!" Sloan splattered the wine in the man's face. "There. Now that ye've had your wine maybe you can answer my question. Why is Gearlach the only Draecna casualty?"

Swiping at his face with the back of his hand, Corter sputtered and licked his lips. "Draecna are not the easiest creatures to kill. Their lives can only be taken by one o' their own. 'Tis something to do with that friggin' magic flowing through their bloody veins."

"I was promised the power of the Waerins was great. I was assured their abilities would secure the safety of my throne." Sloan tired of this bothersome game. His castle lay in ruins. During the battles, he'd taken to following the skirmishes in this less-than-adequate tent. He enjoyed his luxuries and grew bored with the constant noise and grime of this utter foolishness. It was high time they all gave up and died so he could return to his accustomed standard of living.

"A Waerin's no match for a Draecna, m'lord." Corter backed closer to the flap of the tent and ducked as Sloan lobbed the wineglass directly at his head.

"Then ye'd best be figuring out a way to trap more Draecna to use against each other. Must I tell ye every step to take? Why the hell do I allow ye to live?" Sloan paced across the length of the tent, scuffing his slippered feet against the thick carpet. "I'm bored with this battle. I want Taggart gutted and I want the guardian's body impaled on the poles in front of Tiersa Deun."

With a nod, Corter edged his way under the heavy flap of the tent. "Aye, Sloan. I'll see that it's done."

She opened her eyes to suffocating darkness. What was different? Hannah turned her head and strained all her senses. Then she knew what had changed. The darkness rendered nothing but total deafening silence. The bone-jarring echo of exploding blasts had finally come to a halt. All that shattered the stillness of the shelter was the steady rhythm of William's breathing spiked with the occasional snore. Hannah tried to move her leg. With a start, she real-ized her leg had moved. That meant the three days had passed. Taggart had said the spell would lift in three days. If she could move, that meant they had at least passed the third day or possibly even more. She shifted and tested the other leg. With a bit of protest, that leg obeyed as well.

Sitting up, Hannah winced as her muscles let her know in no uncertain terms she'd been idle for entirely too long. If Taggart still lived by the time she found him, she'd wring his neck herself.

"William!" Hannah croaked out into the darkness. "William, wake up!" How in the world could he sleep at a time like this? It sounded as though he'd gone into hibernation for the winter.

Hannah massaged the feeling back into her legs and arms, willing her muscles to come to life. "William, WILL YOU PLEASE WAKE UP!" Good lord, if shouting didn't work, she'd have to crawl over there and beat him.

"I've been awake. I'm guarding you, remember?" William released a loud, creaking yawn with a great smacking of his jowls. "Is Taggart back yet?" Shuffling sounded in the darkness to Hannah's right, followed by a series of popping farts.

"No. Not yet." Hannah swallowed hard and forced herself to ignore the dread gnawing in her chest that told her something was deadly wrong. "William, can you make a flame yet? Even a small one to create some light?"

"I'll try," William mumbled, not sounding too confident as he scuffled around in the dark.

Hannah heard him inhale a great rumbling breath and then exhale with a mighty gush. Nothing happened. Velvety darkness weighed in all around them like a dense, eternal blanket.

"Dammit," William muttered.

"It's all right, William. One of these days, your flame will come. It's just not ready yet." Hannah reached out, found the young hatchling's side, and gave him a reassuring pat.

"It's not just that, Mother," William sniffed as he rustled

around in the darkness beside her. "The glowing stone Gearlach gave me to use in the night doesna work anymore."

Feeling her way up the wall to stand, Hannah edged her way toward where she thought the door might be. "Well, maybe once things settle down, he'll be able to give you another."

"Ye don't understand, Mother." William's voice cracked as though he struggled to speak through emotions clenching at his throat. "If the magic has faded from Gearlach's stone, it means Gearlach is dead."

Hannah leaned against the wall and closed her eyes. Denial closed off her throat and tears stung the back of her eyelids. Surely, William had to be mistaken. "Maybe the stone just got damaged in one of the blasts, William. We mustn't give up hope."

"The stones cannot be damaged, Mother. What I tell ye is one of the tenets Taggart drilled into my head. I promise ye, Mother, I know this for certain."

Hannah raised a shaking hand to her face and cradled her head. Gearlach gone. What else had happened in the three days of her incapacitation? She dreaded finding out. "I know you're certain, William. I'm so sorry. I guess I just don't want it to be true."

"I know, Mother." William's sniff echoed through the shadows. "Gearlach always played the fool. . . ." William coughed and rumbled into the darkness. "But he made the very best sort of friend."

Hannah wilted against the rough gemstone walls, the ache in her heart piercing more painfully than the unpolished crystals cutting into her back. She closed her eyes tight against the heat of tears and forced the rising hysteria back into its tiny box at the back of her mind. Now wasn't the time. She had to find Taggart. As far as she knew, he still lived and would know what they needed to do. She had to operate under that theory.

Taking a deep breath, she swallowed hard and twisted to slide her dagger out of the back of her dress. "William, I know you're hurting. I am too. But we've got to save our grieving for Gearlach for later. We've got to find our way out of this pit of darkness and join the others."

"But Taggart said to wait until one of them came for us."

"I'm not waiting any longer. Now, you can either come with me or sit here alone where you can't see the end of your nose. Which is it?" Hannah knew what William would choose. He feared the darkness and being alone more than anything else.

"Which way do ye think we should go? I don't remember the way we came in. We've been in here too long."

Biting her tongue to keep from screaming, Hannah reminded herself William was very young. It had been three days since he'd carried her into the shelter and he'd probably curled up and gone to sleep as soon as he'd dropped her into the pile of pillows.

"William, this is a shelter. Do you remember seeing anything in this room we could use to find our way out? Do you remember seeing tables with lanterns or anything before the lights went out? Candles with Draecna flints lying beside them? Anything?" She could strangle Taggart and curse him with his own catatonic spell! He'd closed her eyes after he'd paralyzed her and she'd faded in and out of consciousness for the duration of the spell. She vaguely remembered the sounds of the bombing, but that was about it.

She heard William shuffling about. He sounded like an oversized rat; his rear claws scraped on the slate floor and then thumped as his feet thudded onto a carpeted area. A crash sounded, then a louder clunk and screech as William collided with what sounded like a solid piece of wood furniture.

"I found the table, Mother."

Hannah clapped her hands together. "Good job, William!" She just hoped he hadn't cleared it of the contents whenever he'd *found* it.

She heard him pawing the top of the table; his claws clattered as he tapped the surface of the wood. "Careful, William. If you knock anything off onto the floor, you'll never find it in this darkness."

A warm, yellow glow illuminated the darkness as William struck the shutter on a Draecna lantern. "Look what I found, Mother." He tapped the cone-shaped top of the crystal cylinder and gave Hannah a toothy grin.

The light eased the tension in her chest. Hannah rewarded William with a laugh. The darkness fed the demons of her mind and the brightly burning lantern held the terrors at bay. "Excellent job, William. Now let's get out of this hole and try to find the others."

They broke through the rubble blocking the passage and shoved their way into the main hall. Grunting, William heaved aside a collapsed column and held Hannah back while he looked to the ceiling to make sure the passage itself wouldn't implode.

Hannah ripped another strip of cloth from the bottom of her dress to wrap around her bleeding hands. The shattered gemstones and crystals scattered throughout the caverns were razor sharp and sliced her flesh every time she steadied her hands against a wall.

William helped her tie the latest rag, shaking his head as he cleaned more blood from higher up on her arm and shoulder. "Ye need Draecna hide, Mother. Ye're going to be ripped to shreds before we get out of here."

"I'll be fine, William." Hannah winced; some of the

shards embedded themselves deeper into her flesh like tiny slivers of glass. She'd worry about it later. There wasn't time now. They had to find the others.

A movement in the debris beside the hearth caused another stalactite of crystals to crash to the floor. As the echo of the crash faded off into silence, a distinct moan filtered up through the wreckage.

Picking their way through the rubble, Hannah and William slid across the gem-scattered floor. Hannah shook her head at all the rubies, amethysts, and carnelians winking in the light of the Draecna lantern. The jeweler of Jasper Mills would've gone into sensory overload. Hannah swallowed a bitter laugh. She hated gemstones. They were slippery wicked little beasts that tripped you when you walked and ate your flesh whenever you touched their jagged edges.

Hannah grabbed William's wing as she lost her footing and stumbled in a rockslide of the treacherous debris. "Dammit!"

"Get on my back, Mother. It will be better if I carry ye. With my weight, I do not slide as ye do."

With a sigh, Hannah relented. "Just until we get over to whoever that is that needs our help." Grabbing hold of his wings, she pulled herself up on his shoulders and wrapped her arms around his muscled neck. "Okay, William. Let's go see if we can dig them out."

William plowed through the wreckage as though he were a bulldozer. Hannah held on, clamping her arms around his neck and onto his wings as he lurched from side to side.

"I think it's Gilda, Mother." William wrinkled his nose and raised his snout higher into the air. "Take a whiff, she always smells like swamp water."

"William!" Hannah hissed as she slid off his back. "That's not a very nice thing to say."

"Well, it's true." William raised his nose again. "All ye need to do is take a big whiff. Dinna ye smell something like a bit of mildew?"

When this was all over, she was going to have a long talk with William about speaking his mind and how his words affected others' feelings. "Okay, William. I'll take your word for it. Let's just see if we can get some of this wreckage off her and see if she's all right." Hopefully, Gilda wasn't conscious enough to have heard what William said.

William hefted the column pinning Gilda against the hearth and scooped away the crystals burying her head. "Gilda? Can ye hear me? It's William and Hannah."

"The goddess," Gilda whispered.

Hannah knelt beside Gilda's head and used cloth ripped from her dress to brush crushed crystals from the Draecna's mouth and eyes. "We haven't seen her, Gilda. You're the first one we've found so far."

"No." Gilda struggled to shake her head, her eyes closed as a frown creased the brow line between her horns. "The goddess has sifted to the heart of the battle. Her son, your mate, is in grave danger."

Hannah closed her eyes as a wave of dizziness threatened to topple her from her feet. *Breathe.* She had to breathe. She had to think. Now wasn't the time to panic.

"Did she tell you where, Gilda? Did she say where the heart of the battle was located?" Hannah forced herself to choke back the bile burning in the back of her throat. She wanted to scream. She couldn't lose Taggart. She would not contemplate life without him.

"The Baelaon Fields," Gilda whispered as she wet her trembling lips.

"The Baelaon Fields," Hannah repeated using William's wing to pull herself to her feet. Hugging her bleeding arms to her sides, she released a shiver that had nothing to do with the cold. The name of the place sounded like death. Her sixth sense tingled at the base of her brain. A feeling of dread gnawed at her gut; a sense of loss already hammered at her heart.

"Dig her out, William," Hannah instructed as she stared off into space. "Settle her somewhere with food and water while I try to find some provisions to take with us. But hurry. We don't have much time. We've got to get to the Baelaon Fields."

"I want to know the traitor who killed him!" Taggart raged with his wings outspread. He glared at them all standing below him. It could've been any one of them. Which one had betrayed his beloved friend? Taggart paced the short length of the rock ledge he'd chosen as his podium to address his gathered Draecna troops. Fury raged through every fiber of his tensed body as he flexed and stretched his wings. From this vantage point, he could just make out Gearlach's head where it dripped on a pike outside of Sloan's tent. Taggart sheathed and unsheathed his silver-tipped claws, wishing Sloan stood in front of him so he could rip him open from his throat to his gonads. "I expect an answer!" Taggart thundered, his voice echoing across the valley.

"Do ye actually think the traitor is foolish enough to confess?" Isla shimmered into focus on the ledge beside him.

"Now is not the time, Mother," Taggart hissed.

Isla bowed her head, glanced at the troops, and lowered her voice so only Taggart could hear. "I know ye are in pain, my son. But ye know in your heart this is not the way to find Gearlach's murderer."

"They must all realize the danger they are in now that Gearlach is dead. As long as there is one Draecna out there killing for Sloan, none are safe."

With a nod, Isla folded her arms across her stomach and

her image started to fade. "I agree. Ye need to warn them as I am now warning ye. Hannah and William are on their way. Your spell has run its course. Hannah fears for ye and she comes to save ye."

Taggart closed his eyes. By all that was holy, the three days had passed. There would be no stopping Hannah now. He should've paralyzed her for a year. He could've reversed the spell once the war had ended. He didn't need this. He had a traitor in his midst and now Hannah in the middle of the fray. Opening his eyes, he returned his gaze to the gathered troops still standing at attention. Which one of them could be the traitor?

Septamus appeared by Taggart's side as though he knew he was about to be bidden. "What are your thoughts?"

"Ye know my thoughts, Septamus." Taggart snorted with a bitter huff. The old Draecna knew him better than he knew himself.

"Until we find which Draecna the Waerins have turned, we cannot act. All plans to attack will be reported to Sloan and thwarted." Septamus stroked his claws through the strands of his silver beard as his eyes narrowed into speculative slits.

"There is another complication." Taggart drew a heavy breath and clicked his claws against his armored face. Gads, how had things managed to get so out of hand?

Septamus shot Taggart an exasperated look and heaved a disbelieving sigh. "More complicated than a traitor in our midst?"

"Hannah and William are on their way to see us."

"Well, that's just lovely now, isn't it?" Septamus swept the ledge with his tail and waved his claw at the troops. "Report to your stations and stand at the ready! I want to be notified of anything out of the ordinary." Turning back to Taggart, he fixed him with an irritated glare and poked him in the center of his chest with his claw. "That is *ex-*

actly why *I* never mated! They are entirely too much trouble!"

Crossing his arms over his chest, Taggart returned Septamus's irritated look. "Weren't ye the one telling me to sleep with the woman? To get on with my life? I think I should hold you partially responsible for this mess."

"I told ye to bed the lass! I didna tell ye to keep her for life." Septamus turned his back to Taggart and climbed down from the ledge. "I canna help it if ye didna listen to me properly."

The cold, barren ground scraped rough against her belly as she wormed her way to the edge of the cliff. Here under the scrub, beneath the trees, she could remain unseen and still see what went on below. Hannah wished she had her pair of binoculars from back home. But this vantage point and her twenty-twenty vision would just have to do. The wind rustled in the trees, blowing leaves and dust into her face. Thank goodness, she'd landed upwind of the battle.

Curious, Hannah sniffed, wondering if it would do any good. After all, with the gift of immortality, they said she'd received the gift of seeing Waerins for what they truly were. Perhaps she'd also been given the Draecna's heightened sense of smell. Sulfur, decayed leaves, refuse of some sort, and *whew*—rotted meat. Hannah covered her nose and gagged. Craning her neck, she scooted around a bush, wincing as a stick poked her in the side. What stood in front of that tent? She couldn't quite tell. Something perched on a pole. Inching farther over the edge of the cliff, she hung on to the bush as she focused harder on an object crawling with flies.

"Oh my God." Hannah collapsed against the side of the cliff and vomited into the scrub.

"Mother!" William grabbed her around the waist with his tail and yanked her back up the side of the cliff.

"Don't look, William," Hannah gasped as she rolled to the ground at the top of the cliff.

"I already saw him," William replied, offering Hannah a drink of water from one of the skins hanging around his neck.

"That must be Sloan's tent," Hannah rasped. She shuddered as the vision of Gearlach's flyblown head battered at her mind. Sloan had to die. She'd never considered herself capable of murder until now, but it was kill or be killed. Sloan wouldn't expect Hannah. He'd be too busy fighting Taggart and his army of Draecna. Her fingers curled around the haft of the dagger melded to her waist. She could do this. She could do this tonight.

"What are ye thinking, Mother? Taggart says ye're dangerous when ye get quiet." William shuffled back and forth in front of Hannah, peering down at her with a worried look on his face.

Hannah broke from her daze and glared up at William. "Oh, he does, does he?" Standing up, she dusted herself off and reached for the bag she'd hastily stuffed with clothes while William settled Gilda with food and water in a portion of the cavern left intact. "Don't you worry about it, my fine Draecna son. I'm going to change into my darkest set of clothes and as soon as the sun sets, I'm going on a little visit to Sloan."

His forehead wrinkled between his horns as William held on to the bag and pulled it out of Hannah's hands. "I don't think Taggart would want ye to do that. That doesn't sound safe at all."

With her hand held out, Hannah snapped her fingers. "Give me the bag, William. Taggart isn't here and I know what I'm doing. I'm going to end this once and for all."

Shaking his head, William held the bag out of her reach. "Why do you no' wait until we reach Taggart and ask him. I would feel much better if we could ask Taggart."

William might feel better if he could ask Taggart, but Hannah knew *exactly* what would happen. Adopting her sternest, most motherly tone, Hannah snapped her fingers again. "William, have I ever led you astray?"

"Well—" William paused, the worried crease deepening between his twitching horns. "No, not really."

"Then give me the bag. Once I've left, if it will make you feel better, why don't you find Taggart's tents? Take to the sky, William. I've no idea which direction they took, but once you're aloft, I'm sure you'll be able to find them."

William looked at the bag, looked at Hannah's outstretched hand, then turned and scanned the horizon. Gnawing on his thick lower lip with one of his fangs, he finally edged the bag over into Hannah's grasp. "I hope I'm not messing up again."

"It's going to be fine, William. I promise." Hannah smiled as she hugged the bag to her chest. "Now turn your back while I get changed. We've got some work to do."

The stench burned her eyes and made them water. Hannah blinked hard and tightened the black scarf hanging around the lower half of her face. Clamping her lips shut, she took shallow breaths as she belly-crawled through the darkness to the rear of Sloan's tent. His tent abutted a grassy rolling hillside. What an arrogant bastard. Sloan just dared his enemies to challenge his authority. The undulating hillocks adjoining the open hillside made perfect channels for hiding Hannah's midnight run.

The moonless sky assisted her journey; the cloak of its shadow proved to be her friend. Hannah glanced up at the roiling storm clouds blocking the stars and relaxed even more. Karma seemed to be on her side. She'd end this misery tonight.

She paused as she reached the flat stretch of ground making up the last few yards to the back of Sloan's tent.

The campsite appeared as silent as a graveyard. There wasn't any movement around any of the other tents. Her heart hammered against the walls of her chest drowning out any other possible sound.

Squinting, Hannah spotted dazzling crystal obelisks mounted beside the stakes of the tents. As she watched them, the obelisks periodically fired into the darkness without revealing any obvious source of power. Their brightness fluctuated with a steady rhythm of a slowly beating heart.

A movement near the tent caught Hannah's attention. She held her breath as a lizard the size of a small dog slithered out of a nearby stand of grass. The unsuspecting reptile meandered into the barrier between the obelisks. The firing rhythm of the stones synced and a blinding line of white light reduced the lizard to nothing more than a puff of smoke. Hannah flinched in time with the zap. Poor lizard. If only he'd had better timing, he might've made it.

No wonder there wasn't any movement outside of the tents; the crystal sensors worked better than any guards. Now what was she going to do? She couldn't stay here forever. Propping her chin in her hand, she released a frustrated groan while she watched the obelisks fire a beam of light around the tent. She hated technology. Then the laser disappeared just as quickly as it had connected the sentries into a glowing arc. Hannah sighed and settled more comfortably into the hillock and observed the sensor's process three more times. If she timed her entry just right, she could be under the tent flap before the beam detected her.

Hannah edged closer to the tent, waited a few seconds, allowed the sentries to fire again, then rolled under the edge of the canvas right into Corter's hairy leg.

"Well, looky here at the little piggy that just rolled into me feet! Looks like I'll be gettin' to gut ye after all!"

CHAPTER THIRTEEN

"**I** made it, Taggart." William edged his way through the tent flap and stopped just inside the door.

Taggart's head snapped up. "And Hannah? Where is your mother, William?" He didn't like the way the young one avoided looking him in the eye. What had Hannah talked poor William into doing now?

William stared at his feet and chewed on his lip as he worried the end of one of his wings.

"William." Taggart gripped the edges of the table until his knuckles cramped. "I'm going to ask ye one more time. Where is Hannah?"

"We spied on Sloan's tents on our way here." William dropped his head lower and dug a hole in the dirt with his biggest toe.

"And?" Taggart prompted. The Draecna had best spill the rest of his story soon or Taggart was going to strangle him.

"When she saw what he did to Gearlach, she decided to sneak up on him tonight and kill him herself." William pressed his lips together and folded his claws tightly across his belly.

"She's decided what?" Taggart threw the table out of his way as he lunged for William's shoulders.

William scrambled just out of Taggart's reach, his eyes

widening as Taggart morphed into his Draecna form when he lunged across the room. "She *told* me she was going to *visit* Sloan. But I know what she's truly planning. She thinks I'm just a baby and that I can't figure things out. She said it would be okay and that I should just come and get you."

"The woman is going to drive me insane!" Taggart roared, destroying the side of the tent with a furious swipe of his claws. Turning back to William, he shook his clenched fist. "Did I no' tell ye to watch her, boy? Did I no' tell ye to keep her out of trouble?"

"She doesn't bear watching easily, Taggart. Have ye ever tried doing it?" William unstrapped the bags Hannah had forced upon him, threw them to the floor, and shot Taggart a bullish glare.

"Sounds like someone is finally growing up," Septamus observed from his seat in the corner.

Narrowing his eyes into venomous slits, Taggart whirled to snarl at them both. "It's well past midnight. I've no time for your snide observations. I fly to Sloan's tent on the winds of the storm. Follow me if ye dare." Spreading his wings, he launched himself into the sky through the gaping hole in the tent. Fueled by his fury, he faced into the bitter wind, praying he'd reach Hannah in time.

"I truly appreciate your making it so easy for us." Sloan shot a sadistic smile over his shoulder as he poured a glass of wine. "Now I won't have to hunt ye down to crucify ye in front of Tiersa Deun."

Hannah tested the ropes binding her wrists behind her back before she answered. Not that tight, and they hadn't found her dagger hidden against the small of her back. Good. Her possibilities still abounded. "Glad I could help you out, Sloan. You seemed to need it."

Corter kicked her to her knees. "Mind your tongue, bitch! Show some respect to yer betters."

"Now, Corter." Sloan clucked his tongue as he sauntered across the length of the tent. "We mustn't be cruel. Not just yet. Help her over to the settee. Undo her hands so she might join us in a glass of wine."

Corter yanked her to her feet. He sliced through the ropes with a short stubby knife drawn from his belt, then shoved her closer to Sloan. With a glance at the blade, Hannah darted a look around the room and noticed no other weapons. Good. Corter's paring knife was no match for her Draecna dagger. Adrenaline fueled her quickening heart rate as her plan unfolded in front of her.

Watching Sloan and Corter, Hannah eased one hand behind her back and slipped her dagger into her palm as Sloan poured her wine. It melted into her hand and snuggled against her wrist as though the blade understood exactly what she wanted. Rubbing her wrists as though they ached from the bite of the ropes, Hannah shrugged as both men glanced at her from across the room.

"Ye do like wine?" Sloan asked, holding up a bloodred crystal decanter.

"Oh, absolutely," Hannah replied. She wouldn't miss this glass of wine for the world. Her heart raced as Sloan filled the glass. Her stomach churned like a restless sea. She focused on Sloan's chest as he meandered toward her. She ignored the victorious leer on his face as he prowled closer. She'd aim for the soft spot just below his breastbone. Her hand flexed tighter around the bejeweled handle of her dagger as she imagined the lunge of the killing thrust.

"Your wine, beloved Guardian," Sloan sneered as he extended the glass.

"Your death," Hannah hissed as she buried the dagger to

the hilt. With a grunt, she twisted it farther under his rib cage. She held his eyes locked in her gaze as she rotated the blade even deeper.

Sloan spewed a series of short, surprised gasps. His mouth opened and closed and his head bobbed down as he stared at Hannah's hand. The wineglass slowly slipped out of his grasp and tumbled to the floor. With a shudder, he coughed out a spray of bloody droplets. His hands clutched toward her throat as Hannah twisted the knife again. The jewels in the handle of the dagger hummed and radiated a visible energy field as Sloan crumbled to the floor.

"Sloan!" Corter barreled from behind the wine cabinet and pulled his short blade from his belt. "Ye bitch, I canna believe ye've killed him. But I'll tell ye right now, I'm no' as soft as him."

Hannah yanked the dagger free of Sloan's body and whipped it around toward Corter's face. "Come on, Corter. I'd love to carve you up too."

The front section of the tent exploded into flames. Sloan's gaudy oil paintings hanging from their golden cords along the tent poles burst into blazing squares of art. Wine bottles exploded and metalwork melted into dripping, orange molten curls as the heat intensified into an uncontrollable inferno. The white-hot blaze incinerated all it touched.

"I'm gonna kill ye," Corter swore as he lunged toward Hannah's face.

Hannah twisted to the side, slashing as she did and opened a long gash down the side of the man's grotesque, mottled body. Corter rounded, slapped his hand against his bleeding side, and rushed at Hannah again. Just as Corter bore down upon her, Hannah dove straight at his short, stubby legs.

Corter stumbled over her, his misshapen limbs churning as he lost his balance. His bleeding, obese form lurched to the side and landed in the burning wall of canvas. Corter screamed as the material burned into his flesh, entrapping him in a blanket of flames. Hannah cringed and turned away.

"Sorry, Corter, you know what they say about payback."

"Hannah!" Taggart's roar echoed beyond the raging inferno eating the sides of the canvas. He burst through the wall of flames, his wings outspread like an avenging angel from Hell. He gathered Hannah against his chest, gently touching her face as though he feared she wasn't real. The longer he gazed into her eyes, the fiercer his scowl became. "Woman, when I get ye back to my tent I am going to turn ye across my knee and fair beat ye until ye learn to do as ye're told!"

Hannah couldn't resist a mischievous grin up into his eyes as she pressed deeper into the sheltering curve of Taggart's outspread wing. "Promise?"

With his wings outspread, Taggart slowed their descent and touched down in the center of the dusty encampment. Hannah's heart fell at the sight of the barren ground beaten to a pulp by constant marches of the Draecna guards. They'd be lucky if anything ever grew here again. She wrinkled her nose at the overpowering smell of Draecna scat. Then smiled when she remembered she'd first discovered that scent at the shores of Taroc Na Mor.

Even though the night had traveled well past the twin moon's zenith, all the Draecna had gathered in the middle of the village of tents to stand vigil until Taggart returned. She grinned. Apparently, word had traveled fast of her midnight raid and Taggart coming to her rescue.

"It is over," Taggart announced as he eased Hannah's feet to the ground. "Sloan lies dead. His tent city smolders, fully burnt to the ground. Sloan and Corter's bodies lay cremated within it."

Isla stepped forward. "Are ye certain? Truly certain? Your brother and his executioner are both finally dead?"

"Hannah?" Taggart smiled and pulled her forward into the circle of the firelight.

With a weary nod, Hannah held up her dagger. The blood on the blade reflected a purple-red haze in the flickering light of the fire. "Sloan is truly dead and so is Corter. Both of them tasted my blade."

The Draecna raised their snouts and shot flames high into the ebony darkness of the sky as Taggart hugged Hannah to his side. "Erastaed is free. We can start to rebuild and now the people can live their lives without fear."

A pushing and scuffling deep in the group worked its way to the front of the clearing. Several of the younger Draecna soldiers nearest Taggart parted, smiling and nudging each other as Dasim shoved them aside.

"Can I see the blade?" he asked, his eyes darting from side to side as he held out a shaking claw.

"Of course, Dasim." Hannah smiled. Isla had explained that Dasim was somewhat special.

Turning the knife over and over between both his claws, Dasim's brow wrinkled between his horns as he shook his head. "This is Sloan's blood on this knife?" he asked as he tapped on the blade with a shaking claw.

"Yes, Dasim. Sloan is finally dead." Taggart spoke quietly to the Draecna peering at the knife.

"Then I must mix it with yours." Dasim lunged and buried the blade deep in the center of Taggart's chest and twisted.

"NO!" Hannah screamed and jumped on Dasim's back. She pounded and beat him across the head while he whipped his neck to shake her free. "What the hell have you done?"

The other Draecna clustered and pulled him off Taggart, while Septamus caught Taggart by the shoulders and lowered him to the ground. The gemstones encrusted on the dagger's hilt vibrated and glowed in the dark just as they had when Sloan's life force had left. Hannah crouched over Taggart's body as the knife hummed and whirred in his chest. She watched the handle, terror clenching at her heart as she recognized the killing magic at work. No! It couldn't be happening, not now, not when their future had looked so bright.

"What do I do? You promised me you couldn't die. Tell me what I can do to save you." Hannah cradled Taggart's head into her lap as his glazed eyes fluttered open and closed.

A weak smile played across his shaking lips as Taggart struggled to speak. "Only another Draecna could take my life, sweet love. The odds of that happening seemed verra slim indeed. It seems now my time has ended after all. I'm so verra sorry, Hannah. But I canna stay with ye as long as I once thought I could."

"You can't leave me, Taggart. You promised me you would never leave me!" Hannah sobbed against the cooling flesh of his throat. This couldn't be happening; his body already felt so cold. "I need you, Taggart. Please don't leave me. You can't expect me to live forever without you."

"I am so sorry, my Hannah." Taggart shuddered with a gasping cough. "Please forgive me, my love. Ye know I will be forever . . . yours."

A keening sob tore from Hannah's throat as she tightened her arms about Taggart's limp form and pulled him to her chest. An explosion of flames burst in the clearing in front of them, followed by a piercing howl. William had finally found his first blaze and ignited Dasim's body.

The builders paused, lowered their tools, and bowed their heads in her direction. Hannah tightened her lips in a strained smile of approval at the elaborate funeral pyre.

They had erected the structure inside the largest cavern of the Goddess Isla's stronghold. The cavern would protect the ashes from the slightest gust of wind during Taggart's ceremony. She traced her fingers across Taggart's urn, a gift from the artisans of Erastaed. They had intricately carved an ivory bone box telling the story of how Taggart had given his life to save them from Sloan's evil rule.

She released a shuddering sigh as she hugged the box to her chest. She'd run out of tears days ago. She'd forgotten exactly when. All that remained inside her was an empty ache that never hoped to heal.

"Mother?" William's voice interrupted her tortured musings.

"What is it, William?" Hannah whispered, not bothering to take her eyes from the uppermost level of the pyramid.

"What are your plans after the ceremony?"

Hannah pressed the ivory urn to her chest so tight the inlaid lid dug into her breasts. She welcomed the pain. It took her mind off the deeper ache breaking her heart into a thousand pieces. "Why, William? What does it really matter?"

"The people need to know."

Hannah closed her eyes. Hadn't the people taken enough from her? "Septamus and Isla are handling everything, William. It doesn't really matter what I'm doing. I'm sure it will be just fine."

"I am not a child anymore, Mother. Please don't speak to me as if I am." William moved in front of her and blocked her path so she couldn't walk around him.

Hannah looked up and saw her sorrow mirrored in the depths of William's great dark eyes. "I'm sorry, William. You are absolutely right and I'll try to remember that in the future." Turning back to face the nearly finished pyramid, Hannah gave a weary shrug. "After the services, I haven't decided what I'm going to do. There is one option I'm considering, but if I do that it would be pretty major. So I haven't really settled on anything just yet."

"Septamus wondered if you were going to go back." William encouraged with a nudge of his wing.

"Are you talking about me behind my back?" Hannah nudged him back with her elbow.

"*I'm* not." William rewarded her with a toothy grin. "As the Erastaed's new council, Septamus and Isla met to discuss what they thought you might do."

"If I go back," Hannah began, "Isla can only send me back alone and she can never bring me back to Erastaed again. You realize what that means?" She wanted William to understand he might have to go on without her. She loved her Draecna son with all her heart, but Jasper Mills would be hard-pressed to accept him as one of their own. Of course, she could always make her home at Taroc Na Mor. William would always fit in at his birthplace if the gateway ever became usable once again.

William nodded. "I understand." Strolling along beside her, his claws clasped behind his back, he scowled down at the floor as he continued, "But Septamus and Isla both remarked the portal is in the process of being repaired. Eventually, the gateway to Taroc Na Mor will be restored. Then I could see ye again."

"Eventually?" Hannah asked.

"Give or take a few hundred years."

"I see." Hannah pinched the bridge of her nose. Well, with her curse of immortality, she would live long enough to see them all again.

"I would miss ye, Mother," William whispered.

"I would miss you too, my son."

A crimson silk banner draped across Taggart's body as it balanced on the shoulders of six young Draecna. Each of the bearers wore golden circlets around their arms and their horns. They marched in unison as though he weighed nothing, heads held proud, eyes straight ahead. They carried their leader to the top of the one-hundred-and-eleven-step funeral pyre and lowered him to his honored resting place.

Hannah walked beside them, her eyes locked on Taggart's face, her heart begging him to open his damn eyes. She wanted it to be some cruel joke. Some magic spell someone had cast to spoil their joining ceremony. But no, his body remained motionless, his features frozen in the eternal mask of death.

Isla swayed along the other side, her great luminous eyes filled with the stark pain of a mother who'd lost her last child. Septamus limped his way up the steps. He closed the processional march. He looked as though he felt each and every one of his three thousand years.

Hitching his way over to her side, Septamus gave Hannah a sympathetic shrug of his wings. "They . . ." He nodded toward the throng of faces pressed into the caverns. "They would hear ye speak if ye are able. Are ye so inclined?"

Hannah gazed out at the sea of followers; her mind whirled at the swarm of colors buzzing around them. "Please just tell them Taggart loved them more then he loved his own life. And he'd be honored at how they supported him through all of this."

Septamus nodded his approval. "I will see that they hear your words. The translator speaks it even now."

A deafening murmur hummed through the crowd as they all rose and filled the cavern with thunderous clapping.

"Please just let this be over," Hannah begged.

Septamus agreed with another nod. "Draecna, it is time to send your leader home."

The six bearers stood, faced Taggart's body, and removed their circlets of gold. They placed the rings on Taggart's chest and touched their claws to their foreheads. Once they'd each performed this ritual, the six returned to their positions lined up on one side of the pyre. In unison, they inhaled chest-expanding breaths and ignited their hottest blaze.

The blue-white flames licked and danced to the ceiling as the Draecna exhaled for what seemed like forever. The inferno blazed; sparks crackled and spun up into the darkness until nothing remained on the platform but ash.

Hannah shuddered, her body shaking with the emptiness of lost love. She had no tears left to cry. She watched the glowing embers swirl with the updraft and disappear into shadows. The hollow sound of footsteps shuffled toward her. Hannah clenched the urn tighter in her hands until her fingers cramped. If she gave it over to them, they'd shovel the last of him inside and then force her to shut him away forever.

"Please, Guardian."

Her throat ached from the emotions eating away at her soul. Hannah choked back a dry sob. With shaking hands, she forced the box into Septamus's waiting claws, never taking her eyes from the ornately carved lid.

"I want it back once he's placed inside."

Septamus paused; a rare look of surprise shadowed his wrinkled face as he gently pulled the box from her grasp. "That is not usually done, Guardian. Prince Taggart's tomb awaits him beside the River Ursia Diuan."

Hannah yanked the box back out of Septamus's grasp, her heart hammered against the lid. They had robbed her of the love of her life; she'd be damned if they'd deny her this. "Does my word mean anything in this world or not?"

With an apologetic bow of his great horned head, Septamus retreated a step. "Of course, Guardian, your word means everything. Please forgive me."

Extending the box again, Hannah steadied it with both hands. The ivory case suddenly seemed much lighter. "Then please do as I ask, Septamus. Once Taggart is inside, return him to me. Don't take him away from me again."

"As ye wish, my Guardian." Septamus bowed his head, took the urn, and turned to lay his friend to rest.

"If ye select one of the humans that pleases ye from the surrounding provinces, I will bestow the gift of immortality upon them. Then ye willna be alone for your eternity. Just pick whichever one of them ye like." Esme's dry, logical voice jarred her from her thoughts as she perched in the cushioned seat of the window.

Pressing her forehead tighter against the cool pane of glass, Hannah wished Esme would just go away. Select a human. What did she blather about? At the moment, a jackhammer ratcheted inside her head, and there wasn't an herb in all of Erastaed that matched the strength of the prescription medication she used to take back in Jasper Mills when it came to stopping one of her migraines.

"Esme, what are you talking about?" Hannah sighed and closed her eyes. Esme needed to just go away. The migraine yanked her stomach into the act, the excruciating pain sickening her until she almost retched. If Taggart had been here, he would've healed her with a wave of his hand. Her eyes burned behind her closed eyelids. No. She couldn't cry. It would only increase her misery. Besides, she'd promised herself she wasn't going to put herself through the if-Taggart-were-here game today.

She heard distinct shuffling about the room and cracked an eyelid just as Esme picked up a pile of scattered clothing and rearranged several tossed-about pillows.

"Do the servants not tend to your private rooms? This place is a disgrace." With a look of disgust, she displayed her fangs as she heaved several plates of questionable food into the hearth and ignited them with a disinfecting fireball. Turning back to where Hannah sat curled up in the window seat, she refolded her shimmering wings against her scaly back. "I have noticed ye appear to be unable to function well without a mate. If ye will select another human that ye believe would be suitable for an eternity, I will gift them with immortality since ye already have an extended lifespan."

Massaging her temples, Hannah tightened her eyes shut again. Esme just didn't get it and her heart ached too badly to attempt to explain. "It's not that simple, Esme. You don't just go get another human like you're replacing a pet that just got hit by a car."

"I fail to understand this pet-hit-by-a-car comparison ye reference. Please explain." Esme circled the room again and swept up more scattered clothing with her tail.

"Esme, I feel like shit! Would you please just leave me in peace for now?" She'd reached her limit. Grabbing the silver ice bucket off the table, Hannah slung out the ice, clutched it to her chest, and lost what little breakfast she'd been able to force down earlier.

A cool damp towel pressed against the base of her neck until her retching spasms ceased. "Forgive me, Guardian. I didna realize ye were so unwell."

Another damp towel wiped against her mouth and a glass of water pressed against her lips. "Take just a sip to rinse your mouth and spit it into the bucket before I take it away."

"I'm sorry, Esme. I didn't mean to bite your head off." Hannah eased back against the pillows of the window seat as Esme removed the pail. Now guilt hammered alongside the unbearable pain drumming inside her skull. "Please just hand me Taggart and give me some time to myself. When I feel better, I'll explain it so you understand."

Esme scowled down into Hannah's face, then cast a wary glance at Taggart's urn where it rested on the mantel across the room. "The prince's remains should be in his tomb. It is not natural that ye keep them in your rooms. All the Draecna speak of it. Even Isla has mentioned her son should be properly laid to rest."

"Okay, that's it. Get out of here, Esme. I've had enough of your lectures for one day. I'm in no mood for any more of your insolence." Hannah drug herself off the bench, clutching the wall to maintain her balance. "The people of Erastaed stole my last chance at happiness for the price of their own freedom. I'll be damned if they tell me what to do now." If she wanted to keep Taggart's ashes in her room, it wasn't anybody else's damn business.

Esme's eyes widened as she backed toward the door; the scales of her body flushed to a deeper shade of blue. "I only tell ye these things so ye know the truth. Without the truth, ye canna make wise and logical decisions."

Hannah held her head as she staggered toward the mantel, where she stretched to slide Taggart's urn down into her arms. Have mercy but her head pounded. She'd not had one this bad since her freshman year of college. She'd had to go to the ER and get a shot to ease the pain of that one. She cradled the carved ivory box against her chest and slid to the floor. Squinting her eyes, she glared up at Esme and brought her knees up to support the base of the box. "I pity you, Esme. I pity you and your pathetic logic and I hope someday, you figure out what to do with your heart."

Esme's eyes narrowed as she lifted her snout. "From what I have observed, logic is far superior to your so-called heartbreaking love." Then she jerked her head down in a nod and slammed the door behind her.

"I thought she'd never leave," Hannah muttered to the chest in her arms as she settled it more comfortably in her lap. For the thousandth time, she stroked her fingers across the carved images across the lid. With a bitter laugh, she lingered on the one panel that looked painfully like Taggart's profile. "If I keep this up, all the pictures they carved of you are going to be worn away."

The smooth ivory warmed to her touch; Hannah calmed with the weight of Taggart pressed against her body. Her fingertips tingled as she stroked the lid; when she noticed it, she shifted positions on the floor. "I must have a nerve pinched or something," she muttered. Rolling her shoulders, she rubbed her fingers together then suddenly realized her headache had completely disappeared.

Hannah stared down at the chest, then massaged the back of her neck. Surely not. It couldn't be. Her headache must've just run its course; she'd puked and then it went away. Taggart couldn't heal her from the other side.

"Taggart?"

She stepped out of the lily-scented water and reached for the heated towel waiting on the steaming rocks. "I've made my decision and I have to say I feel much better now that I've finally settled on it. So, I'd appreciate it if you two would support me." Hannah listened and glanced toward the outlined forms of Isla and Septamus against the rice paper divider as they waited on the other side of the room. She knew they wouldn't like what she told them, but as the saying went, they'd just have to get over it. Blotting the moisture from her legs, she heaved a sigh as Septamus finally reacted. She knew he'd be the first to fight it.

"She canna do that. Can she do that? Take his remains back to Taroc Na Mor? The portal hasna been repaired yet. And besides, it just wouldna be right for his remains to be on the other side." Septamus paced around the edges of the oval, wool rug centered in the room. With a frown, he scratched behind a horn as he glared at Taggart's remains on the mantel.

"Apparently, she can do whatever she wishes." Isla paced right behind him, her arms folded across her glistening belly.

"I can hear you clearly," Hannah called from behind the rice paper screen. "And I can see you both through this thing. The light's on that side, remember? Did you forget that I was still in here?"

"No, I did not," Septamus snapped. "I just thought we spoke low enough so you couldn't overhear us." He motioned toward Isla to move closer to the door and farther away from the screen.

"And I am *still watching* the outline of your body through the rice paper. Actually, it's pretty see-through. Can you see me? Stay over here where I can hear you," Hannah added. The stodgy old Draecna needed to realize her decision was best for all concerned. "Besides, what difference does it make if Taggart's remains are in Erastaed or Taroc Na Mor? You two have an entire country to rebuild. I would think you've got a lot more to worry about then an urn full of ashes."

"The people need to be able to pay their respects," Isla admonished in a reproving tone.

Hannah exploded from around the screen, shaking the shirt clenched in her hand to within inches of Isla's snout. "I think the people have taken their fair share from me! Don't you dare stand there and tell me to give them one damn bit more." How dare they lecture her on what the people needed! As far as she was concerned, the people had taken everything she had.

Isla blinked, backed up a step, and laced her ornate claws across her tiled belly. "Perhaps you are right. Perhaps we could build an image or something for the people to visit in memory of Taggart."

Shaking out the shirt still clenched in her hand, Hannah nodded. "There you go. I think that sounds like a fine idea." After she folded the shirt, she hugged it to her chest and frowned at the scattered clothes on the satin-pillowed bed. "I am concerned about William, though. I'm worried about leaving him behind. He's still very young and immature."

"William has matured more than ye think. The revolution aged him quickly. He has his fire now. It's time he put some distance between the two of ye. It would be the same if he'd known his natural mother. The time of separation has come." Septamus clasped his claws behind his back and resumed his pacing about the room.

"But I'll never see him again," Hannah argued as she tossed the shirt to the bed.

"How can ye know that?" Septamus shot back. "Ye have the years of a Draecna ahead of ye and we have sworn to ye that we shall repair the portal. Taroc Na Mor is the ancestral home of us all and in several hundred years there will be a new batch of eggs ready to replenish the nursery. The portals of time must be maintained."

"Well at least now we've got an immortal guardian," Isla observed. "Why didn't we think of that years ago?"

"Great. I can see it now." Hannah muttered, plopping down on the end of the over-stuffed settee. "I'm going to be a bitter, heartbroken old woman with a castle full of lizard eggs."

"What did she say?" Septamus asked.

"Never mind." Hannah shrugged as she shoved her clothes into the bag. "It doesn't bear repeating." So this was her destiny. Matriarch over the keepers of the portals. She wished Grandma had warned her. It sounded like a lonely lot for the next several thousand years.

★ ★ ★

Since Sloan's death, the entire world of Erastaed appeared greener, as though the realm itself exhaled with relief. Hannah, Septamus, Isla, and William looked out across the blossoming valley at the winding River Ursayus as it glistened its way out to the sea.

A warm gentle breeze ruffled Hannah's hair; it reminded her how Taggart had combed his fingers through the strands. Her throat ached with the threat of another onslaught of tears. No more. She'd promised herself, no more. She couldn't stay here. This was Taggart's world. She couldn't live here without him. The sooner she left this place the better. She stood a better chance of surviving his loss back at Taroc Na Mor.

"Is it time yet?" She glanced to the horizon, then turned to Isla.

Isla cast a narrow-eyed glance at the position of the sun, then turned to search for the rising of the second moon. "Almost. The two almost share the sky. We have but another moment to wait."

Turning back to Hannah, Isla gave her a toothy smile and gently touched her claw to Hannah's cheek. "I shall miss ye, my brave daughter. Take care of yourself until it is time for us to meet again."

"Thank you for everything, Isla." Hannah swallowed hard and pressed her face into Isla's claw.

"Take care of yourself, Guardian," Septamus instructed. "And do not doubt that we *will* see each other again."

"I know, Septamus. This long lifespan will just take some getting used to. Now I'll finally have time to read all those books." Hannah hugged the stodgy old Draecna's chest, smiling as he grudgingly patted her on the shoulder.

"William, you know I'm very proud of you and you know how much I love you." Hannah wrapped her arms around William's neck, breaking her promise to herself that she'd shed no more tears.

"I love you, Mother," William whispered as he clutched her to his chest. "I'm going to miss ye with all my heart, but I promise I'll do ye proud so I can tell ye when I see ye again."

"I know you will, William," Hannah choked as she wiped her hand across her eyes.

"'Tis time, daughter. We must cast it now or I canna assure ye will land in Taroc Na Mor." Isla nodded to the sky, where the sun and the moon shared the horizon.

"Tell Esme not to be angry with me. Someday, I hope she'll understand," Hannah reminded Septamus as she stepped onto the center of the octagonal ceremonial stone. Esme hadn't understood why she'd chosen to leave. She'd been quite adamant that Hannah's duty to the people outweighed anything as foolish as heartache or pain. Esme had a great deal to learn about emotions. Hannah hoped someday she'd see Esme again and that the young female would find the path to her feelings.

"I will tell her," Septamus groaned. "For what good it will do."

"Good-bye, daughter. Long life and peace be with you until we meet again." Isla blew a cloud of shimmering flames around Hannah. The circle swirled and gradually tightened until it completely enveloped Hannah's body.

Hannah inhaled the warmth of Isla's spell; she closed her eyes against the confusing myriad of sparkling colors. Her mind swirled and her heartbeat roared in her ears as she felt a sudden lurching shift beneath her feet.

CHAPTER FOURTEEN

Hannah regained consciousness on the edge of the ocean just as a wave crashed into the ledge. "Ugh!" Spitting out seawater, Hannah wiped her eyes and checked to make sure Taggart's urn hadn't taken on any water. "Thanks a lot, Isla."

The wind lashed her wet hair across her face and threatened to douse her again with more salty spray. She had to move now, before she had a chance to figure out where she'd landed, or the waves would souse her again. If she paused to gather her bearings on this ocean-drenched shelf, she'd end up either soaked or drowned. Picking her way up the steep embankment, Hannah vaguely remembered the rock-strewn hillside. As she reached the top, she glanced around. The tension knotted in her chest loosened a bit. She was back. She'd arrived home. This steep cliffside stood just to the north of Taroc Na Mor.

She remembered this to be the embankment she'd wandered down the day Taggart had revealed himself as a hybrid. Hannah squinted against the eye-watering wind as it whipped her hair into her eyes. They'd made love that night. The heat of the memory flooded need through her body. Her nipples tightened and she ached deep with wetness. He'd never touched her again. Pride and circumstance had kept them apart and now her wondrous lover was gone.

She hugged his urn against her chest and rubbed her cheek against the carvings. Maybe Taroc Na Mor wasn't such a great idea after all. His ghost walked here as well. The pain of the memories ached even stronger.

Scuffing her feet in the scattered clumps of grass, Hannah made her way back to the keep. Hannah cringed as she glanced about at the deserted grounds. Had they been gone that long? Taggart would be horrified. The bushes and shrubs had sprouted and overgrown into masses of leafy monstrosities. Additional masonry had chipped away, leaving the foundation eroded and exposed. A part of the roofing had shifted in one spot and looked in danger of sliding off to the balcony on the second floor.

"Wow." Hannah spun on one heel as she circled around to the inner courtyard. "This place is worse than it was before we left. Look!" Holding up Taggart's urn as if it were perfectly natural, she pointed it at the building.

Realizing what she was doing, Hannah tucked the box back under her arm. "I have lost my mind," she muttered aloud as she made her way up the broken steps.

She shoved against the door, bouncing twice with her shoulder until the sticking wood gave way, then stumbled her way into the dingy hallway. Glancing around at the cobwebs curtained down from the rafters, she wrinkled her nose at the smell. Just as she remembered, except maybe quite a bit mustier and covered in a thick layer of dust.

Home. Hannah settled Taggart on the hallway table. "We're home, Taggart." She laid her hand atop the box. With a frown, she leaned closer and placed her other hand on top of the cover as well. It seemed extremely warm. It must've been the passage back to Taroc Na Mor. Isla's spell must've heated up the urn. Hannah shrugged and caressed the box. That had to be what had warmed it. That and the fact, she'd been hugging it to her chest ever since she'd crossed back to Taroc Na Mor.

Rubbing her arms, she glanced around the room. The urn might be warm, but the keep certainly wasn't. She had to find out if the gas was still on or at least light a fire in some of the hearths. It was almost dark. Her clothes were soaked from the welcoming wave and the damp chill had seeped into her bones.

If she remembered correctly, the kitchen was the warmest room in the keep. Hannah paused as she turned to pick up Taggart's urn. That room held even more memories. Gritting her teeth, Hannah took a deep breath. She couldn't very well avoid the kitchen forever.

Tucking his box under her arm, she made her way down the dingy hall. Her footsteps pinged on the tiles as though her shoes were made of iron. The sound reverberated down the passageways. Hannah had never realized an empty house could carry so much sound. Halfway to the kitchen, she slipped off her shoes. She couldn't handle any more castle acoustics. The echoes traveled for days.

Hannah settled the ivory box in the center of the kitchen table and swallowed her misgivings as she scanned the room. Her gaze fell first on the spa in the corner. Biting her lip, she forced herself to turn away and move to the icebox squatting in the corner.

Opening the door, Hannah stuck her head inside and just as quickly jumped back. "Ugh!" That was a mistake. She covered her mouth and tried not to gag as she quickly bounced the door shut with her behind. *Whew.* She'd have to clean that thing out tomorrow or haul it outside and burn it.

She opened the cupboard doors and found a tin of sardines and a slightly gnawed box of crackers. "Well, we have breakfast." Drumming her fingers on the countertop, she spotted an unopened bottle of wine.

Now there's what she needed. Taking a deep breath, she steeled herself and risked another look at the spa. She'd find some candles. Take a long hot bath and drown her sorrows in a bottle of wine. Two times a widow, she deserved a one-night pity party, and what better place than where she and Taggart had first made love?

Rummaging through the cabinets, she loaded her arms with thick, pillared candles, a bar of soap, and several towels to prop behind her head. As she turned to pile them on the kitchen table, she frowned as she noticed Taggart's urn had slid to the very edge of the table toward the spa.

"I never noticed this table being unlevel," Hannah muttered as she slid the box back to the center of the table. A chill teased its way up her spine as she noticed one of the pillared candles lying on its side beside the box in the middle of the table. With a narrow-eyed glare at the candle as if it was pulling some sort of trick, Hannah picked it up and turned it so it could roll to the edge of the table. It didn't. She turned it again and nudged it just a bit. The candle stayed in place.

Snatching up the candle, Hannah picked up the rest of the items she'd scattered across the table. "I'm just tired," she announced to the room as she hurried over to the spa.

She set up the candles on the end of the tub, lit the wicks, and exhaled as the peaceful glow flickered about the room. She started the water flowing into the tub and piled the towels on the other end. As she turned to gather her glass and her bottle of wine, Taggart's urn careened to the edge of the table again.

"Will you stop it!" Hannah slid the box back to the center of the table and held on to it for a moment with both hands. It was warmer this time than it had been in the hallway. Glancing up at the ceiling, Hannah laughed at herself. No wonder. She'd placed the urn directly under the light.

A whooshing sound caused her to turn. Every fire pit around the spa roared to life with a crackling blaze. Hannah forced herself to take a slow deep breath as she stared at the dancing flames. Gas logs. They had to be gas logs on some kind of thermostat. That had to be it. Edging closer to the tub, she refused to acknowledge the ash and debris from the popping wood at the base of the yellow flames.

"I'm just going to drink my wine, take my bath, and I'll worry about everything tomorrow." She looked around the room as she spoke, as though daring the entities to spoil her evening.

Hannah stripped down and slid into the tub. The scalding water soaked pure tonic to her bones. As she closed her eyes and leaned back against the towels, the healing spring water eased some of the agony from her heart. She sipped her wine and watched the flames dance on top of the water spanning across her body. The more she drank, the sleepier she got. It would be so easy just to slip her face beneath the surface and let all her worries and heartaches be over.

"Hannah!"

As Hannah jumped awake, her arm knocked Taggart's urn into the tub, scattering his ashes across the water. "Oh my god! What have I done? How did you get over here? No! No! Now, I don't have anything left of you at all. Oh, Taggart, no."

Hannah sobbed into the spring water, her tears splashing into her hands as she filled them with Taggart's muddied remains where they floated atop the water. As her teardrops fell, the water effervesced and the spa bubbled into a glowing energy froth. Hannah backed up into the farthest corner, as the reaction in the spring grew more frenzied. She gasped as a form rose up out of the glowing chaos and smiled into her eyes.

"Ye brought me back, my love. I've been waiting for ye to figure it out."

Hannah didn't move. It couldn't be real. It had to be the wine or she had drowned and gone to heaven. She took her fingernail and dug it into the flesh of her inner arm, wincing when it hurt like hell. "Please tell me this is real. Please don't let it be a lie," she whispered.

Taggart stroked the curve of her cheek with his thumb. "I promise, Hannah. 'Tis real. Your magic brought me back. I am verra much alive."

Hannah dove into his arms and cradled his face between her hands. Searching his eyes, she touched his cheeks, his lips, and stroked his hair, while he chuckled and stroked her back. "How, Taggart? I don't understand." She kissed him hard before he could answer, then finally came up for air. "How? I don't have any magic."

With a carefree shrug, he smoothed her hair out of her eyes while he shook his head. "The magic of Scotland? Our love? Our immortal union? All I know is I've returned because you and I have much unfinished business. I felt the pull once Isla sent us back. But, Hannah, I never truly left ye."

With a delighted sigh, Hannah wriggled on Taggart's lap and pressed against his chest. "I don't care as long as it's real. I'm just glad we're right back where we started and I'm never going to let you out of my sight again."

"We've an eternity to watch over one another. Now stop talking and kiss me, woman."